THE LAST
THING SHE
EVER DID

Center Point
Large Print

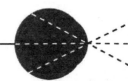

**This Large Print Book carries the
Seal of Approval of N.A.V.H.**

THE LAST THING SHE EVER DID

GREGG OLSEN

CENTER POINT LARGE PRINT
THORNDIKE, MAINE

The text of this Large Print edition is unabridged.
In other aspects, this book may vary
from the original edition.
Printed in the United States of America
on permanent paper.
Set in 16-point Times New Roman type.

ISBN: 978-1-68324-841-5

Library of Congress Cataloging-in-Publication Data

Names: Olsen, Gregg, author.
Title: The last thing she ever did / Gregg Olsen.
Description: Center Point Large Print edition. | Thorndike, Maine :
    Center Point Large Print, 2018.
Identifiers: LCCN 2018015015 | ISBN 9781683248415
    (hardcover : alk. paper)
Subjects: LCSH: Large type books. | GSAFD: Suspense fiction.
Classification: LCC PS3615.L724 L37 2018 | DDC 813/.6—dc23
LC record available at https://lccn.loc.gov/2018015015

*For David Downing, who always knows
the right button to push.*

Twenty years ago

Beetles never stop. They gnaw silently and relentlessly.

Guilt is like that too.

Less than two hours from Bend, Oregon, Diamond Lake is a spectacular sapphire blue with a tawny shoreline ringed by ponderosa pines. The pines there struggled to survive against the scourge of a plague of unseen beetles that insidiously burrowed through the bark and into the cambium, a tree's growth layer where the rings in the trunk are formed. For years the attack by the tiny army went unnoticed, picking away, weakening a once-mighty stand of timber until the trees began to slump into deadfall.

A slow, quiet death.

Unseen.

Until it was all too late.

For Liz Camden, too late happened when she was only nine.

Shards of memory returned every time she passed the sign indicating the turnoff to the lake. Liz was always a passenger when this occurred, because she never, ever drove that route on her own. It was a pact she made with herself, a way out of remembering all of it and preventing the splintery, jagged pieces from stabbing at her. Whenever they did, despite her best efforts to forget, the memories assembled themselves into a cracked mirror.

And it all returned . . .

Liz's mother, Bonnie Camden, and neighbor Miranda Miller planned a day trip to shop in Portland, three hours from Bend. Liz's father, Brian, was away on business, though due home that night.

Miranda's husband, Dan, a doctor with a thriving practice in town, had been looking for an excuse to take out his new boat while the women were "off spending all of our hard-earned money on diamonds and furs." It was a joke, of course. Dan was always one to exaggerate Miranda's spendthrift ways and trumpet his own frugality. Except for that boat.

He'd wanted one for years. He'd sit on the deck overlooking the Deschutes River and roll his eyes at the tubers who passed by. He wanted a boat with an outboard motor. Why float when you could command the water with an engine's roar?

"For fishing," Liz remembered Dan telling Miranda when the Camdens were over to celebrate the end of the summer.

"You can fish from the shore like everyone else," Miranda said.

She could always deliver a deadpan line. She had a knack for it. Or she could make her point with a simple gesture, a roll of the shoulder, and what they all knew and loved as "the Miranda look." A dart at her target, then away, with a slight smile across her face. Never mean. Always effective.

"I want a boat."

"I want a new refrigerator."

"Oh really?" he said.

"That's what I just said."

Liz remembered how three days later a delivery came from Hansen's Appliances. The day after that, Dan pulled up in front of the Millers' house with a boat trailer and the apple of his eye. It wasn't new. But the sixteen-foot Bayliner Capri was the most beautiful thing Dan had laid eyes on.

"God, I love this boat. I might even sleep in it," he told Miranda as the neighbors gathered to ogle his purchase.

Miranda rolled her shoulder, flung her dart—"Well, I hope it's comfy, because there's no 'might' about it, buster"—then slipped away with her wry smile.

She wasn't mad at her husband. Not ever. That's just the way they played. Liz always liked the Millers' banter. Her parents were mostly silent. A quiet and somewhat sweet stalemate. When the chance came to hang out over at the Millers', she always looked forward to it. She knew it would be fun.

The trip to the lake was executed like an army reconnaissance mission, which wasn't surprising. In his life before returning to Bend to start a medical practice, Dan had served in Vietnam. He never talked about that experience, at least as far as Liz knew, but his crew cut and the jangle of the dog tags he still wore telegraphed his history without words. Dan was a lean man with sinewy arms, who was softened by his ready smile and pretend irritation with all the things Miranda threw his way.

As the big day approached, Dan gathered the kids who were not away at church camp—Liz and the Millers' son Seth, both nine, and Liz's older brother Jim, eleven—to talk about the finer points of trout fishing and water safety. Dan could be long-winded, and most everything he said seemed pure overkill. But that was the way he was.

The blast of heat that week had toasted the high desert. When thunderclouds rolled in the night before the big trip, everyone felt the relief that comes with the promise of rain. The TV weatherman, a glad-hander with an endless procession of bow ties, indicated a storm would move quickly through the area.

And, for once, he was right.

The tempest passed through Bend early Friday

morning, slickening the roadways, filling the Deschutes, and pounding the eardrums of those unable to sleep through the cracks of thunder.

That morning Bonnie and Miranda went out ahead of Dan and the kids. "I need to get to Portland early if I'm going to empty Dan's bank account," Miranda said as they drove off.

Years later Liz could still see her mother and Seth's mom as they had appeared when they left in the Millers' Cadillac. They had dressed up for the occasion. Her mom seldom did that. But that day Bonnie Camden looked like a movie star. Indeed, both women did. They wore new summer dresses. Bonnie had made hers from a Butterick pattern she'd found at a fabric store in the town of Sisters. It was a solid sky blue with white piping. Miranda had ordered hers from an expensive catalog from a store in New York. It was white linen that she accessorized with a pale green leather belt. Liz wanted to touch the linen, but she didn't dare. She wondered when she'd be old enough to wear makeup and put on a gold necklace and shoes that clattered when she walked on the stone entryway of her grandparents' house.

Of all Liz's scattered recollections from that day, the one of Mrs. Miller and her mother was unique in that it was the only one Liz didn't mind revisiting.

The white Ford station wagon reeked of a sweet, spicy scent when Liz and Jimmy got inside to join Seth and his dad. Cloying. Heavy. By the end of the day, the scent had imprinted itself on Liz's brain in the way that the odor of the first alcohol that gets a new drinker really, really drunk can later turn their stomach at the slightest whiff. Yet, sitting there, she couldn't determine exactly what it was. Spice like her dad's Teaberry gum? A sachet in her grandma's drawer?

Dan stopped at McDonald's on the way out of town and ran inside while his son and the Camden kids waited. Liz would later remember thinking it was an auspicious beginning to the trip. An Egg McMuffin was a treat. Her mom never let her children eat fast food.

"She says it isn't good for you," Liz recalled saying to Dan when he handed her a McMuffin wrapped in oily paper.

"Beer isn't, either," Dan said. "But you'll drink it anyway when you're older."

Liz sat in the front next to Dan. The radio played country music. At the time, Liz—with her Egg McMuffin and not having to sit next to her brother—thought the moment could hardly be improved. Well, at least the fast food was awesome. The smell and country music, not as much.

The wipers went on when it started to rain a few

miles before the turnoff to the lake. At first, small droplets smeared the brittle remains of dead bugs over the surface of the glass. The droplets grew larger and then suddenly multiplied into such fearsome numbers that individual drops could hardly be discerned. The pelting water sounded like a hundred nail guns hitting the roof.

"We don't need no stinkin' sunshine," Dan said, sipping his now-tepid McDonald's coffee, which earlier had been too hot to drink. Taking his foot off the accelerator a little, he put down the cup and leaned forward to swipe the inside of the windshield with his fingertips in case condensation was contributing to the difficulty in seeing the road ahead. "Man," he said, glancing at Liz next to him and the boys in the backseat, "this is some cloudburst."

The wipers fought wildly against the rain, but it only kept coming faster and faster. The car was enveloped by a continuous sheet of water.

As the vehicle eased up an incline, Dan lowered the driver's window and looked to the sheer walls of blasted basalt on either side as a guide.

Liz couldn't be sure, but later she came to believe she'd been the first one to feel it. A slight rumble. Maybe something was wrong with the radio. Jimmy liked to turn the bass up real high on the dial on their parents' stereo system. But it wasn't the radio. Liz looked at Dan and their eyes met for a second. Was it the sound of the tires on the roadway? She didn't think it could be. The road had been freshly paved. It looked smooth, like black licorice. Without warning, the wheels began to shake.

"Crap," Dan said, moving his gaze to the rearview mirror. "Boat trailer must be dragging that back taillight. It was loose when the dealer sold it to me. Said he'd fix it. I need to pull over for a second, guys."

Just as the car and the trailer stopped, it suddenly turned dark, as if Liz's mother had pulled her blackout shades against one of her all-too-frequent migraines. It would always be difficult to accurately place what happened in those moments when the wall of water first hit the front of the station wagon. It was fast and fierce. Liz and the boys screamed.

Everything was staccato in her eyes. Dan's terrified face. The rising water. Even the roaring sound emanating from outside seemed to come in pops or flashes.

Dan, who had not yet opened his door, yelled, "Hang on! Flash flood!"

The vehicle lurched from its resting spot. It was a cork. It was a feather. The force of the water shoved it back down the highway. Bumper pool. A steel ball in a pinball machine. The station wagon and the boat trailer careened back down the highway.

Dan stretched his arm over to Liz as though he could protect her.

Washing machine.

Dryer with shoes inside.

Liz looked out her window, and the boat trailer appeared next to her before snapping off and hurtling away with the dark water—along with logs and what might've been a capsized horse trailer. All of it passed in the kind of frightening blur that doesn't allow the mind to fully comprehend what one is seeing.

Shards of memory.

Debris of all kinds pelted them as they rattled backward down the highway. Liz was wondering if that had really been a horse trailer, when, through the filthy windshield, she could suddenly make out the image of an immense horse as it lunged at them. Its hooves hit the glass, and the animal let out a terrified scream, the likes of which Liz would never forget but never be able to describe no matter how hard she tried. It was sharp and guttural at the same time.

After hitting the windshield, the animal rolled over the top of the station wagon. Were they *underwater* now? It was impossible to tell.

Then a small red car was coming at them, at the last instant sweeping to Liz's side of the station wagon. A young woman pressed her hands against the window and called out for help as she passed. Her eyes were more white than blue. So open and full of terror. She was young. Maybe still in her teens. Her gaze caught Liz's for a second before turning back to wherever the churning water would take her.

Liz screamed, "We have to help her!"

The roar of the water outside the car obliterated her words.

Sleeping bags. A cooler. A child's dinosaur-shaped flotation device roared past the Ford in a soupy mixture of water, mud, foam, and all of the things that lake goers would have enjoyed throughout a lazy day on the shore. The pod off the top of a car had dislodged and split open, sending suitcases, clothing, and backpacks into the torrent that carried away everything in the road that had become a spillway.

And then, finally, the station wagon stopped. It had come to rest listing on an outcropping that had been blasted into the basalt when the road to the lake had been forged.

Now that their progress had halted, the pace of the flood outside flew into a much higher gear. Every few seconds, the water surged against one side of the car or the other, sometimes with enough force to rock the vehicle on its perch.

"Everyone okay?" Dan yelled out.

Liz, who had somehow ended up in the backseat with the boys, was the first to respond. "Something's wrong with Seth," she said, shaking as water began to pour inside.

"I'm okay," said her brother. "Seth? Wake up."

The boy, who looked so much like his mother—and often had a quip ready—opened his eyes. "I'm not dead yet," he said.

Even in the chaos of the car, Dan's gasp of relief was audible. Water had begun to pool at their feet. Despite the summer day, it was ice-cold. He rolled up the window.

"We need to remain calm," he said.

"We're going to drown, Dad," said Seth.

"No. No, we're not," Dan said. He undid his seat belt and peered through the condensation and muddy stain of the driver's-side window. The windshield itself had been transformed into a spiderweb of broken glass. "We're going to get out of here. We're going to be just fine."

Liz wiped her eyes. "Promise?" she asked.

Dan studied the boys and managed a calming smile. "We're going to have a hell of a story to tell. I'm going to get out of the car now," he said. "I'll get out and up onto that ledge. Then I'm going to get you out. All of you. One at a time. We need to do this very carefully. All right? One at a time."

None of the three in the backseat said a word.

"Is that understood?" he asked, his voice finally betraying the fear that was eating at the edges of his normally calm resolve. The crack in the veneer of his can-do persona had begun to widen: slowly at first, then quickly to a chasm. Liz could see it. The boys too.

17

Yet they all nodded.

The water pooled from the floorboards and now reached knee level. Every moment or so the noise and jolt of something hitting the car rattled them.

"This will need to be fast," he said. He rolled down the driver's-side window. More water poured inside, and the sound of the roar of the river that had been the road filled their ears. It was a roar punctuated with the din of rocks hitting metal.

Later, Liz would wince at the noise of a friend's rock-polishing tumbler as the girl turned agates into smooth stones, which would be fashioned into key chains for her parents, a bolo tie for her granddad. The relentless noise reminded her of that terrible Saturday excursion to the lake.

Dan hoisted himself out of the car by grabbing the top edge of the doorframe and pulling himself up and backward through the opening. The water grabbed at him, but he made it onto the ledge of rock he'd been aiming for and turned back their way.

The car started to move and the kids screamed.

A second later Dan was outside the back window on the driver's side, fighting the torrents, his eyes full of terror. Kids don't often see grown-ups looking that way. Never had Liz seen a grown man appear as though he was going to fall apart. He pounded on the glass and motioned for Jimmy, who was sitting next to it, to roll down the window.

"Now!" Dan yelled. "Goddamn it, do it!"

"We'll drown," Jimmy said.

"Open it," Seth said. He was sitting between Jimmy and Liz.

"Open the window, Jimmy," Dan said, "or you *will* drown. When I get you out, you're going to go on the roof of the car and from there . . . from there, over to that ledge and then up above the road. The water's not going to get higher. It's going to recede. We'll be fine there until help comes. Okay?"

The car moved again.

Jimmy, shaking, did as he'd been ordered and rolled down the window.

Their laps were now covered with the murk of the unexpected tide that had filled the car.

"Take my hand," Dan said. "Right now!"

Jimmy did, and in a second he was out the window. Liz could hear him crawling on the roof, then silence.

"Where's my brother?" she called out past Seth.

Dan's face appeared again. The flood had battered him. A cut above his eyebrow and on his cheek had turned some of his light-colored blue shirt to a violet hue. "He's good," he said. "Your brother's fine."

The car moved a little more.

Liz heard Jimmy scream her name. "You got to get my sister! Get Lizzie out!"

"She's coming, Jimmy!" Seth yelled back.

"We need to get you out of this car right now," Dan said, his voice now more urgent than it had been a moment before, when Liz had been all but certain she was going to die. But when he thrust his hand in blindly for his son, Seth lurched away from him, grabbed Liz by her shirt, and dragged her over him. It was Liz Dan took hold of and yanked through the window. He winced when he saw her emerge into the chaos outside, and then both of them looked back into the station wagon. The last things she saw were Seth's terrified eyes and his *Have a Nice Day* T-shirt with its image of a smiley face.

And that was it.

Nothing after that.

Nothing except what had been told to her and what she'd read in the paper when she was in high school and the Bend *Bulletin* went online.

Local Boy Drowns in Flash Flood
    An outing turned into tragedy yesterday morning when a nine-year-old Bend boy drowned on a canyon road off US Highway 97 near Diamond Lake. The boy, his father, and two other children were caught in a flash flood.
    "The father managed to save the other two children but, despite valiant efforts, not his son," said Oregon State Police

lieutenant Wilson Donaldson, who led the rescue and recovery team.

The driver told police that the group was on the way to a day of fishing at the popular lake when a flash flood hit.

"The car they were driving was carried more than fifty yards by the floodwaters. It got caught on some rocks, and the driver proceeded to evacuate the children to higher ground," Donaldson said.

After the man retrieved two children, the car apparently dislodged, sweeping both the man and his son away with it.

The father was found unconscious downstream, where an off-duty fire-fighter from Redmond rescued him. The deceased boy was found in the vehicle. All involved were taken to the hospital and are expected to be released shortly.

Officers also reported one other fatality: a horse. The animal's owners and another young woman in a separate car were recovered without injury.

The names were withheld until the Tuesday paper. That article was brief and indicated that the police had conducted an investigation and found that there had been no wrongdoing on the part of the driver. The last mention of the incident was the funeral notice.

And yet, to all of those who were there, and both families, the incident clung like a mark that could never be washed away. Dan and Miranda retreated from Liz's family. Liz and her brother were reminders of what they'd lost.

Only once did Liz ever hear her parents directly talk about Dan Miller and the accident that had claimed his son's life. They were grateful, of course, that their own children had survived. More than grateful: overjoyed. But instead of sympathy for another's loss, Liz's mother took an approach that would define her in her daughter's eyes. Her mother could be a selfish and spiteful woman, always looking to blame others in an effort to boost her own mood. It seemed at times that being negative fueled her sense of joy.

"I don't know," she said. "*You* don't know. Dan might have been drinking that morning. He might have been impaired—seriously so, for all we know. I mean, honestly, you have no idea what happened and neither do I."

Brian Camden immediately dismissed Bonnie's unkind and judgmental remarks. "His drinking early in the day started after the accident, honey. You know that, Bon. Be fair."

"I don't trust him," she said as she swirled the last few sips of a martini in her glass. "Letting Seth die. Killing your own kid like that."

Liz's father was used to his wife's cruel streak

and often just let it roll off him. Not this time. This time he just couldn't.

"He *didn't* kill him. It was an accident. A terrible tragedy." Brian stopped and regarded Bonnie. "Honestly, what's *wrong* with you? He saved our son and daughter. Are you really forgetting that?"

She motioned for another drink. "Of course I'm not. Get a grip. I don't like it when you dismiss what I have to say out of hand. It's demeaning. Really, think about it. You can't say that he doesn't have blood on his hands."

"It was an accident," he insisted.

"That's going to follow him for the rest of his life."

"Only because people like you keep reminding everyone and twisting it into something it wasn't."

"I'm only saying what others think."

That last line was so typical of her mother. Liz thought that her mom somehow derived a perverse sense of dignity from dispensing a mean remark. She managed to do it with a smile on those Elizabeth Arden–pink lips of hers.

"Others don't think that," Liz said.

"They do," she said. "They always will. Whenever he's out and about in town, all of them think it. They all remember what happened. No amount of drinking will ever erase what happened. Nothing that he did that day will ever go away."

PART ONE
BLAME

Where did the blood come from, Carole?

—*David Franklin*

Chapter One
JUST BEFORE

Liz Jarrett lifted her head from her grandparents' old dining table. A spiky jolt of adrenaline traveled through her body. Her fingers found her cell phone, and she looked at the time. It was a little after 10:00 a.m. *Shit!* Liz peeled herself from the chair and went for the shower. As fast as she could, she stripped off her T-shirt and sweats, not even waiting for the water to warm before jumping in. A blast of cold was what she needed. Ice ran down her spinal column as she steadied herself in the stall. Liz needed to shock herself into alertness. She had been up all night, mixing coffee with Adderall, poring over books and her laptop for the most important test of her life.

Her second attempt at it.

I can't screw this up again. The thought of the exam she'd taken three months before contracted her stomach into a tight, burning nut. *I have to pass.* As the cold water rushed over her, her internal monologue shifted. *I will pass. I'm smart. I can do this.*

At twenty-nine, Liz was no longer young—at least not by the standards of her law-school class at the University of Oregon. Certainly there were older candidates for a law degree. In the beginning, Liz had placed those in their thirties or older somewhere along a spectrum between pity and admiration. She'd even caught herself thinking it was "cute" that a grandmother from Wilsonville had made it through the admissions process. *Really, Liz? What's* that *about?* Someone starting over late in life, working like a dog at it, "cute"? *Someday that might be you.* Chasing a dream. Never getting there. A dangling carrot that her fingers could only graze.

Move.

Like a crazed marionette, Liz jumped from the shower and pulled a towel from atop the train rack over the toilet. No time to use the hair dryer. Working at her dark brown hair under the fluffy weight of the white terry cloth, she looked at herself in a mirror that did not offer the benefit of the concealing condensation a hot shower would have provided. She winced. She looked wired. *Ugh.* Her hands shook as she applied deodorant, and for the life of her she couldn't step into her underwear without sitting on the toilet. The room was spinning a little, and for just a flash she thought of the carousel at Disneyland, where her parents had taken her and her brother when they were kids. She'd gotten sick and thrown up on Jim. He never let her forget it. She felt that same queasiness now.

Liz needed to get to the testing center. *Now.*

28

The location was a hotel conference room in Beaverton, more than three hours away. She'd need to risk a speeding ticket to get there on time.

Jeans finally on. Top on. And only one shoe. Liz hobbled through the house, looking everywhere for her other shoe. She stumbled and leaned against the doorjamb. *Where is that shoe?* Finally, back in the bedroom, she found it next to Owen's side of the bed.

Owen! She could kill him just then. Why had he let her sleep? Why hadn't he shaken her awake at the table? He knew the importance of this exam. It was everything to her. It was the pathway to all she wanted to be. It would provide the proof to her husband that she could fulfill a dream.

That she had a goddamn right to one too.

As she slipped her foot into the second shoe, though, Liz recalled Owen speaking to her that morning. The memory came to her through a gauzy veil. Everything about the night before was a little foggy. The pills. The coffee. The reciting of case law out loud until her voice was a rasp. The fishing through the refrigerator for orange juice because she thought it would give her more energy than a Red Bull. Only because she was out of Red Bull.

Yes, Owen had tried to wake her that morning. He had. *Great.* Her lateness was her own fault.

Liz remembered him actually lifting her out of the dining chair. "You are zonked out, babe," he said, hooking his strong hands under her arms. "You need to get yourself together. Get cleaned up and go."

"I need to sleep," Liz told him, resisting his help and sinking back into her chair. "Test tomorrow."

"More like today," he said. "Four hours from now, right?"

She looked at him. Her eyes were sore and dry. She knew she looked like a junkie at a 7-Eleven, watching the hot dogs on heated metal rollers as though they were as fascinating as a breaching whale.

"Four hours?"

He held out his phone, showing her the time.

"Shit," she said. "I've got to get going."

"Yeah, you do. And so do I. I have that meeting with Damon and the other principals this morning. Got to be there on time."

Even now, in her addled state with both shoes on and the memory of his attempt to rouse her, Liz couldn't suppress the feeling that Owen had always put his needs before hers. It had been that way since before their wedding. He had told her over and over that they would live large—and not because of her skills as an attorney.

"Lawyers are a dime a dozen," he'd said more than one time. "No offense, babe. Technology is king. You'll see."

She hated technology. Sometimes she hated

Owen. He was so sure of himself, so insistent that he was on his way to something very important. Something big.

With his firm about to go public, Owen had started a list of all the things money could buy. A Ferrari. A month in Fiji in one of those grass huts that stuck out over the ocean. It went on and on. She went along with his dreams, mostly because there was no point in arguing. Either they'd happen or they wouldn't. Only one item on his list had made Liz push back: Owen planned to bulldoze their little house on the river. However, it wasn't at the top of his ever-growing list, and for a long time she had hoped that he would forget he'd suggested it.

Liz couldn't argue that the house didn't have its problems. Dry rot had weakened the beams under it. Indeed, the floors slanted in the kitchen so steeply that once when she dropped a cherry tomato it rolled to the corner with such velocity that it could've been an outtake from *Poltergeist*.

"We have such history here," she would remind him.

He'd wrap his arms around her as though he loved her and understood. "We'll make our own," he'd say. "Who wants to live in someone else's dream?"

Liz would nod as if she agreed, though she didn't. Her grandparents had built the two-story Craftsman bungalow in 1923. She'd spent every summer there. On the drive over from Portland, she'd watch the forest from her place in the backseat until they reached Bend, where the Deschutes sparkled like someone had sprinkled broken glass on a slate-gray table. The house was small, but every inch of it held some kind of memory. Even as a child, she'd felt it was *her* house. Her refuge. When her grandparents died, they left the house to her mother and father. After they passed in a car accident in Eastern Oregon, Liz and Owen bought out her brother, Jim. It took every penny they had and left them with a mortgage payment that stretched their already tight resources nearly to the snapping point. She'd thought Owen had fought to get the house for her. It was only after the deal was done that Liz understood how her husband of four years really felt about the house.

Owen saw a fortune instead of a quaint old house stuffed with memories. He was constantly reviewing the neighborhood homes on Zillow and Redfin. Over and over he'd tell her the house wasn't worth a penny, but the land was suitable for a million-dollar-plus home. When one of the houses a few doors down passed the two-million-dollar mark on Zillow, he made love to her like they were celebrating a windfall of their own.

A few summers ago, they'd sat on their porch and watched as the house next door, nearly a twin of their own, was devoured by the jaws of a wrecker.

"That'll be us one day," he said.

Liz had sipped a beer as a paddleboarder's wake lapped at the riverbank. She didn't tell Owen that it was bone-crushingly sad to watch that house vanish. The old places built by previous generations were being eclipsed one after another by enormous megahomes that took up every square inch of their lots and blocked out the sun for those who hadn't yet given in and erected their own behemoths. Joined the fight to see who could be bigger. Boxier. More obtrusive. More show-the-world-what-I-have. Liz finished her beer and tried to let go of the past as David and Carole Franklin removed the house next door like it was a pimple on a chin.

She'd wanted to hate them. But she couldn't.

Sure, David and Carole were nice enough. New people almost always are—at first. David ran a restaurant downtown. Carole was a textile artist, but that was a recent affectation. Previously, she'd held a senior management position at Google. It was their little boy, Charlie, who provided the bridge between Liz and Carole. He was blond, had blue eyes, and seemed to delight in all the same things that Liz held dear. He loved the river. He collected dozens of pebbles from the riverbank. Charlie didn't seem to see any difference between an agate and a chip of basalt.

"He's into quantity," Carole once told Liz as they watched the boy drop another bucket of his treasures on the sweeping redwood decking of the Franklins' house.

"Owen's into quantity too," Liz said. "He likes money."

Both women laughed.

Liz was a blur as she hurried across the gravel breezeway to the garage, dialing Owen's number as she went. The call went to voice mail. She pushed the button to open the garage door, and as it slowly rose, she left a message.

"Owen! I'm late! You know how important this is to me. *To us.* I would never have let you down like this. How could you leave without *making sure* I had my ass in gear?"

She slid behind the wheel and turned over the engine of her RAV4. The radio went off like a bomb, blasting a pop song so loudly it made her want to scream as she scratched at the volume control. The music was nearly silenced, but Liz's heart kept hammering so fast and so hard that she wished for a Xanax. Despite her cold shower, sweat collected on the nape of her neck. Scratch the Xanax. She knew that she was so hyped up on pills and so rattled from the sleepless night of studying that polluting her bloodstream with anything more couldn't possibly help.

Goddamn it, Owen!

She put the car in reverse and pressed the ball of her foot against the accelerator. As the car rolled out of the garage, Liz felt a hard bump and slammed on the brakes.

The thump against the rear bumper had been muted but solid, decisive. Had to have been a dog or a cat. She'd even heard a kind of muffled cry when she applied the brakes. Oh, *God,* she hated the idea of hurting an animal. She'd never gotten over the time Owen ran over a fox terrier as they pulled off the freeway one late summer day a couple of years back.

At first he'd resisted Liz's pleas to stop the car. When he reluctantly did, he'd stayed inside while Liz scooped up the animal and wrapped it in her jacket.

"Poor baby," she murmured to the trembling creature when she returned to the open passenger door.

"Oh, *hell* no," Owen said, glaring at the bundle in her arms. "I'm not taking *that* to the vet."

"*That,* Owen, is someone's precious pet," she said, shifting her arms so he could see the wounded canine's scared brown eyes. "You have to. Otherwise it will be a hit-and-run and you'll face charges." That was probably a stretch, but she knew her husband needed a possible consequence to motivate him to do the right thing. Owen Jarrett was, at best, a reluctant rule follower.

She got in the car and shut the door.

Owen glared at the dog in her lap. "I do not want to get stuck with the bill, Liz."

"It's always money with you," she shot back.

"Cheap shot."

The dog whimpered some more.

"You hit an animal," Liz said. "You have to help it. What if it was *our* dog?"

Owen looked at her and blinked. "We don't have one."

"If we *did.*"

"Fine. Fine," he said. "We can take the dog to the damn vet." He put the car into gear and drove slower than he normally did. It was a disgusting thought, but Liz wondered if he was stalling in the hope that the dog would die before they got to the vet.

No such luck.

The terrier patched up and the owner contacted, Liz wondered how it was that Owen hadn't understood—or cared—that the dog's life had mattered to someone. An elderly lady. A little kid. He'd been worried about the cost of it all. Or maybe the inconvenience.

Doing the right thing wasn't that hard to do.

Around that time, Liz started volunteering at the humane society in Bend. She'd always loved animals. Except horses, of course. Horses always frightened her. They reminded her of what she would come to consider the second-worst day of her life.

CHAPTER TWO
MISSING: TEN MINUTES

From the gleaming redwood deck where she drank her morning espresso, Carole Franklin watched her three-year-old, Charlie, stalk a heron along the river's edge. The steel-gray bird with legs that disappeared into the late summer mat of reeds let the little boy get close before launching herself with her massive wings, hovering above the river's surface, and planting herself ten feet farther down the Deschutes. As she looked on, Carole wondered just how intelligent that particular bird was; *birdbrain* certainly didn't seem to apply. A smile came to her as the act repeated itself.

The heron and Charlie were playing a game.

The tranquil water that passed by her home was mostly glass at that time of the morning. That would change. Within an hour the paddleboarders, the inner-tubers, and the hordes of tourists with their air mattresses lashed together, music blaring and beer-can tops popping, would put a stranglehold on the scene. Morning was the best time of day—really, the only time when many were reminded of what had drawn them to Bend, Oregon, in the first place.

Carole and her husband, David, were among a flood of newcomers, and as such couldn't freely join in to complain about how things had changed in the Central Oregon city. Although they'd never admit it to anyone, they knew they were part of the problem. People like them arrived in Bend with armloads of cash, bought high, and propelled taxes upward on cottages and small riverfront homes that had been modest family vacation retreats for generations.

Carole's gaze was drawn across the water to where Dan Miller, a Bend native with a bristle brush of white hair and a wiry frame draped as always in a way-too-large Hawaiian shirt, sheared the blades of his perfect lawn with a push mower. Dan's wife, Miranda, had died the year before of cancer. Carole and David had tried to befriend the Millers, but the older couple had grown tired of welcoming new people into what had been an insular world. The very presence of newcomers like the young couple and the skyrocketing property values they triggered had forced many of their friends to leave. It was a quiet war, an impasse that left the old-timers with the realization that new endings for their stories were being written by people other than themselves.

Carole and David knew all this because Dan had actually said as much when he and Miranda ran into the Franklins at a downtown gallery opening.

"No offense," Dan had said, turning his University of Oregon baseball cap as though tightening it in place over eyes locked steady on the Franklins, "but people like you are going to force us to sell. We're seniors. We're on a fixed income. Our place has been in my family for forty years. I thought I could leave it to my family, but now all they see is dollar signs."

There had been nothing subtle about Dan Miller. Carole knew this dig about his children was really directed at what she and David had done when they purchased their property, a modest two-story that had been owned by longtime friends of the Millers and the Camdens.

Miranda tugged at her husband's shoulder. "That's enough, Dan," she said. "This is just the way the world is now."

Carole understood where the couple was coming from. Her husband, not so much.

"I wish they'd just quit complaining and appreciate what they have," David said as the Millers disappeared from the gallery.

"They do," Carole said. "Or, rather, what they had."

"Things change," he said. "It's called progress."

"Right. Progress. But it isn't progress to them, David. It's a sharp stick pushing them out, and people like us are on the other end of it."

David just raised his shoulders a little and

39

sipped some O'Doul's. "Sounds like it's his kids he should be bitching to."

Carole didn't say another word. She couldn't think of anything to say.

While Charlie made his way along the riverbank, trailing the elusive heron, Carole waved to Dan Miller as he pivoted his push mower toward her and the next row in the nearly perfect argyle design he was cutting into his lawn, crisscrossing to ensure that every blade had been trimmed to uniform height in what surely had to be the most pristine yard along the river. From her vantage point, the old man looked like he'd been carved out of soapstone. His eye drawn by her wave, he looked up and offered a curt nod.

"Beautiful day," she called out.

"The weather's changing," he said, before carrying on.

"Yes," she answered. "I can feel it."

It was nearing the middle of September. The daytime highs still flirted with triple digits, but in Central Oregon's high desert a chill comes at night and lingers into the morning even on late summer's hottest days. That time of year it sometimes cooled to such a temperature that the surface of the Deschutes would emit a slight puff of steam where it wound under the bridge just to the north of the Jarretts' place. Looking at that bridge now, Carole saw a couple of vacation-rental teens crossing it and a lone early-morning tuber sliding beneath it on his downriver float. A man in a canoe with a nearly white cocker spaniel hugged the shoreline along Dan Miller's sliver of beach, paddling upstream.

The river was a slowly moving circus, water and people melding into an ever-changing spectacle from the put-in just above the Old Mill District to its conclusion at Mirror Pond in Drake Park. Along its banks, property owners and vacation-rental managers positioned benches, docks, hammocks—almost any sort of perch on which to sit and watch the show.

Carole's phone rang and she glanced at the number, then called over to Charlie, "Remember, you can't even get your feet wet. Not even a little."

The little boy nodded, the sunlight illuminating his blond hair like a Gothic halo. "Okay, Mommy!"

Carole knew the number. The caller was an insurance adjuster. The four-thousand-square-foot house had a leaky pipe in the downstairs guest suite, and David was on a mission to get the insurance company to pay for the damages. The adjuster was equally insistent that it was a problem caused by the builder, not something they'd cover.

"Look," she said to the man after they'd exchanged pleasantries, "just pay the claim. You don't want us to get a lawyer, do you?"

No answer.

"Do you?"

The adjuster's response disintegrated into static.

Carole made a face. "You're breaking up," she said. "Hang on."

"Okay," she thought she heard him say.

It made no sense to her, but lately cell reception was often better inside the house than out. If this kept up, she'd be making calls from the crawl space.

Charlie's attention had drifted from the bird to a bunch of pinecones that had fallen during a thunderstorm a few days prior. "Stay where you are," she called over to him.

The boy was sitting on the lawn. Next to him was a burgeoning collection of cones. "Okay! Okay, Mommy!"

Carole smiled and slipped into the kitchen, keeping Charlie in her sight through the window. "How's this?" she said into her phone.

"Loud and clear," the adjuster answered, "but I don't think you're going to like what you hear."

"Well, I don't think you're hearing *me*," she said, and then, although she loathed such trivial confrontations, she spent the next few minutes reiterating her husband's position on the damage.

The fact was, she felt sorry for the contractor who had done the work. She considered him conscientious and meticulous. As far as she could tell, there was no blame to be placed anywhere. "Shit happens," she'd told David when he dumped everything in her lap.

"Not to us," he said. "Not anymore. We're done being anyone's patsy. People take advantage of people like us because they look right at us and all they see are dollar signs. I'm done with that."

She knew he was referring to a Lexus that had been nothing but trouble. It took a year of back-and-forth—heated phone calls, nasty e-mails, and a face-to-face at the dealership that could have made the news—to get the dealer to concede the car was indeed a lemon and make good on the warranty.

But this situation was not *that* situation. Besides, they had the money to fix the problem themselves. They had more money than they needed in a lifetime. Her position at Google had been very good to her. It had funded the house. The restaurant. The cars. Their entire lifestyle.

Carole walked from the kitchen to the living room, her eyes fastened on her son's blond hair, a golden bouncing ball.

"You don't really want this to escalate into some legal battle," the adjuster said. "Do you?"

Carole didn't. David had kept pushing for her to make a stand, but it didn't feel authentic to her. She knew what things were reasonable and worth fighting for. This wasn't one of those.

"Can't we just forget this?" she finally told the adjuster.

"No, ma'am," he said. "Once you open a claim, we have to see it to the end."

"Please. Just never mind," she said. "I wish to un-report this, or whatever the term is."

"Not able to do that," he said. "Has to go through headquarters."

Carole was ready to pull the plug on the whole thing. Although she probably wouldn't tell—*definitely* wouldn't tell—David about this attempted change of heart, she was all for giving the insurance company and the contractor a free pass, absolving anyone of any wrongdoing. She just wanted to get the pipe fixed, make the damaged drywall repairs, and get back to a life unencumbered by details that took her away from what was really important. What she most wanted to do.

"I'm so tired of all of this," she said, running her fingers over a weaving of Jacob's sheep wool that she'd finished the previous week. There was something lacking in the piece, and she wondered about it just then. *Needs more black fibers,* she thought. *Maybe birch twigs?*

"I hear you," the man said. "I'm sorry. It's a process. Like everything."

"All right," Carole conceded, a sigh leaking from her lungs as she disconnected the call.

No one seemed to hear her at all anymore. At

Google she had led four international teams over a seven-year period. She was the glue that held everything together. No one made a move without her—not because she demanded submission, but because she'd earned respect from team members and suppliers.

Respect had been elusive lately. The Jacob wool weaving was her latest project. She longed to be taken seriously for her art, but it was slow going. Her weavings were good but not special enough. One time she overheard someone call her the "millionaire artist wannabe" at a dinner party, and it had crushed her. David encouraged her to keep on with her dreams, but sometimes she wondered if he really held the same view as those party snarks.

"Good work," he'd said one time when she was working in her studio. "Too bad you can't sell this for what you've put into it."

"It isn't about the money," she said.

He ran his hand over her weaving. "It's always about the money."

"It's about the creating, David."

The ice in his drink tinkled as he tilted the glass of soda so he could get the last drop. "Sure," he said into the glass. "Creating."

Carole had turned away and returned to her work, ending the conversation the only way she knew how: by ignoring David. He would never understand her need to make art. He could never see what she saw in the white, russet, and black fibers that she wove, tufted, and twisted into something only she saw in her mind's eye.

Now she went back to the deck and called out to Charlie. "Where are you?"

She scanned the yard, the riverbank. The heron had vanished. So had her little boy.

Chapter Three
MISSING: FIFTEEN MINUTES

Liz Jarrett could not escape it. It hadn't been a dog or a cat. It had been the little boy next door. She'd felt the air drain from her lungs as she threw herself to the driveway and cradled Charlie Franklin in her arms.

"Oh, God," she said in a controlled whisper. "Charlie. No. No. Charlie."

Every synapse in her nervous system was firing. A carpet-bombing. She tried to breathe, but it was as if her lungs had been sealed off with something impenetrable. Though she didn't let out an audible cry, tears streamed down her cheeks. Liz gently twisted Charlie's shoulders as if by doing so she'd revive the boy so that he could open his eyes, so that he could speak.

Peekaboo. Come on, Charlie. Snap out of this!

Liz held him close. She kept her voice low. "Honey, wake up! Wake up now!"

Yet nothing happened. Charlie's lips stayed immobile. His eyes stayed shut. The thin fabric of his Mickey Mouse shirt appeared motionless across his chest.

"Wake up!" Liz said, more command than plea. But nothing. Nothing at all.

Everything was spiraling around her.

No, it was Liz who was spinning. She was a washing machine. She was a Ferris wheel. A blender. She'd only known such disorientation once in her life—the flood on the highway to Diamond Lake. She tried to stand up, but she couldn't force her legs to lift her. She pressed her hands against her breasts. Maybe this was a dream. Maybe she was dead. She wasn't sure if she was really breathing just then.

She let it pass through her mind as she knelt there that none of what had just happened had occurred at all. But there was the proof. The limp body of the little boy next door was right there. Liz called over to the Franklins' house, but a plane passing overhead swathed her words in a blanket of noise. She reached for her phone to call 911. Her fingertips trembled so much that she couldn't hit the right sequence of numbers.

This can't be happening. This didn't happen. I didn't do this.

Liz crawled around the car, trying to lift herself up.

What's wrong with me?

Charlie needs help.

I *need help.*

From her place on the driveway, she eyed the workbench in the back of the garage. She needed to pull herself together. Her thoughts came at her in pieces, a smashed dinner plate in the driveway of a yard sale. Pieces everywhere. They could be scooped up, reassembled, but never, ever, would any of it be the same. She had done the unthinkable. That was true. But it *was* an accident. She didn't see Charlie. Not even a glimmer of the boy had caught her eye. Liz thought back to the night before and the pills she'd taken to prepare for the test. She knew that whatever was coursing through her bloodstream just then was partly to blame for what had happened. Saying so would only invite questions from the police. She'd tell them over and over that it was an accident. She was in a hurry. They'd pounce on every detail, shredding her explanation into a million tiny pieces. Each piece, when assembled, would make her out to be either careless or drugged out.

Liz saw no way out of it. She hoisted herself up and stood there, her head bowed over the boy. Blood oozed from the back of his head.

The RAV4 had hit him hard.

She looked over at the workbench once more.

She glanced down at Charlie.

The spinning had stopped. Liz gripped her phone. She could call for help, or she could put Charlie in the car to get him to St. Charles Medical Center. Driving him would be faster. It would get him to where he'd receive the medical attention that he needed.

If something could be done.

But even as she stood there deciding what

to do, Liz Jarrett thought about herself. Later she would wonder what had moved her toward being that person. A person who would go into a self-preservation mode that was really a collision course to personal annihilation. A person who put ambition over responsibility, kindness. Decency. It was in that moment that Liz considered what was at stake in a hotel conference room near Portland. She thought about the test she had yet to take. She thought about Owen telling her that she was a screwup and that she'd really messed up this time. That she was never going to be anything. She was going to be known forever as the woman who killed a close friend's son.

Tiny pieces of gravel were stuck to her palms from crawling on the driveway. She brushed them off, then noticed tiny blood droplets on her jeans. Charlie's? Hers? She sucked in some air. She opened the front passenger-side car door and moved the seat up, then opened the back door.

She hooked her arms under Charlie's tiny body and lifted.

You are so stupid, Liz.

You are going down.

The police lab will find Adderall in your bloodstream.

You will fail the test.

You will be a pariah in your own neighborhood.

You will go to prison.

It happened so fast. Faster than a blink. It was nearly a magnetic force that drew her to the workbench instead of the backseat of the RAV4. She set the body down, gently, on the workbench. Sweetly, even. Even though nothing but darkness was passing through her mind, Liz leaned over and kissed the child's forehead. A tear splashed on the boy's blond head.

What have I done? Fuck me! Kill me!

A blue tarp her father had used when he painted the house and stained the front porch caught her attention. She unfurled the stiff, paint-splotched fabric and placed it over Charlie.

She'd killed him. She hadn't meant to. It had been a terrible accident. It really had.

She knew what she was doing would only buy her time.

Got to take the test. Got to figure this out. Got to. Got to. Got to.

As she approached her car, Liz could hear Carole's voice calling out for her son down by the river.

God, no.

It was an ice pick in her chest.

"Charlie!" Carole called out.

Liz slid behind the wheel and started backing out.

Carole's voice was louder, more forceful. Closer.

Liz pushed the button on the garage-door

opener, and the door rolled downward. She caught a glimpse of a woman's face in the rearview mirror. Her own reflection seemed foreign to her. A stranger's face.

Again Carole calling out for her son.

"Charlie!"

Liz pressed her foot on the gas slowly and continued backing out. As she cleared the space in front of the garage, she saw the bucket of cones that Charlie must have been carrying when she struck him. She also saw a small pool of blood on the gravel driveway. She could feel the pills and coffee make a play for her esophagus, but she managed to suppress the urge to vomit. She'd lost control of everything else.

She'd lost everything.

"Charlie!"

She got out of the car, picked up the bucket, and kicked a couple of the errant cones into the flower bed that flanked the driveway. She put the ball of her foot on the blood and spun around on it, grinding it into oblivion. The spot left behind was no longer red but a damp, dark stain. Liz hoped it would blend into the driveway. She put Charlie's bucket in the car. She needed air. She could barely breathe. She returned to the car and got inside. She rolled down the window and put her foot on the gas.

And she was gone.

• • •

Liz pulled over on a quiet side street just before the highway that slices through Bend and rolled up the opened window. All she could see in her mind's eye were images of Charlie. Playing in the yard. Following after his mother when Carole came for a visit next door.

He had been an angelic child.

Now he was an angel.

As the car idled, Liz screamed as loud as she could. Tears rained from her eyes. She had no idea why she'd panicked. It was an *accident,* a terrible one. One that she'd made a million times worse by her actions after the car hit Charlie.

She dialed her husband one more time. This time when she got voice mail she didn't leave a message. She didn't know what the message should be. She knew that the right thing to do was to return home, call the police, and face Carole and David. Tell them how sorry she was. Tell them that she loved Charlie too. Beg them all for forgiveness. Plead for mercy.

For she'd done something she could never explain to anyone. She'd put Charlie under a damn *tarp* in the garage and drove on to Beaverton and the bar exam.

Chapter Four
MISSING: TWENTY MINUTES

If only.

There is a moment when the parents of many, if not most, missing children recognize an irrevocable mistake they made. They can pinpoint the split second when something they did changed everything in their world. Mistakes are dominoes, falling on one another in a mechanical, unstoppable progression. Those moments never leave them. The echo is a ticking clock at the end of a long wooden hallway. Pounding. Reverberating. Mocking. Reminding those parents that terrible accidents or dark incidents caused by others truly rest only on their shoulders.

Carole Franklin told herself not to panic. It would be unproductive to do so. It had only been a goddamn minute since her eyes held the image of her little boy on the green strip of lawn that separated the river from the house. Maybe five.

She walked around the house, searching for signs that he'd come inside. Nothing.

She took a deep breath and let it out slowly. She sipped some water from the sports bottle on the kitchen counter.

"Charlie?" she called out, her voice firm but not scary. If he was playing hide-and-seek, she didn't want to jolt him into digging in and hiding from her because he thought he was in trouble. "Honey?" Her tone was plaintive but with a growing edge.

The TV was on, and she reached for the remote and put it on mute. She strained to hear her son.

"You better come out right now," she said. No, too harsh. "I have a Fruit Roll-Up with your name on it."

As she stood there, alone in her living room, Carole's heartbeat began to accelerate; it felt like a hammer striking a pillow inside her chest. A thud on repeat, building in intensity. She sipped more water.

Finally she made her way out to the deck, filled her lungs, and shouted for Charlie. The hammer continued to pound on the pillow. Harder. Faster. When her calls brought no response, Carole left the deck and ran the length of the yard, which rolled gently down to the soft, grassy edge of the river. She hurried to the space where the landscape designer had incorporated an old river-rock fire pit, scanning the water for something to indicate something terrible had happened under its surface.

But nothing. No bubbles. No shadow of an object drifting below.

Nothing at all.

The water was nearly smooth and transparent.

Carole stood frozen as a lone crow circled overhead. She put her fingertips to her lips. The muscles in her shoulders and throat had all seized up into a single rigid mass. Her heart was heaving against her rib cage. She was a fighter, though, and began doing everything she could to remain completely composed. She filled her lungs and blasted a cry for help over the water. No one returned her call. Dan Miller was no longer mowing his lawn across the river. The argyle pattern of the grass had been completed. She looked over at the Miller house and thought she saw the old man silhouetted in the window, but she wasn't sure. She looked upriver. The teenagers on the bridge were gone. No one was there, and that meant no one had seen anything happen to her son.

Maybe nothing *had* happened.

She called over to the paddler in the canoe with the cocker spaniel, still working his way upstream.

"Have you seen my little boy?"

The man tugged at his earbuds and leaned in Carole's direction. His dog barked. "Say that again?" he asked.

Carole could feel her knees weaken. "My son," she said. "He was playing out front. Right here. Have you seen him?"

"Nope," the man said.

"He's three!" she called out, as if Charlie's age would jog the paddler's memory.

"Been focused on getting upriver," he said. "You're about the only one I've seen in this stretch."

Carole found herself back at *that moment*. The instant she wished she could change. *Damn the insurance adjuster!* No. She damned herself for taking the call and pulling her eyes from Charlie. She was unsure how long she'd been distracted. Five minutes? *If that.* As she scanned the space where her son had stalked the heron and then collected pinecones, she told herself everything would be all right.

"I'll keep my eyes peeled," the man in the red canoe called out.

Carole thanked him and started pondering the most plausible explanation.

Charlie had gone inside the house.

He was hiding among the arbor of hopvines in the side yard.

He had not gone in or even near the water, because he knew better. She told him over and over the water was dangerous. He knew it. She was sure of it.

After a hurried sweep of the yard and the riverbank, Carole realized that the scenarios she was inventing weren't helping. In her bones she knew that something was really, really wrong.

She punched David's cell number as she went

back inside and then sped through the house, grinding the phone to her ear with such ferocity that her earring tore her earlobe. Blood oozed. *Why in the hell does this house have to be so goddamn big?* There were only the three of them. Why did they have to build a place on the river when she'd preferred a secluded spot on acreage, a site that offered views of Mount Bachelor and posed no threat to the part of their life that meant more than anything?

At least to her. There had been numerous times when Carole doubted the sincerity of her husband's interest in their son. Of course, David said the right things. Fussed over Charlie at the right times. He hunkered down on the floor to play cars with him. He even read to him now and then in the evenings. Carole was grateful. A boy needed his father. And yet there was something rote about David's involvement with their son. It seemed each one of those bonding moments was hastily staged, as though David were checking a box so that he could move on to more pressing matters.

The restaurant.

It was always about that. He was utterly and completely wrapped up in Sweetwater. It was his dream.

His focus and self-absorption had been a good thing during the first years of their marriage, when Carole was deep into her own career. She didn't have time for much more than occasional sex and trips to exotic locales. They talked more on airplanes than they did in their own dining room or bedroom. For a time, that was fine. Even preferable. Carole had things to do too. Her mind was laser-focused on her product team and the launch that always loomed ahead at Google.

Charlie's birth had changed her focus, as babies almost always do. He was the gift from God that Carole Franklin had not dared even to dream about. She was nearly forty when a home pregnancy test kit indicated the right color. Finally. She didn't even tell David at first because she felt that this was her last chance—and the last time she became pregnant, he'd talked her into having an abortion. She was thirty-five then.

"The time isn't right," David told her. "Things are about to pop with my career. I've got my sights on a new restaurant concept. TV interest too. I could be a lifestyle brand. *I know it.* Besides, babe, your career is important too."

The last part of his plea was a bit of an understatement. In fact, her salary and sizable bonuses and soon-to-be-cashed-in stock options had fueled their lifestyle for years. In any event, David hadn't wanted a baby. At least as far as Carole could tell, just not then. He'd wanted to pursue his dream unencumbered by the responsibilities of fatherhood, and she'd gone along with it.

Before the moment that sent her searching the river frontage and every room in the house for her son, Carole thought that her greatest irrevocable mistake had been the abortion. She'd done it willingly. She couldn't completely pin her decision on David. He hadn't forced her, even though it felt that way sometimes. She'd agreed to it because she hadn't really wanted to press the pause button on her own career. Not then. She had moved up to director, and the power and money that came with that was undeniably intoxicating. A drug that she couldn't shake in any kind of rehab. She'd been sucked into a lifestyle that she loved but also knew precluded whatever personal dreams she'd had before joining Google. She loved her job, but she couldn't see a way just then to be both a mother and a rising executive.

Carole let herself believe that she'd terminated the pregnancy at David's insistence. It was, she came to know, a little lie she told herself. She cried a thousand tears after the procedure. She could still picture everything about that morning. The silent drive with David's hand on her knee. A young mother pushing a stroller across the crosswalk as they made the turn to the clinic. A dead bird on the road. The brochure rack in the lobby. An old disco song playing in the waiting room, as though there could be some reason why anyone would ever dance there.

It all came rushing back to her as she searched for her son.

The sound of the technician as she did her work under the shroud of a sheet.

The icy feel of the metal stirrups on her heels and against her calves.

Carole didn't know if it had been a son or a daughter she'd aborted, but she secretly named the baby's spirit anyway. She mourned Katherine and wondered what might have happened had she said no to David.

She was sure she had more time for a baby. But when it became time to have one, she didn't become pregnant. A deep chill went through her. It was payback for her selfishness, for choosing ambition over Katherine. For more than a year, she tried to get pregnant—and nothing. At thirty-nine, she started looking up in vitro fertilization clinics on the Internet—something she'd sworn she'd never do.

But then it happened. It was nearly five years after the abortion when Charlie was born.

When David didn't answer his cell right away, Carole dialed the restaurant's main number.

Amanda Jenkins answered on the second ring.

"Where's David?" Carole asked, her voice sharp and charged with adrenaline.

"Hi, Carole," Amanda said. "He's out of the office right now."

"Where?" Carole asked, her voice rising to nearly a scream. "Where is he?"

"Are you all right, Carole?" The young woman had weathered more than one storm of David Franklin's making over the past couple of years at Sweetwater. She'd juggled staff and customers whenever David asked her to do so. Even when it made no sense. She was good at her job because she was unflappable and loyal. "Take a breath," she said to her boss's wife.

"I can't," she said. "I can't breathe. Charlie's missing. I need David."

"Slow down," Amanda said. "What happened?"

Carole started to spin. She was sure she was going to pass out. She'd fainted once before, when she hadn't bothered to eat in the morning. Low blood sugar. But this was a different kind of wooziness, one brought by fear instead of hunger.

"Amanda," Carole said. "I need my husband."

"He's not here. Can I help? I'll call the police."

"No," Carole said, feeling a wave of nausea in the back of her constricted throat. "No. No. I'll do that." In truth, she admitted to herself, she didn't want to call the police just then. Doing so would elevate what might be, *must* be, a careless mistake into something much more devastating than she could handle at the moment.

She hung up and made her way to the basement.

"Charlie!" she screamed, the words discharged from her vocal cords with a kind of power

62

that she hadn't, up to that second, known she possessed. "Charlie, where are you?"

Carole ran back up and through the main level, then the upstairs. Pulling off the sofa cushions. Looking into the shower stall. The pantry. Under the stairs. Her studio. She scoured every inch as rapidly as she could. She threw herself to the floor next to each bed, looking under the bed frame and pulling herself upright to move as fast as she could to the next room.

The police emergency number was only three digits. She couldn't bring herself to dial them. Not yet. Not to make it real. Not to make it bigger than it was.

She ran over to the Jarretts' little bungalow next door and pounded her fists against the bright pink front door. Her fingertips found her bloody earlobe and she brushed off the blood with the shoulder of her blouse. Owen and Liz were gone. *Of course they were.* Liz had her exam that day—the essay section of the Oregon bar—and Owen had been going to the office early to prepare for an infusion of venture capital money and then an IPO of his software firm.

She returned to the house and went through it a third time. *Nothing.* No trace of her son. Charlie was gone.

This was real.

It was her fault.

Finally, Carole slumped on the upholstered

bench at the foot of the bed and dialed 911.

"My little boy is missing," she said, giving the dispatcher her address. She fought for composure with every syllable as she scanned the surface of the Deschutes.

"Please come as fast as you can," she said, holding the phone with a vise grip. "He's three. I think my little boy fell into the river."

CHAPTER FIVE
MISSING: ONE HOUR

Bend Police detective Esther Nguyen was on her third cup of truly terrible office coffee and working through the least favorite part of her job—paperwork—when one of the department's newest officers, Jake Alioto, notified her that help was needed on a call.

"Boy missing," he said. "Mom's pretty torn up."

Esther set her cup on a stack of papers. "How long?"

Jake was young, with light brown skin that made his white teeth nearly blindingly so. Esther had a hard time not looking at his mouth when he spoke. So white. Perfect. A somewhat struggling goatee accentuated his look.

"Not very," he said. "An hour at most."

"Custody issue?"

He didn't think so. "Dad's at work. Mom's home."

"Where?"

"Riverfront, near the pedestrian bridge by the park."

Esther went for a light jacket that hung on a peg adjacent to her office door. She was a petite woman, just five feet tall, with black hair that she wore blunt-cut to her shoulders. Silver wire-framed glasses shielded her brown eyes. She wore no jewelry but a slender gold necklace that her father had given her, a pendant in the shape of a sea star from a trip the family had made to California when she was a teenager. When she was agitated or nervous, her fingertips always found their way to the pendant. Its golden surface held a particularly bright sheen where she'd touched it countless times.

"An hour doesn't make a missing person," Esther said. "You're aware of that, Jake, right?"

Esther had an edge that made her good at her job but sometimes difficult to be around. Talk around the office was that she might be somewhere on the Asperger's continuum. This was just mean-spirited armchair analysis, but it was a fact that Esther could be direct in the kind of unflinching way that can also signal a lack of understanding of social cues.

Jake stepped aside so she could lead the way. "Yeah, I know," he said. "Of course. But I feel sorry for the woman. She's falling apart."

"Name?"

Jake, who had a teenager's ambling gait even though he was twenty-five, hurried to keep up with the detective. "Mom's Carole Franklin," he said. "She's a local. The missing boy is Charlie. She thinks he might have fallen in the river when she wasn't looking."

"Did she sound drunk?"

"No, ma'am."

Esther gave him a look. A familiar one. "Don't call me that."

"Sorry," Jake said. "My bad."

As they made their way to the cruiser, Esther thought of the case of a little boy in Corvallis, the jurisdiction in which she had started her career. Tommy Walton vanished from his babysitter's backyard. He'd been missing for days when his mangled body was recovered from an abandoned roller rink. Esther had known that little boys and girls were targets of the evil and the insane—but hadn't *really* known it until then.

Esther had worked the case with her partner for six weeks until they arrested the neighbor, a sixteen-year-old boy who'd sodomized and strangled Tommy. He'd done that in the first half hour of the boy's abduction. Esther never forgot that she and her partner had held out hope that the boy would be found alive, certainly during the first few hours and even days of the investigation.

Esther knew missing-persons case rules were a bit of a myth. There was no twenty-four-hour mandatory wait to get started on a search. A small child or a professional person with a spotless record can earn the support of a search team within a few hours of going missing.

· · ·

While Jake prattled on about a girl he was dating, Esther drove past a Thai fusion restaurant on Wall Street that had been the location of her first date with her soon-to-be ex-husband, Drew. She'd never be able to eat there again. The restaurant, known for its legendary green curry dish, would forever represent the start of her personal disaster.

Like other professionals their age, Esther and Drew Oliver met online. Drew was handsome and outgoing and had a kind of glib personality that Esther found so very different from other men she'd dated. Those other guys had been interchangeable. Serious. Smart. Most were computer science and technology geeks and more interested in code than in carrying on a conversation. Esther wanted to laugh. She wanted romance. She wanted a little adventure.

Drew understood all of that. He ran a Bend brewery start-up that was making serious headway but was still far from the steady income her parents required of an ideal suitor for their only daughter. The pair dated for nine months, then moved in together. While Esther was in no rush to get married, her mother's constant refrain that "things don't look right" beat down on her like a headbanger's drumstick. When Drew asked her to marry him, she agreed right away, thinking it would get her mother off her back.

That was a miscalculation.

"Money is more important than a good time," her mother whispered in Esther's ear on her wedding day. "You will never be able to raise a family. A cop and a beer maker—that's just not what I'd consider a suitable combination for a successful marriage."

"We're not having this conversation, Mom."

Her mother fussed with the white meringue tulle of Esther's wedding dress, still on the hanger. "You didn't ask me. So what? It is my job to tell you what I think."

Esther didn't even bother with a response. She hated her mom for ruining her special day, but that was her mother, a negative soul who made a point of slicing the joy from any possible moment with her razor of a tongue.

As she drove past the Thai place on the way to see about a missing child, she was long past denying her mother had been right. When the brewery ultimately failed, Drew's charm and outgoing nature turned inward and sullen. He lashed out at the world. Drank more. Found a hundred reasons to stay away from home. Glib turned into sarcastic. Caustic mutated into mean. When they separated, she knew it was not going to be temporary but the only—the final—solution for their situation.

"We were wrong for each other," she told Drew when she'd finally had enough and conceded that her mother had not cursed her marriage but simply predicted its dismal outcome.

"I'm wrong for anyone," Drew said.

Esther didn't argue. She didn't allow herself to fall into a trap. No more traps. No more fighting. No more feeling sorry about what might have been—and never would be.

Esther parked the cruiser in front of the Franklins' residence. The house was one of those dark fortresses with slits for windows on the street side and splashes of lime-colored evergreens jammed into position to brighten up a space that seldom saw sunlight. A fringe of zebra grass edged the walkway, and a basalt water feature that was all angles and dark spires burbled adjacent to the driveway.

"Some place," Jake said, looking up at the house.

"Something else," she said. An amalgamation of taste, style, money, and the good sense to let professionals do the heavy lifting while allowing the homeowners to think they'd done it all on their own. Esther's mother would love this house, and the people who lived here would be her heroes.

Esther thought that the house, with its perfection, its slavish attention to detail, said new money. People born rich don't try so hard. They know they don't need to. They already have everything they want, and they never have to break a sweat to show it off. Showing it off is for those at risk of ending up back where they started.

They got out of the car. With Jake trailing, Esther turned the corner to walk up to the door as Carole Franklin heaved open the front door and lurched toward them. She was tall—five nine or ten. Her hair was a silvery blond that fell in soft curls to her shoulders. She was trim, with the body of a swimmer or yoga enthusiast. Probably both.

In other circumstances, Mrs. Franklin would have made a stunning, if not imposing, figure. But this morning she looked crumpled. She wore the kind of terrified look that Esther had seen in the eyes of other mothers.

"He was out of my sight for a minute," she said, valiantly fighting to keep any tears from falling from her watery blue eyes.

Esther put her hand on the woman's shoulder. "I know you're scared, Mrs. Franklin. I'm Detective Esther Nguyen, and this is Officer Alioto. I need you to tell me what happened. Take your time."

"There isn't any time," Carole said. "Charlie could be anywhere. Anything could have happened to him."

"I understand," Esther said. "I know it might be hard to believe, but I've been around long enough to know that kids just wander away."

Mrs. Franklin's lips tightened. "Charlie never

leaves my sight," she said, forcing the words from her mouth.

"Right. But this time he did, right? We're here to help. Let's go inside. Tell me what happened."

Mrs. Franklin led them to a living room with floor-to-ceiling views of the river and repeated her story about being on the phone for "only a minute or two" with the adjuster from the insurance company. "We had a leak in the basement. I don't even care about it. I should never have taken the stupid call."

"It's not your fault," Esther said.

Mrs. Franklin fiddled with a stray thread that had come undone from the gray velvet pillow she clutched as she sat on the sofa. The light from the river, now full of paddlers and inner-tubers, flickered in her eyes. A sound system played an incongruently soothing interlude in the background.

"But it *is* our fault. Living here at all. We live on a *river,* for God's sake," she went on. "I never should have turned my back for even a second. I know better. I do. This is my fault," she repeated, still trying to keep her voice from shattering.

"You need to take a breath," Esther said. Her tone was kind, not condescending. She'd interviewed hundreds of witnesses and knew how rapidly a person could go from being able to help a case to being utterly useless. Sometimes even a distraction. She needed Carole Franklin to be the kind of person who fit her tasteful surroundings. Thoughtful. Organized. Self-aware.

"You didn't see any sign that he went into the river, did you?" Esther asked.

Mrs. Franklin watched as police officers gathered by the riverbank. "No," she said. "I called over to a man canoeing with his dog. I saw a tuber on a red Riparian tube go by. My neighbor across the river—he was there. No. No one saw him go in. But, really, where else could he be?"

"Does he have a hiding place?" Esther's tone was calm, full of empathy, Jake noticed. He wished that particular Esther worked at the police department.

"My nephew had a secret hideout," the detective went on, "a fort that he assembled out of cardboard boxes in the basement. My sister had a fit one time when she couldn't find him."

"No," Mrs. Franklin said. "We don't have anything like that. I've searched the house."

The police officer who'd arrived on the scene right after the call approached. "Detective," he said, "we've looked everywhere. In every closet. Under every bed. We even looked in the dryer in the laundry room and the freezer in the garage."

Carole Franklin wrapped her arms tightly around her lanky frame. "The freezer," she said, horror in her eyes. "I didn't look there."

"It's all right, Mrs. Franklin," Esther said. "He wasn't there."

"We've cast a wider net," the officer continued. "We have another pair of officers working the shoreline. Nothing so far."

"All right," Esther said, returning her attention to the woman. "Where is Mr. Franklin?"

"I don't know," she said, watching the water. "His phone went to voice mail. I've texted. I've called. I have no idea."

"Is there any chance he might have come home and taken Charlie somewhere?"

Mrs. Franklin faced her. "You mean to the park or something? Of course not. David's not that way," she said, her tone shifting a little.

"What way?"

"A father who surprises his son. He's more . . . predictable."

"Right, of course. What does he do?"

"He runs Sweetwater. The restaurant on Wall."

Esther nodded and told the responding officer to send someone over to see if David Franklin was at work. "We need him here."

"Thank you," Mrs. Franklin said.

"No problem," the officer said. "We'll find your little boy."

Esther shot the young man a swift but decisive look.

Mrs. Franklin caught it. "You can't promise that, can you?"

Esther didn't think so. "No. I'm sorry. We can't promise. What the officer is saying, though—and what I know from my own personal experience—is that kids turn up."

"Always?"

Esther could feel her desperation. Carole Franklin was grasping at straws, and she needed to believe that everything would be all right.

"More than ninety-nine percent of the time."

Mrs. Franklin nodded. "I need to *do* something," she said, turning to look back at the river, imagining her little boy falling from the bank. Getting scared. Scrambling. Thrashing. Fighting to get to the surface. The images played on a loop over and over, and she couldn't stop the sequence.

"I need to go out there and help find him," she said, getting up.

"No." Esther motioned for her to sit. "Take a breath," she repeated. "You need to let us do our job. We can do this. Is there someone we could call? Another family member?"

The mother of the missing three-year-old looked hard at the detective. Her eyes were outlined in red. She slumped back down and rocked herself a little, thinking before speaking. Perhaps willing herself to be the deliberate woman she'd been in the boardroom. "And tell them what?" she asked. "Tell them that I wasn't paying attention and my son vanished? That I wasn't watching and he fell into the water? I

75

can't. I can't do that. I can barely say that to you, let alone people who know Charlie."

Esther reached over to touch her hand, but the frightened mother pulled away. "We don't know what happened, Mrs. Franklin," Esther said. "It's early. Let's see where we are when your husband gets here. This is traumatic. You need support."

"I can't," she repeated. "I can't even say the words."

"I understand, Mrs. Franklin."

Carole Franklin looked at the detective in a way that indicated she no longer saw her as someone who was judging her lapse in motherhood. She was, in fact, there to help. Yes, she was going to find Charlie.

"Please," she said. "Call me Carole."

Esther nodded, and Carole handed her a photograph that she'd retrieved from the side table.

"This was taken two weeks ago," Carole said. "My dad and his wife were up from Santa Rosa. We went to Lincoln City for the day."

Charlie was standing on a driftwood log, smiling at the camera with that kind of exaggerated smile that little kids make whenever a lens is pointed in their direction.

"He's wearing that same shirt today," she said.

Esther studied the photograph. The boy was wearing a Mickey Mouse pullover, a wild mix of red and black that little ones find cool. He

76

had a crooked smile and light blue eyes like his mother's. "This helps. Thank you. He's adorable."

Carole offered coffee, but Esther declined.

"Let's talk about the water. Is Charlie able to swim at all?"

"No. He's three. We took him to toddler swimming lessons but—no, he's not a good swimmer."

"Has he been known to go into the river? You know, when you are not around to supervise?"

"No," Carole said. "Never. Absolutely not. Look, we live on the river. Our son knows better. I tell him every day. I told him this morning. Don't even think about getting your feet wet."

Carole stopped talking. She sat there quietly. Nearly frozen.

"Then why do you think he might have gone in?" Esther asked.

Carole looked out the window. "I don't know. He shouldn't have. He *wouldn't* have. But he was out there." She raised a finger and pointed. "Out by the river. Where else could he have gone?"

"And that was the last time you saw him, Carole?"

"Right. I said that already."

"But you said he hasn't gone in the water in the past."

Carole nodded. "That's right. I honestly don't know if he went in. I don't think he would. I really don't. And I told him. I told him to stay away from the water. He knows better. I know that. Charlie's smart."

"Did you see anyone out there?" she asked, indicating the river.

She nodded. "A guy on an inner tube. Some kids on the bridge. Someone in a canoe. My neighbor across the river was out there for a while."

Esther asked for more details, and the mother of the missing boy did her best to fill in the blanks. She could barely get her words out.

"Sorry," she said. "Sorry. I'm not like this. I'm not."

"This is a lot to take in," Esther said. "Take a breath."

Esther looked out the window. The river was nearly as flat as a pane of glass. The detective was pretty sure that if the boy had fallen from the bank, his mother would have seen an indication of it. The man paddling the canoe would have. Maybe the tuber floating by around that time. Or the elderly neighbor across the water, pushing a mower.

She turned her attention back to Carole, who by now was very pale, her skin nearly the color of her hair.

"Carole?"

The boy's mother snapped out of her stupor. "I was only away from him for a minute. Really I was."

"I know," Esther said. "I need you to stop saying that, all right? We need to focus on where your boy might have gone, not what mistakes you think you might have made."

Carole blinked. "Thank you."

"Neighbors? Friends nearby?"

"Our closest neighbors are the Jarretts, but they left early in the day. Liz is taking an exam for the bar, and Owen is with a tech firm downtown. The couple on the other side of us stays here only a few weekends out of the year. They're not here now. They rent out the house, but no one's checked in yet for the weekend that I can tell."

"All right," the detective said. "We'll look into everything. Has anything troubled you lately?"

Carole looked confused. "I don't know what you mean."

"I mean, have you or your son received any unwanted attention from anyone? Anything at all?"

"No. Everyone smiles at him. Charlie's a friendly little boy. Please find him. I know he's out there. He's scared. I can feel it inside."

Missing kids came in several flavors, and over the years Esther had worked cases that aligned with each type. The most common were those in which custodial rights played a part. One parent lashing out at the other by taking a child or not returning him or her from a scheduled visit.

79

In most instances, those were easily solved. Charlie's parents were together, so the detective scratched that kind off the list. A runaway was another possible scenario, but Charlie was too young to fit that profile. Next was what social workers and law enforcement called "thrownaway" cases. Those occurred when parents simply abandoned or kicked the child out of the family home. Again, scratch. Sometimes foul play was involved in that scenario, but not all that frequently. Sometimes children simply wandered away from the sight of their parents and got lost at the store, on a camping trip, or even in their own backyard. And finally, the kind that chills even the most seasoned investigator: the abduction case, in which a stranger had preyed upon the most vulnerable.

Local law enforcement from around the region was notified first. Arrangements for an Amber Alert were made, and the National Center for Missing & Exploited Children was contacted. Within hours, Charlie's photograph and description would be everywhere. If the case wasn't solved in short order—as most are—the little boy would be seen on TV, on shopping mall bulletin boards, and all over social media.

Help could come from anywhere.

Across the state.

Right next door.

Chapter Six
MISSING: TIME UNKNOWN

The blond-haired little boy was under the blue water of the ocean. Charlie's warm breath floated from his lips, a pant too weak to extinguish the tiniest birthday candle. Too faint to stir the wisp of a dandelion-seed head, as he and his mother had done the day before when they walked to the playground with the pirate ship.

Too faint. Too weak. But alive.

Charlie tried to twist, but he couldn't move. He looked upward through narrowed eyes, but in his disoriented state he had no idea which way was up and which was down. His tears instantly dissolved in the seawater and he tried to cry out, but the blue of the ocean kept his words close, compressed to his face. His head hurt. He wanted his mommy right then. More than he'd wanted anything he'd ever wanted in his life.

More than a puppy.

More than a chocolate animal cookie.

Mommy! Come and get me! Mommy! I'm in the water. I can't breathe! Get me!

Each word came out in small bubbles beneath the blue.

Yet no one heard him. No one knew where

he was. Charlie didn't know where he was. He didn't understand how it was that he'd found himself in the water, under all of that blue.

He lay there, very still. Thinking his mother would come. He thought of his father and tried that too.

Daddy! Daddy! Come and help me! Get Mommy!

Those words no longer came from his vocal cords. Instead, they pulsed their way through his brain, stumbling along the way. He thought about the pinecones he'd gathered along the Deschutes shoreline—how one had pricked his finger, another had released a whirling seedpod that twirled through the air. He recalled his walk up the hill from the shore, balancing that full bucket of pinecones.

Then everything became fuzzy. His head was wet, but the blue kept him from reaching upward to touch it. No more tears. No more cries for help.

Charlie didn't understand how it was that he'd ended up in the water.

Mommy?

Daddy?

Help me.

The boy closed his eyes to shut out the heavy, heavy blue. His breathing slowed some more. Just a faint, shallow puff. His hope for his mommy or daddy to pull him from the water dissipated as Charlie Franklin, three, found himself fading into the sweet calm of oblivion.

CHAPTER SEVEN
MISSING: FOUR HOURS

It was nearly 2:00 p.m. when Liz Jarrett pulled her car into a spot by a dumpster in the parking lot behind the Shilo Inn, where the bar exam would commence in ten minutes. She could feel her fingers tremble as she turned off the ignition and removed her car keys. She glanced at herself in the rearview mirror. She doubted that she'd ever looked worse a single day in her life. Not even on the longest nights-into-mornings in college, when she drank, smoked, and partied herself into a near stupor. Her eyes looked wild and hollow at the same time. It was like looking at a photograph of someone she didn't know. Didn't *want* to know. *Who was that woman?*

Liz flipped the mirror so she couldn't see herself anymore and scanned her surroundings. A single pedestrian took his time exiting the lot for the street. When he was no longer in view, she reached across the seat and grabbed the small metal bucket that had ridden with her from Bend to Beaverton. A moment later, her heart pounding all the while, she lifted the dumpster's lid and tossed it inside. It fell to the metal bottom with a horribly loud, hollow bang. She cast a panicked

83

look around her but still saw no one. She peered inside the dumpster. Empty except for the little bucket. She wanted to cover it up, but there was nothing there. She let the lid fall. It thundered on impact.

Her heart bounced inside her chest.

Inside the Shilo Inn, the cool air from the hotel's air-conditioning blasted her. Liz imagined running through a car wash just then, the blasts of water and then air taking the sweat from her body. Making her feel as though she were clean, when in reality she'd never felt dirtier in her life.

She flew to the bathroom and doused her face with water. She didn't even want to look at her face.

Pull yourself together. Take the test. Go home. Owen will know what to do.

The paper towel dispenser next to the sink was empty. Really? Everything about this day was wrong. She pulled a pack of tissues from her purse and patted her skin. The mirror grabbed her image. She looked like shit.

She was shit.

Behind a table in the upstairs lobby area, a woman with coral lipstick and eyelashes that scraped her eyeglasses fished for her packet.

"Skin of your teeth," she said.

"Pardon?" Liz answered, somehow holding the tremor in her voice at bay.

"One more minute, dear, and you'd be locked

out. If you pass, remember that judges like punctual lawyers. Come to think of it, test administrators do too."

Liz took the packet. It took everything she had not to respond to the woman in kind, telling her that, with a minute to spare, she was on time. *The law is about technicalities* passed through her mind, and she wanted to say as much.

But she didn't. If there was no way out of what she'd done, then a flippant retort would only cement her in the mind of this coral-lipped, spider-lashed woman who lived to wag her finger and would surely delight in facing the cameras.

"She was disheveled and late," Liz imagined the woman saying to reporters. *"Very strange. I knew something was wrong with her the minute she made a beeline for the bathroom. She didn't even acknowledge me. Something wasn't right with that one. I could see it from twenty-five yards."*

Phones off. Purses and backpacks stowed. The ballroom was a freezer full of people young and old going after a dream. She recognized a couple of people from the last time she'd taken the essay portion of the test. An Asian man from her study group who knew the law inside and out but muffed the essays because of a misunderstanding of the wording of a question. A mother of three was also a repeater. Sally, an Oregon Law class-mate of Liz's. Sally's dad had been a lawyer of some note, and he'd wanted to pass on his practice to his only daughter. Sally had told Liz one time that she preferred running the office to being in court. "Look, I have three kids. I need to be home in the evenings, not burying my face in a law book or reading depositions. My dad doesn't get it. All he cares about now is his legacy. When he dies, I'm selling the practice the next day."

The page in front of her confronted her with a blank stare.

Ten minutes into the exam, Liz got up. She kept her head down and went out the door, passed the woman with the tarantula eyelashes, and went for her car. Sweat dripped down her temples. She kept her breathing shallow, because she was sure if she took in any more air, she'd heave. She sat there trying to get a grip on herself. She turned on her phone. Her hands quaked as she sent a text to her husband.

> Liz: I need you.
> Owen: I got your message. In meeting. Have to wait.
> Liz: I screwed up.
> Owen: No shit? Can't call now. There will be other tests.
> Liz: Not the test. God, Owen. I need to talk to you.
> Owen: See you tonight. Everything will

be all right. Promise. Need to focus
here. Big things happening here. Later.

With a jolt, Liz noticed a message had come in
from Carole—then saw that it had been sent early
that morning. Her heart still hammered as she
opened it.

Just sending you good vibes for the
day. Saw your light on. I know you
pulled an all-nighter. Don't worry. You've
got this. You're going to do great.

Carole had completed the text with a smiley
face and a heart emoji.
There was no emoticon for how Liz felt just
then.

Owen Jarrett had dark hair and dark eyes. At
thirty-one, he was in perfect shape, though
outside of running along the river on Saturdays
and the occasional visit to the local gym, he
didn't really work at it. He drank as much beer
as he wanted, and there was never a time when
he couldn't double down and finish the last slice
of pizza. Thin-crust. Deep-dish. Didn't matter.
Good genes, he'd tell those who marveled at his
ability to stay in fighting shape. Guys who had to
work at it were jealous. Women found themselves
drawn in by his looks but somewhat annoyed by

his relentless pursuit of being the best at whatever he did. A bit of a braggart. Definitely a man who was all but certain he deserved his place at the top of the food chain.

In the offices of Lumatyx, a loft over a downtown Bend art gallery, Owen walked around as if he owned the place. That was fine, as he and his partner, Damon West, actually did own the company. Lumatyx proprietary software assisted employers in determining which potential candidates were best suited for a job, how long they would stay, and at what cost. In essence, Lumatyx software would help companies manage the inevitable employee churn to their advantage. Slash the number of times they got burned by new hires who didn't stay long enough to recover the costs of getting them up to speed. Fewer signing bonuses for hires who could be had without them. Owen, who had majored in computer science at the University of Washington, had met Damon at Microsoft. They'd missed the cash grab at the mega software company, and so they had plotted a way toward a fortune of their own. The answer was Lumatyx. Damon had the coding skills, but Owen had the heart of a marketer. He could talk a good game. It was up to Damon to deliver. That sometimes created a little tension.

Lumatyx was a few weeks away from an infusion of cash from a venture capital firm out of Boston, and Owen was on the precipice of a windfall. The Subaru Forester that he'd driven for the last three years was going to be swapped for a Ferrari the day after the trading bell rang. He already knew the color and model. A black convertible with a red leather interior. Flashy, sure. But he'd earned it. The house he and his wife bought from her family's estate would meet the wrecking ball, and another mammoth dream home would rise up along the river.

Every single day was a tick of the clock closer to the best thing that had ever happened to him.

Damon stuck his head into Owen's office. Owen didn't say so, but he had noticed that over the past few weeks Damon had upped his game in the fashion department. His shirts were no longer Gap but English Laundry. He'd replaced his wireless LensCrafters frames with some thicker, hipper nerd style. He was living off charge cards and the promise of paying them off with a single click on his online banking account. He wasn't really hitting it, though. In those glasses just now, he looked more like an African American Buddy Holly than a digital-solutions tycoon.

"Conference call in two minutes," Damon said.

Owen looked down at a text from his wife asking him to call her. "Coming," he said, Liz's messages vanishing as he powered down his phone.

Chapter Eight
MISSING: FIVE HOURS

"Holy shit, David, where have you been?"

David Franklin dropped a pile of lifestyle magazines and some other papers in a heap in front of Amanda Jenkins. He pulled back a little. Amanda and the lunch waiters at Sweetwater crowded him. That didn't make him the least bit happy. It was the kind of greeting that portended some disaster: an oven that didn't work, the salamander broiler on the fritz. David was dressed in black jeans and a gray linen shirt open at the collar. His shoes were black Italian loafers, and around his wrist he wore a matching woven leather bracelet. He was strikingly handsome, with a head of coal-black-and-silver hair that he let grow just long enough to allow for the gel and the humidity of the day to make his locks curl.

Stylish but not fussy.

That was David's look, head to toe.

"What's going on?" His brown eyes searched the faces of what he called his "superstar" restaurant team.

Amanda was his number one. Not quite an assistant manager, but as close as increasingly strained financials allowed. She was a willowy redhead with green eyes and a band of freckles that crossed the bridge of her nose like a tan mist. She was smart and cautious. She ran the front of the house with precision and didn't suffer any hiccups in service. The food was David's domain.

"Carole's been trying to get you," she said. "We all have. You haven't been picking up."

"Phone's dead," he said. "What's going on? Carole all right?"

"Yes," Amanda said. "I mean no. She's not all right. David, Charlie is missing. The police are looking for you."

David took a step back, as though doing so would turn back the clock and erase what Amanda had just said.

"What do you mean, 'missing'?"

By now Amanda was losing some of her calculated cool. She could feel her heart race a little. This was bad. "Carole can't find him anywhere," she said. "The police are at your house right now. David, where have you been?"

His face went white. "Running errands. Jesus." He turned toward the door, and the keys to his Porsche slipped from his fingers. Amanda dropped down to retrieve them. He held his hand out as she passed him the keys. His hand was warm, damp.

"Can't find him?" he repeated. "Can't find Charlie?"

Amanda's heart raced more. "That's what they said. Carole's frantic. You want me to drive you?"

David shook his head. "No. No. I can do that. You take care of things here. We have a full house tonight. No mistakes." He reached for the handle on the back door, a shaft of light beaming into the restaurant as he swung it open.

"What the fuck kind of response is that?" Mitchell, a sous-chef, asked when the light beam had cut out.

"He's in shock," Amanda said. "He's out of his mind with worry."

Mitchell rolled his eyes. He'd never liked David Franklin. "His kid is missing and he's worried about tonight's service?"

"Stop it," Amanda said. "Can't you see he's in distress?"

"He didn't look all that distressed to me."

"You want to get a new job?" Amanda was used to defending her boss. David could be a tyrant in the kitchen and a charmer in front of diners. "Is that what you want?"

Mitchell, who had been a sous-chef at three other Bend restaurants before coming to Sweetwater, shrugged. He could get another gig. "You banging him?"

Amanda felt her face flame red. She pointed her index finger at Mitchell. "You are fired. Get out."

"Fine," he said. "This place is a train wreck anyway."

"Go!" she said. "Now."

When he'd slouched away, Amanda turned to the servers gawking at the scene from the doorway. "Get back to work! We have a full restaurant tonight. We're not going to let David down."

A few minutes later she planted herself in a bathroom stall. Amanda had tried to hide it, but she doubted she'd been successful: she was shuddering from the confrontation. Her mind was spinning. She agreed that something had been off about David, but she couldn't make any sense of it. *Where had he been?*

That morning had been anything but routine. He'd come in at his usual time, was working on an update to the menu that included some gorgeous chanterelles that had been sourced by a local picker. He was being his old David self, talking about an investment that had gone sideways, a trip to France that he'd been planning as a surprise for Carole, tossing a few darts at the city planners who wanted to limit the number of vacation rentals in town.

"It's vacation rentals that have transformed Bend from a backwater into a going concern for restaurants like ours," he'd said. "We can charge vacationers twice what locals can pay. And the whole city cashes in on all this new money. Fresh

93

money. Money du jour." He'd grinned, pleased with his turn of phrase.

Then, just a little later that morning, things had changed. His mood had shifted with a call, and he briskly announced that he needed to run an errand. He didn't say where or who it involved. "I need to skedaddle." One of his trademark words. "You hold down the fort."

As Amanda composed herself in the stall, she had a funny feeling about David's sudden departure. Before the call, he'd talked about how he wanted to personally check out the quality of the mushrooms being brought in by the forager. "Last time I got some hen of the woods from this dude, they were within a day of going bad. Not up to the standards of Sweetwater, for sure."

"For sure," Amanda had said.

Yet, when that call came, David had just packed up to leave. As though the freshness of the mushrooms were no longer a concern.

"What about the chanterelles?" she had asked.

David grabbed his keys and hurried toward the door. "You check them out. I trust you."

Amanda had stood there, mouth agape. David didn't trust anyone. He was the kind of restaurateur who insisted that no one listened when he spoke. No one followed his precise instructions about the food or the linens or the background music. One time she'd seen him yank a candlelighter from a server in front of the whole house because he said the young man was lighting a tea light wrong.

"Hold the candle at an *angle* when you light it!"

As she sat on the lid of the toilet, Amanda wondered what was going on at the Franklins' house and why David hadn't answered any of his calls. His phone wasn't dead. *It was never dead.* Her boss hadn't taken the calls because he hadn't wanted to.

CHAPTER NINE
MISSING: FIVE HOURS, FIFTEEN MINUTES

It was almost three thirty in the afternoon when David pulled up in front of the house. Two Bend police cars crammed the driveway, blocking the garage, and another was parked across the street. A group of onlookers in T-shirts, shorts, and flip-flops gawked at the scene from the sidewalk.

"I bet that's the dad," said a weekender with muttonchops and a beach-ball belly as he passed by. It was as though he thought he was watching David on TV.

"Nice car," said another.

Before he could make his way inside, Carole was in David's arms, gripping him with the force of a vise.

"Charlie's gone!" she said, her façade giving way, the whole edifice shattering into a zillion pieces. Ruins. Dust. There was no holding anything together. For a second she was a rag doll, and her husband's grip stopped her from collapsing onto the front steps. Her sobs reverberated from the doorway and back out to the yard.

"What's happened, honey?" David said, holding

Carole tightly, letting her sob into his expensive shirt.

Her face remained buried in his chest. "I—I turned away to answer a call. I told him to stay away from the water. I did. He knows better. Really, he does. I should never have taken my eyes off him," she said, gulping for air.

David's eyes met those of a gravely observant woman standing a few feet away in the foyer. Allowing him a moment to calm his wife. She nodded at him.

"Are you the police?" he asked.

She showed her identification and introduced herself.

"What happened?" he asked her.

"We don't know yet," the detective said. "We're trying to find him."

"David, I'm so scared. What if—" Carole stopped herself.

"We'll find Charlie," he said, looking right into her eyes. "Of course we'll find him."

Over the next couple of hours, Jake and other officers from the Bend Police Department continued to search the riverbank, question bystanders, and go door-to-door. Esther phoned a woman in the records department to pull up a report on local sex offenders, just to be sure. Not surprisingly, while there were plenty in Bend and the other little towns nearby, there were none in the immediate vicinity of the Franklins' residence. Real estate prices around the river kept the area pedophile-proof. Unless the neighbor was a very rich pedophile. While the Franklin house wasn't a crime scene—at least, not yet— Esther told Jake to collect the blood drop on the living room floor.

"Mrs. Franklin cut her ear," she said, "but let's be sure the blood is hers, not the boy's. I'll collect the blouse she's wearing. It also has blood on it."

Jake nodded. "Anything else?"

"No," she said. "Not yet. This is a waiting game. We hope the boy is hiding somewhere and isn't in the river and hasn't been abducted. We need to determine where Mr. Franklin was at the time of Charlie's disappearance too."

The veteran detective considered that the neighbors who had been relegated to the shadows cast by the enormous Franklin house were gone at the time of Charlie's disappearance.

"Rental next door downriver is owned by Connie Phillips, Portland," Esther said. "Owen and Liz Jarrett own the little place on the other side. Let's track them down too."

"Got it," he said.

"Before things go from bad to worse here," she went on, "I'll make a run up to the put-in at the park and see who was on the river today. Carole says the tuber that went by just as she answered the phone had a rental from Riparian. The other guy we need to find was in a canoe with a dog, heading upriver."

"Not much to go on," Jake said.

"You got that right," she said, looking out at the traffic jam that had formed in the river. A cluster of fifteen tubers lashed together were drifting by, unaware of what had occurred at the big house they were staring at. One guy with a gut and a beer cooler trailing behind him on a tether noticed the police. "Must be bustin' a party! Cops, go home!" he called over to his buddies and their girlfriends.

"We have a right to party!" said one.

"Yeah!"

Esther rolled her eyes and turned to Jake. "God, I can't stand tourists."

"My dad says the only thing good about them is their wallets."

"I like your dad. He's right."

Esther returned to the Franklins. By then they'd moved to the kitchen. David had made his wife a cup of tea. Carole was slumped on a barstool, one elbow planted on the counter, holding up her head.

"Carole," Esther said, "I know this is hard. I'll need you to change your top."

"My top?"

Esther's eyes went to the blood drop.

"This is my blood," Carole said. "You don't think that it's Charlie's?"

"No. Absolutely not. Since I've seen it, though, and since you're cooperating with the investigation, I need to bring it in. You know, to exclude you."

David spoke up. "Cooperating? Exclude? I don't like how those words sound, Detective. It feels a little threatening."

"No. Not at all. It's procedure. A box we have to tick off."

"I didn't hurt him," Carole said.

"I know," Esther said, although she didn't really. "Please. Just help me so I can do my job and move on so that we can find out what happened to Charlie."

Carole got up from the barstool and disappeared into the bedroom.

Esther focused on David. It was the first time they'd had a moment alone.

"How do you think she's holding up?" she asked.

"She's not," he said. "She feels guilty and she's scared to death."

"Guilty?"

"She thinks it's her fault. That kind of guilty."

"What kind of relationship does your wife have with your son?"

David narrowed his eyes. "How do you mean? A good one. Mother and son."

"Little boys can be challenging sometimes," Esther said. "I have a nephew that pushes my buttons like a video game. There are times when, well, I can hardly stand to be in the same room with him. He gets under my skin. Does Charlie do that to Carole?"

David didn't respond right away. He let the detective's words linger in the air. He looked down at the river and the paddlers and tubers.

"He's a little boy. So, yes," he said, "he's challenging. Just so you know—because I know where you are going—Carole is not the kind of person to be undone by a kid. She worked in the tech space and managed a group of half-autistic crybabies, and she did so effortlessly."

Just then Carole reappeared wearing a light pink sweater. She'd placed her blood-blemished blouse in a dry-cleaning bag. "Here," she said, handing it over. "Now please stop this nonsense and go find my son. He's out there and it'll be dark soon and . . ." Her words fell into tears.

"Sit down, honey," David said. "Finish your tea."

"I don't want any tea. I want Charlie. I want my little boy home right now, right this goddamn minute. Where is he?"

"I don't know," David said.

"We're looking," Esther said.

"Well," Carole said, her voice rising with anger, "you can see he's not here. Go and find him. That's your job."

Chapter Ten
MISSING: SIX HOURS

Cody Turner was the assistant manager of Riparian Zone Rentals. At twenty-six, he was like a lot of the young people who came to Bend. Skiing in the winter and rafting in the summer. Rinse and repeat. He wore his black hair in a ponytail and was working on a pay-as-you-go full-body tattoo that documented the highlights of his life. His dog. A rainbow trout. His brother. The name of a girlfriend who had moved back to Portland. Cody hadn't lived all that much, and his roommate, Hawk, had advised him to leave a little room on his body for some future awesomeness. "That's what my ass is for, bro," Cody said with his raucous laugh, which fluctuated between endearing and annoying, depending on how stoned his friends were when Cody was being Cody.

Esther Nguyen crossed the heat of the parking lot to the rental shack. Two teens ran the processing part of the operation from under a canopy, collecting signed liability waivers and cash, and holding credit cards and driver's licenses as collateral for red and blue inner tubes that had been screen-printed with *Riparian Zone* in bold, black letters. Once the tourists were processed, a pretty girl with dark brown hair and long arms pulled tubes from a stack behind a rope and passed them to renters.

"Manager here?" the detective asked the employees working the cash boxes.

"Cody's over there," said one, indicating the illustrated young man helping a mother put a life jacket on her daughter.

Esther waited for him to finish before introducing herself.

"Yeah," he said. "Word travels fast around here. I heard some kid drowned downriver."

"We don't know what happened," she said. "That's why I'm here."

Cody shifted his weight on his flip-flops. "We didn't do the kid, and even if we did, we have an ironclad waiver," he said. "Last year some showboater from California cracked his skull on a rock and tried to blame us. Said the tube was flat and he lost his balance and fell into the river. Totally wrong on that. We didn't even need to prove him wrong. Waiver's everything."

"I'm looking for one of your customers," she said. "Someone who might have seen something."

"Nobody here saw anything."

"Right," Esther said firmly. "But someone you rented to might have."

"Look, no one said anything and, just between

you and me, the whole idea of a drowning is flat-out bad for business. Look around you. Most of these people are out of shape or half-drunk. We don't need them scared too."

"I see," Esther said, glancing around at the group of patrons lined up to sign waivers to get out on the river. One young man caught her gaze and ditched whatever he was drinking in the trash can. "Should you even be renting to some of these folks? I mean, if they are drunk. Or half-drunk, as you say."

Cody gave up a lazy grin. This cop was smart. Probably smarter than him.

"What do you want?" he asked.

"How long does it take to get to the bridge by Columbia Park?"

Cody computed the time. Numbers had never been a strong suit. He was more the artistic, free-spirited type. His tats proved as much.

Esther wondered if he was mentally counting the minutes on his fingers and toes or if he was actually calculating the flow of the Deschutes. "Cody?"

"Half hour," he finally said. "Maybe twenty-five minutes. Depends on a bunch of stuff: time of year, current, and if you make it through the little rapids without a wipeout."

The time of year was today.

"Fine," she said. "What time do you open in the morning?"

"Ten," Cody answered, this time with complete confidence. "We open at ten. Usually we have a line the second we put out the shade awning."

"I need to know who rented here from opening to, let's say, ten thirty. I'll need to see their waivers."

Cody did a little more of his very slow processing. "Don't you need a court order?"

Esther kept her eyes on his. She didn't think Cody was high. She suspected he just had the kind of empty look that made him appear as such. "You really want me to go to the trouble of getting one? Might trigger other trouble too. You want this place closed down, Cody? Drunk people shouldn't be given a rental." She indicated the young man who had ditched his beer. "It would invalidate the all-important waiver, you know."

Cody looked stunned. Or not. Maybe that was how Cody looked all the time. "You wouldn't do that, Detective. Would you?"

She needed the information and she needed it now. Charlie Franklin's life was at stake. "Trust me, Cody, you don't want to find out."

The tatted young man turned toward the office part of the rental shack and motioned for her to follow. "Fine," he said. "Fine. But you can't keep the waivers. I need them. It's procedure. You know, an important legal requirement."

He disappeared inside and returned a beat later with a folder full of waivers.

"We have sixty-five. Pretty much in order," Cody said. "You know, in sequence of when we get them turned in. The most recent ones on top. The first ones of the morning on the bottom."

"I get it. Thanks."

"Hey, you promise to get those back to me, right? I'm the assistant manager here and I need to follow procedure. It's a superimportant part of my job."

She looked down at the papers. "I know. I'll copy these and get them back to you before the end of the day."

"You better," he said.

"No worries, Cody."

Esther walked across the hot asphalt, got inside the hot car, and immediately turned on the air-conditioning. It had to be one hundred degrees. The last gasp of summer was a scorcher. She practically melted into the seat. As she let the air flow over her face, Esther leafed through the papers Cody had given her. She removed any with female names or whose ages indicated they were children.

Carole wasn't sure about the age of the inner-tuber she'd seen, or really anything about his physical description. "He was white," she'd said. "I really didn't look at him. At the time there was no reason to. He was just another vacationer floating by. Maybe in his thirties. I don't know, maybe older. I don't know."

"Think. Take a second. Nothing remarkable about him?" Esther had asked.

Carole, shattered as she was, came up with one more detail, although she was hazy on it. "I think he had a U of O T-shirt on," she had said, before adding, "but that's about half of the floaters around here."

As the air-conditioning cooled her, Esther identified five names that seemed like possibles among the sheaf of waivers. Their ages ranged from twenty-eight to forty-two. Three were Oregon residents, though not locals. One was from Los Angeles, the other from Dayton, Ohio. All were staying in summer rentals. All included their home addresses on their waivers.

Esther called the names in to Jake, who had returned to the office to enter more details into the national database on missing and exploited children.

"What are we looking for?" he asked.

"We need to know where they are so we can talk to them," she said. "One of them may have seen something. Maybe they didn't even know what it was that they'd seen or why it could be important."

"If they saw something, then why haven't they called us? It's been all over the news."

"Like I said," she went on, "they might not have believed they'd seen anything relevant."

"Or just maybe they're staying quiet because of

something they *did* see. Or something they *did*. Any line on the canoe guy?"

"No," she said. "Carole couldn't remember anything about him except that he had a dog and was listening to music. Riparian doesn't rent canoes."

"Canoe color?" Jake asked.

"Red."

"Anything on it?"

"Nothing. Have PR make sure to get the word out that we're looking for the canoe paddler who was on the river at the time with a dog."

"Okay, I'll work the names."

On her way back to the office, Esther stopped at the Miller place and rang the bell, but there was no answer. The heat of one of the hottest days of the year had turned a pot of geraniums into a brittle, lifeless display. The woman next door called over from her front porch that she'd seen Dan leave for the store.

"You could set a clock by his routine," she said. "He'll be back soon. Like clockwork, that guy."

Esther tucked her business card into the doorway. "If you see him, have him call me."

"Hope you find that kid," the neighbor said, quickly adding, "I have a scanner."

"Did you see anything?"

"Nope. Nothing at all."

Chapter Eleven
MISSING: EIGHT HOURS

Drake Park was Bend's civic centerpiece, a verdant expanse next to Northwest Riverside Boulevard speckled with mature trees and highlighted by a body of water that seldom failed to live up to its namesake. Mirror Pond was created early in the last century as a hydroelectric power source for the growing high-desert city, the largest in Central Oregon. Few think of that when they gaze out at its pristine, reflective surface. They think of the beauty of nature, of the forethought of the pioneer families who settled Bend and had the presence of mind to create a gathering place for all time.

The afternoon Charlie Franklin went missing, a classic car show had commanded nearly all of Drake Park's space along the pond. It was one of the last events of the season, with visitors from all over the state and beyond. Old Fords, Corvettes, and T-birds shimmered in the ponderosa-filtered sunlight as classic rock pummeled the scene from a temporary stage set up for the event. The band, the Rock and Rollers, segued from Steve Perry to Chuck Berry with barely a break between songs.

At first no one noticed the two divers as they

geared up and went into the water. Subtlety was an asset when a city is as dependent on tourist dollars as Bend. The summer season was nearly over, then a short lull before Oktoberfest events, and then the start of the ski season. Distinct seasons and nearly guaranteed good weather were among the area's strong suits.

"What are they looking for?" asked a woman who'd grown bored of the chrome grill on a '57 Chevy that was mesmerizing her boyfriend.

"Dunno," he said, scarcely looking up. "Maybe a body."

"That's so gross," the young woman said, moving closer, unable to look away.

Another man, also fixated on the same old Chevy, a turquoise-and-cream-colored beauty, spoke up: "I heard some kid drowned upriver."

"No," she said.

"Yeah. That guy has a police scanner." He indicated a man in a lawn chair next to his classic Mustang.

"Seriously," she said. "That's heartbreaking."

"Yeah, it is."

"Come on, Carmen," her boyfriend said. "Let's go get a beer."

She stood there for a beat, watching, before leaving for that cold one.

The dive team disappeared under the shimmering surface, then a few minutes later reemerged before repeating the process. They were working in a grid, methodically searching what many considered the jewel of the city. A small crowd gathered as word got out about what was going on. In time, another pair of divers from out of the area joined in the search.

Three young white men with dreadlocks and miners' headlamps at the ready ignored the scene and continued doing what they did every day, methodically picking through the garbage containers next to Northwest Riverside Boulevard in search of aluminum cans, mostly untouched food, and whatever else they could scrounge.

Unable to go right home, Liz Jarrett sat on a bench at the water's edge, watching the scene. It was nearly an out-of-body experience. She couldn't feel her legs. She could barely breathe. A little girl looked at her as though she were a wax figure in a California tourist town. She couldn't go home just then, although she knew she had to.

Instead, she sat there as the divers searched for something they'd never find.

While she was remembering what she had done.

The clock over the fireplace had been Carole's idea. It was a kinetic sculpture that aped Calder. At the moment she hated it more than anything in the world. As the minutes flew by, the hours moved too. She and her husband sat in the living room and waited. There was nothing more to be done. In her direct, borderline cold manner, the Bend police detective had told them that while they could not know what had happened to Charlie, there were several possibilities. All were being worked.

The first scenario was the only one that brought any measure of comfort: Charlie had gone somewhere nearby and fallen asleep. "He might be awake now," she'd said, "but all the commotion may have frightened him."

The Franklins had asked if they should be out calling for him.

"You've done that," Esther said. "He hasn't responded. Doing it any more might only frighten Charlie, if he's hiding."

"We can't just sit here," David said.

"Let us do our job."

It was the kind of shutdown that David hated, but for once he acquiesced.

The second scenario was horrendous, but it was better than the last one that the detective would mention as a possibility. "It is very rare," she said, "but we are also considering an abduction."

"Who would take Charlie?" Carole asked, her eyes red from crying.

David put his hand on her leg. He didn't need to answer.

"As I said, child abductions are atypical," Esther went on. "We've already done an Amber

Alert on Charlie. In most cases, however, those are child custody related. That's clearly not what happened here."

"If he was abducted," David said, "then we'll catch the freak. Right?"

"We'll do our best," the detective said. Clearly she couldn't promise that.

"Maybe it was a kidnapping for ransom?" Carole said with a little hope in her voice. "We can pay. We will pay anything."

"Kidnapping for ransom happens more in movies than in real life. If someone contacts you, we'll need to bring in the FBI."

Then had come the final possibility. Worse than being kidnapped. Worse even than being molested by some deranged man.

"It might be that he did go into the river. You need to process that, Carole—David. The department has already deployed a dive team to search Mirror Pond."

Carole had put her hands on her face. David had reached over and held her. "That did not happen," he said, his voice firm. "Our son is alive. He has to be."

Esther had heard other parents say the same thing.

"That's what we all hope," she had said.

Chapter Twelve
MISSING: ELEVEN HOURS

Liz was on the couch when Owen swung open the front door. He'd tried to call her after he left the office, but she hadn't picked up. He'd been coming home later and later as work consumed more of his time than ever. When he found her, she was curled up like a snail in its shell. A bottle of wine sat on the coffee table. Her fingers clutched an empty glass. She looked up at him but said nothing.

"I heard the news," he said, throwing down his laptop case and jacket. "Why didn't you tell me Charlie was missing?"

Her eyes were puffy. She'd been weeping.

"Sorry," she said.

Owen dropped his bag and went to console her. She was a mess. Her long brown hair had been fashioned into a messy bun. Loose tendrils brushed her shoulders. Her blouse was disheveled. Her makeup was smeared.

"We need to get over there," he said.

Her lips trembled and she reached for the bottle of wine. He pushed it from her grasp. She'd had too much.

"I can't," she said. She clutched their cat,

Bertie, a rescue found in Columbia Park. The gray-and-white tabby's motor played against Liz's obvious anguish.

"We have to," Owen said. "Carole and David need us."

Liz shifted a little on the couch. Bertie jumped to the floor. The smell of the merlot permeated the space. "I know," she said. "I just can't. I don't feel well, Owen."

She'd been drinking. That was obvious. However, she didn't seem drunk. Not the kind of drunk he'd seen her dive into when she couldn't cope with something.

"The test?" he asked. "Baby, don't worry about that. That's small stuff."

She didn't answer, and he backtracked a little.

"Small stuff in comparison to Charlie," he said. "God, I hope he's okay. You don't think he fell into the river? They need a goddamn fence over there."

"I don't know," she said.

"We need to get over there," he said. "You need to be strong for Carole. And David. They must be going through hell. Cops are parked on the street."

Liz's eyes met his for the first time, but she didn't say anything.

Owen nudged her a little. "This is a big deal," he said. "A damn shit storm. Come on. Pull yourself together. They need us."

Liz could hardly move. "And do what, Owen?" she asked. "What are we going to do?"

"I don't know," he said. "Hug them. Bring them soup." He heaved a sigh. "God, you're right. I don't know what the hell we can do. Hope that Charlie's all right."

Liz looked away. "I don't think he's all right."

Owen got up from the couch. "I don't, either. Let's get our shit together and get over there."

It was dusk when Owen and Liz Jarrett pushed past the onlookers who crowded the entrance to the driveway they shared with the Franklins. Liz was more than a decade younger than Carole; her husband twenty years younger than David. While Liz and Carole were at different points in their lives, they had connected in a very real way. It wasn't a mother-daughter relationship, but more like a kind of sisterhood that came from the ups and downs of living next door. Owen got along with David, but he, like his wife, was more aligned with Carole. They were both techies. Her career with Google impressed Owen. His position with a tech start-up about to blow up made Carole a kindred spirit, or at least a tantalizing benchmark of what success might look like. Everything David and Carole had—the cars, the house, the bank account—was within his grasp too.

Liz had never been motivated by money. She

116

was looking for relationships that were born of emotion, not opportunity.

Once inside the megahome, it took only a second for Liz to have her arms around Carole. Only a heartbeat later both women had dissolved into a muted cacophony of sobs.

Owen stayed close to David. "How are you holding up?"

"Not great," he said, looking over at the two distraught women. "Managing, I guess."

"What the hell happened, David?"

"We don't know. He was in the yard and then he was gone."

"Shit. They don't think he fell in?"

"They don't know. We don't know."

Carole and Liz held each other for a long time, letting their tears subside. Silence. Ache. Then regret.

"I took my eyes off him for only a second," Carole said.

"Little boys move fast, Carole," Liz said, still holding her friend close. "What can we do? How can we help?"

"Just pray, I guess," Carole said. "The police are all over this. They'll find him. Everything will be all right."

"Right," Liz said, the word coming out like a cough.

"I saw the Amber Alert," Owen said. "Gave our street. I knew it had to be Charlie."

Carole pulled back from Liz. "Honey, I thought you'd still be in Beaverton."

"I needed to be here," she said.

Carole hugged Liz again. "But your exam . . . you've been working so hard."

"There will be other times for a test," Liz said. "Tests aren't important. You, David, and Charlie are. I can't believe any of this is really happening."

Carole went into mom mode just then. She told David to get Liz a glass of wine and led her to the sofa. "We'll find him. *They'll* find him."

"What can we do to help?" Owen asked David.

"Just be who you are," he said. "Carole is falling apart. I'm not doing that great, either."

For the next hour the two couples sat, mostly in silence. Carole pulled an afghan from the sofa and wrapped it around Liz.

David and Owen went into the kitchen.

"This isn't really happening, David. Is it?"

David understood the question. It wasn't about what had transpired that morning; it was about the worst possible outcome. An outcome neither could say out loud. At least, not directly.

"They searched Mirror Pond," David said. "There's hope that he didn't fall into the river."

"Yeah, that's good."

In the other room, the two women stayed entwined on the sofa. Liz couldn't stop crying. David and Owen could hear her soft cries in the kitchen.

"Maybe I should take Liz home," Owen said.
David didn't think so. "I think it's good that she's here. It's distracting Carole, and I think that's welcome right now."

"If you're sure," he said. "Is the rest of the family on the way?"

David shook his head. "Carole doesn't want anyone alarmed."

"It's on the news now."

"I know," David said. "But it probably hasn't made it to Spain. That's where Carole's parents are, on a trip with friends. My folks are dead. I'll call my sister."

David offered Owen a beer and took an O'Doul's for himself. They stood at the kitchen window overlooking the river.

"Sometimes I just hate it here," David said.

Owen watched the last group of tubers spin lazily in the river, bouncing off each other like balls in a drunken bumper pool game. They kicked and splashed, lying on their backs like overturned sea turtles. "Yeah. I know what you mean. It's like having Middle America in your face all day long. Not cool."

Carole continued to console Liz on the sofa, first with words promising everything would be all right, even suggesting that all of this was only a very bad dream. The simple gesture of holding hands under the afghan provided a little solace in the darkest moment of Carole's life. Liz's too. What happened to Charlie—whatever it was—had brought a deep, throbbing pain in the hearts of both women.

They had been close before tonight, but not in the beginning.

Before the teardown of the old house and the construction of the new place, Liz had been a little standoffish, only friendly enough so as not to be rude. She told the newcomers that the house they planned to raze had been part of her childhood. Her grandparents were close friends of the O'Donnells, the owners of the property before it was sold to the Franklins. Liz's childhood visits to Bend included fly-fishing with the O'Donnells' son Trevor and making s'mores with her family in the river-rock fire pit that Mr. O'Donnell had built, stone by stone. There was never anything but a crush between Liz and Trevor. He was three years older. At fourteen, seventeen seemed old to her.

When the old house came down, Carole purposely left the fire pit right where it was. David wanted it gone, but his wife thought better of it.

"Liz has real memories here," she said when she and David met with the landscape designer and reviewed the plans for the landscaping.

"Who cares what she thinks? She's still a kid. She can make new ones."

Carole pushed back. "Old memories matter, David."

He frowned. "It doesn't go with the architecture. It just doesn't."

"We're neighbors now," she said, looking at her husband. "I want us to be friends."

CHAPTER THIRTEEN
MISSING: THIRTEEN HOURS

The Jarretts walked up the incline past the old detached garage and toward their door. A lid of thunderclouds had darkened the sky, and the temperature had dropped some. The eerie call from a loon came from the river. The couple didn't speak. They only nodded in the direction of the patrol officer who had been stationed on the street. With Carole, Liz had found a new and larger hatred for herself. One that she could never have imagined in a lifetime of disappointments. Owen put his arm around her, but Liz was sure that it wasn't to comfort her, rather to move her quickly past the police and into the house.

She was a leaf—no, a piece of trash—that he was scooting out of view.

With each step, Liz thought of Carole. Her actions had turned her closest friend into a sodden ball of misery. Carole was about to slide into a very dark place. She would have to go into the bedroom where her son had slept and face the emptiness. She'd pass by the cement pad of the new patio with his tiny handprints embedded forever and know they'd never grow larger. That the family Christmas card with the three of them that Carole had sent last year had been a one-off, not the first of a series. Liz had brought all of that on. The thought ricocheted through her mind that maybe none of this had really happened.

That it was a bad dream.

That she was an actor in a play.

That she'd wake up.

That the curtain would rise.

That Charlie wasn't dead on her father's workbench in the garage.

Liz faced her husband. Her brown eyes were on the verge of letting tears fall. She started to shake.

"I have something to tell you," she finally said.

"You're fucking crazy," Owen said. His eyes penetrated her. "You didn't do that, Liz. You couldn't have."

Liz didn't say anything. When she told him what she'd done, each word had stuck in her throat like a dull steak knife. Saying it a second time would surely make her cough up blood.

Charlie's blood.

"I didn't know what to do," she said, her eyes finally flooding. "I panicked."

Owen started pacing. He slammed his fist onto the top of the morris chair that faced out at the river. He couldn't look at her just then.

"You don't run over a kid and then not call an ambulance," he said.

Liz went to him. She didn't touch him. She just stood there. "I didn't run over him. I didn't. I—I bumped him. It was an accident."

Owen spun around. "This is more than just an accident, Liz. Get a dose of reality. You messed up in the biggest way anyone ever could. You made bad into worse. There isn't a word for this disaster."

Liz reached for him, but he pushed her away. "I'll fix this," she said.

Owen took a step back toward the window. "How? How in the hell can you fix this?"

Now Liz started pacing. She went to the kitchen. She hurried back to him. Over to the front door. Then back to her husband.

"I'll tell Carole and David," she said. "They know I loved Charlie. They will know it was an accident. Carole knows me."

Owen tried to hold it together, but his wife's reasoning was completely ludicrous. "Seriously?" he asked from his place by the window. "And then you'll tell them the part that you put their kid's body in the garage so you could go take the bar?"

"I wasn't thinking clearly," she said. "I was messed up."

Owen shot her a look. It was cold. It was meant to hurt. Hurting her just then was the only way that he could stun her into stopping her inane excuses for what she'd done.

"Hopped up," he said. "You were hopped up on those goddamn pills you've been taking. It isn't an accident when a drunk driver kills someone. It's a crime."

Liz's eyes went to the front door. It passed through her mind that she could make a run for it. She could push past Owen, get to her car, and drive far, far away. She could go to some place in Idaho or Nevada. A place where no one would know what she'd done. A place where she could start over. She'd never be a lawyer. She'd lose Owen. She'd live the rest of her life looking over her shoulder while she worked as a grocery checker or motel maid. She'd never be anything in life, and in that moment, she accepted such an inevitable outcome. She deserved it. She could feel the doorknob twist. She could hear Owen yelling at her to stop, but only halfheartedly. He'd want her gone. He'd want to start over with his big money and a wife who wasn't a murderer.

"I'm sorry," she said, crying. "What do you think I should do?"

Owen slumped back down into the chair facing the river. "Let me think. The police are crawling around the neighborhood. Let me think of what to do. Goddamn you, Liz. You screwed up big-time. The biggest screwup in the world."

"What are we going to do?" she asked.

"*We* aren't going to do anything." Owen went to the bathroom and splashed water on his face.

He looked in the mirror, not at himself, but in the direction of his wife, whom he could hear rummaging around for a corkscrew.

"Owen, we can't just leave him there."

"We won't," he said, reemerging from the bathroom. "We aren't. I'm going to clean up this mess."

He didn't say *your mess,* though Liz knew that was what he meant.

"Owen, I'm sorry. I'm sorry. You know that, don't you?"

He barely looked at her.

"Don't do anything," he said, going for the door. "Stay put. I'll fix this. I've worked too hard to lose everything because of something you did." He turned to her to show that he meant what he was about to say and amended his words. "*We've both* worked so hard."

CHAPTER FOURTEEN
MISSING: FOURTEEN HOURS

For decades the front porch of the Jarrett place had been *the* site of countless family celebrations. It ran the length of the Craftsman bungalow, facing the river and the endless parade along it. Birthday parties, the Fourth of July, a nearly annual family reunion had taken place on those wide, old, worn planks.

To Liz, all of that seemed a million years ago.

With her husband gone, she looked in the direction of the water. It was after midnight and she half hoped the next day would never come. Her tears with Carole and David had been genuine. She'd loved Charlie. She knew he'd loved her too. He'd come to show her his pinecones that morning. A few days before, she'd told him that they would make pinecone turkeys for Thanksgiving that year, something she'd done with her mother when she was a girl. Pipe cleaners, gobs of glitter, construction paper, and googly eyes transformed the cones into the kind of treasure that mothers can never discard.

Owen had given her some pills, and now she sat there watching, drinking some wine, and feeling as though a dark lid were sliding over her.

She looked down at her hands, limply lying in her lap. What had she done? How could she have carried Charlie into the garage to hide him away? Who was she now?

She saw old Dan Miller ensconced in his swivel chair across the water, the light from his TV set silhouetting his bushy, white cockscomb hair. He was always in that chair, facing one way or another. Sometimes he held binoculars to his eyes to get a better look. Seeing him like that always gave her a hollow feeling, only served to remind her how after Seth had died he'd simply retreated from life. He'd become one of those people on the outside, looking in. Face pressed against the glass. She wondered if Dan had seen something that morning, anything that she would not want him to see.

Even in her drugged and drunken stupor, Liz traced the sight line from Dan's vantage point to the driveway the Jarretts shared with the Franklins. She wasn't sure, but she didn't think he could have seen what had transpired when she backed out from the garage. He might have witnessed Charlie wander over with his pinecones, the lurching of her car, her panic as she ran around to find the dead boy behind the car.

Liz looked over at the house next door. Carole and David's place had knife cuts for windows on the street and the sides facing their neighbors. The narrow windows were afire with light. Every one of them. She wondered if they were looking in every room again, trying to find something that might indicate where Charlie had gone.

Or who had taken him.

She knew they'd never see him again. Carole's heart would be broken forever. The chain reaction that she'd ignited would reverberate for the rest of their lives. Carole would grieve. David too. They'd do so publicly. Arms would wrap around them. Maybe their marriage would become stronger. Maybe it would disintegrate. Liz had done all of that. She'd lit a fuse, and there was no way of stopping it.

She would live with what she'd done. She'd cry with her friend, but her tears would not come from the same place as Carole's. Owen would stand by her. Wouldn't he? In books, secrets are always a dangerous bond. Would they stay together because of what he had on her? And what she would have on him when he'd fixed the problem?

Liz put the wineglass to her lips and poured the rest of it down her constricted throat. She hated pinot gris, but it was what Owen gave her when he told her to pull herself together.

As she waited for Owen, she prayed silently that God would forgive her and would understand that it had indeed been an accident. That God would know that evil didn't live in her heart. That she'd made a mistake. As the wine and the pills took over, Liz felt her eyelids become heavy and her limbs go numb. The wineglass dropped into her lap. What was happening? She wondered if she was overdosing. She hoped that she was. She didn't deserve to live. She didn't *want* to live. Living would be torture.

Liz looked down at the river.

It was a black snake with a stain of silver from a fading moon peeking through the breaking clouds. It called over to her. *Begged* her. Told her that if she would go into the water, everything would be all right.

Charlie Franklin came to her as she drifted off, sitting on the porch in an old Adirondack chair that her grandfather had made out of lumber from a cedar tree that had died not long after he bought the property.

Charlie had his bucket of pinecones and a big grin on his face as he knelt beside her while she rested. He told her that everything would be all right. That when she got to heaven, they'd make those turkeys together, like she had promised. He spoke to her in complete, measured sentences. Not like a three-year-old at all. He told her that he knew that she hadn't intended any of what happened to him. That she was not the reason he had died. That what had transpired between them on the driveway that morning had been an accident.

"Lizzie," he said, "it'll be okay."

Liz woke up with a start and picked up her empty wineglass, which had somehow managed to hit the floor beside her chair without breaking. She felt woozy and strange. Not herself. She knew she would never again be whoever she'd been.

She hoisted herself up from the chair and held the handrail to make her way back inside.

"Owen?" she called out, her voice raspy and her feet unsteady.

No answer.

She went into the kitchen, the bedroom, the office, even the bathroom, stumbling as she worked her way through the house. As repulsed as she was at what she'd done, it took everything she had to avoid going into the garage to see what Owen was doing in there.

Chapter Fifteen
MISSING: FOURTEEN HOURS

Owen knew he had been out in the garage far too long. For all his furious, can-do bluster with Liz about how he'd fix everything, he was stuck, vapor-locked, just inside the door. An acrid scent permeated the air. He couldn't make himself cross the space to the workbench, and the tarp, and the nightmare beneath it.

Sealed off all day, the garage was stifling, like an oven preheated for a take-and-bake pizza. To let in some air, Owen had twisted the knob on the side door parallel to the river and popped it open. But then he'd had to nod in the direction of a patrol officer who'd parked across the street to keep an eye on things.

He pulled the oven door shut again.

Now all this time had passed, and those eyes were on him. The cop had to be wondering what in hell he was doing. *Great.* This could not get any worse.

Owen had no idea what he was doing, just the words of his wife pushing him there, telling him what she'd done. It was surreal. It was a bad dream. It was the end of a dream too, he knew. Everything that he'd worked so hard to achieve was going to be undone by her actions.

Liz, what a colossal mess!

With seemingly every muscle in his body pulled taut, his movements were labored. Sweat that had accumulated on his brow was dripping down and forcing the salty liquid into his mouth. He doubted that his heart had ever pounded as hard as it was at that moment. Not even when he ran his only marathon, in Boston, when he was in college.

The garage was old-school. Built in the days when families had only one car and no real need for the stuff that accumulates with time and money. Liz's car, the newer of the couple's two vehicles, had been the winner in a coin flip to decide who would dodge the snow and frost in the winter, the weeping sap from the pines in the summer.

Everything would be different if he'd won the toss. None of what had happened would have occurred. He knew that by altering one little detail, the world is changed. Just one little thing. He compiled a list of little things. If Liz had gotten up on time. If he'd parked his car there. If they'd never bought this stupid house or met the Franklins. If. If. If. The contents of the list came at him like an Uzi, striking him in the heart and causing his lungs to gush out all their air. He felt weak. Disoriented. Sick to his stomach.

Liz really, completely, totally fucked up.

How could he fix it? He *had* to fix it. He had everything riding on the eventual IPO, and the slightest whiff of a scandal would trigger the clause that promised morality and fidelity among all the principals of the firm.

A wife killing a neighbor's kid—and then hiding the body!—was going to be front-page news. There would be no way to hide it. No way out.

He turned the dead bolt on the door between him and the cop across the street and flipped on the single light that hung over the workbench. On the bench was the tarp. Under the stiff covering was the body of the little boy all of Bend was searching for.

Goddamn it. Fuck! Shit! Liz, you idiot! What were you thinking?

Owen started to pace, first back and forth and then in a small circle. He had to get rid of the body. That much was a given. He couldn't tell the police that he just stumbled across Charlie in his garage. They'd want to know how he had gotten there. They'd want to examine the car when the injuries that caused the child's death were identified. They'd know. Everyone would know.

He'd have to ditch the body somewhere.

He'd have to run Liz's car through the car wash.

He'd have to do all of that fast.

It was an accident. Liz was a gentle soul. She

didn't mean for this to happen. If she told the truth, then her life really would be ruined.

And, even more importantly, he'd lose his job. The boatload of money that he was about to get. He'd lose everything.

Liz's husband stood there paralyzed—thinking, planning, and arguing with every scenario that came to mind. A drop of sweat fell to the floor. He wiped his forehead on his sleeve. He started moving again, thinking, processing.

And then he heard it: a soft puff of air causing the tarp to rise and fall just a little. It puzzled him. Maybe the window above the workbench was ajar and air had been forced inside by the gentle breeze.

That was a lie that he told himself when he instantly knew better.

Charlie Franklin wasn't dead after all.

The little boy from next door was alive.

The impulse to pull the covering off Charlie and save him was a jolt that came and went. Owen stood immobile in that oven of a garage as the smell of the boy's urine wafted through the air.

Bad had gone to worse. Terrible had become horrendous. An accident had suddenly morphed into an epic disaster.

The sound of a car door slamming startled him.

The cop, finally coming to check on him?

A nosy neighbor from across the street?

A pizza delivery guy.

Any could be his undoing. How in the world could he explain his way out of this mess? *Holy shit.* Liz had backed into a little boy, covered his body up with a tarp, and left him for dead all day in the hell of an overheated garage.

There was no way out of this, no undoing it.

He finally forced himself to move to the workbench. He stood still in front of it, looking closely at the tarp. It was nearly imperceptible, but what he saw couldn't be ignored. The tarp rose and then fell. He watched it repeat the same motion. Up and down.

Alive.

Owen Jarrett played out the scenarios one more time. He wasn't going to lose everything because of one stupid mistake. He stepped closer and put his hands on the tarp. He was going to stop the tarp. Stop the little boy. It was crazy and sick and Owen didn't care about any of it. He was doing what he had to do.

At first Owen felt nothing but the boy's still, fine-boned body beneath his hands. He told himself he'd imagined the breathing. But then Charlie made a mewling sound, muffled by the tarp. The noise jolted Owen, and he pushed down on the plastic. The boy stirred—didn't push back, but remained in barely perceptible, squirming motion. His heart hammering inside his chest, Owen found Charlie's face through the tarp. He did not want to pull off the loose plastic covering. He didn't want to see what he was doing, although the act could not have been more deliberate. He put his hand over Charlie's face and pressed down. The boy twitched. Twitched again.

Goddamn it, Liz! Look what the fuck you are making me do! You bitch! This is your fault!

Sweat from his forehead met the tears in his eyes. He reached for a shop rag with his free hand and wiped his face.

Charlie had been left for dead, but he wasn't giving up. His muted squirming and odd, twitching motions lasted for what seemed like a long, long time. Owen would never be sure just how long. There was a flash in which he almost stopped doing what he was doing. But he didn't. There would be no way of explaining the unthinkable.

The boy stopped moving. Owen stepped away, his heart pounding to near bursting. The plastic covering loosely tenting the body was still.

Owen had to get out of there.

He didn't want to overthink, but he needed an excuse for having come out to the garage and stayed all this time. He scanned the space and retrieved a small box marked KITCHEN and started for the door.

The patrol officer's head popped up as he emerged.

"Found it," Owen called to him. "Holy crap, do I need to clean up this garage!"

"Tell me about it," the cop said. "Girlfriend's been after me to do the same for about a year now. Just never get to it."

"Yeah," Owen said. "Hard to find the time."

As he turned the doorknob to go inside, he made a promise to himself. He'd never tell Liz what he'd done. This was her disaster. She was to blame for Charlie's death. He'd remind her of that whenever he needed to. For the rest of her life.

However long that was.

Chapter Sixteen
MISSING: FIFTEEN HOURS

As if sleeping would erase what had happened, Carole lay still on the California king bed that faced the moonlit river. She'd tossed her pillow to the floor. It was after 3:00 a.m., technically the day after her son went missing, but in her heart and in her soul it was merely the continuation of the day when she'd senselessly turned her back on Charlie. She told her husband and the detective that it had been only five minutes that she'd taken her eyes from him. That hadn't been true.

A look at her phone's call record indicated twelve minutes. *A dozen minutes.*

There was no way she could insist that she'd only turned her back for a second. Twelve minutes was long enough to go to the Safeway and back. Long enough to watch the news until the sports came on. Long enough to microwave four bags of popcorn.

Too long.

Long enough to call her parenting into question.

Her pillow was soaked with her tears. David held her from behind, wrapping his arms around her shoulders as she cried quietly, steadily, into the fabric.

"David," she said, her voice a croak, "I'm so, so sorry."

"Not your fault," he said, pulling himself a little closer. "Everything's going to be all right. I promise."

"Really?" she asked, although she knew the ridiculousness of such a promise. Whatever had happened to their little boy was beyond any promise. "He's all right. He'll be coming home, won't he?"

David tightened his embrace. "Honey, we have to have faith."

She started to move toward the edge of the bed, but he held her close. The divers searching Mirror Pond had found no trace of Charlie. Searchers also scoured the riverbanks on both sides but found nothing there. One ambitious young man with the local search-and-rescue team even dug into the beaver lodge on the off chance that Charlie had somehow become trapped inside.

Dead or alive.

He'd vanished without a trace. Chasing the heron and collecting pinecones and then gone.

"He's alive." Carole shifted in the bed. "We have to do something, David. We have to go look for him. We need to get dressed and get out of here."

David loosened his embrace. "We *have* looked. Everyone is searching. Charlie is on everyone's mind right now. Because of the police. The

140

news. The Amber Alert. Someone must have taken him, Carole. Someone must have hidden him somewhere. I was scared that he might have drowned, but now I know that he's alive." David's voice choked with uncharacteristic emotion and he repeated himself. "He's alive."

Carole untangled his arms from her body and put her feet on the floor. "I can't sleep," she said. "I have to go. Get up, David! We both have to go. You don't understand. This is my fault. We have to find our son! *I* have to find him!"

David watched his once-again frantic wife put on a pair of pants and a shirt. When he could see that she was serious, he did the same, but it was dark outside and he didn't think there was any point in looking until first light. He followed her down the stairs to the front door. The air was cool and still. Only the Jarretts' bedroom lights were on.

The couple walked past a police car and an officer with a paper cup of gas station coffee.

"We need to look," David said to the young man behind the wheel.

"He's all we have," Carole added.

The officer nodded grimly, and they left him behind.

They made their way toward the bridge, passing a "vacation rental by owner" notorious in the neighborhood for its parties. It was stone quiet just then. A clutch of amber glass beer growlers sat in a cardboard box on the sidewalk. A hastily rendered sign read: **FREE TO A GOOD HOME**. Except for a breeze shifting the leaves of an alder, it was as if time were standing still. Carole wished to God that it were, that there was a way to roll everything back to the previous morning.

She leaned against the bridge railing while she and David looked upriver. A crane loomed above a construction site a few houses up from the edge of the playground.

"Maybe he fell into a hole over there," Carole said. "The excavator has a magnetic pull for little boys. You know that's true, David."

He reached for her hand on the rail. "The police looked there, Carole. They told me."

Carole could not be deterred. It was plausible. She could imagine that when she turned her back, he'd gone in the other direction, then right over the bridge and up the river to the construction site. It could have been what had happened.

"Maybe they didn't see him," she said.

David held Carole by the shoulders and searched her eyes. "Honey, they used dogs. The dogs' trail ended at the river. At the driveway. His scent was all over the place. And then gone."

Next they walked along the river and returned to the play area of Columbia Park. In the center of the grass space above the river was a pirate ship climbing structure that offered slides and various interactive games aligned with the pirate theme.

"Charlie loved to find the treasure," Carole said. The treasure was a grouping of six items on a spinning wheel that included jewels, coins, and other nods to the pirate theme.

"Loves to," David said. "He *loves* to."

Carole stopped. "I didn't mean to . . ."

"Mean to what?" David asked, though he knew.

"Mean to say *loved*. Yes, *loves*."

A dog barked in the distance and a car drove by. Other than that, it was only the two of them—the two of them minus their boy who had disappeared.

"Where were you today?" Carole asked.

He didn't answer.

"When we tried to call you," she said.

David looked away. "Out with a supplier," he said.

"Don't lie to me, David."

"I'm not lying," he said. "Where is this going?"

"You know," Carole said. "I don't want to fight about her. Whoever she is. At least I know it isn't Amanda. At least not her alone. She answered the phone at the restaurant. Whoever you're screwing . . . you know I don't even care. I don't. I'm sorry I brought it up."

"You should be," David said, refusing to allow her to bait him. Baiting him was a favorite pastime of Carole's. She did it whenever she drank too much or was angry with someone else. "Our son is missing," he said. "Let's focus on that."

"I needed you," Carole said. "Charlie needed you."

David didn't speak for the longest time. He processed her words. She was looking for a way out of what she'd done: an act of carelessness that caused what he hoped was not a tragedy.

Her eyes were cold, unblinking. "Just who *are* you screwing these days, David?"

David stopped walking. "Are you seriously going to go there? Our son is gone. I'm not screwing anyone. God, Carole. Let's focus on what we need to focus on. Getting our son back. Undoing your mistake."

Carole gave her husband another hard, cold stare.

"I knew you would blame me," she finally said.

"I don't blame you," he said, although his tone contained a hint of uncertainty. She deserved that. "I don't."

"Liar," she said. "You are a terrible liar."

"You always said I was a good liar."

"About fucking," she said. "Yes, a good liar. About things that matter to me, though, not at all."

David could feel his blood pressure escalate. Carole could make him feel as though he were some kind of a voodoo doll that she could prick with words. There were a million reasons why he put up with it, of course.

In fact, more than a million.

"Were you drinking this morning?" he asked.

Carole threw her hands up in the air and shook her head slowly, emphatically. The remark was a direct jab.

And a familiar one.

"Are you always going to go there?" she asked, careful to contain her anger. "Goddamn you, David. I haven't had a drink since before Charlie was born and you goddamn know it. You do. You of all people shouldn't put that on me."

"Really, Carole?" was all he said.

It was all right for her to question his fidelity. It was her go-to accusation whenever and wherever she seemed to feel the need. Sometimes he hated her so much that he would do anything to hurt her. He'd kept his mouth steel-trap shut. That was how he saw himself. Yet, every now and then, David Franklin could no longer hold his tongue. Carole deserved a jab from time to time. The drinking problem was the only thing he could grab on to at the moment. Maybe ever. He'd been in AA for ten years. He'd never so much as had a single drop of alcohol since the day he quit drinking. Never the slightest threat of a relapse. Carole had tempted him with mojitos, Manhattans, and merlot for years.

"Why'd they take your blouse?" he asked, focusing on her eyes.

She spun around and started for home, and he hurried behind her.

"Where did the blood come from, Carole?"

She didn't answer.

"Did you lose control?"

"Don't even dare say another word," she said. "You know better. You know me."

"And you know me," he said. "I'm not playing around on you. It's over. I promised you."

"Over? Really? I doubt you and your whore are done."

"It *is* over," he repeated. "Believe me."

Now back on the footbridge over the Deschutes, Carole and David faced each other once more.

"Look," she said, speaking in a near whisper. "I'm not an idiot, David. I smell her on you sometimes. I do. I really do. And for you to say those things about me being a drunk or some kind of monster . . . I don't think I even know you. I really don't."

David stood his ground. "Let's focus on what we both know to be true," he said, trying to reel in all the ugly words that had crossed his lips. "Charlie. Let's focus on Charlie."

Carole pulled her jacket tighter. "A minute ago you suggested I might have had something to do with whatever happened to him."

David tried to hold her but she shoved him away. "I didn't mean it, Carole. I know you better than that. I *know* you. Whatever we have isn't perfect and hasn't been great for a long time, but we're solid in knowing each other. That counts for something."

A fish jumped, startling Carole and shifting her focus. "The blood on my blouse was mine," she said. "From my ear." She touched her scabbed-over earlobe and winced. "I tore my earring out when I was calling 911."

He nodded. "Yeah. I know. The cops know too. They are just doing what they are supposed to do: eliminate the possibilities. Exclude us. And they need to do that."

"Right," she said. "I know. I'm sorry. I'm sorry for what I said."

"Me too. Me too."

"Charlie's out there, David. He's scared. He's cold. He wants to come home."

"We're going to find him. I know we are. Keep thinking positive thoughts. Know that our boy is only lost, not gone. Not gone forever. He'll come home."

The Franklins had done a good job of keeping their voices as low as possible, but the surface of the river is a good conductor of sound.

Someone could hear every word they were saying.

Chapter Seventeen
MISSING: FIFTEEN HOURS

Owen watched his wife. Out of it. Finally he shook her hard. Harder than he needed to. Nothing. His heart was pounding so hard inside his chest that he was all but certain the police officer planted across the street could hear it jackhammering. Maybe at that very moment the officer was calling some suspicions in to the police department.

"Liz," Owen said, now hovering over her in the dim light. She'd drunk herself into a puddle of tears and booze. The smell of alcohol was heavy on her breath. The pills he'd fed her had left Liz's eyes somewhat vacant. He wondered what he'd ever found attractive about her in the first place. She was a mess.

"We need to get going," he said when she finally stirred and looked up from the sofa.

"What?"

"We need to get out of here now."

"Where are we going?" she asked, her eyelids suddenly snapping open as she remembered what had transpired that day. "We can't run, Owen," she said. "They'll find us."

Owen grabbed her by the shoulders with such

force that she winced. He yanked her to her feet. "We aren't going to run, Liz. Goddamn you, wake up and pull yourself together. We have to get rid of it."

It.

Charlie was no longer a boy. He was now an *it*. A body. Something to be discarded.

Liz started to cry. At first it was the sound of a hurt animal. A dog with its leg in a hunter's snare. A weak dog. A dog that knew that in a few more breaths it would die. Then Liz started to get louder.

"Don't you do this, Liz. You need to get your shit together. The cops outside will hear you. Get that? They will hear you. They'll think I'm beating you up or something. Jesus! You've screwed up big-time. The biggest colossal screwup in the world. Do you know what's going to happen if they find Charlie in our garage? Do you know how long you'll survive in prison?"

On her feet, wobbly but able to stand, Liz looked her husband directly in the eyes. She saw the terror behind his threats. The gravity of what she'd done nearly sent her sinking down to the floor. Her pockets were full of fishing weights. Her chest was wrapped in the lead blanket of the dental office. Just then she felt immobile.

He hurled more at her, but all she saw was the movement of his lips.

"Women get raped in prison too . . ."

Liz stood there, fighting to stay on her feet as she thought of Charlie and what she'd done. Passing out had brought a respite from the trauma of the day before. Trauma she knew was of her own creation. Silent tears fell down her cheeks and watered the floorboards, but no words came from her lips. She wanted to go and get him—not *it*—and carry Charlie over to Carole and David's. She'd throw herself down on the walkway and plead for forgiveness.

While she went through this mental process, Owen was in her face, giving her a steady stream of reality wrapped in blame. He offered it all up in a loud whisper. Owen could be like that. He'd make a big show at the table in a restaurant when the server was out of earshot, letting other diners know what kind of imbecile the waiter had been, but never loud enough for the offender to hear. Confrontation Owen-style was always directed in an environment that he could control. If he was angry at Liz for something she had done, he'd save it for the middle of a car ride when he could berate her, bring her to tears, and then reel it back, tell her how none of it was her fault.

He raised his voice a notch. Not to yell. Only to make certain that she could feel his anger. "You were drugged up. Everyone will look at you as a woman who killed the neighbor kid and then did not do one goddamn thing about it . . ."

Liz caught only fragments of Owen's tirade. Her mind raced ahead as she planned what she would do. She'd drown herself in the river. It wouldn't be a cry for help but a deliberate act to rid the world of the likes of her.

"Come on," he said, tugging at her shoulders once more. He'd watched her unravel enough and softened his tone. But not his request. There was no way that he'd do that. All of this was, in fact, all her fault. "I can't get rid of it by myself."

"Where are we going to go?" she asked.

"Somewhere out of town. I don't know. We can't leave Charlie in the garage."

He had said the boy's name.

"I don't think I can do it," she said.

"I don't see how you have much of a choice, Liz. I need someone to watch and make sure no one sees me. You think I can drive the car, find the spot, get out, dump it, and risk being seen?"

Back to *it*.

"Well," she said. "I can't. I *can't*."

"You've got to. You killed him, Liz. You've got to help me or we're both going to prison."

"But *you* didn't do anything."

"I lied for you. I'm in this mess because of you. I'm an accessory after the fact."

"But it was an accident."

"It stopped being an accident the second you put that kid under the plastic tarp in the garage, Liz."

She fumbled for a jacket from the hook near the door.

Owen told her that he'd open the garage door so he could back in the RAV4. They'd put the body in the back and cover it up with the stack of Bend *Bulletin*s that had been left behind by her grandparents. Liz had saved them. They were at least thirty years old, and she thought the historical society might want them. She'd told Owen a thousand times they couldn't be tossed into the recycling bin. But not that night. That night the newspapers would be used to cover the biggest mistake she had ever made.

"If the cop or anyone else asks us what we're doing, we're going to the recycling center."

She nodded. "Right. The recycling center. Is it even open?"

Owen swung open the door and held it for her. "It's open twenty-four hours."

"We're not leaving him there," she said.

He put his fingers to his lips. "No," he whispered. "We're not."

Liz got in the car while her husband pulled open the garage door. She maneuvered the RAV4 around and backed it inside, keeping her eye on the street in front of their house and the Franklins'.

"The police car's gone," she said, mostly to herself.

Owen closed the garage door and opened the

hatch in the back. He pushed down the seat while Liz watched him through the rearview mirror. He grunted a little as he hoisted Charlie's body into place. The light was shadowy, but for a second Liz was sure she'd seen the little boy's arm dangle from under the tarp. The sight, real or imagined, nearly made her vomit. Every mistake she'd made that day had a moment when she could have done the right thing. This was another one. She could stop what Owen had insisted they do and plead for Carole and David's mercy.

But she didn't. Fear had gripped her. Not the fear of going to prison but the fear that came from knowing she'd be a pariah for the rest of her life. That there would never be a way back in.

A second later, the hatch slammed shut and Owen opened the garage door, motioning for her to pull out of the garage. He shut the door and jumped in on the passenger's side.

"Get on the highway and head south," he said.

Heading south on US Highway 97, Owen was mostly silent. They'd changed positions in the car on the on-ramp when it became clear that Liz, despite the adrenaline that coursed through her body, hadn't sobered up completely. She'd creased a fender on a mailbox in their neighborhood.

She looked out the window as the blur of nighttime lights came at her. She thought of

Carole and David and how they were probably wishing to God they'd never moved to Bend. Liz wondered if the Franklins had played the game of what-if, as she had herself. If they'd run through the morning Charlie went missing and thought of all the ways that it could have been different. The one little change that could have altered what happened . . .

Liz had done it. She knew that she'd do it every day for the rest of her life. *Her life.* Her suffering. She deserved all of it.

"I think there's a place we can get off up here," Owen said.

Liz nodded in her husband's direction.

The car filled with light as another vehicle approached from behind.

"We're going to get caught," she said.

"Shut up. We're not."

Owen kept his foot on the gas but eased up a little, allowing the other car to pass.

"We are. Someone will see us," she said. "Someone will wonder what we're doing when we get off the highway. No one gets off the highway here. They'll think we're in trouble."

"We *are* in trouble, Liz," Owen shot back. "And you're the cause of it. Shut the hell up. I'm going to cut the lights and slow down. I'm going to take the turn fast, so you'll need to hold on. No one will see us."

Liz didn't say anything. Although she wanted

to die, she found herself checking her seat belt to make sure it was secure. Her eyes had flooded again, and the stars over the high desert swirled in a messy mix of light and dark. She looked in the side mirror and made note of a pair of headlights a good mile behind them.

Without a word, Owen switched off the headlights. The dividing line dimmed to a faint yellow band. The RAV4 began to slow.

"Hold on," he said. "The turn's right here." He gripped the wheel and cut sharply to the right onto a rancher's road. The right tires lifted slightly from the earth and Liz thought that the top-heavy vehicle would roll over.

She didn't care. She hoped she'd die.

But it didn't roll.

Without tapping the brakes a single time, Owen let the car shoot down the road. It was paved for the first twenty-five yards; after that, it was paint-mixer bumpy.

"Owen, you need to slow down," Liz said.

"You need to get a grip," he said. "I've got this. Can't let anyone see the brake lights, Liz." The car was slowing. "No one saw us, right?"

Liz thought of the headlights a mile behind them.

"No. I don't think so."

The RAV4 rolled to a stop in front of a field of summer-dead bunchgrass framed by a couple of groves of juniper, trees that in the darkness resembled black flames reaching skyward. The desolation of the place hit every mark.

"We'll hide it over there," Owen said.

It again.

After making sure the interior lights wouldn't come on, Owen opened the driver's door to get out, and the chill of the outside air came at her.

"I need your help. Are you coming?"

Liz was frozen. "What about Carole and David? They won't know what happened to Charlie. They'll never know."

"Don't be stupid. Look at the fence line here," he said, indicating the pristine wire-and-wood-post fencing that seemed to run for a mile. "This rancher doesn't let a single weed grow around those posts. He's going to find it. He's going to call it in. David and Carole will think some pervert killed Charlie."

"They'll never get over it," Liz said.

He didn't look at her. "It was an accident, Liz. Wasn't it?"

"Yes, but—"

"We can*not* keep talking about this. You need to find a way to deal with it. You'll need to find a way to deal with Carole and David. You'll never, ever be able to admit what you did. You'll never be able to ask for forgiveness."

Liz didn't say another word. She got out,

moved to the back of the car, and held out her cell phone, casting a faint light downward so he could see. She watched her husband shift Charlie Franklin's tarp-wrapped body from beneath the old newspapers. The wind caught a few of the pages and carried the sheets of newsprint like kites upward into the dark.

A beat later Owen gently set the body at the base of one of the junipers.

A flash came from her phone that seemed to light up the whole outdoors.

"Holy shit!" he said, utterly blinded. "Did you just take a picture?" As his eyesight returned, he found Liz standing by the car, propping herself up with her hand on the hood.

"I didn't mean to," she said, fumbling with the phone. "Deleting. God. Sorry." The wind blew and the tarp rustled.

"What's the matter with you?" Owen said. "Get in the car."

"The tarp," she said, sputtering for breath once they were both inside. "Maybe we shouldn't leave the tarp."

"I wore gloves," he said.

Their eyes met. "I didn't," she said.

Owen turned the ignition. "I'm not going to go back and unwrap him. I don't want to see the mess you—"

"The mess I made," she said. "I know, Owen. I know."

"Just shut up. Let's get out of here. I want this night over."

He turned the car around and returned to the highway, turning on the headlights only after rejoining it and traveling a few hundred feet.

The RAV4 passed a car parked on the opposite shoulder, its headlights off.

Owen did a double take, then turned to his wife. "Liz, did you see that car before we pulled off?"

The headlights, dim and far behind them as they got off the highway, came to mind. It was a fleeting thought, refusing to land in her brain as something related to what her husband was asking. Liz didn't think it could be the same car.

"No," she said. "It might have been there. Probably ran out of gas or maybe the driver's taking a bathroom break."

CHAPTER EIGHTEEN
MISSING: SIXTEEN HOURS

When the RAV4 passed from view, the driver parked on the wide shoulder of the highway turned on the ignition. He started toward the spot where the RAV4 had left the roadway. He didn't bother turning off his lights. He didn't care who saw him. He was there to find out what the couple in the silver SUV had done in the middle of the night in the middle of nowhere.

He flipped on his high beams to trace the tire tracks after the pavement gave way to gravel. He turned the steering wheel in a slight zigzag to illuminate the landscape on either side of the road as he searched for the place where the car had stopped.

As he slowed, he could see where footprints led down an incline. He braked and positioned his car so his headlights would flood the space with light. He got out and stood there in the night air. Down by the junipers, he caught a flash of the paint-splattered tarp.

As he made his way down the incline, he noticed a coyote approaching the tarp.

"You go away! Get! Go!" he called out loudly and with a force that hadn't escaped his lungs in a very long time.

The animal looked at him, its eyes white in the glare of the car's headlights.

The man picked up a rock and threw it in the direction of the coyote, missing, but close enough that the animal retreated.

He bent down, his knees landing hard on the rocky, dry soil. Very gently, he peeled away the paint-splattered cocoon that enveloped Charlie Franklin's body.

"What did they do to you?" he said, looking down. "What on God's green earth did they do?"

The car wash was self-service, which was a very good thing. Owen Jarrett pulled his wife's car into the bay and loaded the coin machine with four quarters from change he'd scrounged from the cup holder in the console. He kept two for the vacuum. Liz slumped herself against the cinder block wall, her eyes no longer raining, but cast downward as though looking at anything other than the pooling water by her feet was more than she could bear. They hadn't said a word to each other for a half hour. The handheld sprayer fanned a sharp stream of sudsy water over the rear bumper where Owen thought he could see the tiniest trace of Charlie Franklin. A smudge. Owen couldn't be sure, but he thought it could be blood.

He hadn't opened the tarp to see the extent of Charlie's injuries. He just didn't want to look at him.

It was the middle of the night, almost morning. Owen told himself that lots of people are so busy during the day that they delay things like washing the car to dead hours like this. As the water ran over the car, he made up responses to any questions he might get if someone asked him what he was doing there.

Although no one would.

But if—if—they did, he'd say that he couldn't sleep and decided to use his time to the best advantage by washing the car. His wife had come along to keep him company. Or maybe they'd just made it to Bend from a long drive and had to get the bug splatter from the hood and windshield.

Yes, that was good.

If his questioner persisted, he'd tell them to fuck off. They were upset about their neighbors' lost boy. Neither of them could sleep.

He used the little brush on the back bumper and across the **MY RESCUED CAT RESCUED ME** sticker that Liz had added the first day off the car lot. Rubbing it back and forth to ensure that any DNA left by the accident had been truly obliterated. He knew that it would never, ever get to that point. No one would ever know what they'd done to make everything disappear.

Owen had taken care of everything. Charlie would be found, of course. And when he was, Owen knew that he and Liz needed to react in the way that they would have if she hadn't done what she had.

If he hadn't done what he had too.

While Liz watched, he got back into the car and inched it out of the bay and parked alongside the vacuums. He opened the trunk space. There was the faint odor of urine.

Owen grabbed the newspapers and deposited the stack into a recycling bin next to the car wash. He returned to the car and fed the machine a quarter and started to vacuum as methodically and as quickly as he could. It was a race against a machine that notoriously petered out just when you needed it to suck up something. He worked in straight, parallel lines. Then he worked crosswise. The sound of the vacuum obliterated what was going on in his mind. Just moving the attachment over the carpet, up on the roof, along the sides. He was getting rid of any trace of Charlie Franklin: his hair, skin cells, fibers from his clothes that might have fallen when the boy's tarp-wrapped body was placed inside.

Back home in their house on the river, Owen Jarrett went past his wife and reached for the whiskey bottle. The hour didn't matter. He needed something to get the taste of what he'd done out of his mouth. His fingers shook as he gripped the glass and poured the amber liquid down his constricted throat.

Liz came to him. She was still drowsy from the pills and the wine, but not so foggy that she couldn't see herself through his eyes.

"What next?" she asked.

He didn't answer. Instead, he took another slug.

"I need to know," she said.

"You need to just let it be. Let things happen."

"What things, Owen?" Her voice was tight, her words fractured.

"The things you started. You need to just back off. Let go of it. React to it like you would if you—"

"We should call the police."

He grabbed her. Hard. He shook her.

"Are you crazy? Look, it's too late for that," he said. "Don't you get it? You killed a kid. We got rid of the body. We're both so screwed here that we'll never get out of this if we get caught. Do you understand?"

"*I* did this," she said. "You didn't. I'll tell the truth."

"Liz, you can't tell the truth now. We can never, ever tell the truth."

"What if we get caught?"

"Let's pray that we don't. Let's goddamn pray that no one saw you back into Charlie and that no one saw us cleaning up your mess."

No one spoke for a minute. They just faced each other.

"They'll find him, right?" she asked. "Carole

and David will get to say good-bye to their baby, right?"

Owen poured himself another. "Yes. I'm sure it will be soon."

"They'll find out," Liz said in a whisper. "They'll know."

"No," Owen said. "*You* might have fucked up beyond belief, Liz, but I'm not stupid. I've never been stupid one second in my life. I've fixed this. I've thought of everything. You are not going down for this. You're not going to end up with a goddamn needle in your arm. I won't let that happen."

Esther lay in her bed, facing the ceiling. It was nearly 4:00 a.m. She could not recall a time when she had been more exhausted. Not even the cruel machinations of her ex-husband as their marriage unraveled compared to the emotional drain of the first day of the Charlie Franklin investigation—and how it reminded her of the Corvallis case that ended with the dead boy and a family changed forever. She traced the steps she'd taken, the people she'd talked to, the interviews conducted with the family.

Mostly she wondered what was really going on in that *Architectural Digest*–class home on the river. *The river.* Divers told her that it was possible that the boy had drowned and got caught under a log, although they'd looked in all the likely points where a body could snag.

"Water's not all that murky this time of year," a diver told her. "Not like it will stay that way when the rains come."

As she lay there, her fingers found the gold sea star pendant, and she reviewed the time line in her head. Phone records confirmed that Mrs. Franklin was on the phone for twelve minutes. It was within that period that Charlie vanished. If he'd gone off with someone, then it had likely been without a struggle. No one heard anything. No one saw anything. If Charlie Franklin walked away, it was with someone he knew.

Who was it? And why did they take the three-year-old?

Across town, the front page of the Bend *Bulletin* was rolling off the presses. The local TV stations had already aired the story of the missing little boy the night before as an add-on to coverage about the classic car show in Drake Park. By the time the papers hit newsstands and doorsteps that morning, everyone in Bend would know that Charlie Franklin had disappeared. Among the readership or the viewers who caught the update on the morning news would be the person who knew exactly what had happened.

CHAPTER NINETEEN
MISSING: ONE DAY

The retriever was more bronze than golden, but she was almost twelve, and the change in her glorious coat came with the territory. Tony Lupita, Jessie's owner, lamented that she no longer darted out at every squirrel or cozied up to the younger dogs when they were out walking to the top of Pilot Butte, an extinct cinder cone that rose almost five hundred feet above its stunning surroundings.

It was before daybreak, the best time to be there—especially after the scorcher of the previous day. It was just fifty-five degrees.

Tony looked at his watch. The sun would pour light like golden maple syrup over the sleeping city of Bend in about six minutes.

A warm glow.

Just like Jessie.

He loved that dog the way that he loved people. In fact, to his way of thinking, she *was* a person.

A couple of tourists in navy-blue running gear came toward the dog walker and the dog, racing to the bottom of the butte. They wore earbuds and the look of self-satisfaction. Tony, a widower in his late sixties, gave them a quick wave. It seemed odd that they'd be coming down the butte before the light show, but tourists were a very weird breed.

The morning air carried a chill. Tony wore old Nikes, faded 501s, and a windbreaker that he would almost certainly peel off once he made it to the top and felt the heat of his own body rev up from the walk. He'd been coming there with Jessie since she was a puppy. The top of the butte had restrooms and a few benches for soaking in the view, twinkly lights eclipsed by the sunrise. Mount Bachelor, the Three Sisters, and Mount Hood cut through the high-desert floor. Before pulling out his water bottle and taking a seat, Tony tossed a stick out for Jessie and she did just as she always did: took a circuitous route to go after it, nose to the ground, before bringing it back.

Tony took out his phone and snapped a couple of pictures, drank some water, then began following the coiling track back down to the parking lot. By then they encountered at least twenty or more who had started up the 1.8-mile hike to the top.

As Tony and Jessie made their way to the car, he noticed a man and a little boy. The boy was crying and the man was telling him to shut up.

"You aren't my dad," the boy said.

He was blond, about four. Maybe a little younger. It had been a while since Tony had been around children, and ages were tough for him to determine. At any age, however, no kid should be treated like that little boy was being treated.

"Shut up," the man said. Tony couldn't make out his face, which was obscured by the bill of his Pabst Blue Ribbon baseball cap.

"Is everything okay here?" Tony said, leading Jessie over to the man and the little boy. Jessie, who loved kids, started to growl at the man. It was out of character for the dog.

"Get that beast away from me," the man said. "There's a leash law."

"She's on a leash," Tony said, taking a step closer. "There's also a law against child abuse."

"Mind your own business," the man said, tugging at the now-crying boy and shoving him into the backseat of the vehicle.

Tony hated confrontation, but the hairs on the back of his neck stiffened. "The boy says you're not his dad," he said. His heart was pounding, and he knew it had nothing to do with the climb up and down the Pilot Butte.

The man turned away and went around the driver's side of the car, opened the door, and got in, flicking away Tony's concern as if it were nothing.

"Screw you," he said through the open window. "Try doing your girlfriend a favor by taking her obnoxious little rug rat out for a little hike. I wouldn't *want* to be his dad. My kids would never be so goddamn lazy. I guess this is what you get when you meet someone online."

Tony glanced at the boy in the backseat. He was crying and pitching a fit. And while he thought the man with the abusive tongue had a complete lack of understanding of how to parent, he had to admit that the kid was pretty bratty.

"I want my mom! I want Daddy! I want to go home!"

It made Tony glad that he hadn't tried to date after his wife died. Who needed the aggravation? Online dating, even at his age—maybe especially at his age—could only bring on the worst of all relationship possibilities. He didn't want to be a grandpa to some lazy kid, either.

The next morning, he couldn't put the little boy and the man out of his mind. Sure, the man was a complete ass, and it was more than likely that the little boy was a terror, but something nagged at Tony and he couldn't quite place it. He ran the encounter through his mind as he brushed his teeth. Something had been off. More than just the hateful words that had been hurled at him.

There had been no car seat for the boy.

He was shoved into the backseat and left there unsecured, like a loose bowling ball, to flail around at any sudden stop. That in and of itself was against the law. It was more than that. Who takes their girlfriend's kid out at that time of the morning? And who doesn't have a car seat for a little one?

Once he made the connection to the missing boy on TV and what he'd seen at Pilot Butte, it only took a minute to let Jessie out in the backyard, check her water dish, and make the short drive to the Bend Police Department. Tony Lupita didn't think there was any point in calling 911. He didn't know much. It was more of a feeling of alarm that had lodged inside him. Yet, while he couldn't be sure that he had seen anything that could help in the Charlie Franklin case, he knew wrong was wrong.

"Those poor parents," he said, sitting across from Esther in her office. "They must be going out of their minds."

"It is very, very hard," she said.

"I can't imagine."

She listened as he related all that he'd seen the previous morning. Unfortunately, and despite his good intentions, Tony was short on the kind of details that would assist in the investigation.

"Average height," he said, when trying to describe the man. "Around forty, maybe? Stocky build, I think. Not sure. He had on one of those down-filled puffy coats. Blue. Yes, blue. Or a bluish green."

"Anything about his facial features?"

"His hat," he said quickly. "He was wearing a beer baseball cap."

It was something but not a direct answer. "His face, Tony. Do you think you could work with a sketch artist?"

Tony looked down at his lap. "I could try, I guess. I mean, all I remember is that he had really angry eyes. Like he hated the world. Sure didn't like that kid. Every look he gave the boy was a glare."

"All right," Esther said, moving him along gently. "Could you tell his race? Hair color?"

"White. Had a tan, though. I couldn't swear to it, but I'd say his hair was more brown than black." He stopped for a beat and then looked at her, embarrassed. "God, I'm such an idiot," he said.

He wasn't an idiot. He was like a lot of witnesses. Even those who were very sure of what they'd seen during a stressful moment could be wrong. She'd had a case where a woman had identified an assailant with the complete assurance that she was "one hundred percent" positive he was the perpetrator, only later to break down on the witness stand and concede that she'd never really gotten a good look at the man's face. *"I was too scared to look at him,"* she'd finally said.

It happens.

"You're fine," she said. "Tony, you're doing fine."

Inside, Esther wished he'd been a thousand

times more observant. He didn't even know the model of the car. Thought it was a Chevy but could have been a Ford. His description of the child—apart from being blond, male, and about three or four years old—wasn't much better.

"If it was a dog," he said, "I know I could have done better. I know my dogs."

Esther took down his contact information and the meager details of what he'd witnessed and thanked him for being a good citizen. She loved animals too, but right now she had a missing child to find. Every second counted, and by that point the case was edging toward hopeless.

"It just came to me," Tony said as he was getting up to leave. His face brightened a little. "The car's plates were from out of state. The one with the stylized sun. New Mexico. Yeah, the plates on the car were from New Mexico! I'm pretty sure. Well, I'm almost pretty sure."

Esther perked up too. That was something. True, there were probably more than half a million vehicles registered in the Land of Enchantment, but they still weren't all that commonly encountered in Central Oregon.

She made arrangements to get a local portrait artist who volunteered to do the occasional police sketch in to meet with Tony, though she held no real hopes for the exercise. While well-meaning, the artist was more of a law-enforcement groupie than someone who could actually render a viable sketch based on the details coaxed from someone else's memory. One time she'd spent most of her time sketching another officer's likeness and signing it along with her phone number.

A white Chevy or Ford with New Mexico plates was hardly a defining clue. It was something, however. Something along the lines of *something is better than nothing*. In Esther's experience, there wasn't time for a slow-burn investigation, the kind in which leads come in dribs and drabs. They needed a breakthrough. They needed something definitive—fast. Esther hoped—and she held this hope deep, deep in her marrow—that Charlie was still alive. But experience and common sense told her time was running out. Time did that. It just doesn't stand still.

She went to the break room down the hall and filled her I ♥ BEND mug with the last bit of coffee from the carafe. Not even a full cup. Whoever had been there before her had neglected to do what the sign said: **LAST CUP? MAKE A FRESH POT.**

It dripped like molasses into her mug. Esther knew it was going to be terrible after sitting on the burner for way too long. She started another pot, and as she poured boiling water over the ground beans, she found herself saying a silent prayer.

Find Charlie. Help us find him.

CHAPTER TWENTY
MISSING: ONE DAY

Carole dragged herself to the door to let Liz inside. Carole's silver-blond hair was flat. She wore yoga pants and a pullover. She didn't look at all like Carole Franklin. She was a wounded animal. The younger woman from next door held some take-out containers in her hands. Neither woman said anything at first. Liz awkwardly put her arms around Carole and hugged her.

"I know it's early," Liz said, "but I know you haven't eaten anything."

Carole pulled away. Her blue eyes were puffy and red. "I'm not hungry."

"I know," Liz said. "But you have to eat. I got your favorite." She opened the box and the smell of pad thai wafted into the air. "Three-star. Shrimp."

"Thank you," Carole said, trying to smile, though she had no intention of eating. Eating would only ensure another trip to the bathroom, where she'd end up bracing herself over the toilet and heaving up anything in her stomach. Or nothing at all, if it was empty. She'd thrown up twice that morning.

"He's out there," she said, tears stinging her eyes once more. "He is."

Liz started to cry too. "Oh, Carole, I'm so, so sorry."

Carole reached for Liz, holding her close while they sobbed. "They'll find him, won't they?" she asked. "He'll be all right. Remember that girl that went missing for ten years? The one in California? They found her. She's all right. She survived. She hadn't been murdered."

Liz could hardly speak. "Don't even think about that. Don't. Don't let your mind go to that place." Tears streamed down her face. She felt sick. Sicker than she ever had in her life. She'd never be well again.

Her hands trembled when she went into the kitchen to make a plate for Carole. Carole stayed planted on the sofa, cocooned in the afghan.

"Where's David?" Liz asked, coming back with the food.

Carole looked up. "At work."

Liz set down the takeout and looked into her friend's eyes. Carole didn't blink. She just looked at her, telegraphing a message that indicated disappointment with her husband.

"He got a call from someone," she said. "Said he was going to see the detective and then go on to work the dinner service at Sweetwater."

Liz sputtered. "I don't understand," she said. "How could he do that? He needs to be here with you."

Carole picked at the Thai food. "It's fine," she

said, her words still splintered by the trauma of all that was swelling around her, sucking her into a whirlpool. A tar pit. "Why should this day be any different than all the others? For all I know, he's off with some girlfriend somewhere, crying on her shoulder, looking for comfort sex. Or just sex, period."

Liz's teary eyes widened. Her friend had never indicated anything like that before. And they were close. Sure, they complained about their husbands, but neither had crossed the line into character assassination. Carole was measured. Thoughtful.

"You don't know that, do you?" Liz asked.

Carole rolled her shoulders. Liz wondered if Carole had finally processed what it was that she'd just said. Her little boy was missing, and she had taken the opportunity to trash her husband.

"I guess I really don't know it for a fact," she said, "but David hasn't been a good husband or a decent father for a very long time. He's had affairs in the past. I think he's having one now."

Liz could scarcely believe her ears. "Do you know who it is?"

Carole put down her chopsticks and set her food on the steel-and-glass coffee table. "I used to think it was Amanda," she said. "For a long time, I was pretty sure that he was sleeping with her. Not so much now. She was at the restaurant when he was out doing whatever it was he was doing when I needed him."

Carole's words hung in the air. Damp clothes on a laundry line, blowing just enough so that they could snap and be seen.

Dirty laundry.

The hours blurred into what would become an endless loop. Losing a child was like no other crime. Police came. People gawked from the street. Reporters showed up. Carole barely registered the attention that swirled around her. Her focus on Charlie coming home alive stayed resolute. She didn't pay any mind to a Bend *Bulletin* story that speculated her son had drowned in the river. That couldn't be true. She felt for sure he was alive. He had to be.

Only one other line in the article stopped her.

Bend Police recovered evidence from the home that has been sent to the state crime lab in Springfield for testing.

She had to read it twice to find the sense in it.

Her bloodstained blouse.

This was at once a truth—the blouse had been sent in for testing—and the vilest lie, in what it suggested.

But that quickly, she brushed even this aside. The heat left her face. Her breathing settled. It was nothing but a distraction. It had nothing to do with finding her little boy.

Charlie was no longer under the blue. He wasn't sure where he was. Not at all. In fact, Charlie still didn't know what was up or down. There was a weightlessness that made him feel buoyant. Happy. Safe. The throbbing pain where his head had been hurt, and that made him cry out and wince with every movement, had abated. Faded away. He felt as though he were floating in warm water. Not on the river. Not a lake. Warm, like the big soaking tub in his mom and dad's bathroom. It was black all around. He wasn't scared, though. He wasn't calling for his mommy anymore. Not his daddy, either. The boy was just floating and waiting. Every once in a while he could see a shooting star, a smear of light, streak across the blackness overhead. There was no sound. He wondered if maybe he was in heaven. If so, where were the angels? He listened to hear them, but there was nothing but silence. A slight hum, maybe? Where were the puffy white clouds that would float him?

He was only three, but in that moment, floating on that soft, warm water, Charlie somehow had the sense that he'd be all right. That everything would be fine. He believed that whatever had occurred was only a moment in time. It would pass.

He would be free.

CHAPTER TWENTY-ONE
MISSING: TWO DAYS

Detectives continued to canvass the riverfront neighborhood and work the phones to determine if there had been anything in the Franklins' background that might have made Charlie a target for a child abduction driven by either monetary gain or revenge . . . and not the attention of a child predator.

As perfect as their home environment appeared, there were indications that the couple's life before Bend wasn't nearly as pristine as had been portrayed. A woman who had worked with Carole at Google told Esther that not only was Carole a drinker, she was a hard and selfish boss.

"I'm totally talking out of school," Cassie Potts said from her office in San Rafael, "but she was a total bitch to work for. She never advanced any of her team members. At least her female team. If you had a dick you had a better shot at moving up."

"So she didn't get along with some of her staff?" Esther asked.

"No," Cassie said. "I mean, I guess people who get that far so fast forget that they were once like the rest of us."

"You don't like her," Esther said, keeping her sarcasm in check.

"No. But that's not why I'm calling. I wanted you to know that she wasn't all that. She's still a Google Alert of mine and I saw the story about her son. I'm surprised she has a kid at all."

"And why's that?"

"She didn't want to be bothered. She actually fired one of her assistants after she told her that she was having twins. Carole Franklin literally said, 'You'll have twice the work with those twins and I'll get half of what I need out of you.' "

"That isn't legal," Esther said.

Cassie let out a laugh. "Half the stuff that goes on in the real world isn't legal. You should know that, Detective Nguyen."

"Was there anyone there who might have wanted to harm Carole, hurt her in some way?"

"A lot of people hated her," she said. "But taking her kid, that's just not something I could imagine anyone around here doing."

"You must have thought you might know something that could help the case," Esther said. "You called me."

"I just wanted you to know that the woman in the papers crying about her kid isn't perfect. That's all. She'd do the same for me."

Jake appeared when Esther set down the phone.

"Got anything?" he asked.

"No, not really," she said. "Unless you count a

coworker from Carole's past that uses a missing-child news article to pour more misery on what I assume to be a former business rival."

"Aren't people super?" Jake said.

"*Super* isn't the word I was thinking but, yes, they are."

Jake stayed planted in the doorway. "Lab guy called. The blood on the blouse is Mrs. Franklin's."

Esther nodded. "That's good. I guess. Doesn't help the case much, but it makes it less likely that the boy's mother did something violent to him. Woman on the phone said Carole was a drinker back in the day."

"Didn't smell anything on her."

"No. I didn't, either."

Jake briefed Esther on his conversation with the insurance adjuster.

"He backs up everything Carole Franklin told us. She was on the phone. Longer than she admitted, but she wasn't off doing something to her son."

"Unless she did it before she talked to the insurance adjuster," Esther said.

"Didn't think about that. Her whole time line might be a lie. She could have done something to Charlie anytime after her husband left the house. Couple of hours there."

"Right. But my gut tells me no, she didn't. I just don't read that from her."

181

Jake shrugged. "Okay. Fine. So where does this leave us?"

"Same place," she said. "We need to find Charlie."

Carole was sitting outside on the front steps when Liz arrived home from another aimless run along the river. Liz was running to escape and knew it. It was a sunny and warm day, but Charlie's mother wore a down vest. Even the puff of the down couldn't conceal her shivering frame.

"Oh, Carole," Liz said, wishing she'd had a heart attack before turning into the driveway. "What are we going to do about you?"

There was no answer for it. It was the kind of stupid remark that people make when they attempt to fill silence. It was only one notch better than asking how the mother of a missing child was feeling at the moment.

"*If,*" Carole said. "You know, *if* they don't find Charlie, or *if*. . ." She stopped.

Liz sat next to her and put her arms around her. An image of the hunter cuddling Bambi's mother passed through her mind. "They *will* find him."

"If they don't," Carole said, "or if he's dead, what will happen to me?"

The question struck Liz as self-absorbed, but who was she to judge?

"I don't know, Carole. I suppose you'll be heartbroken for a long time. Maybe forever. But if it's true—and it's a big if—then you will find a way to live with it."

"But who will I be? I won't be Charlie's mom anymore."

"You will always be his mom," Liz said, fighting her own tears.

"If you don't have any children," Carole said, "you aren't a mother."

"Let's go inside," Liz said.

Carole tried to stand, but she was shaky, so Liz helped her to her feet.

"Thanks," Carole said, her words sputtering from her lips. "I can't sleep. I can't do anything. I need to know what happened. I want to know where Charlie is, and I want to know if he's all right. I want to be his mom. It's all I ever wanted to be. None of that," she said, gesturing toward the big house next door, "none of that matters one whit to me."

Every word from Liz's friend was a poisoned dart in her heart.

Chapter Twenty-Two
MISSING: TWO DAYS

Whoever was at the door was persistent and impatient. The doorbell rang. Knock after knock. Another ring of the bell. From the kitchen where he was searching the refrigerator for something to eat, Owen cautioned his wife with a finger to his lips. He'd told Liz not to answer the door for anyone unless it was Carole or David. No texting. No random phone calls, either. No casual conversation with anyone.

"We need to control the situation," he'd said as they drove home after taking Charlie to his final resting place. "We can't do that if we add other people to the mix."

Liz waited for a long time before she went to peer through the peephole. The front porch was empty.

Who was it?

She cracked open the door and almost immediately a voice surged at her.

"I thought no one was home. Thank God, you're here."

It happened so fast. A woman with a microphone was on Liz. Behind her was a man with a camera.

"We're from KATU," said a young woman with flinty eyes and a red gash of a mouth. "I'm Katrina Espinoza-Jones. You've probably seen me on TV."

Liz had. She tried to step away, but Katrina latched onto her arm.

"You must be devastated," the reporter said. "I've heard you're close with the Franklins."

"Yes," Liz said, "we are."

"Great. Can we do a quick interview?" She looked in the direction of her cameraman. "We need to get the word out. Every single second counts." Katrina didn't wait for an answer. "Rex, are you getting this?"

The cameraman, his head down and eye in the viewfinder, gave a quick nod.

"I really don't want to do this," Liz said, trying to extricate herself from the reporter.

"But you have to," she said. "We have to find Charlie. I need to know what you know. Everyone in Oregon is looking for this little boy. You can help."

"I wasn't home when he went missing," she said. "I was taking the exam for the bar in Beaverton."

"My uncle's a lawyer," Katrina said, as though they now had a connection. "How are the Franklins doing?"

"You need to talk to *them*," Liz said.

Katrina motioned for Rex to get closer. "Oh, we

185

will," she said. "They're talking to us in a few. You're background. What can you tell us about Charlie?"

Liz's eyes started to get wet. She could feel her hands shake, and she put them behind her back and looked into the lens. "A beautiful boy," she said. "That's all I can say."

Just then Owen appeared from behind his wife and hooked his arm around her.

"She's in shock," he said. "Not now. This is a terrible time for everyone."

Without another word, Owen pulled Liz into the house and shut the door.

Katrina turned to Rex. "I bet *GMA* is already working with them. God, we're always so late. I blame you for that, Rex. You are so slow."

The FedEx quick print shop was on the same block as Sweetwater. When Carole and Liz passed by the restaurant that morning, neither said a word about stopping inside. There didn't seem any reason for it. Everything had been an ordeal that day. Reporters at the house wanted a story, but there was nothing more to be said. Charlie was gone. No one knew where. At FedEx, Carole started to break down when she told a young man with a shaved head and a half dozen visible piercings why they were there.

"I need to make some posters," she said.

"Color or black-and-white?"

"Color," she said.

"Do you have your graphics done?" he asked. "We can help with that if you don't. Totally reasonable."

Carole stood mute for a second.

"We could use some help," Liz said, taking Charlie's photo from Carole's trembling fingers.

The employee nodded. All of Bend knew about Charlie Franklin by then.

They followed him to a computer terminal at the back of the store. Liz did most of the talking while the young man scanned Charlie's photo and typed in the information.

"Maybe we should make the word *missing* in all caps," he said. "Like this. And red. I think red would make it more prominent."

Carole looked at the screen. "Yes, red. Thank you."

A half hour later, they were out the door with five hundred flyers that would soon be posted all over town.

"We should have offered a reward," Carole said.

"People will help," Liz said. "They *will*. You don't need a reward."

They dropped a stack off at the police department, the school district offices, the High Desert Art League. They hung them in the windows of shops all over town. The two women ate and drank nothing. They just kept handing out posters and telling the same story over and over.

"He just vanished. He's my son. Someone out there must have seen something. Please help me find my boy. He's scared. I know he is. Tell everyone you know about Charlie. Someone has to have seen him."

No one looked at Carole or Liz without sadness in their eyes. None who saw them that day would have traded places with either of them for all the money in the world. There could be nothing worse than losing a child.

Maybe one thing, Liz thought, then chastised herself. Who was being self-absorbed now? Carole's torment had to dwarf hers.

When all the posters were gone, they sat on a bench at Drake Park, looking at the other moms as they paraded their children back and forth on the pathway that fronted Mirror Pond. Liz had said that they should just go home, but Carole was adamant that she wanted to be in a place that Charlie loved so much.

"Maybe whoever took him will take him here. Maybe Charlie'll convince his kidnapper to bring him here."

Liz didn't know how to respond. In her grief and shame, she'd veered toward the improbable on numerous occasions.

Carole sprang to her feet when she glimpsed a

blond-headed boy from behind. He was the right height and build.

"Charlie?" she asked, running over to the child, who was holding a young woman's hand as they walked toward a massive redwood tree.

"Charlie!" she cried out, bending down and dragging the child into her arms.

"Hey! What are you doing?" the woman said. "Don't touch my daughter!"

Carole froze, then leaped back from the child.

Liz took her arm. "My friend's little boy went missing."

"Your friend scared the crap out of Evie!"

"Sorry," Liz said.

Carole looked completely mortified. "I am. I really am."

Evie was crying and her mother swept her into her arms. "Scaring a little kid like that," she said. "That's really twisted."

Liz felt as if she were going to vomit. If Charlie stayed missing, if there was no end to the story of what happened to him, Carole would roam Drake Park or shopping malls or anyplace where kids congregated, looking for her son. She would be trapped in a kind of hideous limbo. She'd suffer until her dying day.

Dear God, she thought as they walked back home, *what have I done?*

"Jaycee Dugard made it home," Carole said.

"Yes, she did."

But Charlie isn't going to. I absolutely know it.

"I know he's coming home too," Carole said. "He's out there and we just need to find him."

"Right," Liz said.

"I had a dream last night that he was a teenager. I wasn't living here anymore. I'm not sure where I was. Somewhere warm. I was sitting outside on my front porch when I saw a young man walk toward me. I jumped to my feet because I knew right away that it was Charlie. Even though I couldn't really see his face, I just could feel it inside that my son had come home to me. He was so big. A young man. He told me that he'd been held captive and that he'd escaped."

They stopped by the bridge. Tears had puddled in Liz's eyes. Carole's too.

"Oh, Carole," Liz said. There were no other words.

"I know. It was so real. He was so handsome. I told him that I'd never stopped looking for him. I told him that I'd known all along that he was alive, that the part of me that is a mother could not die just because he was missing."

Some paddlers went under the bridge; one of them was playing country music on a smartphone.

"Dreams are powerful," Liz said. She'd had a few of her own. All had been ugly. All had been a product of her growing guilt.

"I know it's just a dream," Carole said, "but I really do think there is some kind of truth in what came to me. That my son is alive. That he will be coming home, and I won't ever stop believing that no matter how long it takes."

Liz wished more than anything that Carole's hopes were true.

But she knew a whole lot better.

Chapter Twenty-Three
MISSING: THREE DAYS

Owen shut his office door behind Liz and pulled the miniblinds on the sidelight. They stuck a little and he yanked hard, nearly pulling the whole unit off the wall. His face was red. Liz didn't care. She was suffering, and he was going on with his life. Owen could come here to his office every day to forget what she'd done. She was forced to sit at home, looking out at the river, comforting Carole.

And now dealing with the police.

Liz folded herself into a chair. She smelled of wine. Her brown hair was a mess; her hastily made ponytail had come loose. Her face was devoid of makeup, her eyes rimmed in red.

"You cannot come here like this," Owen said. "Holy crap, are you drunk?"

Liz glared at him. "No, I'm not drunk," she said, nearly in a growl. "I'm scared, Owen. I'm goddamn scared. I should have told the truth. I should never have listened to you."

He looked past her at the shuttered sidelight. "Keep your voice down, Liz. You need to pull yourself together."

"Keep my voice down? I can't even think

anymore. Look at me, Owen," she said, holding out her hands. "I can't stop shaking. We need to tell the police the truth. They are going to find out. They *are*. I know it. They are going to find out and I'm going to go to prison."

"They aren't and *you* aren't," Owen said, hovering over his unraveling wife and grabbing her thin shoulders. His words came out in a whisper yell, the kind parents use when a kid is acting up in a restaurant.

"I killed him," she said. "I killed him."

"Shut up! Don't say that! You stop that right now."

He shook her, and her body went limp for a second.

"Owen, what I did was wrong." She looked up. Tears streaked her face. She searched her husband's eyes, looking for something that didn't seem to be there. "What we did was wrong."

He ignored her last words. "What did the police say? What did you say to *them?* Talk to me, Liz. Take a breath and keep your voice down. Okay?"

"They wanted to know if I'd seen anything. Or anyone. They just kept pounding me with questions over and over. They were grilling me. They were. I think they know something."

Owen perched on the edge of his desk and leaned toward his wife. "They weren't grilling you. Get a grip. They are doing a routine investigation. They have to talk to everyone. No one knows what happened to Charlie."

"I do. You do."

"No," he said. "We don't. You need to tell yourself that a thousand times over so that you can believe it. We don't know. We don't have any idea. I was at work, and you were taking your test."

"What if they find out that I didn't take my test?"

Owen stopped her. "They won't," he said. "Why would they? We aren't suspects. We loved Charlie. We are the Franklins' closest friends."

"I don't like lying to Carole," Liz said. "It makes me sick inside. I can barely look at her and she wants me to tell her everything will be all right. I know it won't ever be all right again."

"We can't change what's done, Liz. We can't change the people we are and the relationships we have with others. It won't look right. It isn't who we are."

Liz could scarcely believe her ears: *Who we are?* She was a murderer and he was an accomplice after the fact. She could put all of the blame on herself when it came to Charlie's death, but that still didn't mean that Owen had clean hands. They were bloody too.

"They are going to find out," she said.

Owen pushed back. "They haven't even found his body."

"But they will," Liz said. "I know it. And when they do, there will be something there that will point to me. To you. DNA. Carpet fibers from the car. Something."

"There isn't anything. You don't need to worry."

"Owen, this isn't worrying. This is facing up to it."

"You need to go home. You need to shower. You need to pull yourself together and be Carole's best friend."

"I'm a monster."

"You made a mistake. Don't make another. Don't drag us down to a place that we can never get out of."

"We're already there, Owen."

Owen ushered her out of his office and down the hall to the reception area. He could feel the eyes of Lumatyx employees as they traced his movements. Owen used to show Liz off. She was so beautiful. Smart. She could talk to anyone who worked there about whatever it was they did in a way that made everyone feel that she understood what they were talking about. One coder thought Liz was cool. The accounting lead asked Owen one time if Liz had been a model. She was part of what his future was going to be. Not arm candy. She was smarter than that. True, some of that pride had ebbed when she failed the bar. He'd lied and said she'd had the stomach flu that day.

He didn't want his team to think his wife was a failure. That would make him look foolish, as though he'd chosen poorly.

And now Liz had made a spectacle of herself. He was embarrassed beyond words. Angry too. She was a screwup.

He *had* chosen poorly.

"Is Liz all right?" the front desk girl asked as Owen turned to go back to his office.

"Our cat got hit by a car," he said.

"Oh, no," she said, making a sad face. "That's terrible. Is it going to be okay?"

"No," he said. "I'm afraid not. She didn't make it. Liz is crushed. Me too."

Her sad face went into overdrive. "I'm so sorry," she said. "That's super-rough."

He thanked her and went back to his office. Later that day a card addressed to Owen and Liz appeared on his desk. Everyone at Lumatyx signed it:

Sorry about your cat . . .

Linda Kaiser had just about given up on her latest Blue Apron meal. Tuscan-style pear and arugula pizza? Seriously? There was no need to make pizza from scratch when anyone in Beaverton with a phone could get one delivered and ready to serve in half an hour. The pictures made it look easy, but it was nothing short of a major hassle. She put the caramelized pears on the pie and slid it into the oven and poured herself a glass of wine.

She followed the sound of the TV news and joined her husband in the family room to watch. The lead story featured reporter Katrina Espinoza-Jones discussing the case of a missing boy from Bend.

She sipped from her glass as a woman's face filled the flat-screen mounted over a fireplace mantel crowded with framed family photographs and Scottie dog knickknacks.

"I know that woman," Linda said, pointing. "I saw her at the bar exam."

Her husband, Dale, reached for the remote. He preferred ESPN.

"Wait," Linda said, tapping his hand. "Stop it! That woman's lying. Why is she lying?"

"Lying about what, Linda?" Dale asked, although he didn't care about anything she had to say. She always saw trouble where there wasn't any.

Linda snatched the remote. "She wasn't at the exam all day at all. She left after only a few minutes. Came late, too. Something's very wrong about that girl."

"Hey," he said, "why don't you report it?"

His tone was only on the edge of being sarcastic. Too much and she'd smack him. Linda never liked her "rightness," as she called it, challenged. Dale had learned to live with it by allowing himself to be less right.

Even when he wasn't.

Linda was always tweeting a complaint. Calling customer service. Telling a server how to present a dish. Asking to see the manager at a store. Linda always needed her voice heard. One time she called the police about a suspicious package left at her door.

It was from UPS, addressed to her husband.

She took her wine to her laptop and looked up the number for the Bend Police Department. When it came to giving her two cents about anything, Linda refused to be denied.

"It's my civic duty," she told her husband as she punched in the numbers.

Chapter Twenty-Four
MISSING: FOUR DAYS

Over the next few days Carole and David would appear in front of the cameras. Carole would plead for their son's return. She'd hold a framed photo of Charlie against her chest, much in the same way she'd held him when he was a baby, rocking slightly back and forth. David sat there impassively, responding to questions only when prompted, and never when Carole was speaking.

"Our Charlie was our dream come true," he said during the interview with the reporter from KATU. "If you know anything about where he is or what happened to him, please call the Bend Police Department."

When the lights went off, the war between Carole and David would start again.

After a while, only Carole and her precious framed photo would meet the press.

David was nowhere to be seen.

Liz filled the old white claw-foot tub and stripped while the bathroom filled with the dense vapors of the rising water. She sat awkwardly on the edge of the tub, thinking about what to do. She'd lost a couple of pounds since the accident, the only good thing that had happened because of it. Stress had made her hair fall out in the back, and she'd taken to wearing a ponytail to conceal the physical effects of her guilt. Her skin above her breasts broke out in a light pink rash, and no amount of calamine could calm its angry hue.

The bath was an escape more than anything. She *needed* an escape. From everything. And everyone. Especially Owen. He was flopped on the bed reading some paperwork and cursing Damon, who he was all but certain was trying to screw him over.

"He's just a nerd without any game," he said as she slipped away to the quiet of the bathroom. "All of a sudden his balls have grown to grapefruit size and he's trying to push me around. What a joke. He's such a prick. He thinks that he's the one that created Lumatyx. It wasn't even his idea. It was mine. I was the one who came up with everything. He just worked the code and the back end."

She wondered how long this had been going on, how long her husband had been a stranger. She'd been immersed in her law books and her volunteer work at the humane society and hadn't been paying attention.

The water beckoned her with the promise of an end to her misery.

So did the expensive razors that Owen had been buying online.

Liz slid into the water, letting it envelop her. Her head slipped below the surface, and she opened her eyes. The surface swirled, breaking up the light from the overhead fixture. She wondered if drowning victims were able to see the world from the depths before they died. Was it beautiful to them?

She stayed under the surface for a long time before emerging, gasping and sucking in air. Drowning would never work. With drowning there was too much time and too much fear baked into the solution.

A razor glinted at her.

I'm over here! it seemed to say. *Pick me up. Easy. Quick. Never dull.*

She pictured the pool of red all around her. Owen busting down the door. Crying out as if he were so upset about what she'd done. Tears and histrionics as though she mattered to him more than anything on earth. That was a big laugh.

She thought of Carole rushing in and pulling her from the water, because Owen wouldn't know what to do. Or yes, yes he would: he'd stand still, making sure that she was really, really dead.

Her fingertips grazed the handle of the razor. Just the slightest touch. In doing so, she felt a surge of electricity run through her body. She touched it again, this time with more purpose. Yet she couldn't pick it up. Not even to shave her legs. The temptation was there, but not enough to propel her to take that step. Instead, she reached for the bar of lavender soap. She wanted to die. She deserved to die. She couldn't do it, though. She finished her bath and went to bed.

She was grateful that Owen was asleep when she slid between the sheets. He was naked, a signal that, later in the night, he'd pretend to be reaching for her in his sleep and wanting sex. It was his MO. *A game.* She normally played along, pretending she was sleeping too, and the two of them would make love until the sheets were knotted by their feet, and every fiber of their bodies pulsed with the ecstasy of their touch.

But that was BC.

Before Charlie.

Now Liz couldn't imagine touching him, and she made sure that she went to bed after he did. She went so far as to put an extra pillow between the two of them as a kind of dam to keep him at bay. When he reached for her at night, she said she was having her period and was using a tampon.

He fell for it.

She knew then that her husband didn't know her at all. She'd stopped using tampons a year ago.

And although she'd started the chain reaction of everything that had happened since the accident, she'd grown to despise Owen. She knew that he'd never admit it to anyone—it would reflect poorly on him—but he felt the same way.

It started to rain that night, and Liz lay there, eyes open, listening. If suicide wasn't the way out, what was?

CHAPTER TWENTY-FIVE
MISSING: FOUR DAYS

Liz was not asleep. She was in a foggy twilight of memory.

She had never been so cold in all her life. The cold was always the first thing she remembered when her reflections—thoughts she tried to vanquish—returned to the flash flood.

The chill gripped her as she and her brother clung to a rocky ledge and watched in horror as the waters swept away Dan and Seth Miller. The memory was still shattered glass, and she would always allow herself a way out from it by wondering if she was remembering what had happened at all, or if it had been told to her. Or if she'd pieced things together incorrectly. Had she seen Seth look at her and call out that he was going to be all right? Or had there been a flash of panic in his eyes as he realized that, by saving Liz, he'd be risking his own life?

Over time, memory played tricks against reality. Jimmy insisted that neither of them had actually seen what happened. He said they were crouched down on the rock, holding on with everything they had. The station wagon vanished.

The cold of the water—that she knew to be true.

She, her brother, and Dr. Miller were admitted to the hospital to treat their injuries and the hypothermia that came with the flood. Liz had a gash on her thigh that took eighteen stitches to close, along with a cracked rib and a broken foot that had her in a cast for the first six weeks of the school year. Jimmy had been luckier. His physical injuries were minor. His skin was bruised, but apart from some abrasions on his knees and a fingernail that had been torn off, he was fine.

Liz held memories of her parents and grand-parents coming to see her at the hospital. The look in their eyes had meant to calm her, she later understood, but it sent her into a panic. Never had she seen such alarm in their eyes.

Jimmy was in the same room, a curtain separating them when the nurses came to examine her. Liz hated the sound made by the metal hooks holding up the big white curtain whenever the medical staff drew it open or closed.

"Where's Seth?" she asked one of the nurses.

"Let me get your mother," the nurse said, swiping the curtain open and looking at Bonnie Camden.

"She's asking about her friend," the nurse said.

Mrs. Camden's blue eyes seemed almost gray. Red and gray. She'd tried to make herself presentable, but her makeup had been applied carelessly and her lipstick was a red smear. Liz would think about that from time to time. Wondering why her mother had bothered to put any makeup on at all . . . or if it was the makeup she'd had on from the day before. Liz had lost all track of time while she lay there in the hospital bed, staring, thinking.

"Honey," her mother said, "we have some sad news about Seth."

Her mom waited a beat so Liz could prepare herself for what she already expected after picking up the pieces of whispers from the other side of the curtain while she waited for the doctors and nurses to do whatever it was they had needed to do.

Even so, she asked, "What, Mommy? What happened to Seth?"

Her mother placed a hand on her arm. "I'm sorry, honey. Seth didn't make it."

Her father, a big man with dark brown llama eyes, reached from behind her mother.

"We're lucky that you and Jimmy are alive. None of you should have been up that canyon road with the rains we had."

Liz started to cry. She didn't know what else to do.

Later she would revisit that salvo thrown by her father at their neighbor. There would be others. The Millers would nearly fade from their lives, only to be seen when crossing paths at the store or when Dan Miller would mow his lawn that perfect way that he always did. The Camdens would pounce at every opportunity to cast blame on the man who "could have killed our kids." Others would agree. They'd nod or even corroborate the charge that Dan Miller had been incompetent, drunk, and generally a nefarious character.

Everything changed for everyone who'd been so happy the morning of the fishing trip to Diamond Lake. They hadn't let the rainy forecast or the showers the night before get in the way of what they all thought was going to be an outing to remember—which it became for all the wrong reasons. And now there was nothing but a wall of pain between all of them. What had been a loving and fun relationship was now icy and cold. What had been a bond between two families living across a river from each other had been upended. When the city proposed a footbridge across the river, Liz's father lobbied hard to get it moved a little farther north. He was careful with his words, even suggesting that the resident beavers would be disturbed by the proximity of the bridge— although anyone who lived on the river knew that beavers didn't care one jot about the tourists who had started to pour into Bend.

Liz was a teenager then, but she knew the underlying reason.

Her father didn't want a direct route to the

Millers. His own shortcomings as a father had made him sickened by the sight of the man across the river. A mistake like the one made by Dan Miller was a virus. Liz remembered how the backyard chickens her grandfather kept would relentlessly peck at an injured bird—peck and peck until a small wound turned into an open gash. Until the weakened bird was pushed into the corner of the coop, unable to fend off its attackers, which pecked, pecked, pecked until all that was left was a bloody carcass.

Her parents had been Dan Miller's first stealth assailants. Others followed. Whatever the doctor did was suddenly seen through the smeared lens of something he'd done—or something he hadn't done. His medical practice suffered. His membership in the Rotary lapsed. Kiwanis too.

The lawn fronting the river became the only aspect of the man's life that looked as though the unthinkable had never occurred. It was a velvet strip of green separating his house from the water's edge. The river had become a moat that isolated the Millers.

It was true that Miranda Miller fared far better than her husband. Many pitied Dan's wife. Some wondered if she'd forgiven her husband for what happened or if she reminded him at every turn that Seth was gone. She was seen as a tragic figure, as much for the fact that she was married to Dan as for being the mother of the little boy who had drowned in the flash flood that last weekend of summer. The visits between Liz's mother and Mrs. Miller continued over the years, but only sporadically, and never foursomes with their husbands. No more joint barbecues or outings around town.

Dr. Miller took a break from his incessant yard work one time when she and Owen moved into the old house on the river and gave a slight wave in Liz's direction. She saw him and stood there, doelike, on a roadside with traffic whizzing by. Unresponsive. Not even a blink in acknowledgment. Dan Miller had saved her brother's life and her own, but Liz found herself acting like one of those pecking chickens in the coop.

She came to hate how she'd never reached out to Dan. Wrong, she knew, was wrong.

The call from Linda Kaiser, the Beaverton woman who had managed the registration table for the Oregon bar exam and who insisted that Liz Jarrett had lied about her whereabouts the day Charlie went missing, was one of more than a hundred tips that Esther and Jake sifted through in the first days of the case. Linda said that Liz had just settled in before getting up and leaving.

"She seemed off to me, too," she said. "Like she was upset. Came just before we locked the door. Most are Johnny-on-the-spot and come early. Not this one."

Esther wondered where Liz had gone after the test.

And if she'd just made it to Beaverton before the exam started, had she been in the neighborhood when Charlie disappeared?

"Maybe she saw something," Jake said as Esther pulled into the driveway that the Franklins and Jarretts shared.

"Maybe she was upset by the news. Carole probably reached out to her. They're friends and neighbors."

"Makes sense," Jake said.

"Looks like they're home," Esther said, indicating the Jarretts' RAV4 and the Forester as they stepped out of the cruiser. A breeze blew smoke from a barbecue grill across the river, one of the last smells of summer permeating the air.

A moment later the detective and the officer stood in front of the pink front door. Liz answered the bell with Owen right behind her.

"I saw it was you," Liz said, looking past Esther and Jake. "Not the press. I don't want to do interviews, but I do want to help."

"I know this is a hard time," Esther said.

Owen spoke up. "It is. Hard for David and Carole, that's for sure. Hard for us because we care about them." He reached for his wife's hand and squeezed it.

"And Charlie," Liz said as her cat, Bertie, slid past her to the great outdoors.

"That's why we're here," Esther said. "Can we come in?"

"We were just going out," Owen said, still gripping his wife's hand. "Now we'll have to catch the cat."

"Oh, I'm sorry," Esther said.

"It would just take us a minute," Jake said.

"We really have to go," Owen said. "What is it?"

"Right," Esther said. "You're in a hurry. Understood. We took a call from Linda Kaiser in Beaverton. Do you know Linda?"

Liz's face went blank. "No. Sorry."

"We've never heard of her," Owen said.

"Well," Esther went on, "she saw you on the news, Liz, and she took exception to something that you said."

"What was that?" Owen cut in.

Liz looked down. "What did I say? I was upset. I said I hope Charlie is found soon."

"Of course," Esther said. "Not that. She said that you didn't stay for the exam. That you left almost immediately after getting there."

Owen shook his head. "That's wrong. She took the exam."

Awkward silence filled the space. Liz didn't answer right away. She stood perfectly still. Thinking.

"What's going on here?" he asked.

"I'm sorry," she said, her eyes now brimming

211

with tears. "I should have told you. I choked. I just knew I couldn't pass it. I lied to you, Owen. I went there to take it, but . . ."

He put his arms around her. "Oh, honey . . ."

"I'm sorry," Liz said. "I should have told you."

Esther and Jake took a step back from the couple. The scene was intense. Liz wasn't crying, but it was obvious that she was devastated by her disclosure. She kept her eyes cast downward. There could be no doubt that she was humiliated by her admission.

"What did you do after the test?" Jake asked.

Liz was flustered. Her face was red. "What does that matter?"

"Just trying to pin down the time line," Esther said. "Maybe you got home earlier than you told us before?"

"No," Liz answered. "I took my time getting home. I was in no hurry to tell Owen what had happened. Everything I told you was true. I just didn't stay for the full exam, that's all."

"This is pretty embarrassing for my wife," Owen said, speaking about his wife as though she weren't within earshot. "We've got somewhere to go now. Let us know if there's anything else we can do."

"All right, then," Esther said. "Linda said you got there late."

"I overslept a little," Liz said. "I didn't get out of Bend until nine thirty. I probably broke the speed limit the whole way there."

212

"Before you left, did you see anything?" Esther asked.

"Anyone?" Jake added quickly.

Liz stood there for a beat. "No. Nothing. I really wasn't paying attention to anything. I was late and in a hurry to get to Beaverton."

"The test was important to Liz," Owen said, reaching for her hand.

Tears welled up in her eyes. "I'm really sorry, Owen. I just . . ."

"It's all right," he said, leading her back inside. "There'll be other tests."

Jake turned to Esther as they went back to the cruiser.

"Family drama there for sure," he said.

When the detectives were gone, Owen put his arms around Liz.

"You were perfect," he said.

She pulled away and found a seat on the couch. She grabbed an old embroidered throw pillow to hug. "I don't understand why you want it to look like I lied to you. I told you about everything I did."

He sat next to her. "I just think it plays better this way. It makes it seem more realistic if you are so deeply embarrassed about your failure at the bar exam that you couldn't even tell me."

"It makes me look like a liar," she said, forcing him away.

"No," Owen insisted. "It makes you look real."

Chapter Twenty-Six
MISSING: FIVE DAYS

A thunderstorm that had been forecast had moved over Bend early the morning of the fifth day of Charlie's vanishing, darkening the skies and making the world seem even heavier than it had been when Esther arrived at the Franklins' place five days ago. The thunder was coming from far away. It was the bass of her brother's stereo system, pounding in the background as she kept her nose in a book. She and Mark rarely talked anymore, a casualty of the geography that separated them. He worked for a youth organization with a facility somewhere in the jungles of Belize. She missed him. She missed many things.

Before going to the office, the detective walked up the street to the footbridge over the river. She looked downriver at the Franklins' house. Two paddleboarders passed under as she stood there; a group of tubers floated by the beaver lodge.

Where are you, Charlie? Did someone take you? How come no one saw anything?

Her phone buzzed, snapping her out of her thoughts.

It was Jake. "Detective, we got something. Something big, I think."

"What?"

"Got a hit off the sexual offender database. One of the names off the rental waivers. Brad Collins, forty, Dayton, Ohio."

"Good work," she said. "Where is Mr. Collins, do you know?"

Jake was excited, nearly out of breath. "Got that too," he said. "Called his home number on the waiver and—*get this*—his mom answered. Nice lady. Said that her son is staying at the Pines. Drove out here with a buddy, a kid that she says lived out West and needed a ride home. Said he was even thinking of moving out here. Don't think she knows a thing about her son's past. Used to be a teacher. Said he's always doing nice things for kids."

"I'll bet he does," Esther said. "Good work, Jake."

"I got more," he went on. "I called the manager at the Pines. He's in 22, the cabin on the end, farthest away from the manager's office. He's there now."

Jake was nearly giddy, and Esther couldn't help but smile.

"Meet me there," she said. "Don't drive into the lot. We don't want to scare off Mr. Collins. He might have Charlie."

"Right. Right. I'll be there. Quiet, like."

Brad Collins sat on his bed in his monthly rental cabin at the Pines. He hadn't put up a fight or

215

tried to escape out the back way when Esther and Jake showed up at his door. Indeed, from the moment he saw the Bend detectives, he exhibited nothing but weary resignation. He even invited them to look around the cabin before Esther could ask to do so.

"When things like this happen," Brad said, "I know I'll see people like you. I came here in part for a fresh start. Some fresh start."

Esther and Jake studied the scene. Nothing remarkable. An Ohio State T-shirt hung on the back of a chair. Fast-food wrappers. Coffee in a small pot scented the air. No indication of Charlie Franklin. No sign of the friend he said he brought out to Oregon.

"Cam is nineteen and that's all I need to say about him," Brad said.

"Where is he?" Esther asked. "We might need to speak with him."

"I dropped him off in Madras with his family."

"Do you have an address?"

He nodded. "Yeah. I'll give that to you. Like I said, I'm used to this. Jesus, you people always come sniffing around whenever a kid's involved."

"You might be able to help us, Mr. Collins," Esther said. "Can you come downtown?"

His face went red. "I've been through this before and I've played it both ways. I've gotten a lawyer and I've gone in to be interviewed without, as you say, 'incident,' and either way I end up with nothing but humiliation and, in the case of a lawyer, a big fat bill to pay."

"You can take your own vehicle or ride with us," Esther said.

The Ohio man picked up his keys from the nightstand. "I'll drive," he said.

Brad Collins was overweight, with a receding hairline and hooded eyes that darted around the space with more energy than his girth might have suggested. The Ohio State T-shirt was tugged over the roundness of his stomach, leaving a bare stretch of skin exposed. Esther had watched him pull it down several times on the closed-circuit TV that captured every move he made and everything he said.

Armed with a folder that contained the information posted on a sex offender website, Esther took a seat directly across from Brad. He was being interviewed first as a witness, not yet as a suspect or as that resident of law-enforcement purgatory, a person of interest.

"How did you know about the missing little boy?" she asked.

"I saw it on the news," Brad said.

"Right," she said. "The news. Was it on the TV or in the papers?"

"As far as I know it hasn't been in the papers," he said. "Pretty much everyone knows. Bend's a

217

lot smaller town than where I come from in Ohio. Missing kids are a big deal."

"Yes, they are." Esther kept her eyes riveted to his. Uncomfortably so. She was looking for a window into his soul, a way to measure whether he was being truthful or evasive. He stared right back. "You were on the river that morning, weren't you?"

He folded his arms. "You know I was," he said. "Let's not play games, Detective. I'm here because of my past and the fact that I went tubing down the same stretch of river where the little boy went missing."

"All right," Esther said. "Yes, that's why you are here. Your tone suggests a kind of hostility, and I don't know where that's coming from."

"Really? No matter how clean I keep my nose, people like you are always harping on me. Beating on me for things I didn't do."

"I just want to know what you saw, Mr. Collins. That's all. I'm not here to beat anyone up. I'm here because there's a little boy out there somewhere. He's scared. His parents are scared. That's why we're here. No other reason."

"So you say," he said, barely looking at the detective.

Esther opened the folder. "It's the truth. And I can see that you *have* kept your nose clean. I do see that."

He looked over at the unblinking red light of the camera mounted on the wall.

"I was a student teacher at the time. Twenty-two. The boy was seventeen. It was wrong, not just because he was underage but because I was in a position of authority. In other states it would have only been a lapse in judgment, though. Not a crime." He looked again at the camera's red light. "You have no idea what it feels like to be watched all the time, Detective."

Esther set down the papers. "I guess I don't. Let's get through this so that you can go home, so that we can move this case forward."

"Fine," he said. "Yes, I was on the river. Yes, I guess I went past the house where the kid, Charlie Franklin, went missing."

"Did you see him?"

He stayed quiet for a moment. "Yeah," he said at last. "I did. I saw him. He was playing by the shore. I floated by. That's really the end of the story."

"He was playing," she said. "What was he doing? Was he close to the water's edge?"

"He's a kid," he said. "I barely saw him. I don't know what he was doing. I paid more attention to that big house than anything. I remember thinking that some millionaire had to be living there and that the kid was some rich person's child. You know, how lucky that boy was. Where you start in life matters. Big-time."

She knew what he was saying was true. Her own mother had said so many times.

"I need you to think, Mr. Collins. I need you to think very, very hard."

"I have," he said. "I don't know anything. Really. And if you think for one second that I really had something to do with this, then you better check out the bartender at Anthony's in the Old Mill District. I got out of the water at Mirror Pond, took the bus back to return my tube, and planted myself in front of the TV in the bar to watch the game. I bet my Visa card was swiped by eleven o'clock, if not a few minutes sooner."

Esther's eyes met his. "We'll check into that. Now, I know you've been thinking long and hard about the day on the river. Did you see anything—really, anything at all—that was unusual?"

"I don't live here," he said, shifting in his seat. "I don't know what unusual would be."

"It was quiet that morning," Esther said.

Brad looked away. "Yes. Very."

"Did you hear anything?"

He glanced at her, then away once more. "Some kids were partying up the river, but it was quiet past the little bridge. I thought the kids were obnoxious."

"Upriver?"

"Yeah. Just past those damn rapids."

"What else?"

"Nothing. A guy with a dog. In a canoe. Some ducks."

"Do you remember anything about the boy? Anything?"

"No. I don't. I really don't. I was minding my own business. I'm on a damn vacation. At least, I was."

"How long are you going to stay in Bend?"

"Up to now I was thinking of moving out here. Rented the cabin for a month's stay. Now I'm not so sure. Came here to do a good deed and I get blamed for something I didn't do."

"No one's blaming you," Esther said.

"Maybe not for this, but you blame me. People like you always do. No matter what I do, I'll always be the first person that gets the knock on the door. And for what? A mistake I made a long time ago."

The detective handed the Ohio man her card.

"Let me know if you are going to leave," she said. "I might have a few more questions."

CHAPTER TWENTY-SEVEN
MISSING: FIVE DAYS

Damon West poked his head into Owen's office at Lumatyx. It was after ten in the morning—early for Damon, who favored a workday that lasted until after midnight. A row of red Japanese toy robots on a stainless steel credenza behind Owen bobbled as the air moved. The toys were an affirmation of the geekdom that surrounded Owen. He'd ordered the lot of them from eBay but pretended they'd been collected one at a time. In his heart, Owen Jarrett was not a techie. He could, however, play the part.

"You look like shit," Damon said.

Owen knew that his business partner's assessment was probably on the generous side. He'd had less than three hours of sleep. Before getting dressed, he stood in the shower for a full twenty minutes, letting the hot water cascade over him to peel away the sleep and the stream of consciousness that he had been unable to escape.

Liz. Charlie. Liz. Charlie. Murder. Liz.

"Thanks," he said. "I feel like shit. Twenty-four-hour bug, I think."

Damon took a seat in the Herman Miller Eames chair that was Owen's first splurge in anticipation of the windfall he was about to collect on.

"You've been preoccupied," Damon said, adjusting his new frames.

Owen blinked his bloodshot eyes. "Have I?"

"Everything all right? With you?"

"Yeah, sure."

"Liz?" Damon asked.

Owen glanced down at the face of his phone. A stream of texts from his wife filled its cracked surface.

"You'll find out soon enough. She didn't finish her bar exam. Got sick."

"Shit," Damon said. "She's been studying her ass off."

"Yeah, tell me about it. She's at home now trying to figure out her next move. We both are."

"I'm really sorry that happened," Damon said. "It's just a stumble. We've had them, and now look at us."

"Yeah, the money."

"Rolling in, baby. We're set for life."

"Money's good," Owen said.

"What's the first thing you're going to buy?" Damon asked. "After the car, of course."

"I think I've spent every penny in my head a thousand times over. No idea what I'll really do. After the car, that is. You?"

"I'm going to buy my mom a condo in Sunriver," Damon said with a wry smile. "Close to me, but not too close."

Sweat dripped from Owen's armpits and his head throbbed. Even so, he managed a grin. "I figured you'd do something like that, Damon. The only thing we have in common is code."

Damon laughed as he got up to leave. "Yeah. We're about to have big, fat bank accounts too." He looked closer at his business partner and friend. "Drink some water, Owen. You'll feel better."

Owen doubted that.

"Right," he said.

Owen returned his gaze to his phone and started to scroll through Liz's messages.

She had sent the first one only minutes after he left home for the office.

Liz: What have I done?

The next text came through ten minutes later.

Liz: I don't know how to face Carole.
I don't know what I'll say. I'll tell her.
I think I'll tell her. Owen, I need you. I
need your help right now.

Five minutes passed, then another was dispatched.

Liz: We've made this worse. We're really screwed up here. I've thought about it. I should tell someone. But I won't. I promised you.

Owen pressed his hand against his clammy and pounding forehead. His wife was unraveling when she needed to find a way to deal with the situation. Texting unremittingly was not the answer. In fact, it could make things far worse. *Someone could read them.*

Liz: I'm going to take a valium and go over there. I'm going to hold it together. I am. Please don't worry.

Valium was a good idea, but worry was all Owen could do. He picked up the office landline and dialed Liz's cell. She picked up on the first ring.

"Listen to me," he said, his voice calm and controlled when inside he wanted to drive home and shake Liz hard and get her to snap out of what she was doing. "You need to get rid of your phone and go to the AT&T store and buy us each new phones. You need to do that before you do anything. Okay?"

Liz stayed quiet. "I don't understand, Owen."

Owen kept his cool. He had no choice. His irritation showed on his face but not in his voice. He didn't need any pushback from Liz.

"Smash your phone with a hammer right after this call," he told her. "Obliterate it. I'll get rid of mine too. And, Liz, never text me anything about what happened. Do you understand? I said we couldn't talk about it. That means texting. *Especially* texting."

Silence filled the receiver.

"Did you hear me?" Owen asked.

Finally a response: "Yeah, I did. I'm sorry. I didn't think about that. I just needed to talk to you and I knew I couldn't call you."

"That's okay," he said, lying to her. None of what they'd done was okay. "After this call, we can't talk about anything like this on a phone again. That means texting too."

"I'm going crazy," she said.

"No," he said. "No, you're not."

"I am. Really, I am."

He ignored her. "I told Damon I had a twenty-four-hour bug. I told him that you got sick at the bar exam. Okay? No more stories. Nothing elaborate. Nothing convoluted. Keep things simple. People who've done this kind of thing are always tripped up by what they say after they've done it."

"This kind of thing" was murder, he knew. He wouldn't dwell on that.

He heard Liz swallow. "What about Carole and David?" she asked.

Owen turned his body toward the window. The sidewalks were full of people shopping and finding their way to one of the city's farm-to-table places that had been featured in the *Oregonian*. The car show and the Charlie Franklin story had provided a one-two punch to one of the last summer weekends.

"Be yourself," he said.

"I don't know who I am anymore."

"You're Liz Jarrett. You love Carole. Go help her get through this."

It was not a suggestion but an order.

Liz was a woman who knew how to stand her ground, but she knew that under her feet the ground was shifting and at any moment she was going to fall. It would be a hard fall, one from which she would never recover. She couldn't push back at an order. She no longer knew who she was.

"But—" she started to say, before letting her words drop.

There was no arguing with something as horrific as what she'd already done.

Chapter Twenty-Eight
MISSING: FIVE DAYS

Owen caught a glimpse of himself in his office window. Damon was right. He *did* look terrible. His eyes were accentuated by dark crescents. Stress mottled a smooth complexion that was usually marked only with three-day stubble. Owen needed to pull himself together. He needed to help Liz get herself together. They needed to take a deep breath. Both of them. They needed a moment to stem the grief and shock that had enveloped them. If they didn't, they'd surely get caught. Owen put his iPhone in a Starbucks cup that he'd retrieved from the trash. It was good that he'd bought a twenty-four-ounce drink the other morning. His usual twelve-ounce "tall" would never be big enough to contain the phone. He put the paper cup back in the trash and covered it with a bunch of other papers. That night the janitor would take the trash to the dumpster. He'd tell everyone that he'd lost his phone as he went about the business of reassembling contact names and numbers into a new device.

It was smart not to make any adjustments to his routine.

As he sat there facing the empty Eames chair,

his necessary betrayal played over in his mind. He'd let Liz believe that Charlie was dead when he went into the garage. He'd let her carry the burden of what she thought she'd done. He rationalized his actions as the only way to save their marriage, their very lives. He'd killed the neighbor kid because he knew that he'd lose everything if his wife were arrested for murder.

He'd worked too hard for the Lumatyx deal and the cash that was going to pour over him like the sweetest nectar known to man.

Charlie would have told on them.

They'd never get that big house on the river.

He told himself, *What's done is done.*

Esther felt her phone vibrate as she sifted through reports. She glanced at the image of her mother that appeared on the screen. Lee Nguyen had been calling for days. At all hours. Esther had grown tired of her mother's need to say she was sorry when she really wasn't. After her father died, Esther's mom had sought to strengthen their bond, but each time she'd found a way to remind her of some disappointment—her failed marriage, her dubious career, her casual sense of style.

All of those things seemed so petty, so insignificant. Charlie Franklin was missing. This was no time for her mother to interject herself into her daughter's life. Not when another mother was desperate to find her own child.

Esther felt the gold sea star pendant around her neck and rejected the call.

The swipe of Brad Collins's Visa card and a quick telephone conversation with the bartender at Anthony's confirmed the Ohio man's story.

"He's not our guy," Esther said.

Jake shrugged. "Still a perv, though."

"I don't know, Jake," Esther said.

Jake thought he saw a little sympathy in her eyes. It puzzled him. "You don't feel sorry for him, do you?"

"No," she said. "Just thinking about his case. That's all. He was twenty-two when he got picked up for molesting that student. The boy was seventeen. Consenting. Seems pretty close in age."

"Still a perv," Jake said.

As Esther saw it, the law is always black-and-white. It has to be. The shades of gray distinguishing criminals were the province of the district or county attorneys who handled the overwhelming caseload that came through their offices every day. They alone had the authority to decide the shades. Not the police.

"Yes, the law says so," she said.

An hour later, David Franklin pounced on Esther in the lobby of the Bend Police Department. He was a handsome man, but the anger in his face twisted his features into what reminded the detective of a gargoyle she'd seen on a church in a village in France when she toured there with a high school group. At the time, she'd thought the gargoyle looked like one of their chaperones. Now, however, she saw the missing boy's father as the physical embodiment of the terra-cotta figure. His eyes had narrowed, and his mouth was a slash of anger.

"You found out who took our son," he said.

"No," she said, gesturing for him to follow her to her office. "We haven't. We don't know yet what happened, Mr. Franklin."

"Some pervert got him. I know it. I talked to my buddy at Anthony's. He called me right after one of your officers chatted him up. Told me about his background. I want to know what the hell you're going to do with Brad Collins."

"He didn't take your son," she said, closing the door after him.

"You can't know that. He's got a record. He was on the river at the same time Charlie went missing."

"Sit down," she said. "Take a breath. Please."

"I won't sit down, and I won't have you tell me what to do. Every second matters here and you know it. You need to get that guy in here and grill him."

"We've interviewed him," she said. "He's not involved."

"He's a pedophile," David shot back. "That kind of skunk doesn't change his stripes. He's into little boys. You know that."

She shook her head. "His victim was seventeen. He was twenty-two. He's on the registry—that's right. But there's no indication he's offended a second time."

"There's no such thing as a onetime sex offender and you know it."

"It's rare, I'll give you that," Esther said. "But, again, he was twenty-two and his victim was seventeen. He's never been known to have the least bit of interest in little boys." She could see he wasn't hearing her. He was operating with tunnel vision, and Brad Collins was in his crosshairs at the end of the tunnel. "Now, please go home. We're working this as hard as we can. We're leaving no stone unturned. Really none. How is Mrs. Franklin?"

"How do you think she is? She's drugged up on a sedative and even that doesn't stop her from crying nonstop."

"Go home to her," Esther said. "Take care of her."

"I can't go home right now," he said. "I have a restaurant to run."

Lee Nguyen sat on the steps outside her daughter's condo.

"You don't answer my calls," Esther's mother said. "So here I am."

Esther let out a sigh. "Mom," she said, "I've been busy."

Lee kept her expression even. "Not busy," she said. "Just angry at me."

Lee's black hair was sprinkled with so much white that it nearly looked like a late-winter snowdrift. It was just as stiff. Lacquered by an overabundance of hairspray. She wore black pants, a white blouse, and a bright pink sweater.

"You are my daughter," she said. "You owe me the respect of an answer when I telephone you."

"You drove a long way just to let me know you're disappointed in me again, Mom."

Lee hooked her arm in her purse and faced her daughter. "Your silence kills me every day."

Mom wins. She always does.

"Fine," Esther said. "Come in, then."

Lee followed her daughter to the door of the condo. She was a diminutive woman, but she moved quickly. Esther always considered her mother catlike, showing up suddenly to sharpen her claws and then leave.

"Do you have a view?" Lee asked, a reminder that she'd never been there since Esther broke up with her husband.

"No, Mom," Esther said. "I don't."

Inside, the detective went into the kitchen, where she turned on the electric kettle, a wedding shower gift, for tea. Though the space was spotless and nicely decorated with a mix of contemporary art and furnishings, the look on her mother's face indicated that she didn't approve.

"Small place," she said.

"Really, Mom?" Esther said, thinking back to every other aspect of her life her mother had found fault with. Her career. Her clothing. Her almost ex-husband. It would never end.

"Sorry," she said. "I told myself to make nice, but I think it is hard for me."

The admission surprised Esther. Her mother had never indicated any faults of her own.

Maybe she's trying.

They sat at the dining table drinking tea and picking at almond cookies from a box purchased at Trader Joe's.

Lee put down her cup. "I saw on TV the case you are working on, Esther. I hope that you find that little boy. I hope that you can bring him home to his parents. I don't know what I ever would have done if I lost you."

Esther smiled a little.

Her mom was trying.

"There are lots of ways to lose someone," Esther said.

"Right," Lee answered. "Lots of ways."

"I love you, Mom. I just can't stand your disappointment in me. It hurts me to think that you live in constant displeasure over the choices I've made."

"He was not a good husband."

She was right, of course.

"Yes. But it's done. So if we're going to move on and get along, then we have to let that alone." "You could have been a doctor," Lee said.

Esther smiled. Her mom's refrain was decidedly familiar. "And that too, Mom. Leave that alone. I'm doing what I need to do."

CHAPTER TWENTY-NINE
MISSING: SIX DAYS

Amanda Jenkins was sorority-girl pretty, an all-American beauty with the tone and frame of a young woman who loved sports and didn't have to work out for the sake of doing so. She rented a modest though still expensive apartment above Bend's Old Mill District. She lived in a second-floor unit with a half-dead Martha Washington geranium, a gift from her mother, next to the welcome mat. When she let Esther inside, she did so being very careful not to let Toby, her cat, snake her way between her legs and out the door. The cat tried that every chance she got.

"She'll never come back once she gets out to the real world," Amanda said, shutting the door behind her.

Esther loved cats but was desperately allergic. She wanted to pet Toby, who playfully rubbed against her ankles, but that wasn't an option. Antihistamines made her drowsy.

"I'm glad you called," the detective said.

"It feels right," Amanda said. "Uncomfortable, but right." The young woman found her way to her sofa and sank into its soft, mint-colored velour cushions. She wore faded blue jeans and a white cotton top. Her red hair was pulled back and hung behind her in a luxurious ponytail. She wore no makeup. Around her wrist was a charm bracelet that she'd later say had belonged to her grandmother. She was a young woman who grew up with a solid foundation. Doing the right thing wasn't a stretch.

Even when she'd perhaps done something so very wrong.

Amanda cast her green eyes downward. "I don't want to lose my job. I guess that's my only concern. But I know that I will. You know, once I tell you what I know."

Esther was skeptical about Amanda and David's relationship. Was it purely professional? It was the elephant in the room, and—considering that a little boy's life was at stake—there was no point in mincing words.

"Are you and David having an affair?" she asked.

Amanda bounced to the edge of the sofa. She didn't stand up, but she nearly propelled herself to her feet. "No," she said. "Never. Who told you that?"

"That's not important, Amanda. You can tell me the truth."

"I'm *telling* you the truth. I would never be involved with that man—and it's not just because he's married. He's a complete ass. A jerk. He only cares about one thing and that's his stupid restaurant."

"Really, Amanda? Why call me to come over to tell me what a jerk he is? I think that's pretty much the opinion of half of Bend."

"And the other half hasn't met him," Amanda said.

"From where I sit, yes. Now, we're in the middle of an investigation, and I need to know why you wanted to talk. If it isn't about the affair, then what?"

"There is no affair," she said. "At least not with me. I really don't appreciate your tone, Detective. I'm trying to do right here."

"Sorry," Esther said. "Continue. Please."

"I'm upset now," Amanda said, running her fingertips on her charm bracelet like a silver rosary.

"I'm sorry," Esther said, though she wasn't. She backtracked, though, keeping her voice quiet and respectful. "Tell me what you think I need to know."

Amanda waited a second, calming herself before unspooling a string of observations about her boss. Yes, she was pretty sure he was, in fact, having an affair, and she suspected he'd made a morning date with whoever he'd been seeing.

"He lied about meeting a supplier. He treats the suppliers like dirt, then kisses their asses if they bring him something special. He's always pulling crap on them. Complaining about spoilage. Shorting them. Bad-mouthing them. The one thing he'd never do is miss an appointment with a mushroom or fish guy. That's how he is. You know, it's all about the restaurant. His story about where he was that morning was a complete lie. I'm sure of it."

"So he *is* having an affair. What does that have to do with Charlie?"

"I don't know. You should know about it. It was something else that I heard him say one time when I came in early and he was on the phone. Couple months ago. He was in his office and I was restocking the votive candles for the tables in the little alcove right outside. I could only hear one side of the conversation."

"What did you hear?"

Amanda picked up Toby and proceeded to pet the cat, sending wisps of fur floating into the air. Esther was pretty sure she was going to have a hard time breathing later that day.

"He was talking to someone—I'm not sure who—but he said something about how Charlie had ruined everything."

Esther kept her expression flat, but inside her a storm was building.

"What did he say specifically? Was he talking about his love life? His relationship with Carole?"

Amanda continued to pet Toby. More cat hair

floated in the air. "He said something along the lines of 'Before that brat was born, I could get whatever I wanted out of Carole.' She was, in his words, his 'personal ATM.' "

"Did he say that one time?" Esther asked. "In anger?"

"No," she said, "he bitched about it all the time. When he wanted to get new linens and was short on cash, someone asked if he could get some money from his wife. Everyone knows she made a bundle at Google."

"Why didn't he get money from Carole?"

"Always said, 'The bitch has me by the balls. She made me sign a goddamn prenup.' "

Esther could be a master of the understatement. She let one fly just then. "He wasn't happy with Carole?"

"No," Amanda said. "And she's nice. A little out there with her weaving, but she doesn't know what kind of jerk she's married to. She probably thinks that he loves her for her. I'm telling you, he only loves her for the money. He's all about the money."

"Where was he that morning? Do you have any idea?"

Amanda picked at some cat hair on a throw pillow as she thought. "I just know that when he came back and the police were looking for him, he didn't even seem alarmed. *Like he already knew.* It made me wonder, but I tried to not think

240

about it. I tried to put it out of my mind but I couldn't. That's why I called you."

Amanda's charm bracelet began to shake, and she clasped her fingers around it. She was crying quietly.

The detective gave the young woman a moment to pull herself together. She would have reached out to her, offered some comfort, but Toby was in the way.

"I know this was hard," she said. "I really appreciate your telling me what you know."

Amanda's tearful eyes looked into Esther's. "It's going to be all right, isn't it?"

"How do you mean?"

"Charlie's going to be fine. Right? It's almost a week. Most kids . . ."

"I sure hope so" was the best she could do.

Back in her car, Esther phoned Jake and let him know of David Franklin's scorn for his wife and son.

"Holy shit," the young man said. "That could be big. The motive."

Esther cautioned him. "It's a possibility," she said. "But it wouldn't be easy for David to get home and take Charlie unseen by anyone."

"No, but you said you thought that if someone took the boy, it was more than likely someone familiar. If it were a stranger, he would have raised holy hell. At least, most three-year-olds would. One time my sister asked me to pick up my nephew from day care. I *know* the kid. I was supposedly Justin's favorite uncle. But he flipped out in front of everyone. It was surreal."

"Charlie's dad would have to have returned home to get him, and how could he have been sure the mother wouldn't have seen him do it? She was home with him, watching him."

"I guess. Was Amanda sleeping with the dad?"

"I don't know," Esther said, looking at the time. "I don't think so. She says that he was messing around with someone else but that it sure wasn't her. I doubt she'd let him so much as touch her."

She told Jake to meet her at the Franklin place.

"I need you there," she said, pulling into a traffic circle. "We're going to have a little chat with Carole."

CHAPTER THIRTY
MISSING: SIX DAYS

Esther and Jake dodged the media—Bend's mostly—that had remained parked across the street from the Franklin house for nearly a week. Esther recognized one reporter as a stringer for the *Oregonian*. A missing little boy doesn't generally catch the interest of news editors unless he's white and comes from a wealthy family. Charlie Franklin was tailor-made for the media. When Esther worked the missing-boy case in Corvallis, the boy was half Native American, and she practically had to beg the local TV affiliate to do a story. It was an ugly truth that all police officers knew.

Carole met them at the door with anxious, haunted eyes. "Did you find him?" she asked. She looked tired, wan. She wore the same pink sweater that she'd changed into when she gave up the top she'd been wearing when she tore her earlobe. Esther thought that she smelled of alcohol, but it might have been an alcohol-based mouthwash.

"Is Mr. Franklin here?" she asked.

Carole stepped back a little, letting them in. "He had a meeting," she said. "Do we need him here now? I can try him." She reached for her phone.

"No," the detective said. "We want to talk to you. Just you." Her tone was formal, she knew. She wished that she had a way of communicating with a softer touch, but that morning she just didn't have it in her. The pressure she was feeling was like a stack of stones planted on her chest. One more, and her rib cage would splinter.

"You don't have any news about Charlie, do you? What about that pedophile from out of state?"

"No. We're pretty sure it wasn't him. We're all but certain that Charlie wandered off with someone he knew."

"Who? Who do you think?"

"That's why we're here," Esther said. "We want to find out more about what's going on with you and your husband."

Carole wrapped her arms around her thin frame and looked nervously away. "I don't understand. What are you getting at?"

"Carole, we need some honesty here," Esther said. "What is going on in your marriage?"

Carole stiffened. "Our marriage is solid."

"We've heard otherwise," she said, trying to push gently. "We need to get at the truth."

"What you need to do is find our son. That's all you need to do. The state of my marriage to

David is irrelevant and has nothing to do with what happened to Charlie."

"You don't know that, Carole. Look, we don't like to pry into private matters. We don't. But in this case there are a few things going on that we need to discuss. We need to better understand the dynamics here."

"We're not having this conversation."

"We need to," Esther said.

Jake, inexperienced and impatient, spoke up. "Is your husband having an affair?"

Esther gave him a sharp look but noted that Carole hadn't flinched at the question. Not in the slightest.

"What does that have to do with any of this?"

"Maybe nothing. We need to investigate all possibilities. If there is another party involved, we need to talk to her."

"I don't know," she said. "You should probably ask him that question. And so what if he is? What would that matter?"

"We're trying to figure that out," Esther said. "Do you know who it is?"

"No," Carole said. "Not really. I thought I did—I thought it was Amanda Jenkins at Sweetwater, but as I got to know her, I could see that she really didn't like my husband in that way. Maybe not at all. Besides, I don't think she is the type of girl who would waste her time on a married man."

"Then who?" Jake asked.

"Look," Carole said, "if there is someone, I don't know who it is. David's a private man. My family says *secretive* is a better word for the way he operates. I say *private*."

Esther leaned closer. "But you suspect he's seen others."

"Of course," she said, again without hesitation and with just a glance at the detective. "He had a fling with a girl before we moved here. It was messy. She turned aggressive about it. I wasn't about to lose my husband. In part, it's why we're here. We had to get away from her."

Carole got up, her gait unsteady, and observed the river, the current slowly propelling some paddleboarders toward the old beaver lodge.

"We should never have moved here," she said. "It was David's idea. I shouldn't have listened to him." She fell silent, appearing to forget they were there. "God," she said to the window, "I want Charlie to come home."

He ran his fingers over his fashionable stubble and took a deep breath. Owen Jarrett felt his own handsomeness, a chin that was chiseled just so. Another deep breath filled his strong, runner's lungs. He reached for his new phone and scrolled through the latest messages from Liz. While she was refraining from directly referencing what had triggered her meltdown, her neediness had been accelerated by what she'd done. And by what she'd forced him to do. She was drowning and wanted a lifeline.

He wanted to throw her an anchor.

> Can you come home? I'm falling apart here.

He was tempted to write back to her: *You've ruined my life. I don't want to come home ever.*

Instead, he shut her down with a terse two-word message.

> Working late.

He swiped a finger against the glass of his phone and sent out a text to a different contact.

> I'm going through a lot here. Don't you even care?

He put his feet up on the desk and waited for an answer.

None came. He put his palm against his forehead and rubbed at a throbbing pain.

> Answer me!

He texted again.

> I promise. I'll be free of her.

No answer.

His rage began to fester. He hated being ignored. Everything he'd ever wanted was all out of sequence. It all teetered because of Liz and what she did.

He told Paula, who was on the phone at the front desk talking to her boyfriend, that he was heading out for a bit. The young woman smiled and waved. With Damon off getting an eyebrow wax or something, Owen felt it was safe to take a minute to think.

To plan what to do next.

He drove down Wall Street and around the block to Newport, where he crossed the river. A couple of miles out of town, he pulled over behind a brewery that had somehow managed to fail in a town that's a magnet for brewmasters— and beer drinkers. It was the only place he knew would be deserted and available for what he knew he had to do.

He rolled up the windows and faced the mirror.

"Oh, God, no!"

The words had stuck in his throat. He took in some air and tried it once more.

"Oh, God! My wife! You need to come quickly. I think she's dead. She's dead. She's really dead! Hurry!"

That was too definitive. And why would he say "Hurry!" if he'd thought she was dead? Do-over.

"I think something's the matter with her. I

just got home. She's unresponsive. She's been depressed lately. Really depressed. I never thought this could happen. Please hurry. She's all I have."

Owen looked at himself in the rearview mirror. He'd have to do better. He'd have to find a way to ramp up the anguish and release some actual tears if he were going to be believable.

Liz was never going to make it through the investigation into the disappearance of the neighbors' boy. It had been obvious nearly from the first day. In fact, when he thought about it, his wife had been fragile before the incident. Unsure. A second-guesser at everything. He wondered what he'd seen in her in the first place. She'd idolized him. That was true. She'd been an available sounding board when he talked about his grand plans, a ready lover when he wanted sex. She was beautiful. And she was smart. But all of the things that he had found appealing were now coming under more scrutiny. His. Others'. She'd failed the bar twice. She talked about how humiliating that had been. She'd never once acknowledged the shame he felt. All of the people in his circle at the office and in the industry were unquestionably A-listers. She could have been one too. She looked it. In the way that a jeweler can tilt a diamond to conceal the flaw, the experience with Charlie had revealed something so deep and so wrong that there was no fixing it.

She'd crack and fall to pieces, and while Owen knew that she loved him, she could be only a liability to him now. She'd blundered into quicksand and, in her blind panic, would think nothing of pulling him in with her.

Owen looked in the mirror again. He had always liked what he saw. Right now, however, he knew his world was about to change. He was on the verge of a dream come true. And while he knew there had been a time when he truly loved Liz, that had been eclipsed by the mistake she had made. He furrowed his brow and tightened his lips. He put his hand on the wheel and let out a scream that came from deep inside. It was the kind of scream that could send a flock of geese flapping into the sky, that would make the bravest dog run and hide under the bed. His eyes popped a little.

Still, no tears. Not a single drop. It was much harder to do than he thought.

"Help me," he said in a raspy whisper. "I just got home. My wife . . . she's not breathing. Oh, God, please hurry. I think she overdosed on pills. Hurry."

Better, Owen thought, but he'd still need to find a way to turn on the waterworks. Or at least give the appearance that he had cried just before the paramedics arrived.

Onions occurred to him.

CHAPTER THIRTY-ONE
MISSING: ONE WEEK

Matt Henry waited in the lobby to see the detective handling the case of the missing little boy. The young man with shoulder-length brown hair and morning stubble wore a red fleece, khaki shorts, and Birkenstocks.

When Esther emerged, he introduced himself as the "canoe guy" the news said was being sought in conjunction with the missing little boy, Charlie Franklin. She led him to an interview room where the air-conditioning was working too hard. The room was an icebox.

"Sorry for the chill," she said. "Maintenance is on the way."

Matt said he was fine. "Had a good workout," he said. "Took a run along the river this morning. That's when I heard on my Oregon NPR podcast you were looking for me. I'm totally behind in my podcasts. Anyway, that's when I figured I might have something that could help. I think I might be the paddler in the red canoe you're looking for."

"Tell me about that morning," she said.

"Right. Okay. Me and Chelsea were playing around that morning. Chelsea's my dog. We were paddling in Mirror Pond and, I don't know, I just got a wild hair and decided to head up the river. Just testing my new toy."

" 'New toy'?"

"My GoPro. Got it for my birthday."

She nodded, familiar with the make of camera. "What time was that, if you remember?"

Matt thought for a beat. He liked to be precise. He worked for a local engineering firm.

"We got a late start," he said. "Chelsea chased a rabbit in the park and, well, we didn't get into the water until after nine thirty. Beautiful morning. Lots of commotion around Drake Park, though. You know, with the car show. I'm not much into cars. More of a cycling kind of guy."

"So you decided to head up the river." Esther wondered if he paddled in a straight line or a leisurely, circuitous route. He sure talked in circles.

"Right," he said. "We started up the river. I listened to some tunes and set up my equipment."

"What kind of equipment?"

"The GoPro. I told you. I figured it would be cool if I shot some footage from Chelsea's point of view as I paddled. It's a lot harder to paddle upstream than I thought. I don't think I'll ever try *that*—"

"You have video?" Esther asked. Adrenaline charged through her nervous system.

Matt gave a quick nod. "Yeah. I remember the

woman calling over to me. That's on the vid. She was pretty upset. I didn't see anything. I thought she was drunk or something. Seems like that's all people do around here: drink. Not good for you."

"Where is the camera?"

Matt retrieved the camera from the pocket of his fleece and the two of them huddled awkwardly over the device to watch the playback on its minuscule screen. The first images were of the morning's jog up Pilot Butte with flashes of the dog's hindquarters featured prominently.

"Let me speed past all that," Matt said. "You been up there? Awesome view. Well worth the effort. Sunrise is the best time to go. I've been up there two hundred and six times. More than that, actually. That's when I started keeping track. Had to start somewhere."

"We all do," Esther said. "And, yes, I've been up there." She was tempted to give some kind of bogus number, just because Matt Henry's OCD seemed to beg for it, but she didn't.

"All right," he said. "Here. It starts right here." He tapped his finger against the screen as though the detective needed prompting to get her complete attention.

Esther bent closer. It was agonizingly slow going, and the dog had the attention span of a mosquito. She could hear the sound of the water and see the tip of the canoe as it moved upriver. A mallard landed, and the camera went nuts while the dog barked.

"Whoa, Chelsea!" Matt could be heard exclaiming. "Do *not* go in the drink with that camera on your head!"

The dog settled down and the paddling continued. Just past the beaver lodge, the camera picked up a glimpse of the shoreline. While it didn't show the Franklins' house, it was unmistakably their property. The lower third of the river-rock fire pit flashed by.

"See that?" he said. "I think that's the kid."

Esther didn't say anything. She could see Charlie's sneakers walking away from the shoreline.

The camera spun around, and the canoe went back to the beaver lodge. In doing so, it picked up the image of a man with binoculars looking across the river. Matt talked incessantly to his dog the whole time, telling her what a good baby she was and how he didn't want her to go after the beavers.

"If we get lucky enough to film them, we can put it on YouTube," he said.

After ten minutes he started upriver again.

Carole's voice could be heard now, calling out, "Have you seen my little boy?"

Matt didn't reply right away. "Say that again?"

"Here," Matt told Esther, pointing at the video. "I pulled out my earbuds right there. I didn't answer the lady right away because I didn't know what she was talking about. She seemed a little out of line. You know, yelling like that."

"I'm going to need to keep this camera," Esther said.

"I'll get it back, right? You won't keep it forever, will you?" He looked skeptical.

"Yes, you'll get it back. We'll copy the video. All right?"

"Was there anything on there that was helpful with the case of the missing boy? I know that some people think he might have gone in the river, but I think if he did, Chelsea would have barked at him. She's a barker. She barks at a leaf when it blows across the road."

"Yes," she said. "You've been very helpful."

Esther didn't say so, but one thing struck her as particularly odd. The old man with the binoculars was Dan Miller.

What was he looking at? And why hadn't he said anything to her about that when they talked?

Esther ran into Jake outside of the records section. Jake smiled at her, but she didn't return the gesture. Smiling was almost never her first reaction to seeing someone.

"Canoe guy came in," she said, handing over the GoPro. "Took some video."

"What's on it?"

"Charlie."

"No shit?"

"He's walking away from the water. He doesn't go in—at least, not at the moment he was being filmed. He's carrying a bucket. Can't make out much more than that. And Dan Miller. He's on the tape too. You need to download it so we can see it on a larger screen."

"On it."

"Good."

With that, Esther returned to her office to drink more coffee and scroll through messages. Media calls, mostly.

Charlie almost certainly had not fallen into the water. The canoe guy and Brad Collins would surely have noticed that. That was good. That meant the child hadn't drowned. On the other hand, that meant that it was more likely than ever that he'd gone somewhere under his own power—or with someone else.

Someone, she thought, that the boy almost certainly knew.

Chapter Thirty-Two
MISSING: ONE WEEK

Dan Miller opened the front door wearing a Hawaiian shirt, khaki shorts, and flip-flops. The retired doctor's white hair apparently hadn't yet decided on a direction to lie in that day: it was all over the place. In one hand he held the remote control to his television set. While Dan had talked to other officers, he'd never responded to her request to get in touch when she'd talked to the neighbor and left her business card.

Esther was circling back. The GoPro video was a good reason to make another run at the old man.

"Golf is on," he said, opening the door wide and revealing an interior that looked every bit the authentic Old Bend the house portended from the street. It wasn't a faux cabin with fake moose-antler chandeliers and bear silhouettes stenciled on parchment-colored lampshades. It was real. Heavy beams supported the soaring ceiling. Dark oak flooring, scarred from years of people coming and going, led to a stone fireplace whose firebox, circled by a heavy shadow of black soot like a teen girl's heavy-handed mascara, indicated decades of memories.

"I'm here about the Franklin boy, Dr. Miller," she said.

Dan motioned her inside and shut the door. "Been sitting in my chair, watching the river and the goings-on over there," he said, indicating a leather chair that swiveled from the picture window to face the TV. He had a front-row seat to all the action, on both the Deschutes in front of the house and the links on the large flat-screen, his only apparent nod to modern technology. He muted the TV, although it didn't matter much. Golf is the quietest of any broadcast sport, with whispering announcers barely registering above a suppressed cough.

Dan offered Esther something to drink, but she declined. It wasn't a social visit. Esther didn't do those anyway.

"Mrs. Franklin says you were out doing yard-work when her little boy disappeared," she said.

The old man fiddled with the remote for a second. The joints of his fingers showed signs of arthritis. Twigs with tiny burls. He set down the remote.

"I was cutting the grass, yes," he said, "but I don't know a damn thing about the kid disappearing. I was busy. I was 'in the zone,' as the kids say. It takes focus to do things the right way. Even mowing the lawn needs to be done right." He paused before adding, "I try not to look over in that direction much anyhow."

"Why's that?"

Dan gave his head a little shake and then stepped to the window and pointed. "Seriously?" He turned to meet Esther's gaze straight on. "It's like I told the other young officer." He pointed toward the window. "Look at that monstrosity, sticking up like a middle finger between the homes that have been there for forty or fifty years. Excuse my French, Detective, but I look at that house and the people who live there as a big middle finger to the rest of us. Or at least what's left of us. New people with their glitzy homes and European cars are ruining this town. It's just a matter of time, and this place will be a city without children, populated by people who look at the Internet all day long and have nothing of interest to say to anyone."

Dan was on a roll, and as much as Esther enjoyed his rant—and could see the truth in what he was saying—she needed to guide him back to the subject at hand. "So you saw nothing," she said. "You were right outside. You waved to Mrs. Franklin before she went inside."

"I don't recall waving to anyone," he said. "And if I did, it was only because I'm polite to a fault. Mom raised me that way. Truth is, I can't stand those people over there. Not even Carole. I mean, from what I've seen and when I've run into her and her husband in town."

"You're not sugarcoating a little for me?"

Esther asked with a friendly smile, to soften her sarcasm. Or at least try to.

Dan caught it and smiled back. "The little boy's all right," he said. "The parents? Jesus, that David is a piece of work, and Carole's useless. They fight all the time. It's like living across from some kind of movie-of-the-week trash that's always on and with no way to change the channel."

"How so?"

Dan didn't say anything. He sat down heavily, mute.

"How so?" she repeated.

"You don't want to know," he finally said.

"But I do," Esther said. "I actually need to know."

Dan looked away, back out the window to the river. "Well, then I don't want to say. I'm over seventy, but I won't use the old-guy's trick of really speaking my mind and then pretending I'm too senile to know I did it." He pointed across the river. "You can see a lot from here."

The detective and the old man watched as, as if on cue, the couple with the missing boy faced off in the kitchen. David was saying something in what seemed to be a spirited fashion, but it was hard to see if he was angry or upset. Esther noticed a pair of binoculars on a table next to the swivel chair but didn't think she should pick them up to get a better view.

"You saw something," she said.

"Not anything important. Nothing that has to do with anything that really matters here, Detective. I've seen things, but nothing that would help you."

"A little boy is missing, Dr. Miller. I need to know what you know. I understand you don't like the parents much, but beyond the big house I can't see why you'd despise them so much. Seem like a nice couple."

Dan leaned into his leather chair and swiveled it in the direction of the detective. "Like I said, he's a jerk and she's a moron. Do I need to spell it out?"

"I think you do," she said. "Yes."

The elderly man wasn't a shrinking violet by any means, but he shifted uncomfortably before speaking. "He's a player. I think that's the word you use today."

Esther pushed a little. "What do you mean?"

"I've seen him over there with a woman. Not his wife."

"Are you sure?"

"Yes," he said. "My eyesight isn't as bad as you might think, and though it's been a while, and most all of it is from memory, I know it when someone is having sex."

"When did you see that?" Esther asked.

"Honestly, I couldn't count the times. Maybe ten."

"Recently?" Esther asked.

He shrugged. "No. Not really. It stopped a few months back. The two of them got into a knock-down, drag-out fight. I almost called the police—I guess that would be you—but I didn't. I was hoping that they'd get divorced and move away. Still be stuck with that piece-of-shit house, though. Excuse my French again."

"Do you know who the woman is?" Esther asked.

He said he didn't. "I'm not even sure if it was the same one. Girls these days change their hair and dress different. My wife had the same hairdo from high school to the day she died. Wore a skirt too. Never pants. My Miranda was a genuine classic."

He fiddled absentmindedly with the remote.

"You must miss her a lot," Esther said.

"That's an understatement," he said. "Every second of the day. What can you do? She wouldn't want me to lie down and die. Life goes on. Those two across the river don't know what Miranda and I always knew."

"And that was?"

Dr. Miller took a deep breath. "That a marriage is between two people. Bring a third into the mix and you're bound for trouble."

"You don't mean Charlie, I presume," she said. "You mean another woman or another man."

"*Of course* that's what I mean. I had a family.

It was everything to me. Kids are the greatest things in the world, though these days nobody seems to give a rat's ass about them."

Esther smiled to herself. Apparently *ass* wasn't French.

"I hope they find that little boy," he said as he got up to lead her to the door. "Still wish they'd move, though."

"About the day Charlie went missing. You told the officer you were home, but you didn't see anything."

"That's right. I didn't."

"I don't know if that's entirely true, Dr. Miller."

"What do you mean?"

It was time to mention the GoPro.

"We have video. It shows you watching from the window." She indicated the pair of binoculars. "You were using those."

"I don't know if I was or wasn't, but I sure didn't see anything. If I did I'd have called the police. Calling the police or an ambulance is the decent thing to do."

Across the river, Liz called the humane society to let them know that she couldn't come in to volunteer that afternoon. It was the first time she'd ever missed a day.

Animals had always been her great love. Throughout her childhood she'd raised just about every kind of creature available at a pet shop. She was not a cat person or a dog person. She was an animal person. One time she'd found an injured otter, and she nursed it back to health. For years after his release, she was sure that every otter she saw was Ollie.

She held her cat, Bertie, on her lap when she left a voice message for the volunteer coordinator. The cat's outboard motor purr ordinarily calmed Liz when she was feeling stressed.

But no longer. Nothing could calm her.

"We've had a tragedy in our neighborhood," she said, picking her words carefully as she thought of Owen's advice. *When you talk to anyone, never give details. Details will trap us.* "Our next-door neighbor's son is missing. I think I'm going to stay home and see if there's anything that I can do to help out."

Liz hung up and went over to the window that faced the Franklins'. That enormous house punched at the sky. It looked dark and foreboding, even more so than ever. She remembered the day the framers came and how, board by board, the structure shut out some of the light that had poured over the river and spilled onto the Jarretts' shoreline. She'd gotten used to the change over time, mostly because Carole, David, and Charlie brought some joy and their own kind of light to the neighborhood. She tried to erase from her mind what she'd done. She wanted to tell herself that it had been a nightmare or even a stray recollection from a movie she'd seen.

Liz watched from the window while police came and went. Owen insisted that everything would be okay.

For Carole and David, she knew it never would be.

PART TWO
SORRY

Blame me. Fine. That's how weak you are.

—*Owen Jarrett*

CHAPTER THIRTY-THREE
MISSING: EIGHT DAYS

A little over a week since Charlie vanished, and they had nothing. Just Matt Henry's GoPro videotape strongly suggesting that Charlie Franklin had not gone in the river. And that was shot from his dog's point of view. No one had seen anything. Not a single verifiable sighting. The man from Pilot Butte with the New Mexico plates and the screaming little boy was a Match date disaster. Local police had questioned him. Nothing. Nothing at all. Esther and Jake decided to return to where it had all started.

"Let's revisit the Jarretts. Liz is Carole's closet friend, at least here, locally."

"She wasn't home when it happened," Jake said, looking at his notepad. "She'd left around nine thirty to take the test."

"The bar exam she didn't stick around for," Esther said.

"What more do you think she could tell us, then, if she wasn't home?"

Esther wasn't sure. "Let's pay her another visit and find out."

They drove across town and parked in the

driveway, looking down the stretch of gravel that led to the Franklin place.

"Man, that house is huge," Jake said.

"It sure is. Pretty soon little places like this one will be a thing of the past," she said, indicating the Jarretts' house.

She knocked on the door. Liz answered. She was still in her bathrobe and her hair hadn't been washed.

"Sorry," she said, realizing she looked like a wreck. She ran her hands over her hair, trying to flatten it out, but it was no use. It was a twirl of snarls. "I haven't been myself since this all started."

"Can we come in?" Esther asked.

Liz kept the door stationary. "The house is a mess. Just like me. Probably not the best time."

"We don't mind, Mrs. Jarrett," Esther pressed, taking a step closer to the door. "We won't be long. We're just revisiting some things, trying to find out anything that we can. A little boy's life is at stake here. Can we come in?"

Liz couldn't refuse. Rebuffing an interview would make her look indifferent. The fact was she was shattered inside. She could feel her heart rate escalate and her face grow warmer.

"All right," she said, "but you'll have to excuse the place."

She led them to the living room. She could barely look at her visitors.

"You mind if I put on some clothes?" she said. "Lost track of the day."

"That's fine," Esther said.

The detectives surveyed the room while Liz disappeared into the bedroom. The living room was fairly neat. Esther couldn't see any reason why Liz would have felt it was in disarray. Esther was only an indifferent housekeeper and would have considered the Jarrett home perfectly fine for receiving company. A denim-blue camelback sofa faced the river, its back against the river-rock fireplace, which, judging from the black soot on the lintel, got plenty of use in winter. Over the mantelpiece was a painting of a group of skiers. Family photos adorned the shelf. Off to the side, near the dining room, was a set of free weights—thirty pounds each.

When Liz returned, her hair was in a loose ponytail and she'd put on a pair of jeans and a dark blue V-neck T-shirt. She caught Esther's gaze as it lingered on the weights. "My husband does curls while he watches TV."

Liz reached for the coffeepot and offered the detectives a cup, but both declined.

"I don't know how I can help you," Liz said, filling her mug and looking straight ahead at the wall of cupboards. "Like I told you, I wasn't home when it happened. Drove up to Beaverton early that morning. Didn't get home until late."

"Yes, that right," Esther said. "Let's focus on

what you might have seen in the days leading up to Charlie's disappearance."

Liz sat, set down her cup, and folded her arms. "You think he was kidnapped? That's what I think too. I think someone came and snatched him right out from under Carole."

"We really don't know what happened," Esther said.

"Has there been a ransom demand?"

"No," the detective said. "Let's focus on what you can tell us."

Liz leaned forward, steadying herself with a hand placed squarely on the armrest of the old morris chair. "I didn't see anything."

"Maybe a car out of place?"

"There are always cars out of place around here. We're overrun by tourists this time of year."

"What about Charlie? Did you see him with anyone in the days before he went missing? Maybe talking to a stranger?"

"Oh, no," Liz said. "Not at all. He was a very well-behaved little boy."

Esther glanced over at Jake. She wondered if he had noticed the same thing she had.

"I know you are good friends with the Franklins," Esther said. "You and your husband both. Right? You are close."

"We are," Liz said. "Nearly from the time when they first moved here."

"Right. I know this might be hard to do, but we

need to know if there's been any trouble between the Franklins. As far as you know."

Liz shifted in the chair. "I don't want to gossip about people I care about."

"Of course not," Esther agreed. "I get a sense that you and Carole are especially close."

"David's pretty busy with the restaurant. Carole and I have had a lot more time together. She's helped me prep for the bar. I've helped her get her studio in order."

"Good friends."

"Very."

"Sometimes good friends confide things to each other. Has Carole ever confided anything to you about her marriage?"

"Like what?"

"You know what I'm talking about, Liz. About her marriage to David."

"None of this has anything to do with their marriage," Liz said. "Some freak came and took their kid. That's what happened."

"Probably. But we need to know if that freak, as you say, might have been someone that knew them. Maybe someone from David's restaurant. Or someone from Carole's past."

"Carole doesn't have a past. She worked her ass off at Google and married David."

"What about David?"

"I don't know what you're getting at. Really, I don't."

"Has David been faithful, as far as you know?"

Liz bristled a little. "Look, there was a time when he wasn't," she said. "I think. It was before they moved here. Carole told me about something, but I really didn't pay it any attention. She complained about her husband the same way I complain about mine. He's too busy. Too distracted at times. I wouldn't know if he's played around behind her back here or not. She never said so."

Esther looked over at Jake again, giving him the signal to ask a few questions of his own.

"You live next door," he said. "You must have seen something."

"I don't know what you mean. I told you I wasn't home."

"Not that. I mean *before*."

"Oh," Liz said. "I still don't know what you mean."

Jake clarified. "A stranger. Something or someone that just seemed out of the norm. Something that maybe you look back on now and can't quite make sense of."

"I wish I did," she said. "I wish you could bring him home right this very minute. I just can't help you. I hate to chase you out of here, but I have an appointment that I need to get to. I'm already late for it now."

"All right," Esther said, handing Liz her card. "Please call me if anything comes to mind."

Liz said she would.

• • •

"Did you notice that she talked about Charlie in the past tense?" Jake said as they returned to the car.

Indeed Esther had. "It doesn't necessarily mean anything, other than the fact that she thinks the boy is gone for good."

They'd reached the car. Jake looked back at the house. "Why would she think that?"

"Because most kids who've been missing this long *are* dead. Some are never found. Dead nevertheless." She got in behind the wheel.

"You think Charlie Franklin is dead?" Jake asked when he'd joined her inside.

"I don't know," she said. "But yes, probably. He probably is. I hate saying it, Jake, but this is the world we're living in now. Not very many miracles these days."

"That's pretty jaded, isn't it?"

His remark made her wince a little. He was right. "Sorry," she said. "It doesn't mean that we won't fight like hell to try to find him and bring him home. God willing, he will be alive. I want to be hopeful. Wishing for something doesn't make it so."

Esther put the car in gear, and they drove downtown to a coffee shop. Her pessimism about Charlie's fate bothered her. She wondered if thinking that the case might be hopeless would affect how she handled it. No, she decided. The

Franklins needed their son back, but they didn't need false hope that all would be all right. It was her place to toe the line and always tell family members that she and the other members of law enforcement had locked arms and were working every single second on solving the case. There were lots of cases, though. And sometimes cases cooled.

"Did you notice something odd about the way she spoke about Charlie?" she asked while they waited for their order.

"You mean apart from that it was in the past tense?"

"She never said his name. Not once. A little odd, I think."

"What are you getting at?"

"Nothing, really," she said. "Just a little strange."

He poured three servings of cream in his coffee, turning it from dark brown to a light beige. He added sugar too.

"I noticed something else," Jake said.

Esther took a drink of her coffee. "What was that?"

"She couldn't wait to get rid of us, just like last time," he said, stirring the pale mixture. "She said she had an appointment to go to, but I really don't think so. She wouldn't have gotten dressed if we hadn't shown up. I bet she didn't have anywhere to go."

"Maybe she ran out of wine," Esther said.

"Yeah," Jake said. "I smelled that too."

The detectives left, and Liz stood immobile by the front door. She kept her eye on the peephole until Esther and Jake disappeared. She listened for their car to start and waited for the sound of the tires moving the loose gravel over the surface of the blacktop. Their appearance hadn't been unexpected. She knew there would be a time when the police would circle back. She thought she'd be prepared for it, but it had been hard sitting there, telling them lie after lie. Her hands were shaking, and she held them together while she went back to the kitchen to get a drink. She needed to steady her nerves. She was in serious trouble. Just one glass of wine, and she prayed that God would help her figure out what to do. She was so sorry for everything she'd done. She knew it was impossible to undo any of it. It was beyond grotesque.

One glass turned into two. She paced around the house, glancing at the river every now and then, squinting her tired eyes as the sparkles of light bounced through the old glass of the original window. The laughter of some kids floating on the water turned her stomach. Maybe it was the wine? No, she knew, it was the fact that she'd killed a little boy. She imagined for the thousandth time telling Carole what she'd done, but there was no scenario in which she could imagine forgiveness. Not even a little.

I need to do something.

Owen *needs to do something.*

She put down her wineglass and retrieved her purse from the bedroom. A painting her mother did of her brother and Seth mocked her. Bonnie Camden insisted it was her best work. It showed the boys sitting in a red canoe on Mirror Pond.

It was an accident.

People say that, and those involved cling to it. A tragedy's main players have no control over how other people might choose to perceive an error in judgment. The parents who leave their child in a hot car "only for a minute," the teens who double-dare a buddy to jump from a cliff "because if you don't, you're a wuss"—no one means to do harm, but those outside of the scenario are always quick to assign blame.

Her parents had done that to Dr. Miller.

Others would do that to her. The difference was, while what happened to Charlie was absolutely an accident, what she did afterward ensured that she'd never escape blame.

She got into her RAV4 and started for Lumatyx. Outside, the world was bright, sunny. The radio played an upbeat pop song. Everything was at odds with how she felt.

When she got inside Owen's building, the

receptionist said her husband was at an off-site meeting.

"What off-site meeting?" Owen hadn't mentioned anything. But then, he hadn't told her much about what was going on at work. She could feel him pushing her to the sidelines. "Where?"

"He can't be disturbed, Liz."

Liz balled her fists and pounded the surface of the receptionist's desk, as if she needed to make some kind of gesture to show how urgent the situation had become. Words couldn't be used because every sentence that carried the truth was an indictment.

"Look, I need him," Liz said. "It's important."

"Sorry," the young woman said.

"Everyone is sorry," she said, raising her voice. "We're all so goddamn sorry!"

The receptionist blinked. Owen's wife was scaring her.

"You need to see someone," she called after Liz as she hurried away. "You're coming unhinged."

CHAPTER THIRTY-FOUR
MISSING: EIGHT DAYS

The Liz drama lingered. Everyone at Lumatyx talked about it. After the off-site, the two partners returned to the conference room. It was after 8:00 p.m. Damon West shut the big glass door and turned around to face Owen, who sat at the end of the massive live-edge Douglas fir conference table.

"Thanks for sticking around," he said.

"Fine. Seems serious. What's up?"

"It *is* serious, Owen. Ordinarily it would be none of my business. I've got plenty on my plate right now. Now this . . . this needs addressing right now."

Owen knew Damon enjoyed poking his nose in everyone's business. He dug in deep like a tick. Always acting concerned. Soulful, caring eyes. In reality, Damon was no different from Owen. To be fair, he might have been at one time. But not now. Not when dollar signs replaced the work behind their ambitions. Owen studied everyone's weaknesses. His arm around an employee's shoulder was often a choke hold.

They didn't know it, of course.

"What does?" Owen asked.

"This is hard for me," Damon said.

You love this and you know it.

"What is it, man?"

"Just a reminder," Damon said, looking serious and very concerned. "We have a lot at stake here. The VCs can get very touchy. They don't want any trouble."

"Trouble?" Owen leaned forward. He was not about to be pushed around by his backstabbing partner. "Why are you saying this to me? I get that. I know it as well as you do."

"Do you, Owen?"

"Get to the point, Damon."

"Your wife," he said. "She's becoming a problem. I know she's wrapped up in the missing neighbor kid's case. I'm sorry about that. Really I am. She scared Paula. She's losing it, big-time, and people are starting to talk."

"Talk about what? What do you mean? Get to the point already!"

"When she can't get you on your phone, she calls the front desk. She's always frantically trying to reach you. I don't know what is going on with her, but it's hit the office gossip circuit."

Which you run like a side business.

"She's devastated."

"She seems to be unstable."

"Don't talk about her like that," Owen said. *Although you're right,* he thought.

"This wasn't easy for me. We're on the cusp

of something big and I don't have to remind you that if either of us makes a mistake that causes the money guys to have the slightest concern, we're dead."

"Not both of us, Damon. The one who causes the problem."

"Morality clauses are vague. But yes. The one who gets in the way of everything we've fought for is out. Left with nothing."

Owen quietly seethed.

"Just get her to pull herself together," Damon said. "All right?"

Chapter Thirty-Five
MISSING: EIGHT DAYS

That night, Liz and Owen barely spoke. They sat in the living room for a long time. The sound of some last-of-the-season vacation renters roasting marshmallows a few doors down from the Millers' leaked through an open window facing the river. Not a single word was uttered about what had happened at the office. Or what Owen had been doing when he was at his off-site meeting. It was hard to trust him when every time he spoke it was a suggestion on how to lie.

Despite his lies, Liz counted on Owen. She hoped against hope that everything would be all right—as he'd promised.

That night when they went to bed, Owen moved close to her as she lay on her side, facing the wall. He pushed his pelvis against her, a signal that usually indicated that he wanted sex. She wondered how he could even contemplate such a thing at a time like that. She could think of nothing but the couple next door and the little boy she'd accidentally killed.

Owen had told her that everything needed to be normal. Yet there was no normal anymore. She didn't feel like making love to him. She wondered why he'd even want to touch her. She was poison.

Instead of tugging on her shoulder to roll her over, Owen leaned in and whispered in her ear.

"You need to toughen up," he said. "If you crumble on me, I'll kill you."

Liz didn't say a word. Didn't breathe.

"I swear that I will, Liz," he went on. "I'll make sure your name is dragged through the mud before I do it, too. Your mistake is not going to cost me."

He stayed close for a moment, feeling her body shiver under the sheets.

"You seriously need to get a grip," he whispered before rolling over. "Tomorrow we need normal. Not drama."

"Okay," she said.

Liz didn't view her husband's words as a threat. She saw them as a promise. She'd earned each and every word. A silent tear fell onto her pillow, and she studied a blank wall as though there were answers there. She looked at her phone and watched the time roll by. She didn't want to dream of Charlie. She was afraid that she'd see his face again. His eyes shut. The pinecones he'd so proudly collected scattered on the driveway. The tarp from her father's old workbench, a plastic envelope in which to hide him. She wanted none of that in her mind.

She willed herself not to think about it for a second. For two seconds. That was her record.

For the longest time, her efforts to find refuge from her thoughts proved futile.

Finally, after two in the morning, Liz fell into a restless sleep.

This time Charlie didn't come to her. Instead, she dreamed she was in the station wagon with her brother, heading out that morning to Diamond Lake. Country music filled her ears. The Egg McMuffin felt warm in her small hands. And then the roar of the flash flood as water poured over her, Jimmy, and Dan and Seth Miller. In her dream she could make out Dan Miller's bloody face before he went after the car carrying his son away. His eyes met hers for what seemed like a very long time. The memory was freeze-framed. It was hard to know how long the doctor hesitated before he went after it. He was going to die saving his son, although it didn't turn out that way. Seth died. Dan survived. She wondered what he would have given to trade places with his son. She'd give anything if Charlie could be home, warm in his bed with the *Star Wars* duvet, and if she were the one wrapped in a tarp and discarded off the highway in the howling cold of the high-desert night.

The accident when she was nine years old was no longer the worst moment of her life.

Something else had replaced it. It, too, had

been an accident. That truth was something she needed to hold tight inside.

That night Liz had a second dream. She was sitting with Carole at the breakfast table. David was gone. Owen too. It was only the two of them. Carole wore white. Her face was lined, her eyes vacant and sad. Liz looked down at her own hands. *Age spots.* Liz felt a bump protruding above her left breast, just below her shoulder. *What?* Her fingers found an implanted port used to receive chemotherapy medications. *Cancer?* She was dying and before her was this sad angel, Carole. She moved her lips to tell Carole what she knew she should say, but nothing came out.

"It's all right," Carole said. "When you go, don't worry."

She tried once more, but again no words came out.

"I forgive you," Carole said.

Liz pushed herself up from the table. She was weak and undeserving. She could not accept the kindness that Carole was offering her. She was unworthy. She clawed at the port, somehow ripping it from under her skin. Blood splattered over the table and onto Carole's white hair and white dress.

"It's all right," Carole said. "I would have forgiven you no matter what."

Chapter Thirty-Six
MISSING: NINE DAYS

It was easy. The little boy and his mother had decided on the black-and-white terrier mix. It was love at first sight. The dog was a rescue picked up behind the Bend Walmart, fittingly dubbed Wally. He was one of those dogs that practically smiled when he looked up at someone, treat or no treat.

Usually those moments brought Liz Jarrett such joy. This time, however, tears came.

She'd been volunteering at the Humane Society of Central Oregon, just off Twenty-Seventh, for the past year. When she'd told the staff there she was studying for the bar, she laughed and said she was going to represent animal rights. "And if those dogs and cats in the kennel don't get ten hugs a day," she teased them, "I'm coming after you."

The little boy was wearing blue jeans and a green and navy Seahawks T-shirt. His blond hair curled a little over his ears. Liz wondered how that mom with the dark hair could have a blond boy. And yet those two fit together the way Charlie and Carole had. Her eyes dampened a little, and the mom, a pretty woman with short black hair and a slender face, put her arm on her shoulder.

"What is it?"

Liz snapped out of her misery. "I'm sorry," she said, drying her eyes. "There's something truly beautiful about a boy and his first dog. A precious bond is being made right now."

She watched as the dog nuzzled the boy and heard the belly laugh that came right along with it.

The mother smiled. "It *is* a beautiful thing."

"Yes," Liz said, easing herself from the joyful scene. "I think I'll need to be excused right now. I'm really sorry. Wally is a great dog. I know he's going to a good home. Sorry. I'm sorry. Tamara can help you with the paperwork."

"Okay. Take care," the mother said, surprised at the sudden departure of Wally's adoption coordinator.

Liz hurried to the storage room and locked the door. She was grateful that there was no mirror in the space. She couldn't stand the sight of her own face. Seeing that little boy laughing with that dog had been a knife in her heart. She sat on a pallet of dog food. She was numb. She was no longer a person.

If she could stay there forever, she would. Never come out. Curl up and die. Turn to dust. Any of that would be a relief from the agony she'd caused the Franklins.

Over and over, eyes closed or open, Liz kept seeing Charlie's face. The tiny slits made by his eyelids. The blue of his lips. The bucket of spilled pinecones. The tarp. All of it. She had robbed Charlie of his life and she'd taken the coward's way out. If anyone had ever told her that she could have done that, she'd have punched them.

A half hour later, Liz emerged from the storage room. She handed her key card and photo ID to Tamara, the woman in her fifties who managed the facility.

"What's this?" Tamara asked.

"I think I need to take a break."

"I know you're close to Carole, Liz, and I can't imagine all that they and you are going through, but animals are good therapy. For people. People hurting."

Liz knew her manager was right. She'd seen it a thousand times. A widower coming in to get a dog after his wife succumbed to cancer. Empty nesters filling the void left by the last kid off to college. A young woman heartbroken over her breakup with a longtime lover.

"The animal part is fine," she said. "Just kind of breaks me up when the little ones come in here. Makes me think of my friend and her son. I don't think I can do this right now."

"What about working in the back office? We could sure use some help back there. Paperwork doesn't love you back, but it's a necessary evil around this place."

Liz removed the white smock that she wore over her street clothes. She handed that over to Tamara too. "I don't think so," she said. "I'm not good for much of anything right now."

"They'll find Charlie," Tamara said. "I just know that they will."

Liz didn't know what to say. It seemed that every word that came out of her mouth when she spoke about Charlie was a lie. She even questioned her own tears. She wondered if they were solely for her. If they had nothing to do with the death of a child she'd loved so much. She was barely hanging on. Lying to oneself is an exhausting task.

There was only one thing harder, she now knew: keeping a dangerous secret.

Liz stopped at Safeway on the way home. She moved quickly, as if she were a contestant on one of those shopping-spree shows. Her first stop was her most important. She filled her cart with bottles of wine. She didn't shop labels. She didn't look for the highest number of points. She grabbed whatever was at eye level. Then she plowed through the produce aisle and picked up some bagged salad. Grabbed some milk. Some chicken.

Her hands trembled as she swiped her debit card at the check stand. The cashier, a man with a penchant for small talk, asked her the question that genuinely kind people frequently do. "Are you all right?" When she didn't respond right away, he paused in his scanning and studied her eyes.

Liz didn't think there would be a time when she'd ever be all right again. No matter what her husband said.

"Yeah, I'm fine," she answered.

The cashier kept his eyes on her for another second. Then the conveyor belt started moving once more. "Okay, then," he said.

When Liz got in her car and started to drive away, it took everything she had not to reach across the seat to twist off the top of the bottle of a hideous Riesling that had somehow found its way into her cart. It was a poor choice. She'd made plenty of those lately.

Before Charlie and the accident, she knew the biggest mistake she'd ever made was in the hospital after the flash flood, though she wasn't exactly sure if she had been tricked or if she'd remembered correctly.

The officers and doctors were a blend of sympathy and accusation as they tried to determine what had gone wrong on the drive to Diamond Lake. Though no one could deny that the flood was an act of nature, there somehow was a need to lay blame. Blame made people feel better. Move on. Act superior. And maybe make them feel just a little safer.

An Oregon State Police officer, a woman with bright red hair and penetrating eyes, sat next to Liz's bedside while her parents hung back just beyond the privacy curtain.

Later, Liz would find a transcript of the notes made the day after the accident. It was in her mother's things, with the two newspaper clippings about the accident.

Officer: You like Dr. Miller, don't you?
Witness: Yes. He's nice.
Officer: Did you notice anything unusual about him that morning?
Witness: No.
Officer: Did he have anything to drink?
Witness: Coffee. We stopped at McDonald's.
Officer: Did he put anything in his coffee?
Witness: No.
Officer: Did you smell anything on his breath?
Witness: No. He smelled real nice.
Officer: What kind of smell?
Witness: A good smell.
Officer: Can you describe?
Witness: Like my mom's mulled wine. Sweet like that.

Officer: You smelled wine?
Witness: I guess so. Dr. Miller always
    smells like that.

Reading those words, Liz could see the officer's green eyes roll over her, taking in everything she said, sizing her up and egging her on. The officer said she was after the truth, but when Liz said that about Dr. Miller and the woman's eyes lit up, Liz knew that she'd just been looking for her to say something ugly about Seth's father.

In the background, Liz caught a glimpse of her parents shaking their heads in disgust. The officer went to them while a nurse checked on Liz's vitals.

"We're pretty sure he was drinking," she said, her voice low, but not low enough. "Blood tests were taken too late to get a reading on any alcohol. We waited too long. We won't be able to prosecute, but I'd watch that one. He might seem like a good guy, but anyone that would take a nip in the morning wouldn't be anyone I'd want my kids around."

Dr. Miller had been drinking that morning. The police and her parents said so. They said so in a kind of whisper. A whisper is a very effective way of making sure everyone hears.

CHAPTER THIRTY-SEVEN
MISSING: TEN DAYS

Carole was a nighttime migrant. She slept on the couch. In a chair in front of an infomercial on pressure cookers that played early in the morning. Finally, she found comfort in her son's bed. It was as much to get away from David as it was to be close to the boy who had disappeared from the river's edge. Questions from the police and innuendo she saw online suggested that David had been cheating on her. That hadn't really been news. He'd done it before they moved to Bend. A leopard, her mother told her more than once, could never change his spots.

For the longest time Carole had been all but certain that her husband was seeing Amanda Jenkins. So pretty. So young. David's type. She saw the way he touched her lower back at the restaurant one time when he was presenting the menu to the servers on opening night. It was a gentle touch, a pat that lingered too long. Carole had wondered if there was a lower-back tattoo in the place that he'd touched. If he'd seen it while he made love to her. Was it at the restaurant, in the pantry? Carole and David had done the same thing before they got married. Was it at the girl's

294

apartment? Or had they slept together there, in Carole and David's home?

When she got to know Amanda, she decided she was too smart to fall for her husband. If nothing else, surely he was too old for her. And when it came down to it, it didn't really matter. Carole had her art, and then Charlie. David had been little more than a distraction from the things at the center of her universe. At times, a fun and even sexy distraction. That was a while ago.

Carole didn't have it in her at the moment to create a scene by launching a slew of accusations. She was so done. All of her emotions had been wrung out like a bar rag, and there was very little anger to throw at David. Their son was gone.

What did anything else really matter?

She knew he'd look for her in Charlie's room when he got home from Sweetwater, so she waited in the little bed, smelling the pillowcase scented from the baby shampoo that she still used on his precious head at bath time.

Charlie, come home to me. Charlie, you are my only real joy. My sweet little love.

A few minutes after midnight, David's beloved Porsche came down the driveway, the engine over-idling in that show-offy way that stroked his surprisingly fragile ego by commanding everyone in earshot to look up and admire all that he had. David never did anything without making sure others could see it. If he bought a piece of jewelry for his wife, it was only so he could point to it and talk about the good deal he'd been able to negotiate. David lived to brag, but he'd never admit that. To be a braggart was gauche. He saw himself as far too sophisticated for that. Carole listened as the garage door went up. She could feel the slight vibration that came with the sound of the chain pulling the door upward. A beat later it went down. Next, David disarmed the alarm. He was getting closer. For some reason her heartbeat quickened a little. She'd do what she needed to do. She didn't see that she had any other choice.

He made his way to the kitchen. Opened a bottle of nonalcoholic beer. Silence as he took a drink.

Everything David Franklin did was very predictable.

Just as his affairs had been.

"Babe?" he called into the darkened hall that led to the bedrooms. His footsteps found his way to her. "You in here?"

"I'm here," she said.

He stood there. Moonlight seeped in through the miniblinds, marking the walls and Carole's face like war paint.

"You going to sleep in here again tonight?" he asked.

Silence. Her heart was broken, and she didn't want a fight.

He looked down at her, crumpled as she was in their son's bed. "Carole?"

She stayed quiet, the bands of light from the blinds shifting on her face. "We can't stay together," she finally answered, barely looking at David. She ran her fingertips over the grosgrain edge of the *Star Wars* duvet; it had been Charlie's favorite for building forts in the dining room. "I don't think so. Not now."

David sat on the edge of the bed and reached for his wife, but she stiffened and pushed him away.

"What are you talking about?" he asked.

Again the bars of light moved across her face. "David," she said, "you know."

But he didn't. Or at least the look on his face indicated as much. Her words were a riddle, and he didn't understand Carole.

"Our son is missing," he said. "We need each other right now."

There were a million things she could fling at him, but she chose only one. "You go to work like nothing's happened, David. You're carrying on like it was nothing. Like Charlie was nothing. There's something seriously wrong with a man who would do that."

"I asked the detective," he said. "I asked her what I could do. She told me that I needed to stay focused and clearheaded. That I needed to take care of business."

"That's not what she meant. Trust me: no one

297

loses their son and goes to work as if nothing happened."

"You're wrong. Charlie's on my mind all the time. He's right here," he said, touching the beer bottle to his chest.

Carole didn't want to fight. She wanted to save all of her energy for the investigation and, God willing, Charlie's homecoming. "You have to go," she said. "Stay at a hotel."

"I'm not going anywhere," he said, getting up and standing over her.

Carole stared at him. She'd faced tougher adversaries in the boardroom. She knew how to take the emotion out of her words. A tone of resignation was better than an avalanche of aggression. "Look," she said, picking her words carefully, "let's not fight. Let's not say something that we will never forget or forgive."

"I want him home too," he said.

"I need you gone."

"I won't go," David said. "I tell you, I won't."

Carole held her tongue. She didn't tell him to go sleep at his girlfriend's place. Whoever she was. She didn't want to make her growing hatred for him be about another person outside of their marriage. This was a family matter. She could see his disinterest in their son from the day that he came home from the hospital. She saw the way he'd always feigned wishing he had more time with Charlie.

But he was too busy.

Too busy with the restaurant.

Too busy having sex with some woman not smart enough to see through his lies.

"Fine," she said. "*I'll* go."

"Where will you go?" David asked, a response that only confirmed what she'd thought of him all along. He had no capacity for love. He only thought of himself. He didn't tell her that she should stay: it was her money that had paid for the house, after all. He just asked where she would go.

She went to an overnight bag that she'd already packed. She took her robe and a jacket and uttered not a single word. She simply fought to keep her resolve that when Charlie came home, she'd kick David out the door as fast as she could. She'd pull the credit line from the restaurant and she'd kiss him good-bye.

For good.

"Don't do this," he said.

Carole turned the latch on the front door.

"It will look bad, babe," he said. "It will look like there's been something going on here. Now's not the time for this kind of drama. Think about Charlie."

She spun around and looked hard at her husband.

"David, Charlie is all I think about. I don't care what other people think. I don't want to fight and I don't want to bad-mouth you. I just don't want to see your face. Not right now."

● ● ●

It was one in the morning when Owen Jarrett climbed out of bed to answer a tentative but persistent knocking on the door. He fumbled for a pair of sweatpants in the shadowy light and hurriedly put them on. Liz, startled by the commotion, started to get up.

"Stay here," he said. "I'll find out what's up."

"It's the police," she whispered. "They've found me."

He slipped a T-shirt on. "Be quiet," he told her. "It is *not* the police. Someone's car broke down or something. Or some kids are shit-faced and can't find their way home. It isn't the police. Just wait here."

Liz put her head back down on the pillow and pulled up the covers.

Owen opened the front door.

It was Carole. She stood there with a small suitcase. Owen could instantly see what was going on. She'd left her husband. She looked more embarrassed than upset.

"Owen, I'm sorry," she said. "I know it's late. Can I come in? I don't want to spend another night in that house with David. I just can't."

He opened the door wider, and she came inside.

"Sure," he said.

"I'll figure out what I'm going to do tomorrow. I mean later this morning."

"Let me get Liz," he said.

Carole put her hand up. "No, don't bother her. Let her sleep."

A beat later Liz appeared in the bedroom doorway. "Carole, I heard your voice. What happened? What's going on?"

"She and David had a fight," Owen said. "She's crashing here."

"It wasn't really a fight," Carole said. "I'm sorry, Liz. I just can't stand being in the same room with David. I don't trust him. I don't trust him anymore."

Neither of the Jarretts asked why she didn't trust David. They just let the words hang in the air.

"I'll make up the bed in the guest room," Liz said.

"No. I can sleep on the sofa."

"Don't be silly. The bed is supercomfortable. I take naps in there sometimes."

"I don't want to be a bother. Of course, I know I've already been one. It's so late and I am sorry. The sofa is fine."

Owen started for the bedroom. "I'm going back to bed while you two figure out the winner of this little battle. Early meeting in"—he looked at the time—"six hours. I should be fresh as a daisy, don't you think?"

"Sorry, Owen," Carole said. "Really, I am."

Liz put her arm around her friend. "Come on, I'll get you settled." She led Carole into the small back bedroom that she and her brother had shared when they stayed for the summer. The room was full of memories. On one wall was the acrylic painting that her mother had made of Jimmy and Seth. They wore oversize orange life preservers that nearly swallowed their bony torsos. It was inspired by a photograph she'd taken a few years before the accident near the turnoff to Diamond Lake. It had hung over the fireplace in the living room at first. When Miranda stopped coming over, she told Bonnie it was because of the painting.

"I love it," Miranda said, doing her utmost to hold her emotions inside. "I think you did a beautiful job. Maybe too good a job. I just have a hard time looking up and seeing him. Dan too. It just hurts." Her voice cracked a little, and she looked away. "It's a lovely tribute, but it still makes my heart ache."

Bonnie had felt sick about hurting her friend. She apologized profusely and put the canvas in the bedroom that very afternoon. It didn't seem to make much difference. Miranda and Dan Miller didn't return much after the painting was moved out of sight.

Over time, the doctor and his stylish wife all but disappeared.

Chapter Thirty-Eight
MISSING: TWO WEEKS

The morning of the finalization of the funding by the venture capitalists, Owen tried not to wake his sleeping wife. She'd taken some pills after putting Carole in the guest room and had tossed and turned most of the night. At the moment she was snoring, and he was glad. As long as she was snoring, she was asleep. As long as she was asleep, she would make no trouble for him. He couldn't have any trouble. Not on the biggest day of his life.

The night before, he had unzipped the protective plastic garment bag that held his new suit. It was a rich cocoa-brown Boglioli that he'd bought online and had tailored by a local seamstress. The suit had cost almost a thousand dollars, more money than he'd ever spent on a single article of clothing in his life. That would change, of course, with the cash coming from the East Coast and the promise to spin off Lumatyx into a multimillion-dollar enterprise. He ran his fingers over the soft fabric of the jacket. It was something Don Draper from *Mad Men* might have worn. Cool. Hip. A sixties vibe. If clothes make the man, then Owen Jarrett felt that he was unstoppable.

The only thing in his way was snoring in the bed.

He showered, shaved, and dressed. When he was done, he looked at himself in the mirror. He was everything he wanted to be. The money would come all at once. After today the tap would be turned on. He'd get that new car. A new house. The respect of his family, who had considered the high-tech industry a world populated by spoiled millennials who didn't know how to do anything except make money, spend it, and talk about it all the time. His father had run a landscaping business, and his hands showed it, with calluses and a nail that had broken off an index finger and never grown back. Owen, his father once remarked, had the hands of a woman. The comment burned him. His hands were soft because he took care of them. He worked hard on having a man's body. His new suit clung to his ripped physique. When he undressed at night, he found himself gazing at his abs, running his fingers over the six-pack that he'd nurtured by running, lifting weights, and eating right. He looked damned good.

And now he was going to be rich.

Fuck Dad. Fuck them all.

He made his way to the kitchen for a cup of coffee.

"You clean up good, Owen."

It was Carole.

"You're up early," he said.

"Couldn't sleep," she said. "Made some coffee. Pour you a cup?"

"Thanks," he said.

Her skin was pale, like her hair. She tugged at her robe as she filled his travel mug.

"Big day for you," she said, then started to cry. "I'm sorry. I'm sorry."

He stepped closer and touched her hand. "It's okay," he said.

"I keep seeing Charlie," she said.

Owen didn't know where to go with that. He wished to God that she'd just go back home. Seeing her and her constant tears ate at him. There was nothing he could say to make her feel better. Every word that came from his lips felt hollow. Just empty.

"Is there anything I can do?" he finally asked, although he knew there wasn't. Besides, he'd done enough already.

"No," she said, backing away toward the sink. "And this is your day, anyway. I remember what it was like to launch a new product in a new country. How it felt to put on a game face and go meet the people who had the power to get you what you came for."

He was grateful for the change of subject. "Right," he said, trying not to look at her. "Any advice?"

Carole was silent for the longest time. "Not

305

really," she said finally. "Enjoy every minute of it. Everything can change in a second. Savor all of it."

Her tears started again.

Owen knew Carole wasn't talking about the venture capital team. She was referring to her son and everything that had happened since the morning he went missing. He patted her shoulder and she drew close to him and started to give him a hug, then stopped herself.

"Sorry," she said, backing off. "Don't want to mess up your suit."

"That's all right," he said, though he didn't mean it. He pulled a paper towel from the dispenser behind her and dabbed at the streak of tears she'd left behind.

"I'm worried about Liz," she said. "She's hurting pretty bad."

"I know," he said. "We all are, Carole. We'll just have to continue to keep Charlie in our prayers and know that he'll be found. He'll be safe."

"You really think so?" she asked.

Owen patted her once more. "Yes," he said. "I know it in my bones."

"Thank you, Owen. Thank you so much."

Owen turned the engine over and sat in his car. He gulped in some air and tried to keep his cool. He gripped the wheel of his soon-to-be-ditched Forester. A stranglehold. He looked at his white knuckles and thought of his father again. *Goddamn him!* His old man never respected anything that you couldn't see or touch. So literal. Always so sure that he was right and Owen was wrong.

Jesus! What did I do to deserve these people in my life?

He took in more air and started for the office. Things were spinning dangerously. He'd expected Charlie to be found within days. It had been two weeks! And he certainly hadn't expected Carole would move in with them. Liz was fragile as hell as it was. Her fragility had made the situation escalate. He'd done things he'd never thought he could do and now he was on the cusp of everything that had ever mattered to him.

Charlie.

The devastation resulting from the boy's disappearance was a festering open sore. Carole and Liz were saltshakers dumping their worries and sadness onto him when he needed to focus on what was really important. Charlie was gone. End of story. Owen's life was just beginning. He needed to be *on*. As much as he admired Damon's intelligence and knew that Lumatyx would never have happened without him, Owen was getting the distinct feeling that his partner believed he had the leading role in its success. Sure, he was always effusive about the partnership that had led to the development of the product. Still, there were signs that he viewed his role as more important than Owen's.

"Without code you have nothing," Damon had told a *Wall Street Journal* reporter who was doing a story about the emergence of Bend as a new high-tech center. "Ideas are great, but at Lumatyx our achievement is building a tool that actually delivers on promises."

Owen was in the conference room during that interview and inserted himself in the conversation, but it was awkward.

Later he asked Damon about it. "Man, it felt like you were taking total credit for what we've done here."

Damon blinked his big brown eyes. "Not at all. Just giving the reporter a story. Fanning the flames. Getting the VC community to consider our intellectual property as the value driver here, Owen. That's all."

Owen didn't buy it.

As he drove to the office, he thought about what he'd done to the little boy next door and how easily he'd been able to put it all behind him. It was like the affirmation cards he'd used in college to get him through a tough exam. Visualizing a goal was the way to make something happen.

It was eight thirty when Owen arrived. Paula

at the front desk looked as if she were going to burst with excitement. An enormous bunch of calla lilies in a clear cylinder vase dwarfed her. "Look what they sent us," she said. "They must really like us."

"Boston?"

She nodded. "I've never seen a bigger bouquet. Must have cost more than two hundred dollars!"

"I'll bet," Owen said.

"You look great, Mr. Jarrett," she said.

Owen feigned an appreciative smile and looked past the receptionist to Damon's office down the sandblasted brick corridor. The lights were off and the door was shut.

"Damon's not in?"

The young woman peered up from behind the wall of flowers. "No," she answered. "He's at the early breakfast meeting. I thought you just came from there."

Owen didn't know a thing about any meeting. The agenda for the visit had been planned weeks in advance. The venture capital team would arrive around noon, sign the agreement, and chat with various employees. A celebratory dinner at Sweetwater would conclude the day.

"No," he said, trying not to give in to a display of sudden fury. "Had some things at home I had to do this morning. Buzz me when Damon gets in, all right?"

She promised to do just that.

When Owen got to his office, he texted Damon right away:

WTF? What meeting?

Damon answered a minute later:

No biggie. Asked for reco of a breakfast place. Told them Chow and they asked me to join them. See you in a few. Great guys. You'll love them.

Owen swiveled in his chair and looked out the window at the street below. Everything he believed about Damon was probably true. His old pal and business partner was a backstabber. Damon was going to make sure that he was first in line to get whatever he could. He was a selfish, egotistical prick.

There was no way that Owen would be cut out of what he knew rightfully belonged to him. He turned on his laptop and checked Damon's calendar for the morning. His face went red with anger.

7:30–9:00—Private appointment.

He sat there and seethed.
So this is how it's going to be. Seriously?
Owen sat there drinking coffee and staring out the window, getting angrier and angrier.

310

• • •

Owen shut his office door and sat down at his desk. He couldn't get any of what had happened in the garage and in that field off the highway out of his mind.

She had done this. All of it.

He turned over a silver-framed photo of the two of them at Crater Lake. Looking at her made him even angrier.

His anger was like a hand behind him, urging him to take care of business. He'd felt it that morning at home. When he stopped for coffee at the drive-through just before Drake Park. Over and over he was reminded that he alone could fix the mess that was taking him down. Deep. Into quicksand. He was being pushed into doing something that he hadn't planned on doing. He didn't like to be pushed. He didn't care one bit about being spur-of-the-moment, although he had manufactured a persona that thrived on spontaneity. With everything he did, there was a calculated payoff. He pulled a sheet of blue paper from the Prada messenger bag that he'd bought used online.

He would never buy used again.

He thought very carefully about what he was going to write.

What he was going to do.

Each word had to count.

Everything he did from now on would allow for no mistakes.

Chapter Thirty-Nine
MISSING: FIFTEEN DAYS

Owen had pleaded with her, exhorted her, even threatened her: when the boy's body was found, she absolutely had to react as though she was as shocked as the rest of the world. After Owen went to work and Carole went back to her megahome to get some more of her things, Liz observed her reflection in the bathroom mirror.

"No," she said, "it can't be."

She put her hands to her face. "Dear God, no. What happened? *How could this happen?*"

He had told her not to say too much, just convey the obvious emotional responses: shock at the discovery, grief on learning that the boy was dead.

"Be yourself, Liz," he told her. "That's all you have to do. Don't add to the drama by saying any more than how devastating all of this is. That's it. Nothing more."

Her hands trembled as she faced the mirror. She *was* devastated. She'd been grieving over what had happened since the second she realized what she'd done. She couldn't eat. She couldn't sleep. When Owen told her to be herself, she didn't know who that was. Not anymore.

She tried again.

"Carole, David, I'm so sorry. *I'm so, so sorry.*"

That felt right. She *was* sorry. She was sorry she had killed Charlie. She didn't have to say that last part. She could think it.

Yes, that would work.

She could tell them how sorry she was.

Liz found herself increasingly unnerved that Charlie's body hadn't been found. He'd been out there in the elements for two weeks. Owen had insisted the night they had left him there that the rancher would find him right away. The next day, even. But he hadn't. No one had. Surely animals had found the body. Carole and David were never going to get the opportunity for closure that the boy's burial might bring. The brutal waiting game going on next door had to stop. Carole was convinced that Charlie had been abducted by some child molester or was being held captive by some fiend who was going to trade the boy's life for money. She clung to that with everything she had. Bend detective Esther Nguyen emphasized several times that abductions like that were exceedingly rare, and in any event, no ransom demand had been received.

"Not yet," Liz heard Carole tell her. "But it could come."

"In most cases, ransom demands are made within twelve hours after the abductee was last seen."

"Then you think he's dead," Carole said.

"I'm not saying that," Esther countered. "I'm saying that you and Mr. Franklin need to be prepared for any possible outcome."

"What about Jaycee Dugard?" Carole asked. "She was found."

Jaycee. Elizabeth Smart. The women in Cleveland.

All were mentioned by devastated parents as proof of a miracle.

"Yes, she was. Like I said, the vast majority of cases don't end that way. We have hope that we'll find him and that we'll find him alive. I need you to prepare."

All of it had to end.

Liz dressed in jeans that were suddenly loose and put on a tank top. Although she hated the drive toward Diamond Lake more than just about anything in the world, she got into the RAV4 for the trip. She was grateful that Carole wasn't outside when she backed out of the driveway to the street. It seemed every time she saw her closest friend, a lie came out of her mouth. Lies when they weren't even necessary. It was as if even the simplest, most innocuous truth had to be covered in gratuitous subterfuge.

She scanned the highway shoulder for the cutoff they'd taken the night she and Owen hid Charlie's body. She remembered the slight rise in the road before a curve. But it was daylight now. The world was a completely different place at night. Then she remembered the most distinguishing elements of the site. The rancher's fence line had been pristine. Its wires were guitar-string taut. The posts were clean and well maintained, unencumbered by a fringe of native bunchgrass. And the junipers. The evergreen spires lined a section of the field where the cattle gathered for refuge during a storm.

Liz was in a storm of her own making, and she knew it.

And there was the road. She pulled off the highway and followed the paved portion to the section of gravel, slowing down near the stand of junipers. Even though the sun beat down and covered the field with flat, even light, she was absolutely sure that she was in the right place. She parked.

Charlie's body was a magnet. It was drawing her close. She could almost imagine that he was calling out to her, not in anger, but in the hope that she'd come to him.

That she'd bring him home.

Liz turned off the ignition, swung the car door open, and breathed in the air. It was rugged and scenic, and as far as a final resting place could be imagined, it was beautiful. She looked up and down the road. She was alone. She supported herself on the RAV4's hood. Owen would kill her if he knew she was there. She started this.

She'd set it all in motion. She had to know why the boy's body had not been found. She couldn't wait for things to just happen. She couldn't stand another second of looking into Carole's hopeful eyes when she knew that Charlie was dead. There was wrong and there was immoral. And beyond that? That's where Liz had wandered. The path she was on was so dark and twisted she'd never be able to find her way out. A million lies could never cover the blackness of her heart.

She started down the incline toward the junipers.

"Hey, you!" a man's voice called out.

Liz spun around, the air leaving her lungs in a gasp.

A man on horseback was approaching her. He had bright blue eyes, white hair, and a mustache. If he were heavier and had a beard, he'd be a department store Santa. If he were younger, a tobacco-company cowboy.

"What are you doing on my land, lady?" he said.

"Arrowheads, sir." Her grandfather had taken her and Jimmy out to hunt arrowheads in the high desert one time, and the memory had snapped to the front of her mind. "I thought I'd look around."

The rancher got off his horse. "Thought you were one of those damn geocachers. They come out here like they own the place. Which

316

they don't. I do. Land's been picked over for arrowheads. Doubt you'd find any even if I gave you permission to hunt here. Which I'm not. Seeing how you didn't ask me anyway."

If Liz had had an arrowhead, she would have stabbed herself in the heart with it.

"Sorry," she said. "I was just driving home and, I don't know, I just thought about it. Something my family did years ago."

He nodded slightly at that, looked around them, and showed the first hint of a smile. "Mine too."

Then he drew up and scowled. "Shit," he said. He was looking over at the grove of junipers. "Looks like someone's been camping here."

Liz's heart hit the parched ground. She'd only wanted to know if animals had scattered Charlie's remains. Now she was there with a man on a horse, and his curiosity was drawing him to a place he might not have visited for a very long time. Now she was going to have to react. She would need to explain why she was there in the first place. Hunting arrowheads would never work. She *knew* the victim. He had lived next door. It would take the world's worst detective about ten seconds to turn a purported coincidence into an accusation.

She stood immobile as the rancher went to where Owen had placed Charlie.

"Damn those kids," the man said. "Come out here to drink and think nothing of leaving a big

317

mess. Out here because there's no house for miles and they think no one gives a crap. But I tell you, we folks out here do."

He bent down and tugged at something.

"Oh, God," Liz cried out. "What is it? What did you find?"

The man with the white hair and the wizened face glanced over his shoulder. "Simmer down, girl. Just some trash. Empty beer carton." He looked around and made a funny face. "Strange that there's no bottles or food wrappers."

"Is there anything else?"

"Nope," he said. "Just trash."

Liz turned away from the man. She felt dizzy. She needed water.

"I'm sorry about looking for arrowheads without asking," she said, still unable to meet his gaze.

"No problem," he said.

As Liz got into her car, he called over to her.

"Hey, you can come by and hunt anytime," he said.

Liz sat in the living room drinking more wine than she should while she waited for Owen to get home. Carole had come and gone throughout the day. Home. To the police station. To check to see if posters were still up.

Liz stared at her phone, waiting without much hope for him to respond to her innocuous text.

She didn't know what else to say. He'd told her to be careful, and she was doing just that. Yet she'd done exactly what he would have never wanted her to do. She'd returned to the dump site. She thought of Poe's story "The Tell-Tale Heart" and was certain that she'd fallen victim to her own paranoia. She'd literally returned to the scene of the crime. Even criminals on the most stupid reality shows knew better.

The front door swung open, and Owen, wearing a new suit and tie, came inside. She hadn't seen him leave in the morning. She didn't even know he had a new suit or why he'd wear one in the first place.

He caught her look. "Investors came today."

"You look great," she said, nudging a glass of wine in his direction.

"You all right?" he asked, appearing to notice the tremor in her hands.

"Yes. No. I'm not sure."

"Is this multiple choice?"

She looked at her glass. "No. Owen, I did something stupid today, but before I tell you, I want you to know that I'm sorry and it worked out and I'll never do it again."

"Liz," he said calmly, "what did you do?"

"I went to where you—where *we*—put Charlie." The correction was necessary. She was

319

responsible for Owen's involvement in this mess. "I went back there. I had to find out why no one had found him. I couldn't take it another minute. You don't know what it's like over there at Carole and David's. She's hanging on by a thread and I don't think she can take another minute of not knowing what happened to her little boy."

"You killed him," he said flatly, "and now you want to be the one to find the body?"

"It was an accident, Owen. Don't you ever say that I killed him! I didn't mean to do any of it. You know that. *You know it.*"

"But it's true," he said. "That's what you did."

Liz was tired of tears. She was angry with her husband for acting as though he'd been a paragon of virtue in the debacle their life had become. She pushed back at him for the first time.

"Don't judge me."

"Don't be a moron. What if someone saw you?"

"Someone *did*. In fact, I talked to the rancher."

"Holy shit," he said. "You're off the rails now."

"Sometimes I don't know why I married you."

"I have that same thought," he said. "Especially since you killed the neighbors' kid. Great move, going back to the body. Did you act all shocked in front of the rancher? Did you cry when the police came?"

"None of that happened, Owen."

"Why not?"

"Because the body was gone."

His eyes locked on hers. "Gone where?"

She held his gaze. "Gone. I don't know where."

Owen took a second to think.

"Maybe coyotes or a pack of dogs got the body," he said finally.

She drained her glass and eyed the now-empty bottle. "That's disgusting. Don't even say that. Charlie was our little friend."

"A little friend that you killed with your car, Liz. Don't get sanctimonious with me. Was there any blood or bones?"

She set down her empty glass and went to find another bottle in the kitchen. "You think I would have withheld that from you?"

Owen followed her. He had a knack for yelling at her in a whisper, and he did that now.

"Don't ask me that, Liz. I don't even know you anymore. I have no clue what you are or who you are. The Liz I knew wouldn't have done half the things you've done since Charlie died."

Chapter Forty

MISSING: SEVENTEEN DAYS

Esther Nguyen put down her phone. The call from the Oregon State Police was the kind that no one looking for a missing child wants to receive.

"Human remains were found south of town," the officer had said.

"We have a missing boy," she'd replied, knowing that just about every jurisdiction had their eyes wide open on the case since it had started nearly three weeks prior.

"Right," the officer said. "Medical examiner is en route now."

Esther could feel her adrenaline spike. "Is it our boy?"

The reporting officer said he didn't know. "Better notify the parents before you get out here," he said. "News crews will be coming. This'll be all over the state in the next hour."

She put down the phone and went for Jake, who was trying his best to figure out the new coffeemaker in the break room.

"We might have found Charlie," she said.

"That's great!"

"Not great."

Jake's face fell. This was not the ending he sought for his first major case. "Jesus," he said. "I thought we'd find him."

Esther had hoped for the same thing. "We need to alert the Franklins," she said. "This is going to blow up all over the news."

"What are we going to tell them?" he asked as he followed her down the hall.

"Human remains were found off 97 and there's no way of knowing if they are Charlie's."

Jake's face went white. "Holy shit, body parts? What the hell did the freak who took Charlie do to him?"

"Animal activity, Jake. They think that the body was dumped out there and coyotes got to it."

Jake got into the passenger seat while Esther turned the ignition.

"I guess that's better than someone cutting up the kid with a chain saw or a hatchet," he said.

Esther looked over at Jake, and he flushed a little. She let it go, knowing his graphic description was his cover for being sick to his stomach about what she'd just told him.

"I'll do the talking when we see the Franklins, all right?" she said.

"Yeah," he said. "You can do that."

"After we let the parents know what's going on, we're heading out there to the site. You going to be okay?"

Jake puffed himself up a little. "Yeah. I'll be

fine. Thanks for the warning. I need to psych myself up just a little."

She offered a grim smile and drove on.

David Franklin answered the door. He was dressed for work in a shirt that was so new, Esther could see the telltale folds that indicated it had not been laundered yet. Just out of the package.

"Mr. Franklin," she said, "we need to talk to you and Mrs. Franklin."

"This isn't good, is it?" he asked, his voice hoarse. "I can see it in your eyes. Especially yours." He raised his chin, indicating Jake, who hung back behind Esther.

"Is Mrs. Franklin home?"

"No, not exactly. She's next door. You want me to go get her?"

"That would be a good idea," Esther said.

While the detectives stood there, David went over to the Jarretts' place and knocked.

"That was kind of weird," Jake said.

"What are you thinking?"

"He said *not exactly* when you asked if she was home. That's a weird response."

Esther agreed. "Yeah, it is."

Carole was still in her bathrobe when she and her husband made their way back to the front door of what had once been a dream home. Carole, who had looked so together the first time Esther saw her, was a mess. Her hair was flat on one side of her head. She'd clearly slept in her makeup. Mascara smeared her cheekbones. Before Esther even said a word, Carole was crying.

Behind them was Liz Jarrett, hovering close to offer support, but not so close as to be part of what appeared to be a serious development.

"You found him," Carole said. "You found our Charlie?"

"Let's go inside," Esther said. "All of us."

"Just tell me," Carole said.

"There isn't anything to really tell you. Nothing conclusive. I'm here because of a discovery made late last night. A trucker pulled over off the highway and found something that indicated a crime."

"What do you mean, 'indicated a crime'?" David asked.

She ignored him for a moment. "Look, I'm here because news people no longer wait for anything conclusive before jumping ahead with speculation and innuendo."

Liz leaned into Carole at that point. Both women were unraveling.

"All right," David said. "Did you find my son? Did someone kill my boy?"

Esther said she didn't know. "What I can tell you is that some remains were found in a ditch. The medical examiner is probably just on the scene now."

"Some remains," Carole repeated. "Some remains. Did the trucker find . . . what did he . . ." Her words caught in her throat, and she stopped, unable to go on. Liz helped Carole inside and over to the sofa, where the two of them sat down.

David stayed put. "What exactly did they find?"

"Remains, Mr. Franklin. The trucker found only a partial body. That's all I know."

"I want to go there," Carole said, getting up. "I want to be there if it's Charlie."

"You all need to stay here," Esther said, looking from Carole to David and back again. "I'll let you know everything that I can as soon as I am able."

Back in the car, Jake spoke first.

"That was weird," he said again.

"Be more specific."

"Mrs. Franklin was over at the neighbors' in her bathrobe."

"So I saw," she said.

"She didn't look like she'd bathed. Her hair. Makeup. I don't think she slept at home last night," he said, his voice rising a little at the end of the sentence as though he questioned his statement.

"Maybe she went over to the Jarretts' this morning just before we got there."

Jake was on a roll. At least he thought so. "I

don't think a lady like that would ever go visiting anyone without looking all perfect like she does all the time."

Esther looked in the rearview mirror and caught a glimpse of Carole and Liz returning to the Jarretts' house.

"Something's going on," Jake said.

"The strain of a missing child is immense," Esther said, thinking back to her Corvallis case and its aftermath. "It's beyond the ability of many to cope. Few couples can weather the storm that comes at them. Even fewer marriages can survive when the loss is their only child. You're right, Jake. Something is going on."

Chapter Forty-One
MISSING: SEVENTEEN DAYS

While Liz put her grandmother's copper kettle on the stove, Carole stayed quiet. She had said little since the detectives mentioned what had been found along the highway. David had gone back to Sweetwater, his Porsche letting everyone know of his exit.

"Chamomile?" Liz asked.

Carole barely indicated a yes.

"All right. Just a minute." Liz fished through the cupboard for some sweetener. She knew that Carole liked agave or stevia—natural sweeteners. She'd always been a proponent of whole foods, natural products, for herself and her son.

Carole sat there at the kitchen table, her brain running over all the same scenarios again and again. How she should have kept her eyes on Charlie the entire time she was on the phone with the adjuster. How turning away, even for just one minute, had set off the series of terrible events. Her lapse had given some creep the way in that he needed to take her son. It allowed evil to walk right in and take control. And now, although she steeled herself with the tiniest shred of hope, she knew her mistake had led to whatever hell her son had suffered after he was taken from her.

"Who does this to a child?" she asked Liz.

"Don't think the worst, Carole," Liz said. "You don't know what happened."

Carole's eyes stayed riveted on her friend's. "You know it," she said. "I can see it in your eyes."

"I don't," Liz said, turning away for a moment. "I don't. Really. I have faith."

It stunned her to lie like that. She wouldn't have thought it possible, but the magnitude of what she'd done was growing larger and larger. Her words were an ice ball rolling down a mountainside, building into an avalanche, hurtling toward innocent people.

All completely unaware of what was heading their way.

"I saw the look in your eyes when the detective said they'd found something off the highway," Carole said. "I saw the hope—the faith, as you say—leak out of you. If *you* can't believe he'll be found, what can *I* do? I'm alone in this, Liz."

"You're not, Carole. Owen and I are here. David's being a prick, but you know that he loves Charlie. You have to hold on to all of that right now."

The ball of ice was becoming larger. It was unstoppable.

"Hold on to what?" Carole asked, setting down

the steaming graniteware mug. The smell of chamomile filled the air. It was a grandmotherly kind of smell. Sweet and soothing. Liz hoped that Carole would sip the hot drink, calm herself just a little. Maybe lie down and try to get some rest.

"I don't know," Liz said. "I'm just trying to be helpful."

"I know, Liz. I know. I'm sorry. I couldn't get through this without you. You are the only one who seems to understand how I feel. You'll make a very good mother to a little boy or girl someday."

Liz didn't know how to respond to that without crying. They sat there in silence for a long time, drinking tea until their cups were empty.

Finally Liz picked up Carole's empty cup and turned to the cupboard. She took her time preparing another cup of tea, then set it down in front of her grieving friend.

"Is it wrong of me to hope that they found someone else's boy?" Carole asked. "What would God think about that? Wishing that some other family will get the worst news of their lives."

Liz didn't know what to say.

"I know what you're thinking," Carole went on, filling the void in their conversation. "I know that you think I'm a terrible person. I can't help it. It's not logical. It's not moral. And yet there's a part of me that hopes that if another child dies, then maybe Charlie will live. Like out of all of the kids who are stolen, you know, one or two make it home."

"I'm not thinking that," Liz said, getting up. "I'm thinking that there aren't enough prayers and hopes in the world for everyone to have everything turn out all right."

Carole drank more tea.

"I need to lie down, Liz," she said. "Wake me up if the police come back."

CHAPTER FORTY-TWO
MISSING: SEVENTEEN DAYS

A caravan of emergency and police vehicles from an array of jurisdictions, along with the Oregon state medical examiner's familiar white van and a couple of news crews from Portland and Bend, lined the highway. At the head of the procession was a large Ryder truck. Cars slowed and necks craned as passersby tried to see the reason for all the commotion. Before the body was found earlier that day, the place was completely unremarkable. No one would have stopped to look. Rabbitbrush and sagebrush competed for water. A hubcap that rolled off someone's vintage VW had settled there. Litter clung to a fence like ratty laundry on a line some twenty yards off the highway.

A silvery white tarp over a broad aluminum frame covered the spot where the trucker had pulled over to take a leak. His dog, Jo-Jo, had found an arm.

"Yeah," the driver said to a reporter as Esther and Jake passed by, "it made me sick seeing that. Something really wrong about people these days. Tossing someone into a ditch like they was nothing but trash."

The sun was high in the sky, illuminating the tent like a big white beach umbrella. The side panel facing the highway had been dropped to obscure the view, although it wasn't likely that anyone could see a thing from the roadway. Whoever had been left there was in pieces. Small yellow numbered evidence markers dotted the vicinity of the tent.

"Evidence, Jake," Esther said as they approached the tent. "Whatever we see here, think of it as pieces of evidence. Don't let it play with your head. If the pieces belong to our missing boy, then that's all they are: pieces. Not him."

Jake made a sound of agreement behind her.

She saw the medical examiner's assistant, Mirabella Condit, working the scene. They'd met at a conference a few years prior. Mirabella was a striking woman who always dressed as if she were going out to dinner no matter where she went. "Look," she once told Esther as they took lunch together on a conference break, "I'm in the lab all day long doing this and that to dead people. It's grim. No doubt about it. My pushback is that I dress up. People say it's about respecting the victims, but it's really because it makes me feel good about myself. Reminds me I'm still a person too."

Now, out on the highway, Mirabella smiled and gave Esther a friendly look. "I thought I might see you here."

"You know about our missing boy."

"Sure. Everyone does. At first I thought it might be him."

"'At first'?"

"Yeah," she said. "Unless your three-year-old has a tattoo on his wrist and is female, then I'd say it's not him."

"No tattoo," Esther said.

"No vagina?"

"Guess not."

The medical examiner's assistant knelt down and pointed to the happy-face tattoo on the mottled wrist. "Beyond tragically ironic," she said.

Esther looked at Jake. "You can go back to the car and catch your breath, all right?"

Jake, looking grateful for the dismissal, turned and hurried away.

"Newbie?" Mirabella asked.

"Yeah," Esther said, her smile joyless. "As green as his face right now."

The two women talked for a few minutes. Searchers found a leg and the torso, but the victim's head hadn't been recovered. Coyotes, Mirabella said, often like to drag those back to their dens for further gnawing. "It takes a while to crack the skull and get into the brains," she said. "A real treat, evidently."

"What do you think happened to her?" Esther asked.

"Don't know," Mirabella said. "We have a little decomp going on here. As the boss likes to say, 'a little softening around the edges.' Exam in the lab will tell us what we need to know. Or some of it. My guess is that we've got a girl here, maybe fifteen or sixteen."

"A runaway, maybe."

Mirabella agreed. "A runaway that ran in the wrong direction."

Esther and Jake returned to Bend, first stopping at the Jarretts' place.

"Weird that Carole is always over here," Jake said. "Her own house is practically a mansion."

"It isn't the same thing, but after I broke up with Drew I actually stayed with my mother for a few days. Didn't want to be alone."

Jake knew how Esther felt about her mom.

"That's saying something, for sure," he said.

Carole ran toward them.

"No," Esther said. "It wasn't your son."

"Oh, God," she said, hooking her arms around Liz, who was just behind her. "I told you that he's alive. I told you!"

CHAPTER FORTY-THREE
MISSING: SEVENTEEN DAYS

Owen looked up from his desk as he rubbed his stubbled chin. Liz stood in his office doorway with a look on her face that he placed somewhere on the raw continuum between terror and anger. Her hair was disheveled, and she wore no makeup. He got up from his chair as fast as he could and pulled her inside, shutting the door.

"What are you doing here? You look whacked-out," he said, dropping the miniblinds that provided some privacy from the prying eyes of the office staff as he ushered her to a chair.

She slumped downward.

Rag doll.

Jell-O.

Noodle.

"The police came," Liz said, her voice cracking. She tried to get up, but Owen pressed her shoulders downward. "The body wasn't Charlie's," she said. "Where is he? You told me, Owen . . . you told me . . . animals took him. Carole thinks he's alive. This is going too far. Too far, Owen. Really."

Owen slid the other visitor's chair up next to his wife's and sat down. His eyes were wide, and he supported himself by keeping a hand on her shoulder.

"Right," he said. "I told you that animals got him. That didn't mean he'd never be found."

She put her face in her hands and started to sob. It was guttural. Constricted. The kind of ugly cry that comes from something very deep and broken.

Owen's eyes darted to the miniblinds and the shadowy figure he thought he saw linger outside the window. He needed to calm Liz. Keep her quiet.

Shut her fucking mouth.

"I guess I was wrong," she said when she'd managed to at least marginally compose herself. "I mean, I wasn't wrong, because it *was* gone. Some animals tore him apart and they found parts out there off the highway. I don't know what parts. It's on the news already."

Owen tightened. "Where are David and Carole?"

"He's at work, I guess," Liz said. "She's home. At our place. She's asleep."

"Asleep?"

Liz turned her eyes away. "I put something in her tea, Owen."

"Something in her tea?"

"Yes, Owen. Damn it. Valium," she said, her voice rising from a whisper to a normal voice. Then a little louder as she found her footing on

337

the shifting sands of what she'd wanted to say. "I know it was wrong," she went on, "but I just can't stand lying to her. Pretending everything will be all right. Acting concerned when she runs through a litany of the mistakes she made that day. You have no idea what it's like. You can leave. Get away from both of them. Come here and get on with normal life. Me? I'm trapped because I messed up in the biggest way possible."

Owen kept his eye on the slightly parted slats of the blinds. "Lower your voice, Liz," he said. "People can hear you."

His words seemed to embolden her a little.

"Really?" Liz asked, although she took the volume down a notch. "I don't care. I really don't. I'm not able to turn off my feelings the way you are."

"I have feelings too," he said. "I hold them inside. Because if I didn't, I'd smack you so hard for what you've done. How your fuckup has encircled me like a goddamn noose."

The office door opened, and Damon came inside. He looked concerned as he studied the two of them through his Buddy Holly glasses. "Everything okay?" he asked, looking first at Liz, who wouldn't even glance in his direction. "Owen?"

"Yes," he said. "Fine. Just a disagreement about where we're going on our celebration trip. She says Tahiti, I say Bora-Bora."

338

Owen was a facile liar. Liz had always known that about him. She wondered how many times he had turned on a dime and lied to her. He was too quick. Lying was second nature to him. Maybe first nature. It probably took more effort for him to tell the truth.

"Sounds like a lot of disagreement going on here over some pretty good travel choices," Damon said. "Why don't you go to both? You can certainly afford it—that is, if you can risk the time off."

"Right." Owen forced a smile. "Great plan. Right, Liz?"

"Yes," she responded, still not making eye contact with her husband or his business partner. "Sounds great to me."

"Conference call in ten minutes," Damon said. "Nice seeing you, Liz."

He shut the door and disappeared.

Liz got up. "You have a line for everything, Owen. I see it. I also see how everything you do is for you. You pretend it's for us. I know better. I did something terrible and probably completely unforgivable. Carole is about to find out her son's dead. For all I know, there's some goddamn DNA or fibers or something that will circle back to me."

"We were careful," he said.

"*You* were careful, Owen. You always are. You cleaned up my mess for yourself. Not for me."

Owen tried to hug her, but she pushed him away.

"You need to chill, Liz," he said. "Go home. We can ride this out."

Chapter Forty-Four
MISSING: EIGHTEEN DAYS

To Owen Jarrett's way of thinking, running a restaurant was among the stupidest and riskiest of business endeavors. Not only that, there was no way of getting around the fact that you had to deal with the public every single day. Listening to a litany of complaints while reveling in only occasional praise. The staff problems. The cycle of rinse and repeat for every single lunch and dinner service. While he admired David Franklin's house, car, and standing in the community as someone everyone seemed to know, he knew that none of what David had had been earned entirely on his own. His wife's money had kept Sweetwater afloat. It had paid for every single thing the older man had.

Everyone who lived there knew it.

Owen scrolled through the news alerts he'd set up for Charlie's case. He'd returned to one in particular several times.

Ohio Man Questioned in Boy's Disappearance

Bend police detectives questioned a registered sex offender in connection with the disappearance of Charlie Franklin, the three-year-old Bend boy reported missing by his parents, David and Carole Franklin.

Bradley Collins, 40, of Dayton, Ohio, was interviewed for two hours.

"Collins was cooperative and has been cleared," said Rick Massey, public information officer for the police department. "He's one of many leads detectives have been following."

Massey said that they have no evidence that the boy drowned in the river, was abducted by a stranger, or met with some other foul play.

"We don't know what happened to Charlie Franklin," Massey said.

Liz was imploding, and if she totally blew, then he'd be ruined. She'd started this mess, and now it was up to him to find a way to end it all.

He had been sure that Charlie's body would have been recovered long ago. Finding the body would shift the case to a full-bore abduction/murder investigation. No one on earth would suspect that they would be involved in anything like that. But a registered sex offender, who'd been there on the river when Charlie went missing? Bradley Collins would surely get a very intense second look, from both the cops and the media. Fresh meat for them, instead of gnawing away next door on the only bone they had: what had happened the morning Liz's RAV4 hit Charlie.

Owen couldn't wait any longer for the desert to give up the boy's bones. The longer things festered in uncertainty, the greater the chance that Liz might ignore his warnings and tell the truth.

Only the truth that she knew.

That she had killed the boy.

Which, of course, wasn't the truth at all.

He had.

Owen left his office at Lumatyx and made his way down the street to Sweetwater. The restaurant was quiet when he arrived, the lull between the early afternoon and early evening rush. Amanda Jenkins, her red hair flowing down her back, was up on a step stool, stretching to reach a blackboard that promoted Alaska king salmon and Ellensburg rack of lamb. As her arm lifted the colored chalk in her hand to gracefully loop out the specials, her short skirt rode up a little to reveal more of her upper thigh than she probably would have liked.

If she had an audience.

Which she suddenly did.

"Been a while, Amanda," Owen said.

Startled, she turned around and gave him a look.

He held out his hand, but she refused it.

"Yeah, Owen, it has," she said, stepping off the step stool. "Lunch is over. Sorry."

"Didn't come for lunch."

"What do you want?" Her tone was colder than it needed to be.

"Jesus," he said. "Don't be such a bitch. I came to see David. He in?"

"Right," she said, taking her eyes away from him. "Yes. In there." She indicated the doorway leading to David's office. "Sorry about that just now. Things have been crazy around here."

David was on the phone and motioned Owen to sit. The windowless space was crammed with piles of papers, invoices, order forms, and letters organized into three different piles.

"Right," David was saying. "I need a little more time. I've been going through a lot around here. Ever read the paper?" He hung up and looked at Owen. "Jesus! Two minutes late and you'd think the bank would have to close down."

"Idiots," Owen said, concealing his surprise.

David relaxed a little. "Been a nightmare lately."

Understatement on all fronts.

"How are you holding up?"

"I don't know," David said. "I don't even know what to do anymore. Carole wants me to act one way. The police have nothing. I sit around here, because every time I go out on the floor, someone offers condolences for something that hasn't happened."

"I can't imagine," Owen said.

"No one can," David said. "I couldn't. You think you would feel a certain way if something really bad like this happened to you. But you really can't fathom what to feel. You know what I mean?"

Owen didn't, but he said he did. "Lots of forces at work," he said. "In the end, it's really only about getting your son back home. That's all that matters."

David put his elbows on the desk and rested his chin in his hands. "I think someone took Charlie," he said. "I don't think for one second that he fell in that goddamn river and drowned. He's a smart boy. He knows that the water is dangerous."

"A kidnapping, then?"

David shook his head. "No. I think a pervert took him. You saw that story in the paper, right?"

"The Ohio guy?" This was perfect, Owen thought. The guy was primed.

"Damn pervert out here on a vacation, on the goddamn prowl. A registered sex offender! This is what we get for being a tourist destination."

Owen didn't say anything. He let David rant.

"I bet half the people I serve here have been convicted of some goddamn crime."

Still not a word.

"Owen? You all right?"

Owen pretended to snap back to the moment. "Yes, fine. Just thinking about something. Probably nothing."

"About what?"

"I don't know," Owen said. "Probably nothing."

David looked hard into Owen's eyes. "You know something."

"No. No, I don't. I mean, when you said Ohio . . . my mind flashed on seeing Ohio plates at Columbia Park the morning Charlie went missing. I remember because we seldom see cars from the Midwest. Seems those folks vacation in Branson, Missouri, or places closer to home."

David got up. "You sure? Did you notice anything else? The car?"

"No," Owen said. "I was running, pretty much didn't look up. Just saw the plate. It was Ohio. That's for sure. Pretty weird, huh? Should I tell the police?"

"No," he said. "They've pretty much ruled out the guy. Goddamn them. I just feel it in my bones that he's the one that took my son."

"What are you going to do?" Owen asked.

"Do?"

The two men locked eyes for a long moment, and then Owen shrugged. "If he's the one."

David picked up his keys, knocking over one of the three piles of envelopes. Owen could see PAST DUE stamped on several. Loan documents from Washington Federal had been shoved aside.

Owen had thought that David and Carole had it all, but now he began to have doubts. She'd made a pile from her time at Google. The house. The cars. The Venetian glass collection. But that didn't mean it would last forever. Maybe they really had nothing at all?

"I don't know," David continued. "The guy's staying at the Pines. He might have stashed Charlie somewhere." He rubbed his face, hard. "He's the last straw. I swear to God he is."

Five minutes later Amanda caught up with Owen on his way out of the restaurant. She looked anxious and scared at the same time.

"Did they find Charlie?" she asked.

Owen barely slowed. "Huh?" he asked.

She put out her hand to stop him, but he kept going.

"David went out of here like a bat out of hell," she said. "What did you tell him? Is there news?"

"No," Owen said. "No news."

At least there wasn't any just yet.

CHAPTER FORTY-FIVE
MISSING: EIGHTEEN DAYS

The Pines was one of the last places David Franklin ever thought he'd visit. Sex with some tourist who flirted with him at the restaurant? He'd do better than the Pines. Hell, just pull her into the pantry. He recalled the time that his server Carla had rubbed her ass against him—*accidentally,* she insisted—when she tried to wedge her way past her boss in the kitchen. Rudy, the cook, caught it and gave David the look, said something along the lines of "Why don't you tap that?"

"Who says I haven't?" David shot back, although he hadn't.

Not yet.

"Everyone else has," Rudy said, leering at Carla as she made her way out of the kitchen, arms loaded with plates of food for a noisy four-top in the front of the restaurant.

The truth was, David hadn't even considered having sex with Carla before Rudy opened his flytrap. She was pretty and all. Cute figure. Wide-set eyes that literally smiled when she talked about the things that made her happy: her new car, her half-marathon finish in the top ten for her age group, the way she could defuse an unruly customer and still get a big tip.

To David's way of thinking, Rudy's comment was a challenge. David was like a compulsive gambler: any challenge fueled behavior over which he had no control.

Rudy said it. David acted on it.

A week or so later he and Carla messed around in the freezer. He pushed her against one of the lockers and the two hooked together like frozen Velcro. He told her she was sexy. She told him he was hot. She leaned into him and he acted as though she was the only thing he'd ever wanted. When the Velcro unsnapped, they stood there acknowledging almost at once that neither one of them really cared for the other.

Carla had thought she'd get a better shift, the one after eight, when the well-heeled tourists from California and Seattle got tipsy, ordered more alcohol than they should, and ran up a bar bill that always translated into the fattest tips of the night.

David had thought that by screwing Carla he'd feel like more of a stud. Now in his fifties, he felt those feelings beginning to wane unless injected with the excitement that comes with exploring a body firmer than his own. Carole had been sexually adventurous when she was with Google and needed to unwind fast: they'd made love on every form on transportation, including a helicopter and a snowmobile. Their lovemaking was rushed and exciting. When Charlie had arrived, and when the house in Bend was finally finished, Carole had all but cut him off. Certainly no more Adventureland. No more blow jobs in the car.

Carole never said so, but the implication was always more than clear: *Moms don't do that.*

As he parked his Porsche, deep down David knew that he'd been challenged by his wife. She'd made him feel like shit with her comments about their teetering marriage and his apparent lack of devotion to Charlie. He loved his son. Yes, he complained about the fact that he no longer got to enjoy Sunday morning sex. He'd whined about how she controlled him with the money. None of that meant that he didn't love Charlie.

On the passenger seat, nestled in a bag on the black leather of the Porsche, was a bottle of Old Grand-Dad. He'd drunk that from college through the failure of his first restaurant. He'd sworn on his life that he'd never take another sip. And for years now, he hadn't, though the thirst for alcohol never abated. In a way, it propelled him to be even more successful at Sweetwater than he'd ever been. He couldn't drink, so all of his energy and all of his angst drove him to work harder. Work filled the place that alcohol had once staked out.

But that bitch Carole. She'd pushed him so

hard with her cruelly insightful remarks. Even when she didn't say the words, she'd challenged him all right. She'd questioned his manhood. His fatherhood. His role in a world that she'd bought and paid for.

David reached for the bag and pulled the bottle from it, settled it in his lap. Its bright orange label was a roadside warning cone. He ignored it. His hands shook as he twisted the cap, the tiny metal prongs holding it to the neck snapping like firecrackers. He seethed. He knew that he was about to undo everything that had gotten him as far as he'd gone with Sweetwater. He didn't know for sure, but the industry rumor mill had him short-listed for a James Beard Award. The Portland PBS station suggested he might appear on a local version of *A Chef's Life*.

"What you do with razor clams, sherry, and cream is a culinary gift to the people of the Northwest," the producer had said. "A rethinking, a reimagining, of the flavors that make us unique. That we love."

David held the mouth of the bottle to his nose and hesitated before taking in the sweet, oaky, and acrid smell of the alcohol that had been his downfall so many times. A hint of citrus filled his nostrils. He flashed to the time he sideswiped a parked car and kept going, rubbing the smudge of paint from the passenger car door with an old rag. Red paint. It had looked like blood. Inside, he knew it could have been. He thought of the time he nearly had a heart attack coming home from the restaurant after drinking well past closing. How the sound of a police siren sent waves of fear through every fiber of his being. He imagined a score of passersby gawking at him as he stumbled heel-to-toe, heel-to-toe, while trying to walk a straight line, or as he tried to blow into a Breathalyzer tube, or as he slurred his speech while arguing with the police officer. The handcuffs. The mug shot. The newspapers publishing an item about it.

Yet somehow—by the grace of God, he once believed—he'd avoided all of that. The police car swept past him, and David Franklin stopped drinking because he knew that if he didn't, there would be nothing left but disaster. His life would be as empty as those pearlescent razor clam shells that were discarded after he'd proudly collected all of those rave reviews. He'd attended the meetings with those he once looked down on as losers, when really they were only different versions of himself.

Now whatever he thought he'd found when he'd pulled himself together had been eroded by the fact that Charlie was missing and that Carole somehow blamed him for everything. She might as well have taken a pair of her orange-handled Fiskars scissors to his balls and mounted them on one of her weavings.

The man from Ohio had mentioned to the chatty bartender at Anthony's that he was staying at the Pines. He'd passed that information on to the police.

He also told David Franklin.

A Toyota Camry with Ohio plates, grimy from a nearly cross-country trip, sat parked in front of cabin 22; a **NO HATE IN OUR STATE** sticker was affixed to the back window. Inside, David was sure, the man who took his boy was doing whatever freaky, disgusting thing that he did. David took a full, deep drink from the bottle. It was nectar coating his throat, reminding his body what alcohol did for him. It gave him the kind of calming rush that made him feel ten sizes bigger. A kind of power surged through him.

I'll make that freak tell me where my boy is, he thought, taking another drink before getting out of his car.

Chapter Forty-Six
MISSING: EIGHTEEN DAYS

David had cut his right hand. Blood oozed onto the leather-covered steering wheel, making his hand slip as he drove. The last thing he wanted was any attention to his driving—or to what he'd done. He'd ditched Brad Collins at the hospital and the Old Grand-Dad bottle somewhere between the cabins of the Pines and home. If he'd expected to feel more like a man for having beat the shit out of a pervert, he found the opposite to be true.

Fuck. Fuck. Fuck!!!

The expletives were useless, but they kept coming while he replayed what had taken place at the Pines as he tried to get home without getting pulled over.

Brad was caught completely unaware. The Ohio tourist was watching *Judge Judy* in his boxers when a rage- and alcohol-fueled David shoved open the cabin door. It swung so abruptly that David was uncertain if it had been unlocked or if he'd been given some kind of superhero boost from the bourbon that he'd guzzled in the parking lot.

"Hey!" Brad said, dropping his feet over the

edge of the bed and standing as if at attention. "You're in the wrong room, buddy!"

David pulled the door shut behind him and wheeled on him. "You pervert! You took my boy!" he said, then lunged at him, jumped on top of him. It was lightning-fast. Superhero-fast. It was faster than a man of his age could normally manage.

"I didn't do anything to anyone!" Brad said as David, bolstered by the booze and powered by the contempt he had for himself and the world, pummeled the younger man over and over.

Brad tried to fight his attacker, but David Franklin was like some kind of machine. He just kept punching, emitting a grunt like a prizefighter with each swing. At one point his hands found a T-shirt and he shoved it inside the bloody man's mouth.

All while demanding answers.

"Tell me where Charlie is!"

Brad had no idea, of course, and the T-shirt made speaking impossible. He tried to shift his weight and slither out from under his attacker, but David was relentless.

"You sack of shit! You know where my boy is and I'll goddamn kill you if you don't tell me! Where did you put him? Where in the hell did you put my boy?"

Brad managed to extract the T-shirt from his mouth. His lip was torn so badly that it hung like a piece of tenderloin on a skewer. Blood oozed like a ketchup commercial.

"I told the police," he spat out. "I don't know anything."

David hit him again.

"Liar!"

Brad coughed up more blood.

"Not lying," he said. "Not . . ."

They struggled a bit longer, and David finally got off him and sat there, gasping for air and snapping out of his rage. His victim's eyeballs were white marbles rolling backward in a sea of red. He grabbed the man by the shoulders and shook him again.

"Don't you die on me without telling me where Charlie is! Where did you put him?"

Brad lay still. He couldn't move. "I don't want to die," he finally said.

And just like that, like the flicking of a light switch from full glare to complete blackness, terror seized David. He was gripped and slapped hard by the reality of what he'd done.

He'd nearly beaten a man to death.

Bloody and weak, Brad Collins fought for air. It was a sickening sound. A trash fish caught in a gillnetter's line, fighting for life.

"Jesus," David said, "what did I do?"

"Doctor," Brad said. "I need a doctor."

David sat there on the floor next to the other man, who was slippery with blood. His own hand was bleeding, and there was blood spatter on his face. He wondered who, if anyone, had seen him at the Pines. He wondered if the guests in the next cabin over had heard him land blow after blow, or if in places like the Pines people just minded their own business. He got up, surveyed the cabin. He wondered what evidence he would leave behind. How long it would take Brad to die. The cabin had an old-school rotary phone, and David grabbed it, yanking its cord from the wall.

The pervert wouldn't be able to call for help.

David staggered toward the door, still coming to grips with what he'd done, and knowing that there would be consequences.

I shouldn't have let Carole get to me.

I should have been a better father.

I shouldn't have screwed the waitstaff at Sweetwater.

I shouldn't have killed Brad Collins.

Brad stirred and David turned around. Doing the right thing after doing something so wrong was the only right choice. "Can you get up?" he asked. He held out his hand.

The bloody man tried to move on his own, terrified by his assailant, but he was too weak.

David knelt down and pulled Brad to his feet. He helped the man into a pair of jeans and flip-flops, then swung his arm over his shoulder and staggered with him out of the cabin to the car. A woman and a man fifty yards away, heading to their own cabin, barely glanced at them. David's mind was racing. He wondered if they thought Brad was drunk.

Lots of drunks in Bend this time of year, he reasoned.

"You didn't take my boy?" he asked as the gravel spun under the black car's tires.

"No," Brad said. "No."

David looked over at him, the bottle rolling on the floorboard beneath Brad's feet.

"I'm sorry for what I did to you," he said.

Brad's eyelids had started to swell, but he returned the gaze. "Hospital," he coughed out through bloody teeth.

"Right."

"You're not going to kill me, are you?"

David returned his eyes to the road. Though it was a thought. Killing the man in the seat next to him would ensure that what he'd done might never be found out. It would silence the one person who could ruin his life. It passed through his mind over and over as he drove down the highway and to the hospital. By the time he exited the off-ramp, his passenger was unconscious.

Maybe he would die.

Maybe he'd never tell anyone what David had done to him.

David stopped the car under the wide portico in front of the emergency room entrance. It was deserted. He looked over at the parking lot. All quiet there too. He honked his horn a few times. He expected a swarm of attendants to besiege him with gurneys, stretchers, and wheelchairs.

No one was there.

He opened the passenger door and hooked his arms under Brad Collins's and pulled him from the car.

Still no one.

What should I do?

David dragged the unconscious and bloody Brad Collins to the big double doors. The glass-and-steel jaws opened wide.

A moment later he was back in his car, heading home to the house on the river.

The big house was empty, and David thanked God for that. He tore off his bloody clothes and put them in a yard waste bag in the garage. Dried blood colored his hands like a bad spray tan. He ran the shower and jumped in before it had even warmed. The blast of cold water numbed him. Hell, he was already numb. Numb from the alcohol. Numb from the beating he'd given a complete stranger. The water turned pink and swirled down the drain. As the temperature rose to near scalding, David stood there and let the hot water flow over him. He didn't try to step to one side and move out of the way. It burned, but he still stood there, immobile. Letting it happen. He didn't care if the water cooked him alive.

He turned off the water and stood in front of the mirror. What had he just done? As the condensation on the mirror began to fade, the eyes of a stranger stared back from its smeared surface. Who was this man? He took a step back—so far back that he nearly hit the opposite wall. His paunch sagged over the white skin of his beltline. His pecs had become pancake breasts. Bags hung under his eyes. David Franklin was no longer anything but middle-aged. He was never going to be anything as great as he had been before his son went missing. The tug-of-war inside of him—whether he'd be better off if Brad Collins died, as it was his only chance to weasel out of what he'd done, or if it would be better if his victim lived so he wouldn't be guilty of causing the man's death—was over. He hoped that Brad Collins survived.

He hoped that his son was not dead. Tears came to his eyes.

There was nothing else to do but dress and wait for the doorbell to ring. He put on a pair of black jeans and a white linen shirt. He combed his hair without the assistance of any product and looked in the mirror. Whoever that man was, he would never, *ever* be what he'd once been.

Most certainly, he'd never be what he'd wanted to be.

Chapter Forty-Seven
MISSING: EIGHTEEN DAYS

Amanda Jenkins opened her apartment door a crack. It was late, and she wore a pale blue terry cloth robe; her luxurious red hair was pulled back, and she was half-asleep. She didn't even speak. She looked at him and sighed. Considering all that had been going on with the investigation and the staff problems at Sweetwater, Owen Jarrett on her doorstep was the last thing she'd wanted to see.

"Can I come in?" Owen asked, edging forward.

"No. What do you want?" she said, opening the door a little wider but not letting him inside.

Owen was wearing a T-shirt and shorts. Sweat bloomed under his arms and across his brow. He'd been out running.

"Seeing you at the restaurant . . ." He started again: "I'm under a lot of pressure, Amanda," he said. "I need to talk. My wife's falling apart. Damon is screwing me over."

Amanda started to close the door, but he stuck his foot in the gap.

"You never want to just talk, Owen," she said.

"Not when there are other things we can do."

Amanda had made a big mistake in sleeping

with Owen and had kicked herself a thousand times since their affair ended. He'd played her. He'd used her for sexual release. As a quasi confidante. He'd told her time and again how Liz was so wrapped up in her "loser dreams" of pursuing a law degree. "She should be focusing on me," he'd said. "I'm her ticket."

Encounters with Owen had been one massive dose of self-importance after another that, looking back, were laughable. Sure, he was handsome. He was confident. He seemed so smart. But he was a liar. A narcissist who saw the world as a place that existed solely for his pleasure. Amanda, with her beautiful red hair, ivory skin, and green eyes, was nothing but an attractive accessory.

It was true that their sex had been dangerous and exciting. Owen liked to take risks. He complained that Liz was too white bread, too tightly wound. "Amanda, you know how to let go. I like that," he'd said.

Being adventurous was one thing. Being stupid was another.

They'd had sex in his office at Lumatyx. At the restaurant after hours. Owen's favorite place to have sex was on the Franklins' property when they weren't home. One time, Owen held her from behind when they were on the Franklins' deck overlooking the river as a group of paddleboarders passed by. She'd braced her hands on the deck rail and tried to contain her ecstasy.

"I think that old man knows what we're doing," she whispered, indicating a silhouetted figure across the river.

Owen looked over at Dr. Miller.

"Doubt it," he said. "The old coot's blind as a bat."

Amanda started to shove the door closed, but Owen's foot stayed firmly wedged between it and the jamb.

"We're done, Owen," she said. "I've told you that over and over. I'm not doing this anymore."

"But I need you," he said. "I'm going through a lot."

"You need help, Owen," Amanda told him, flatly. "You're selfish. Being with you was destructive. The biggest mistake I've made in my life. Every time I see your face, I get sick inside. You're like whiskey to me. I got drunk on it so bad that whenever I smell it now, it all comes back to me. You're human whiskey."

"You're so dramatic, Amanda."

"Go away," she said, raising her voice only a little. She didn't want the neighbors to hear.

"Can't we have one last time?" he said, pleading now, a little desperate. It was hard to say with Owen: Was he pretending or was it real?

Amanda was never going there again.

"I'll tell your wife," she said.

He stared at her, letting her wonder what he was thinking. Finally, he spoke. "I wish you would," he said. "She's suicidal."

Was he really hoping she'd tell? Did he actually want her to push the woman over the edge?

"Did you just say what I think you did?" she asked.

Owen just grinned. It was a smile that she used to think was sexy. At the moment it seemed dark, evil. It was the kind of look that he'd flash at her, and she'd come running.

"I feel sorry for Liz," Amanda said. "But I don't feel sorry for myself anymore. I'm better than this. Now get the hell out before I call the police."

Owen stepped back, and Amanda slammed the door.

Chapter Forty-Eight
MISSING: NINETEEN DAYS

The man in the hospital bed was unrecognizable. His face had been rearranged by a brutal attack the likes of which was seldom seen in mostly quiet Bend. The city had its share of brewpub and barroom brawls, but this beating went far beyond that. It was all but certain that whoever had done this to the man in the hospital bed had meant to kill him. The victim's eyes had puffed up to the size of clamshells and his lower lip was torn so badly that it took a surgeon more than an hour to stitch it—and his left ear—into place.

The man lay motionless while tubes crisscrossed the space behind him before plunging into his arms and his mouth. A respirator forced air into his lungs with the sick sound of machine against man. Up and down the device pulsed.

"He had your card in his pocket, Detective," said Della Cortez, the attending physician. "That's why I called you. I was hoping you could identify him. No wallet. No ID."

If Esther Nguyen had to go by the man's face alone, her answer would have been an emphatic no. As she stood there, she could see things that indicated familiarity. Yes, she knew him by the

Ohio State Buckeye tattoo visible on his exposed shoulder.

"I'm pretty sure it's Brad Collins," she said. "He's a tourist from the Midwest."

"How come he has your card?" the doctor asked.

Esther's mind raced back to the interview she'd conducted. She'd asked him to let her know if he left Bend. She didn't tell him that she thought he was a guilty party in the abduction of Charlie Franklin. At the same time, she hadn't told him she thought he was innocent, either.

"I talked to him about a case we're working," she said somewhat stiffly. "Asked him to stay close."

"He's not going anywhere now," the doctor said.

The detective moved a little closer, looking at the man's injuries as she tried to determine what had caused his face to become twice its size, his fingers swollen and colored like grilled hot dogs.

"What happened to him?" she asked Dr. Cortez. "Did he say anything when he was admitted?"

Dr. Cortez was a tall, slender woman who wore her black hair in an impossibly tight bun that she fastened with a silver clip. She wore no makeup. Esther liked her right away. No-nonsense and compassionate. Dr. Cortez stuck a pencil behind her ear. Her eyes were dark brown and kind. Some doctors exude warmth, others confidence.

Dr. Cortez did both.

"No," she said, picking up her iPad and scrolling through it. "Says that someone dropped him off. Didn't even call for an ambulance. Didn't wait, either. Just dumped him out front and took off. An orderly just coming on shift saw him. Cameras would have caught whoever dumped him here. If the cameras were in service, that is. But they aren't."

Esther swallowed her frustration about the cameras. "How bad are his injuries?" she asked next as she watched the respirator pulse. "He's going to survive?"

Dr. Cortez held the tablet at her side and focused on Esther. "We're watching the swelling in his brain right now," she said, measuring her words carefully. She looked at her patient. "Somebody showed no mercy. Someone fixed it so that he'll need a urine drainage bag."

Esther blinked at that. "They didn't castrate him, did they?"

"Oh, no," she said. "They might as well have." She took hold of the edge of the sheet but thought better of it. "I'm not going to show it to you. Someone pounded this man's penis with a hammer or some other heavy object."

Esther couldn't think of anything to say.

The doctor was just getting started. "I know it's not my job to insert myself into your investigation," she went on, "but this is a hate

367

crime if I've ever seen it. And I've seen plenty. My own brother's gay, and he got ambushed by a couple of drunken teenagers a few years ago. He wasn't doing anything wrong, just went out to meet a friend. They beat him with a metal pipe. Knocked out his front teeth. Never caught the guys."

Esther said she was sorry. "I hope your brother recovered."

"It was a while ago," she said. "He's fine now. He says so. As fine as anyone could be if you live in a world in which some random person can just come and beat the crap out of you for fun."

"Did he make a report?"

"No," Dr. Cortez said. "Cal just wanted the whole thing to blow over. My brother's that kind of a guy. I begged him to tell the sheriff, but he just wouldn't. Didn't think it would matter to anyone."

"It matters to me," Esther said. "It matters to the other officers I work with every day."

The doctor nodded. "Thanks. I appreciate that. Times have changed. Or rather, they are changing. Don't let that happen to this guy. Okay? Find out who did this and put the bastard away."

Esther didn't tell the doctor that she was pretty sure this flavor of hate crime was directed at Mr. Collins because of his past record as a pedophile.

"I better notify his family," she finally said.

A nurse came in, and the doctor gave her some instructions while Esther waited.

"Good idea about the notification," she said. "I hate making those calls, but someone has to. Just between you and me—and them, I guess—I suggest they get out here as soon as they can. No telling how long he's going to last or what he'll be like if he survives."

"How do you mean?"

"There's very likely brain damage here, Detective. He may not be able to tell us who did this. If he survives, he might not even be able to tell you his name."

Esther went downstairs to check with hospital security. A young man in a dark blue security uniform with shoes that had been shined to a mirror finish greeted her with the kind of earnestness that indicated an interest in putting on a real uniform one day. Dr. Cortez had been right: there were no working cameras in the hospital. There hadn't been any for months.

"We're switching over to a new system in the first quarter of next year," the officer said. "Hospital administration didn't want to upgrade a system they were about to shut down."

She thanked him for his help.

"Hey, don't tell anyone about the cameras, okay? Administration doesn't want the word to get out. Thinks that we'd be a target for break-ins. I told them no one wants to come to a hospital unless they have to. But they remind me every day that we're a target for addicts who'll stop at nothing to feed a habit."

Esther sat in her car in the hospital parking lot as an elderly man helped his unsteady wife into their car. It was a touching moment, and she was glad for it. The world was turning upside down. She dialed Jake, feeling sick about what had happened to Brad Collins. She told him she was going to take a look at cabin 22 at the Pines to see if there was anything there.

"I need you to do something for me, Jake," Esther said. "I know this will be hard, but there are a lot of moving parts going on right now and we need to act quickly. I need you to call Brad's mother and let her know that her son's in very bad shape. She'll need to talk with Dr. Cortez to get the particulars. You let her know that we're going to do our best to find out who hurt him."

Jake took it all in. "All right," he said. "I'll call her."

"Thanks. Be sure to get the hospital's main number and give her Dr. Della Cortez's name."

"Esther?" he asked before hanging up. "What if this is related to what happened to Charlie Franklin?"

"I'm not following."

"Like maybe he got caught messing with some other kid. What if someone saw him do something really, really bad and just worked him over in some kind of vigilante move?"

"Anything's possible, I guess, though again, his record doesn't suggest he'd do anything of the kind. Even if it did play out like your scenario, would that justify this beating? We still need to work this assault just as hard as any other case, Jake. Even the bottom of the barrel deserves that. Our job, thank God, isn't to judge. That's for the courts. We're in this to round up the people who have no regard for the law, no matter how distasteful we may find their victims."

"Yeah," Jake said. "I knew that. Sorry."

Esther started to drive toward the Pines.

"Call his mom," she said. "Meet me at the office later." She hung up.

Jake looked up the hospital's phone number so he'd have it ready as Esther had instructed. Then he started to dial. The phone rang about ten times before Mrs. Collins picked up. He'd hardly gotten a word out beyond the fact that Brad was in the hospital when Mrs. Collins let out a wail that he was certain could be heard from Ohio to Oregon. It was so loud that he pulled the phone from his ear until she stopped.

"I'm really sorry to bring you this news," he said.

She cried a little more.

"Really, I am," he said. "I have the hospital's

number right here. Let me give it to you so you can call. Okay?"

"Thank you," the woman said. "I appreciate it. What happened to him? Was he in a car accident? He's not a very good driver."

"No, as far as we can tell he was assaulted. We don't know what happened but we're going to do our best to find out."

"He's going to be all right, isn't he?" she asked, spitting out the words one at a time as she caught her breath between her sobs.

"All I know is that it's very serious, Mrs. Collins," Jake said, trying to wind down the call. "You'll need to talk to the doctors at the hospital."

There was a slight pause on the line, long enough for Jake to wonder if the victim's mother had dropped the phone.

"Mrs. Collins?" he asked.

When she finally spoke, her words were choked with tears. "Did someone hurt him because of the way he is?" she asked, calming herself with a deep breath. "Is that what happened?"

"We don't know," Jake said, wondering if she meant because of her son being gay, or a pedophile. He couldn't see anything to be gained from asking for clarification.

Another longer pause. Mrs. Collins stopped crying. She said she was a caregiver for an elderly sister with cancer and it would take her a couple of days to arrange things to come to Oregon.

"It's pretty serious, ma'am," Jake said. "Doctor says to hurry."

She reiterated her responsibilities with her sister and said she'd get there as quickly as she could.

"He's a good boy," she finally said. "He really is. I don't think it's anyone's business who my son runs around with."

Liz saw Charlie's face everywhere. In the swirl of foam in her coffee. In the line of kids waiting for a turn to skateboard at the park. On TV. In Carole's eyes.

Especially in Carole's eyes.

Liz went for a run to try to bolster her weakened self back into someone who could—and would—do the right thing. As she ran, she kept coming back to how betraying Owen and her promise to him would only serve to visit more misery on an innocent party. He didn't deserve to have his world collapse because of what she did.

CHAPTER FORTY-NINE
MISSING: NINETEEN DAYS

Esther didn't need the help of the Pines office manager to let her inside the cabin where Brad Collins had been staying. The door was ajar, and she eased it gently open, looking around the small space—at the bed, the chair, the nightstand, the tiny kitchenette—to be sure that Brad Collins's attacker was gone. What she saw momentarily took her breath away. It was as if a bloody cyclone had rearranged the furniture and splattered red on the sheets. There could be no doubt that the man fighting for his life had endured his beating there.

She dialed Jake.

"We'll need some techs at the Pines to process the scene," she said. "Big mess here, that's for sure."

"Rage beating," Jake said. "That's pretty messed up."

Esther exhaled. Her blood pressure was up. "That idiot Massey should never have told the paper Collins's name," she said. "I told him how messed up that was. Might have made Collins a target of some vigilante. Wouldn't be hard to find him, drive around any motel and look for Ohio plates."

Her eyes landed on the phone jack that had been pulled out of the wall.

"Check with dispatch to see if any 911 calls were made from here," Esther said.

When she ended the call, Esther again scanned the room's wreckage. Yes, it was sadly possible that this was the work of some kind of vigilante, spurred by the media coverage of the Franklin case. But it could also be something totally random. Maybe Brad Collins met someone locally and things went very wrong. Maybe he'd tried to pick up the wrong guy—a vigilante of another stripe. While Oregon was very liberal, things were a lot more conservative in the central and eastern parts of the state.

"Are you sure you don't want tea?" Liz asked as she lowered herself into the sun-bleached Adirondack chair next to Carole's on the Jarretts' riverfront porch. Her eyes stayed on the gleaming surface of the Deschutes. Looking at Carole only made the bile in her stomach rise.

"No," Carole said. "Wine is fine."

Carole didn't seem to need or want any eye contact anyway.

"Charlie's out there," she said.

"I know," Liz said, pouring herself a second glass from the bottle she'd set on the deck next to her chair.

"He's coming home," Carole said, reaching

over to Liz but still not looking at her.

"Yes," Liz said, shrinking smaller and smaller. "That's right."

"Who took him? Who would do that to a little boy? What kind of evil do we have here?"

Carole was like a mother cat that had been dumped at the humane society not long ago. She stalked every corner of the facility, calling out and trying to find where her babies had gone.

"We don't know everyone," Liz said. "Not like we used to."

"Strangers come here for a good time," Carole said. "They come, they go." The alcohol was working its way into her system. Calming her. Numbing her. Not that Carole needed an excuse. "They take our peace and quiet with their drunken paddling, and then they take our children."

Liz took a gulp of wine. The bottle was nearly empty. She'd need more. They both would. There was likely nothing she could say to quell her friend's unbridled agony. She was a sham of a sounding board, and she knew it. She could nod. She could sprinkle a few words here and there to show her closest friend that she was listening. But there was nothing she could say that would even begin to approach the truth of what had truly happened.

"There's a special place in hell for those who harm children," Carole declared.

"Yes. I agree," Liz said. "We're out of wine. Stay here and I'll be right back."

Carole tilted her head backward and emptied her glass. "You're a good friend, Liz."

Liz slipped through the old screen door and made her way to the kitchen. She deposited the empty bottle on the counter and went into the bathroom. She turned on the sink tap the way some with shy bladders do to mask the sound of using the toilet. She gripped the edges of the pedestal sink and hung her head over the now-steaming water. The hot vapors primed her tear ducts. She stood there crying as quietly as she could. She looked up at her reflection, then swung the mirrored door open so she could no longer view herself. She would have smashed that mirror without hesitation if she could have done so without making any noise.

Silent screams are the most gut-wrenching of all. She deserved every bit of the pain that she was feeling at that moment. She was the most loathsome creature on the planet. The cause of Charlie's death no longer mattered. So what if it had been an accident? She'd killed the boy in her carelessness and weakness. So what if none of what had transpired after that had malice attached to it? Had she known that her effort to retreat and save herself would ultimately prove futile, she'd never have attempted it. But she had. It was like the tightest knot, a noose around her neck: there was no undoing what she'd done.

Owen's threats were a cobra striking her: "He's gone. He's over. You'll be over too. David and Carole will be in agony but they, too, will get past this. Our lives will never, ever recover. Think about that, Liz. Don't be so selfish. Doing the right thing means keeping this all between the two of us."

Her knuckles were white as she gripped the edge of the sink.

"You okay in there?"

It was Carole.

Her hands were superglued to the porcelain. "I'm okay," she said.

"Are you sure?"

"Something didn't agree with me," Liz said, flushing the toilet.

"Sorry. All right then," Carole said, her footsteps fading from the bathroom door as she made her way to the kitchen.

A bottle of pills beckoned from the medicine cabinet's center shelf.

All she had to do was open the cap, swallow them all, and tell Carole that she wanted to lie down. She'd set the stage for such a plan by saying she didn't feel well and by spending all this time in the bathroom. It would take a while for the Percodan to ease her away from what she'd done, but if Carole was the kind soul that Liz knew she was, she'd let her sleep.

I could leave a note. I could write something and stick it under my pillow.

She amended her plan. There was a chance that Owen would find the note and then he'd dispatch it to the trash.

Or maybe slip it into Carole's purse, she considered. That way only Carole would find it. Only Carole mattered anyway.

She steadied herself in front of the shuttered medicine cabinet. She was ugly in every way possible. Death would be a relief she knew she didn't deserve. Her suicide would truly be a selfish act. She only hoped that she could come up with the words that would deflect any blame on her husband.

She worked it out in her head, line by line:

Dear Carole and David,
God will never forgive me for what I've done. You won't, either. I want you to know that what happened to Charlie was a terrible accident. It was my fault. I didn't see him. I swear I didn't. I was backing out of the garage on the way to my test that morning and I felt a bump. I'm sorry. I just didn't know what to do. He was gone. I must have hit him so hard. I don't know how to explain what happened next. I panicked. I put him in the garage. I was

in shock. I don't even know who I was when I did it. I was a stranger to myself. Later I put his body out under the stars off the highway. I thought that someone would find him and that you would know he was gone. I loved Charlie so much. I love you so much. I never told Owen what I'd done. I should have gone to the police but I just couldn't. As I write this I know you will hate me forever. I am sorry. I really am.

Liz

She took the pill bottle and the idea for the note and went back out to the kitchen.

Carole was in tears. "I know you don't feel well," she said. "I just need someone to talk to. I can't get through this without you. Without someone."

Liz put the pills in her pocket. She put her arms around her friend.

"I'm sorry," she said. "I'm so, so sorry."

In a way, she was saying the words for what she'd done. The pills could wait. So could the note. She held her friend and they both cried.

Chapter Fifty

MISSING: TWENTY DAYS

Esther found Jake in his cubicle typing something on Facebook.

He did that a lot.

"If I can tear you away from that, we need to get going."

Jake jumped up. "Sorry. Just checking my feed."

Facebook. Twitter. Instagram and Snapchat. She didn't get the attraction of any of it.

"Dr. Cortez called," she said. "Brad Collins is conscious."

"Wow," Jake said. "I thought he was going to die."

"Me too. He might still. She says it's touch and go. This is our window to find out if he knows who attacked him."

Dr. Cortez intercepted the detectives just outside of ICU.

"We're taking him in for surgery. You have five minutes."

"That's fine. Appreciate it," Esther said. "Did he say anything to you? The staff?"

"When he opened his eyes—and honestly

they're still so swollen and bruised that I don't think he can even see much; maybe some light— he said something about how he wanted to see his mother."

"She's on her way," Jake said. "She had affairs to settle, then needed to take the bus from Ohio."

"That's good," the doctor said. "Too bad she couldn't be here before the surgery."

"Is he going to make it?" Jake asked.

The doctor didn't know. "That he can even speak is a minor miracle. And, to tell the truth, we don't deal much in miracles around here. Go in. Five minutes."

The sounds of the machines keeping Brad Collins alive filled the space around his bed. The bruises on his face had shifted from red and blue to a mosaic of purple and yellow. A no-nonsense ICU nurse hovered nearby.

Esther identified herself and Jake, telling the patient that they were there to help find out who had done this to him. She asked Brad if he could hear what she was saying, and he nodded slightly.

"Mr. Collins," she said, leaning a little closer to where he lay, "your mother is coming from Ohio. She wanted you to know that. She's on her way."

The man in the hospital bed gestured for Esther to come closer.

She bent down, turning her head so that she

could hear him better. He whispered in her ear.

"Charlie Franklin's father."

"Are you sure?"

He gave a slight nod and then closed the slits of his swollen eyes.

"I think he's had enough," the nurse said.

Jake looked at Esther. "What did he say?"

She told him.

"Holy shit."

"You can say that again."

Two minutes later they were in the car for the drive to David Franklin's restaurant.

"What a mess," Jake said. "Successful business-man. Seemed like he had his shit together."

"You say *shit* too much," Esther said. "But, yes, you would think."

Jake cracked the window. "He must have gone berserk."

"Uh-huh."

"Losing your kid—that's pretty heavy," Jake went on. "But Collins isn't our guy. We told Franklin that."

"Right," she said. "But for whatever reason he decided that we were wrong. He's not thinking clearly."

"Who could? You know, given the circum-stances. I thought about what I would do if my little sister had been taken and if I knew who did it."

"And?"

"And I thought that I just might want to beat the shit out of him."

"That word. We going to have to set up a swear jar for you?"

Jake laughed. "Sorry," he said. "My point is I'd want to get him to tell me everything he knew."

"I suspect that Brad Collins did just that. He told Franklin everything he knew about Charlie's disappearance."

"Which was nothing."

"And now look at Franklin. Talk about making matters worse. He's about to be picked up for assault. DA could charge him with attempted murder. Or worse. We don't know if Collins is going to make it."

"Wow," Jake said. "Losing your kid and then killing some poor SOB out-of-towner. That's bigger than making matters worse. That's creating a shit storm."

"That's a buck, Jake."

Jake grinned. "I barely make enough to pay my bills. Cut me a break, Detective."

She looked at Jake and gave him a half smile. She liked him. He was a nice kid.

"Okay. Grace period. Now let's go to Sweetwater and see David Franklin."

David Franklin was at the hostess's desk with Amanda when Esther and Jake arrived. David's eyes stayed fixed on the pair of investigators, and the life seemed to drain from his body.

"You aren't here for dinner," he said.

"No," Esther said. "I'm afraid not."

"Did you find my boy?"

Esther shook her head. "No. That's not why we're here. You know that, don't you, Mr. Franklin?" Her eyes landed on his bruised and scraped right hand.

"I couldn't stop myself," he said. "I was sure that freak took Charlie."

Esther motioned for the restaurateur to come from around the desk. "I need to see your hands," she said.

"What are they talking about, David?" Amanda asked. "What's going on here?"

"Can I call my wife?" he asked, refusing to look in her direction.

"From my office, of course," Esther said.

Jake retrieved a pair of handcuffs. They were still shiny and new, and he'd looked forward to clasping them onto someone's wrists from the moment they'd been issued.

"No, Jake," Esther said, shaking her head slightly. "We'll be fine without those."

"What's happening here?" Amanda asked again. Her voice had grown louder, and it carried past the hostess's desk. The two patrons sitting closest to the door looked up to see what the commotion was all about.

"Amanda," David said, his tone calm, words measured, "I need you to handle things until I get back."

She started to shake. "Where are they taking you?" she asked, pushing past the detectives and standing next to David. "What did you do? Did you do something to Charlie?"

He turned around just as he was about to be taken outside. He looked around the entrance to Sweetwater and then over at the young woman.

"Never," he said. Her words had stung. "Not Charlie. Not ever."

The next morning, Carole sat in the Jarretts' kitchen and stared at the paper. Her phone had gone off what seemed like a hundred times during the night. Some were texts from her husband, but most were media requests. She'd ignored them all. There was nothing left inside of her but the ache for her missing son. Everything else felt like a pile-on that was burying her. Bertie folded herself on Carole's lap and purred.

Liz emerged from the bedroom. She wore her running clothes; her hair was in a loose ponytail. Each day she felt worse than the day before. She knew how things would go. Carole would cry. She would cry. Carole would rage about David. She'd complain that the police weren't doing enough. She'd remind Liz over and over that there would be no point in going on without Charlie.

That morning, though, there was no instant litany of those same old subjects.

"What is it?" Liz asked, sliding into the chair next to Carole.

Carole tapped her finger on the screen of her phone, showing the latest post from the Bend *Bulletin*.

Liz read, occasionally taking her eyes away to meet Carole's.

Restaurateur Charged with Assault of Ohio Man

David Franklin, a popular Bend restaurateur, was arrested on suspicion of assault in the beating of Bradley Collins, an Ohio man recently interviewed by police in connection with the disappearance of Franklin's three-year-old son, Charlie.

"If this goes to trial—and we think it won't get that far—then David Franklin will be a very sympathetic defendant," said Stephen Richter, Franklin's attorney. "No one knows what happened to his son, and no one knows the kind of grief and distress that kind of uncertainty causes. I'd probably do whatever it took to get answers, too."

Franklin was released last night.

"He didn't, Carole? He didn't do this, did he?"

Carole nodded. "He did. He texted me."

"My God," Liz said. "I'm sorry."

"Me too. He's done now. When Charlie comes home, David will never be alone with him again. I knew he was self-absorbed. Selfish. A jerk. But I never thought he had that kind of hate or violence in him."

Liz set all of this in motion, and she knew it. She wondered if there would be any way out of what she'd done now.

"He was trying to find out what happened to Charlie," she said to fill the air.

Carole put Bertie down. "Doesn't matter. He almost killed someone. I can't see any circumstances where I could forgive that."

CHAPTER FIFTY-ONE
MISSING: TWENTY-TWO DAYS

From his DoubleTree hotel room, David could see the medical center. The sight of the sprawling building with the illuminated white cross made him ill. He'd been booked and released on bail that tapped the last bit of his cash reserves. Such as they were. All without a word from Carole.

She'd ignored his calls and texts.

He caught the sight of his bruised knuckles as he pulled the heavy curtain and took a tiny bottle of scotch from the minibar. He'd beaten a man nearly to death. For his son? For himself? To prove he was the equal of his wife, a former Google executive? He stared at the bottle, trying to decide if he should twist the little red wax cap and sink down even lower. He'd heard that Brad Collins would likely recover. If he did, it was a kind of gift that David didn't deserve. And though he didn't live and die on the patronage of local diners to keep the restaurant afloat, he knew that word would get around and people with a justified sense of righteousness would abandon Sweetwater. Whatever had been so important was ebbing away. His lawyer said the prosecutors would probably give him probation for a guilty plea.

"A jury will hate what you did, but they can be made to see that your anguish over losing your son was a mitigating factor," the lawyer said. "At least I think so."

He dialed Carole's number again, but she didn't answer.

I can't explain why I did what I did, he texted. I'm sorry. I'm really sorry.

A moment later, a text came back.

Sorry isn't enough. Bye, David.

Carole had been ignoring the calls from Washington Federal. They had been persistent and completely annoying. Whoever had been trying to reach her obviously didn't know that there were more pressing matters than whatever it was the bank was trying to tell her.

Finally, she could take it no more.

"Look," she said, before letting the caller say a word, "I don't mean to be rude, but now is not a good time. Please stop calling."

"I'm so sorry, Mrs. Franklin," a young man said. "I've been trying to reach your husband."

She wondered if the caller had seen the news. Her husband was unreachable because he'd been arrested for aggravated assault.

"He's indisposed," she said. It was the only polite way of putting his unavailability to a stranger, especially someone who didn't have a clue about what had been going on.

"Oh," he said. "But I have good news. I need to let him know that we've approved the loan we met about."

"I'm sorry, I don't know what you're talking about."

"Oh. The line of credit for Sweetwater."

"What line of credit?"

"Mrs. Franklin," he said, "you're on the paperwork. I see your signature right here."

"You do?"

"Right," he said. "The line of credit should keep the restaurant going until Mr. Franklin's TV appearance kicks off his platform. Exciting times."

All of this was news, of course. She knew cash was tight at Sweetwater, but David had insisted she didn't need to pull out any more funds to keep it afloat.

"I can do this on my own," he told her.

"It's our money," she'd responded.

"Not really, Carole. It's yours. And that's okay. I need to make a go of it on my own."

"Mrs. Franklin?" the loan officer asked.

Carole snapped back into the moment. "Yes. Sorry."

"Good. I thought something might have happened to you. The phone felt like it had gone dead."

Carole slumped into a chair. "No, I'm here," she said. "When did my husband meet with you?"

"Let's see. This has been ongoing. We've had several meetings. This is tricky stuff. No one wants to bankroll a restaurant. Not even in a cool place like Bend."

"Right," she said. "When was the last meeting?"

When he told her, the blood drained from Carole's face. It had been the morning of Charlie's disappearance.

David hadn't been out screwing another barmaid.

He'd been out fighting for his dream.

Chapter Fifty-Two
MISSING: TWENTY-TWO DAYS

Carole and Liz faced the Deschutes. It was dusk. They'd already emptied a couple of bottles of wine and a bag of tortilla chips. No salsa. Just dry chips from Safeway. The air had cooled. Liz got up and retrieved a couple of old coverlets that her grandmother had made during her knitting phase.

"Fall is just around the corner," she said.

"My favorite time of year, Liz."

"Me too."

"Charlie's going to be a pirate for Halloween," Carole said.

Liz took a breath. "Right. That will be great."

Carole sipped her wine. She didn't have to pretend not to drink to support her husband any longer. "I know," she said. "I think I'll make his costume. Last year was store-bought."

"That will be great, Carole."

A pair of mallards landed in the river, and the two women watched the ducks in the dim light.

"What's Owen up to tonight?" Carole asked, filling her glass. "Another meeting?"

"Yes," Liz said. "In a way I'm glad."

"I noticed things are tense between you two."

"I guess. Sometimes you need a break from

your husband." Liz looked over at her friend. "I'm sorry."

"That's fine. I know what you mean."

"Did you talk to David today?" Liz asked.

"No, not really. He texted. I don't know what to think of him. I don't know, no matter the reason, if I can be with anyone capable of so much violence. After he beat up Mr. Collins, I've wondered if he'd done something with Charlie. A fit of rage. An accident. But he couldn't have. He wasn't home. Charlie's gone because of me. David's in trouble because of himself."

Liz kept her eyes fixed on the water, which was turning gold and black. The picture in front of her was the same one that had been imprinted in her mind when she was a girl. The Deschutes was a gold-and-black snake flowing past the house, down to the bridge, then into Mirror Pond.

It looked the same. But it didn't feel the same.

She lifted her eyes from the water. "Dr. Miller must be sick or something."

"Oh? I hadn't heard." Carole looked across at the Miller place. "Maybe he moved without saying something."

"Maybe. But his car was there. No, he'd never leave that house. He was going to die there before selling it." She shook her head. "He's never out anymore. His yard is a mess."

"That's all he cared about," Carole said. "I wish he *would* move away."

Carole had become increasingly bitter as the investigation stalled. Liz tried to bolster her spirits, but everything she said hid the underlying truth of what she'd done. She was a fraud sitting there patting Carole's hand and telling her she'd be all right. For her part, Carole couldn't see anything good in anyone. Everything was negative. No one could blame her.

She'd lost something precious that could never be replaced.

Liz thought of reminding Carole that Dan Miller had lost a son too, but she knew it would come off as a tit for tat.

Carole only wanted Charlie home.

And that, Liz knew, would never happen.

"Never cared much for the man," Carole said. "All he ever did was complain about how big our house is. Funny, now I kind of understand, after staying here with you and Owen. A smaller place does feel more like home."

"Your house is fine," Liz said. "It's all Owen talked about after you guys showed up here with your architectural plans. He wouldn't shut up about it. Wanted to tear this place down that very night. Thankfully we didn't have the money."

Carole smiled a little. "God, you must have hated us, coming in and changing the way things are. You never think about the impact on others when you do something big like that. You just come in and do what you want to do."

Liz poured some more wine for herself. "It's fine. Really. I'm over it."

Carole stayed quiet for a long time. Another pair of mallards careened downward and planted themselves on the shimmering water as though replacing the first pair. The women watched in silence while the birds floated down with the river's current.

Carole got up and leaned against the porch rail overlooking the water.

"Wish we never came here," she finally said. "It was a mistake. We should have stayed in California. David wore me down. Told me it would be better to raise a family in a place like Bend. You know, a place where everyone knows everyone."

Liz joined Carole. "Bend isn't like that anymore. Maybe no place is." She put her arm around her friend. It was another of the rare times that they'd started a conversation that didn't begin with Charlie's name. In essence, he was in every word that Carole said. Although not by name.

"You think it will rain?" Carole said.

"Looks like it." Liz craned her neck so she could see the driveway. "I hear Owen's car. Let's go inside. It's getting chilly."

"You go in," she said. "I'll be a minute."

It was after 9:00 p.m. Owen set his keys on the table by the front door and watched his wife as she came through the old French doors that led to the river side of the house. By then Carole had gone to bed. She'd been going earlier and earlier. She told Liz that she thought that sleep was a better escape than wine.

"I talked to David today," he said, keeping his voice down. "He really wants to talk to Carole."

"You mean he wants to make sure he's got her money for his defense," she said, also in a whisper. Owen gave her a look that was meant to put her in her place, but she wasn't going to let him do that. "Don't give me that," she said. "It isn't the same thing."

"You could be where he is," he said. "With what you've done."

She wanted to throttle him right then and here. She wondered if that was how David had felt when he confronted Brad Collins. A warning. A twinge of fear. The kind of emotion that pushes you to a place you ordinarily would not go.

"You're agitated," he said. "We can't have that, Liz."

Just then Carole emerged from her bedroom. She made her way to the kitchen to get some water for the sleeping pills she'd come to rely on.

"Hey, Carole. Talked to your husband this afternoon," Owen said. "He's a wreck. Restaurant's empty. Looks bad. Says you won't call him back."

"Let it go, Owen," she said. "I want to keep my

focus on what matters to me. Charlie. Not David." She turned to face them from the doorway to the guest room. "I don't give a flying fuck about David. I know what he's about. I always have. That's my sin in all of this: not choosing a better man when it came time to finally get married and start a family."

"He loves you, Carole," Liz said, though deep down she'd doubted it.

Carole looked at the Jarretts. They were a young and beautiful couple. While they had problems, they weren't insurmountable. They weren't encumbered by the fight to have everything all at once. The way her husband had been.

The way, she realized, she had been too.

"David loves David," she said, her voice flat and husky from the wine. "He's never wanted anything that didn't move him forward in his dream. A little boy with a mind of his own never fit into his scheme of things. Sometimes I wonder if he was half-glad when Charlie was taken. It sure freed him from a lot of the annoyances that got in his way."

Carole returned to her room and shut her door.

Liz turned her attention to her husband, still standing where he'd deposited his car keys.

"We are destroying them," she said.

"Don't go there," he said quietly. He raised his hand and motioned for her to stay calm.

Owen always wanted her to be quiet.

"I promise," he said, moving away from her and to the kitchen. "It will be over soon. Anything to eat around here? You can't believe the lousy day I had."

CHAPTER FIFTY-THREE
MISSING: TWENTY-FIVE DAYS

Liz could no longer tell if there was something different about Owen or if it was merely the way she'd been processing everything since the accident. He'd told her repeatedly that she was being paranoid and that there was nothing to be done but wait out the police investigation. At night, when she would lie next to him, feeling the slight heaving of the mattress as he breathed in and out, she wondered how he was able to sleep. *She couldn't. At least not at night.* In the dark, she'd taken to moving from the bed to the sofa, then back to the bed, then back to the sofa again. Her movements were the manifestations of her guilt. She knew that. She was a nomad in her own home. An unworthy interloper. Each day she hoped for the resolution that her husband had promised.

His words played on an endless loop.

They'll find him. It will be bone-crushingly sad when they do. But it will be over. And it'll never lead to us. Not ever.

Liz had agreed to all of it. She knew she couldn't blame Owen for what she had done. She had been the guilty party. He was only trying to help her.

And still it wasn't right. In her heart she knew what they had done was every kind of wrong.

"We need to talk," Liz said one morning while Owen dressed for work.

"Can't it wait?" he asked, making a face as he noticed a small blemish on his chin. "I need to get to the office."

"I've been thinking," Liz said. "And, no, I don't think it can wait. It's about Charlie."

Owen drew closer. His face was hard, his lips tight. Although the bedroom door was closed, he looked around to ensure that what he was about to say was heard only by her. Then he grabbed her by the shoulders, a move that was meant to focus attention on his words.

Instead, it hurt.

"Leave it alone," he said. "Now is not the time."

"You're hurting me," she said, trying to pull away.

"Sorry," he said. "I didn't mean to." He relaxed his hands and let go.

He was lying. Liz knew it. Owen's grip on her shoulder was a reminder that she'd turned over all of the power she'd held in the situation. She'd given in. She'd acquiesced to his plan.

"I think I should tell the police what I did, Owen. I can't live like this."

His eyes drilled into hers. "That would be the biggest mistake of your life. Worse than what you did on the day of your bar exam." He didn't even want to say the words, didn't want to name the things they'd done.

"I'll say that *I* hid him," she said. "I'll leave you out."

Owen let her words hang in the air. He let out a sigh and then, a little more gently this time, led her to the edge of the bed.

"Sit," he told her, and that's just what she did. "We did what we thought was best. I did what I thought was best for you and our future."

"I know," she conceded, wanting to believe him. "But you don't know what it's like. The only thing that's keeping Carole alive is the hope that Charlie will be found alive. I can't keep lying to her. I can't keep pretending that hope is even possible . . . not when I know it isn't."

Owen softened a little. "Look," he finally said, "I get it. I understand. I hate it too. It's what we agreed to do. You can't go changing your mind, Liz. You have to be stronger than that. I need you to stay focused."

"If I told the police everything, except the part where you helped me—"

"They will put you in prison," he said. "They'll put both of us in prison."

"But I won't tell about you," Liz said. Her eyes welled up with tears, but none fell. "Not a word. I'll say it was all me, because it is all me, Owen."

"They will find out, Liz."

She buried herself in his chest.

"No," she said. "Not if I don't tell."

Owen could feel the tension in his wife's body, the wetness of her eyes staining his English Laundry cotton dress shirt. He gently pushed her away and looked into her eyes.

"If you tell the police—tell anyone—so help me, Liz, it will be the last thing you ever do."

The words hung in the still air. Liz wasn't sure if it was a prediction or a threat. Something in her husband's tone confused her. It was so matter-of-fact. So cold. She didn't exactly know how to respond.

Owen could see Liz struggling to process his remark. He'd gone too far, threatening her so overtly—though God knew, he wasn't bluffing. He could so happily strangle her right now. He'd walk it back a little, though. Set them on another track. "There's too much at stake here."

Still Liz was unsure.

"But it's the right thing to do," she finally said.

Owen put his hands back on Liz and held her.

"Babe, you need a sedative," he said.

Liz could feel herself falling into a black hole. Medication had been her husband's answer for everything since the accident. She had no idea where he got the meds. She'd taken so many pills, she wondered if she was on her way to becoming addicted to them. Before the accident she had judged others who relied on pills to get through the day. They were weak. They weren't able to cope with the challenges that come with life. Weak people. Sad.

Now she was one of them.

"I need to tell the truth," she said. "Owen, I need to end this."

"You can't," he said. "You'll waste away in prison. You'll never be a mom. All of our dreams will be over."

"Carole and David's dream is over."

"People like that get up, dust themselves off, and then forge a new life. They've done that with David's career. Google probably fired Carole. She started over. You and I are just beginning."

"Losing your child is not the same," she said. "I killed their little boy. Goddamn it, Owen. Can't you see the difference?"

Owen kept his arms around her, holding her tightly, imagining how much force it would take to end the conversation.

"You know that you don't want your mistake to bring me down, babe. You love me. You'll ruin me. Promise that you won't. That you'll keep everything to yourself. No spilling your guts. Okay?"

Liz pulled away. Her mascara had left a smudge on his shirt.

He unbuttoned his shirt and went for a new one in the closet. "That's my girl. We'll make it. Promise."

Liz was unsure if he was promising she'd survive or if he wanted her to promise not to tell.

Her phone pinged several times as Owen texted her later in the day:

How you holding up?

Doing the right thing sometimes means doing nothing at all.

I'll love you no matter what.

We are going to be fine.

Call me if you need me. Call me if you need me to talk you off the ledge.

For each one of her husband's texts she answered with a sad smiley-face emoji.

Liz had run out of words.

CHAPTER FIFTY-FOUR
MISSING: TWENTY-SEVEN DAYS

Liz stayed still in her RAV4 and stared straight ahead at the sign for the Bend Police Department. Her hands had started to quaver, so she tried to calm herself by gripping the steering wheel. Hard. Her knuckles went from pink to white. Every muscle in her neck contracted as she sucked in air.

She could do this.

On the drive there, she'd practiced what she'd tell the detectives. She would not implicate Owen. She would take the blame for everything. She imagined their responses and how none of what she would tell them would make sense. There would be no use in trying to win them over to see that she had made a terrible accident a million times worse, but the initial act had not been entirely her fault.

She'd leave out the Adderall and the part about how she kept the boy in the garage all day while she went to take the exam in Beaverton. She'd say she'd had a breakdown. It would be true. Or mostly true.

Liz considered how she'd hold her hands out so she could be cuffed. She'd ask to call her husband to confess to him what she'd done. In front of everyone, she'd beg him to forgive her. She'd let Owen out of everything, saying that he'd been so distracted by work that he didn't even notice her obvious reliance on sedatives.

Liz sat there and planned it all. She'd take whatever punishment the prosecutor gave her. She'd find a job in the kitchen of the women's prison, or maybe she'd be able to help the other inmates with legal questions. Maybe there would be some kind of purpose to all of this. Maybe her husband would want to stay with her, but she'd tell him to get on with his life. She knew that marriages don't often survive the truly horrific or the deepest of loss. Carole didn't trust David. She hadn't for a long time. As her friend confided troubles in her marriage, Liz could see that there had been a widening chasm in her own for a long time. Owen was wrapped up with Lumatyx. Late nights. Meetings out of town. Runs along the river that stretched into entire Saturday afternoons. But whatever was going on, he'd had her back. Everything he'd done after she killed Charlie had been done to protect her.

Before going inside. Liz texted Owen a message:

I stole Charlie's future. I promise I won't take yours too.

407

She pulled the key from the ignition and started for the door.

The receptionist at the front desk looked up from his computer, then went back to typing.

Liz could feel the sweat roll down her sides and her back. She held her purse as if it were a life preserver, close to her chest. She was sure she was going to vomit. By keeping the purse close, she felt she could control whatever her body was going to do.

"I'd like to talk to Detective Nguyen," she said.

The receptionist, a man in his late thirties, balding, with a gold hoop in each ear, barely looked at her as he tapped on his keyboard. "Detective Nguyen is busy now, but she should be out soon," he said. "Can you tell me what it is regarding?"

Liz thought of turning around and leaving, but stayed put. "Yes," she said, her voice catching just a little. "Charlie Franklin."

The receptionist's flat affect swiftly turned to keen interest. He studied Liz over the tops of his black-framed readers, tracing her features, noting her fragile demeanor.

"The missing boy?" he asked.

Just then Liz saw herself through his eyes. She knew she looked a fright, but there was nothing to be done about that. "Yes," she said. "I want to talk to her about Charlie."

He locked his eyes with hers. This lady was about to break down. He shifted uneasily in his chair. "Hey, are you going to be all right?"

Liz didn't answer right away. "I guess so," she said finally.

"All right, fine. Please have a seat."

It wasn't fine, of course. Nothing would ever be *fine* again.

Liz sat in a chair next to a silk ficus that needed to be dusted. A stack of magazines, labels removed with scissors to conceal the name of the subscriber, were fanned out on the coffee table. Her phone buzzed.

It was a text from Owen.

Are you at the police station?

She wondered how he knew that. She texted back.

Yes. I'm waiting.

Owen texted back immediately.

Don't do this. Don't.

Owen Jarrett didn't say a word to anyone. He grabbed his jacket and car keys and bolted from Lumatyx as though the place were on fire. Liz was at the police station. Holy. Fuck. She'd promised him. And now she was going to knife him in the back.

She'd said she was waiting. Maybe she still hadn't told anyone anything yet. Maybe there was time.

He'd installed a tracker on her new phone and been compulsively checking it the way some people look at their social media pages for likes and updates.

He'd known he couldn't trust her.

Esther looked at her phone and the message from the receptionist while the safety adviser continued with her mandatory training, highlighting the importance of bending at the knee and not lifting more than twenty-five pounds. The annual training was augmented by a video and opportunities for group discussion and role-playing. No one liked the session or the presenter.

The message stared back at her.

Woman here to see you re: Charlie Franklin. Seems like she's on the brink of a breakdown.

The training session would be over in ten minutes. If the end were twenty minutes away, she'd have gotten up and left. Ten minutes—she could wait that out.

The roomful of clock-watchers sprang to its

feet at break time. Esther motioned for Jake to follow.

"Someone's here with info on Charlie Franklin."

"Cool," Jake said.

The pair wound their way through the building to the reception area. It was empty.

"Carl?" she asked the receptionist.

"They left. You just missed them."

" 'They'?" Esther repeated.

"Yeah," Carl said. "She left with a man. Her husband, I think."

"Did you get her name?"

"No," he said, waiting a beat. "Something better."

He slid Liz's purse over to Esther and Jake. "She left this. Driver's license is in there. Was just about to call. Her name is Elizabeth Jarrett."

Esther took the purse and looked at Jake.

"We'll take it to her," she said. "Let's go."

CHAPTER FIFTY-FIVE
MISSING: TWENTY-SEVEN DAYS

Liz found herself letting the weight of her body press against the door as she looked through the peephole. It was as though she needed something to keep her from falling to the floor.

The detectives from the Bend Police Department were outside.

"Who's there?" Owen called over from the kitchen.

"The police, Owen."

Her husband hurried over to her and leaned into her ear.

"Don't ruin everything," he said. "I'll kill myself if I lose you."

"I won't," she said.

Owen reached for her hand. For a moment she thought that he was about to hold it, to give her some support. Instead, he pressed two pills into her palm.

"Take these. I'll let them in. Stay calm."

Liz nodded and disappeared into the kitchen for some water.

Owen opened the door.

"Mr. Jarrett," Esther said, "we're here to see your wife."

"What about?"

"Well, to be honest, we're not sure."

"She's not feeling well. She hasn't been feeling well for a while now. No surprise. It has been a very hard time for all of us."

"Right," Esther said. "Can we come in?"

"Like I said, she's not well."

"For just a minute," Jake chimed in.

"I don't see any point in it," Owen said, letting them inside and shutting the door.

"She was at the police department today," Esther said.

"Right," Owen said. "She called me to come get her. She wasn't feeling well."

"I see," Esther said. "May we talk to her?"

Owen was about to make some excuse when Liz emerged from the kitchen. Her appearance had changed dramatically since the first day the detectives had met her. She was no longer the picture of youthful beauty. She looked tired. Old. Her skin no longer blemish-free. Her hair dull. Even her outfit was at odds with the young woman who had been fastidious in her appearance. A food stain ran down the front along the zipper of her light blue jogging suit.

"Liz," Owen said, "the detectives want to know why it was that you came to see them today."

Liz stepped closer to the trio by the front door. Her movements were somehow both jittery and

413

slow. She was a machine that hadn't been used in a very long time.

"Right," she said. "I came by to see you."

"Yes," Esther said. "That's right. But when I came out to talk to you, you were gone."

"Owen's right," Liz said. "I wasn't feeling well."

"You left this," Esther said, handing over the purse.

Liz stared at the purse like it was a foreign object, thinking a moment.

"Thanks," she said. "Like I said, I felt sick."

Esther kept her eyes on Liz. "Are you feeling better now?" she asked.

Liz set the purse down and rubbed her temples. "No. Not at all. I think I need to lie down."

"My wife needs some rest," Owen said. "This ordeal has been very hard on her."

"Of course," Esther said. "But first, Mrs. Jarrett, do you mind telling us why you came to see us? Did you have some information that might be helpful about Charlie? Do you know something about his disappearance?"

"I need to lie down," she said. "I really don't feel well."

Esther persisted. "All right. I understand. Then why did you come?"

Owen interjected. "Can't you see she's a wreck? She's heartbroken. She wanted to know why the hell you people haven't found Charlie. It's killing her. It's killing Carole."

Esther ignored Owen. "Is that why you came to see me?"

Liz slumped backward onto the sofa. Her fall was hard, not a soft landing at all. Nearly a free fall. "What Owen said. I just wanted to see if there was anything we could do. That's why."

Esther didn't think so. "It's more than that, isn't it, Liz?"

Liz blinked, and her eyes rolled back into her head.

"Is she all right?" the detective said, turning to Owen.

"She's fine," he said. "She took a sedative before you came. That's how messed up she is by all of this. It's tearing her apart. You can only cry so much before you look for new ways to ease the pain. I think you both should leave right now."

"Maybe she needs a doctor," Esther said.

Owen got up and went to the front door. He swung it open. His movements were abrupt. "What she needs is for you to do your job," he said. "We all need that. Your department is the sorriest excuse for a police force in the state. Little kid goes missing and you do nothing. Shame on you both."

"Well, that was quite a show," Esther said to Jake on the way to the car. "Mr. Lumatyx doesn't seem to want his wife telling us anything."

"She's obviously fragile," Jake said, opening the passenger-side door. "Maybe he's just protecting her."

"That's what he wants us to think. He yanked her out of our office as fast as he could. She didn't even take her purse."

"Maybe she really was having a breakdown and he wanted to save her from making a public scene."

"He's all about appearances, that's for sure," Esther said. "Those jeans he was wearing cost three hundred dollars. The watch, four grand."

"That's a lot of dough," Jake said. "How do you know that?"

"I was married to a guy like that. Everything had to be the best. I wore the same three suits all week long and he had to have a new one every month. My ex was definitely an Owen Jarrett type."

"If she has something to say, what do you think it would be?"

"My guess is that she has information about Charlie's disappearance as it relates to someone close to her. I don't think she witnessed anything. She'd have told us that on the first day. Someone must have disclosed something or she found out something on her own. Look at her. She's a mess because something terrible is eating her from the inside out."

"I thought she was going to pass out," Jake said.

"She knows something."

"Like she's protecting someone."

"Right."

"Then who? Her husband?"

Esther started the car. "Maybe. But I don't think so. He was at work when Charlie went missing."

"And she was at her exam."

"Yes. My guess is that it all ties back to Carole and what happened that morning."

"You think Carole did something to her own son?"

"I don't want to think that," she said. "But we can't account for what she was doing after David left for work at seven and when she talked to the insurance adjuster. She had several hours alone with her boy."

"She doesn't seem to be the type," Jake said.

"The type never seems to be the type," Esther said, wincing at her words. "You know what I mean. You just can't ever know what's in someone's heart, Jake. Not based on how they look, the money they have, their education, whatever. Sometimes there's a lot of ugly behind perfection."

"Carole seems genuinely distraught."

"She does, I'll give you that. The truth is we can't know what's behind someone's emotions. Half the time we project what we think we'd be feeling if we'd found ourselves in the same dire situation. Empathy is often misplaced."

"That's a pretty jaded opinion, Esther. Sorry, but it is."

"I know. You're just starting out. Give yourself some time. What we see up close changes us."

Jake refused to be convinced. "A mother killing her own child? I just don't buy it. Not *this* mother."

"People said the same thing about Susan Smith and Diane Downs."

"Those were genuinely evil women," he said.

"Not to the people who knew them before their crimes. Before the outer layer was peeled off from their personas, they came across as normal, loving moms. Carole Franklin might be like that."

"You think Carole's guilty and Liz knows it?" he said.

Esther shrugged. "They are close. Carole's staying with her. Maybe she said something that got Liz thinking. Maybe she flat-out confessed."

"Well, Carole Franklin's not talking to us."

"Not at the moment. All roads lead back to Liz."

"We need to get to her when her husband isn't around," Jake said.

Chapter Fifty-Six
MISSING: TWENTY-EIGHT DAYS

Liz hadn't been over to the Miller place in a very long time. A decade. No. Much longer. There were times when she had wanted to stop by the place that had been the starting point for so many summertime adventures on the river. One summer she and Seth had it in their minds that they wanted to go inside the beaver lodge that slowed the river to the point where the surface was a sheet of glass a hundred yards downriver. They spent three days preparing for it. Jimmy ruined everything by insisting he and a baggie full of firecrackers would be just the right addition to their plan. He was kidding, he claimed, but the very idea of blowing up the beaver dam was too much for Liz. She didn't want to do anything that would hurt those funny animals. She'd only wanted a closer look inside their home and, truth be told, a chance to hold one of those tiny kits that she'd seen bobbing like glossy-furred corks near the lodge.

It wasn't Jimmy who changed things. It was the tragedy at Diamond Lake that morphed into an impenetrable force field between the two families. She'd thought of coming over to see

Dr. Miller to make amends for the part she might have played in the doctor's downturn.

She even managed to make it to the front door a time or two, but something kept her from knocking.

Not today.

Liz stood on the front porch, catching her breath from her run along the river. Running was the only way she could get away from Carole and Owen. Facing either of them had become more and more difficult. Carole, for what Liz had done to her child. Owen, for what she wanted to do to herself. As the days passed since Charlie vanished, she was spending more and more time alone. Seeing anyone, especially those two, only reflected back the terrible things she'd done.

The Miller house had been so quiet for weeks now. Save for the basement light at night, it almost seemed that the venerable old house had been abandoned. Three copies of the Bend *Bulletin* sat yellowing on the porch.

Liz scooped up the papers and pressed the bell.

No answer.

"Dr. Miller?" she called out, opening the screen door and knocking on the door.

The same Delft blue it had been all those years ago.

"Dr. Miller? Are you all right? It's me, Liz."

Liz tried to twist the knob, but the door was locked. Still holding the newspapers, she went around the house and peered into the garage. The car was there.

He has to be home.

As she made her way around the side of the house, Liz noticed a long, low shape in firecracker colors—red, orange, yellow—pressed down among the nearly spent daisies and daylilies. It was the boat trailer from the day of the flash flood. The long blades of the lilies arched over the long-flattened wheels. Had it been here at the side of the house since it was dragged back by the tow truck while she, Dr. Miller, and her brother were in the hospital?

Liz stepped through the overgrown garden and pressed her palm against the rusted metal of the trailer. Why had Dr. Miller kept that trailer after so many years? She'd have gotten rid of it right away. It had to remind him of the worst day of his life. The unkempt space was in sharp contrast to the rest of his yard, which up until lately had been garden-tour perfection. Here, she thought, was a space that he seldom visited.

She went to the riverfront side of the house. All of the basement blinds were drawn tight. She pressed her ear close to the back door. She could hear a faint noise coming from inside, but with a plane passing overhead, she wasn't sure if she was hearing a television or a neighbor's radio playing. It was very muffled.

Liz looked across the water. The Franklins' place: big and imposing. Her house: small and weak. She remembered all of the good times she and her family had had there. The fire pit sending sparkles of light into the dark sky. The taste of a hot dog roasted to a crunchy blackness. She thought of the time she and Owen had made love on the hammock, only to freeze into silence as some inner-tubers floated by. Standing there was like flipping through a scrapbook and feeling the blast of memory with every page.

Part of her knew that Charlie was the last page.

She turned away and started uneasily for home. There was nothing there for her, but something here seemed wrong.

Mrs. Chow, who had lived next door to the Millers for years, was unloading groceries.

"Tina," Liz asked, "have you seen Dr. Miller lately?"

The short, round woman with a penchant for gauzy shifts and six-inch heels gave Liz a quick nod of recognition.

"No," she said, moving a heavy bag to her hip. "I haven't seen him in a long time. A week? Maybe more? I'm not sure."

"I'm worried about him."

"I didn't realize you were close," the woman said. "He never mentions you."

Liz didn't take the bait. Mrs. Chow could be a negative force, and Liz didn't need that right now. She'd had plenty of that already.

"Well, he's such a fixture in his yard that I got

kind of worried when I noticed that his lawn hadn't been mowed. You know that he practically lives for cutting that grass."

Tina Chow shifted her gaze between the two houses and looked down at the lawn. "You aren't kidding there. I admit, the same thing crossed my mind. First thing I thought was that he'd had a stroke or something, but then I saw the Safeway delivery truck the other day. So I know he's eating. Not my place to get into someone's business. Not yours, either."

Again, no bait taken.

"Right," Liz said. "I didn't know that he was getting deliveries."

Mrs. Chow let out a sigh. Her bag was heavy, and the younger woman hadn't offered to carry in the groceries. She ruminated on how thoughtless the younger generation had become.

"Me neither," she finally said, shutting the car door with a swing of her gauzy hip. "Just started a short time ago. I was going to ask him about it but I've been busy and he hasn't been out messing around the yard. Sure hope he isn't ill or anything. Those greedy relatives of his will turn the old place into a rental, and I'll be stuck with frat parties for the rest of my life."

Liz thanked her and started walking to the street.

"Hey, any news on the Franklin boy?" Mrs. Chow asked.

Liz turned around. "No," she said. "Still missing."

The woman with the groceries made a concerned face. "Poor kid. Poor parents. Seems like the world's a decidedly uglier place these days."

Liz couldn't argue with those sentiments. Nor could she deny her role in the way things were. She thought about her RAV4. She would not keep that car. She would not let it be a monument to an accident the way Dr. Miller had made the boat trailer.

His car was in the garage. Had Dr. Miller become a shut-in? It was the kind of ending that Liz had imagined for herself once she was released from prison.

She'd shut herself in, never able to face another human being.

What happened at Diamond Lake had been an accident. What happened to Charlie had been one too. At least in the beginning. And yet the two events were very different. Only one of them was truly shameful.

Although she'd covered four miles already, she started running once more. Back to the park, along the river. She ran as fast as she could. She could feel her heart work so hard that she was all but certain she would have a heart attack.

That would be the easy way out.

Chapter Fifty-Seven
MISSING: TWENTY-NINE DAYS

The next afternoon, Liz looked in on Carole, who was lying motionless in the Jarretts' guest bedroom. Carole's silvery-blond hair was a snarled mess. A glass of water and those same pills that she'd pilfered to ease her own pain sat on the nightstand. The framed photo of her little boy that she'd clutched in front of the media watched over her.

"Carole?" Liz said, inching closer. "Are you feeling better?"

Charlie's mother stirred but didn't turn her head to look up. "I'm all right," she said, her voice a whisper. "Just sad. Just tired."

Liz perched next to her, her heart beating like a hummingbird's. She put her hand on Carole's and patted it gently. Carole stayed quiet.

Liz sat there looking around the room, remembering all that had happened. All that she'd done. She could hear some dogs barking by the river. A car backfired as it passed by. The low light from the autumn sun cut through the slats of the blinds and made a pattern of narrow bars over the bedspread.

Prison bars.

Everything outside of the bedroom went on as it always had. The river ran past the house, and the day was as beautiful as any day could be.

Inside Liz's belly, the pain raged. She could feel another wave of nausea as her stomach threatened to purge itself once more. She had stopped eating because nothing stayed down. Her throat was raw.

"I'm going to run an errand," she said finally. "I just wanted to tell you that I'm sorry and that I wish I could trade places with Charlie."

Carole squeezed Liz's hand. "I know," she said. "Me too."

Liz didn't say anything more. She'd save her true confessions for the police station and the detective who had been handling the case. She'd go back there and this time she'd tell the truth, because it was the right thing to do. She'd take it all on herself and see to it that Owen would survive this. She gave Carole's hand one last squeeze, leaned over, and kissed the top of her head.

"I love you," Carole went on. "I couldn't get through this without you. I'm hanging by a thread and you are the only one that is here for me."

The bile started moving up Liz's throat.

"I love you too," she said, her voice a constricted whisper.

Chapter Fifty-Eight
MISSING: TWENTY-NINE DAYS

Liz knew something wasn't right with her old neighbor across the river. She crossed over the footbridge. A light, lacy layer of snow had fallen and begun to melt. Bend could be unpredictable like that. Indian summers that can extend to October, or a snowfall that sends a flurry of skiers to the rentals that crowd much of the riverfront.

She stood at the Millers' Wedgwood blue door and knocked. When there was no answer, she reached up to the top of the doorjamb. Old habits like that seldom change. Seth had shown her the hiding place one time when his parents were gone for the afternoon. But there was no key. A living room window was unlocked, and she lifted it open. She stuck her head inside the silent space. A trio of suitcases sat by the door, arranged from largest to smallest. Liz wondered if Dr. Miller had been preparing for a trip somewhere but never made it out the door. He'd vanished from his perch on the deck or the yard that he tended so carefully. So obsessively.

Something's happened to him.

She called out for him.

No answer.

Something felt wrong.

Liz worked her frame inside, landing on the hardwood floor. She was concerned, and the concern for something other than herself, other than her dire situation, made her feel better. Stronger.

Something sweet permeated the air, and she followed the scent to the main bathroom of the master bedroom. What was that? It was pulling her into a dark, paneled space with a big tub and pedestal sink. A toilet commanded the far corner. Dr. Miller's shaving kit was placed on the corner of the sink. A white bottle of cologne with a sailing ship beckoned to her. Liz removed the red top and breathed it in.

Old Spice.

Before she could exhale, Liz was a terrified girl back in the station wagon on the day Dr. Miller drove them to Diamond Lake. The horse coming at her; its hooves shattering the windshield. The terrifying sound of the debris swiping at the car. All of it came at her. She was in the hospital. The angry and concerned faces of her parents. The lady police officer pressing her for a reason to blame Dr. Miller for what happened to Seth.

Liz put her hands on the sink to keep from falling.

She hadn't smelled alcohol like her mother's spiced wine.

Liz had smelled Old Spice.

Reeling, she left the bathroom and went to the kitchen. Everything was put away. The counters were pristine. It was as if the house were ready for a real estate agent to come in with a prospective buyer. Immaculate. Homey. There was even a full glass coffeepot. From the window over the sink, she could see her house and the Franklins'.

Old Spice.

Not booze.

He hadn't been drinking at all.

Tears came, but they were silent ones. The kind that fall without a person really noticing.

She breathed in and tried to pull herself together.

Where was Dr. Miller?

A million-dollar home that held traces of the family that had lived there, but nothing really personal. No pictures. A pair of mallard decoys sat on a small table under the old, yellow wall phone. She touched the coffeepot. It was cold.

As she moved from the kitchen, she could hear the sound of the TV playing in the basement. It had been a long time since she was down there. She stopped at the top of the stairs.

"Dr. Miller, are you down there?" Her voice was weak.

She heard some movement. The TV went silent, followed by the sound of a door closing.

"It's Liz Jarrett, Dr. Miller. I'm coming down. Are you all right?"

It was dark, and when she flipped on the light, she was blasted by a huge number of family photos. The stairwell wall was covered with them. It took her a minute to realize that she was looking at nothing but images of the Millers. It took her breath away. The photos seemed to show every moment of their lives on the river. Stunned, she stepped out of the room and looked around her.

Whoever had put them there—could it have been Dr. Miller?—had spent hours and hours doing so. Seeing it all brought tears to her eyes. It was a very sad labor of love. The family chronicled in that massive array was gone.

She ran her fingers over the images. The photographs were stapled to the paneling, forming a nearly seamless collage. One photo stood out from the others because it was attached with brass thumbtacks and was crooked, as if it had been hastily added. It was a picture of Seth and his father standing in front of the boat. Father and son stood grinning as Dr. Miller playfully mussed his boy's hair.

She couldn't be sure, but it appeared to have been taken the morning of the accident. Seth was wearing his *Have a Nice Day* T-shirt with the smiley face. The image of that shirt had been burned in her memory. It was the last thing she saw when Seth let her out of the vehicle ahead of him.

Saving her life.

Sealing his fate.

Suddenly, Liz wanted to get out of there. Just as she reached the bottom step, Dr. Miller appeared. He wore his customary khakis, Hawaiian shirt, and flip-flops. His white hair was uncombed and his eyes looked sleepy, as though he'd just awakened from a nap. He didn't say anything. He just stared at her, standing very still with his hands behind his back.

"What are you doing in my house?" he finally asked.

Liz didn't move. She was an intruder. A concerned one, but nonetheless an uninvited guest. "I'm sorry," she said. "No one has seen you in a while. I thought something might have happened to you."

His eyes narrowed. "You can see that I'm fine," he said.

"Right." She looked past him. The TV cast light on the side of the basement that was windowless. A rumpled crocheted afghan with zigzag multicolor stripes lay on the sofa.

"I didn't mean to wake you," Liz said. "I was worried."

"That's almost funny, you caring about any-one," he said. "You of all people."

She studied his face. *What was he getting at?*

"Do you need something?" she asked.

"I need you to leave," he said. "I need you

431

to get out of my sight. You make me sick. You and your revolting husband and those miserable neighbors, the Franklins. . . . You all make me want to puke. Now, get the hell out of my house."

"Sorry. I was just trying to help."

"You can help by going right now."

"Fine," she said, turning to make her way back up the basement stairs. Just as she took the first step, she heard a soft cry coming from behind her. She spun around. "What was that?"

Dr. Miller pushed her away. "I said get the hell out of my house! Do you want me to throw you out? Because I will. Just try me. I will do it and be glad to."

The cry again.

Liz cocked her head. The cry was coming from behind the door that sealed off the room where the family had kept their kayaks and bikes in the winter.

"What's going on here?" she asked.

The old man blocked her from coming into the basement.

"Get out," he said. "The sight of you—*all of you*—sickens me. But especially you, Lizzie. Every time I see you, I'm reminded of that day."

Liz moved down one step, defying him. They were now eye to eye.

This was a conversation that she'd imagined they would have had after the flash flood.

"It should have been you," he said. "I've held

that in a long time. I just wanted to say it to you and say it to everyone in this godforsaken town. Seth should be here. Not you."

"I know," she said. "I know. He saved me. Seth saved me. He shouldn't have and I wish that he hadn't, because he was good and I'm not good."

"You are despicable," Dr. Miller said. "You and your husband. What you did. I know."

Liz felt the air leave the room. She looked at the old man's face. His eyes were penetrating, cold. "I don't know what you're talking about."

His eyes stayed on hers. "I saw everything that night," he finally said. "I saw what you did."

Liz knew what he was getting at, but, even so, the look on her face was one of disbelief, questioning.

"The boy," he said.

"I don't understand."

"I followed you," he said. "You treated that boy like he was trash. You people have no morals. No sense whatsoever of what's right and wrong. You disgust me, Lizzie."

The cry once more.

Liz could feel those shifting sands under her feet again. "What *is* that?"

She didn't want to use the word *who* because she already knew.

He didn't say a word.

"What are you doing down here, Dr. Miller? What kind of craziness is this?"

"Really?" he asked. "You're going to say something like that to me? After what you did? You know what I did. You know who I have. Who I saved."

She did. The room shrank and the walls closed in. Liz could hardly breathe.

The old man was speaking. Liz watched his lips move, nearly in slow motion, but could not begin to follow what he was saying.

It just couldn't be true.

"No," she said, sucking in a gulp of air.

Suddenly, Dan Miller brandished a scalpel that he'd held behind his back. It shimmered in the light from the television set.

"You should have been the one to die, you stupid, worthless girl."

"It can't be Charlie," she said, her eyes now riveted on the knife.

"I found him where you and Owen dumped him," he said. "You two left him to die. I saved him."

"He was dead," she said, fighting to breathe in enough air to stay alive. She felt as though she were going to fall. "It was an accident."

The scalpel glinted.

"Not dead," he said. "A concussion. A severe one."

The sands shifted again. She was going to fall. She was going to let that man plunge that knife into her heart.

"I didn't know," she said. "I thought he was dead. It was an accident. Why didn't you take him to the hospital?"

He moved closer. Just a step.

"I found him," he said. "He's mine. You threw him away. His parents—if you want to call them that—care more about their cars than their own child. They never should have moved here. I wish to God that their ugly house would burn down."

Liz needed to buy time. She could feel a surge of strength coming to her.

"I hate that house too," she said, thinking that agreeing with him would calm him, stalling him for a minute or two.

But Dan Miller just laughed. "You covet that house," he said. "I've seen the way you have cozied up to those people. You and your husband are nothing but goddamn climbers with no regard for anyone. Only things. That's all you want: a pile of things."

"I didn't mean to hurt Charlie," she said, her tone suddenly pleading. "It was an accident."

"You were careless," the old man said. "You weren't watching where you were going. I didn't see everything you did, but I can add two and two. At first I thought that you packed him up and took him to the hospital. You should have done that. A decent human being would have."

"I was scared," she said.

Dr. Miller gave her a very hard stare. "You were concerned about something other than that little boy."

"I thought he was dead," she said. "I thought I'd killed him. I was sure he was dead."

"Soon *you'll* be dead, Lizzie." He thrust the scalpel at her, and she twisted her body just enough to avoid a slice to her heart. Instead, the blade cut into her shoulder. Red poured from the wound, and Liz let out a scream.

"You shouldn't have moved," he said. "I'm a doctor. I can make this painless and quick. You're going to die, Lizzie. And Charlie and I are going to leave here."

Liz felt a little woozy, but not so much that she couldn't fight for her life. She threw herself at the old man, and the two of them crashed to the polished cement floor. The scalpel flew from Dr. Miller's hand and skittered over by the door from which the crying had come.

The door opened a crack, and Charlie emerged. The sight of the boy took Liz's breath away. He was wearing pajamas. His head was a mess of blond, a little longer than the most recent photos taken by his mom. Otherwise he looked just as he had the day he went missing. He was healthy. Clean.

And alive.

At the boy's feet was the scalpel.

"You're going to die," Dr. Miller said, as he

wrestled away from her and started to crawl after the scalpel.

Liz somehow found the strength to go after him. She jumped onto his back and grabbed his neck, but she was too weak to choke him. She could feel her strength ebb. Dr. Miller rolled her roughly off him and scanned for the scalpel.

She looked over at Charlie.

Chapter Fifty-Nine
MISSING: TWENTY-NINE DAYS

"Don't let him get it, Charlie!"

The little boy, wide-eyed with fear, bent down and picked up the blade just before Dr. Miller's fingertips brushed the stainless steel handle. Charlie took a step back and slumped against the front of the TV, his small body silhouetted against its bluish radiance. He held the blade before him in both hands and stared at them.

For Liz, it was do or die. She launched herself once again upon the old man's back and drove him to the floor. She took the doctor's head in her hands and slammed it forward against the concrete as hard as she could. She imagined that his skull was a hard-boiled egg and that she'd crack it against a hard countertop, shattering the shell. Dan Miller let out a scream and blood poured from his head, forming a dark, viscous pool and mixing with his thick white hair.

"I didn't mean to," she said, pushing herself up and away from him.

He tried to raise himself, but succeeded only in rolling over. His eyes looked upward at her with a kind of fuzziness that suggested he couldn't see.

"Remember what you did," he said, and then his jaw fell open. His glassy eyes remained fixed on the ceiling.

What was happening? Was everything around her a dream? Or had the drugs Owen had been giving her caused her to hallucinate? She leaned over Dr. Miller, her shirt stained with his blood, and felt for a pulse. He was dead. She'd fought him to save her life, not kill him.

Charlie, who was suddenly next to her, said, "I want my mommy."

Was this a dream?

"I want to go home," he said.

Liz sat up straight and held him tightly. He was wearing pajamas. He looked fine. He smelled good. He was all right. She could feel a small lump on the back of his head, hidden under his halo of gold hair. Charlie was alive! This was real! And somehow God had given her a chance to make things right. The police would try to figure out how Charlie had ended up with Dr. Miller. Charlie probably couldn't answer that, but he would tell them what he knew.

She'd tell them.

"Honey," she said, lifting him into her arms, "I'll take you home. I'll take you to your mommy now."

Blood oozed from her shoulder, but she paid no attention to it.

"Auntie Liz," he said, "Dan's hurt."

"I know," she said. "I'm sorry. I'll call for help when I get you home."

Carrying Charlie, Liz opened the basement door facing the river. Adrenaline coursed through her body. Her world was about to change. Carole was on the porch, watching the river. It would be over now. Liz would go to jail for kidnapping or something along those lines, but she had not killed Charlie. She was not a murderer.

Not the killer of a little boy.

Dr. Miller? Well, that was another matter.

"Carole!" she called over the water, her voice charged with emotion. "He's alive! Charlie's alive!"

Carole ran down to the river's edge. She was frantic. Even from a distance, Liz could see that Charlie's mother understood what was happening, that her son was about to be returned to her. That everything she'd prayed for had come true.

He was Jaycee. He was Elizabeth. He was the trio of Cleveland survivors . . .

The water was high and moving swiftly. Carole was about to go in when Liz stopped her.

"No, Carole!" she called out. "Don't go in the water. Meet me on the bridge. Call 911. Dr. Miller had him the whole time. I think I killed him, Carole. I killed Dr. Miller!"

"Mommy! Mommy!"

Liz would never forget the expression on Carole's face as she put Charlie in his mother's

440

arms on the footbridge over the Deschutes. It was a look that somehow expressed disbelief and shock and fear and relief and gratitude all at the same time. Liz took several steps back, leaving them to it. Mother and son stood in the center of the span, the water of the Deschutes running beneath it a gray scarf being pulled out from under them.

Tears streamed down Carole's face.

"Charlie," she said over and over.

"Mommy," he said, "I was calling for you. Why didn't you come?"

Carole held him tight. She breathed him in.

"Honey," she said, "I was looking for you. I was looking for you *everywhere*. I didn't hear you. I didn't hear you call me."

"Liz hurt Dan," he said.

Carole noticed the blood on Liz's shirt, then the gash on her shoulder. "Liz, you're hurt."

"I'm okay," Liz said.

"We need a doctor," Carole said. She gripped her son but kept her eyes on her friend. "We need help for both of you. She saved you, Charlie. Liz saved you."

By then Liz was reeling. She could barely stand. She'd killed someone. This time she really had. Her heart was pumping so hard that her rib cage ached. Inside, she felt as lonely as she ever had. Her secret had eaten away at her, and she imagined she was hollow inside.

"I'm sorry. I'm so sorry," she said, trying to find the words. "There's something I need to tell you."

Carole pulled her gaze from her boy for just a moment. "You saved him," she said. "You saved Charlie. Let's go."

Still searching for the right words, Liz wanted to say more, but Carole wasn't having any of it.

"We need to get him to a doctor," she said. "God knows what's been done to him."

"Okay," Liz said. "Yes."

Liz watched as Carole nuzzled her son as they walked to their side of the Deschutes. Sirens could be heard in the distance and people had started to gather along the river to watch the stunning reunion between mother and child. The onlookers stayed mostly silent as police vehicles and ambulances converged on the scene.

"That's the missing boy," a woman said.

"It's a miracle," said another.

CHAPTER SIXTY
MISSING: NO MORE

Dan Miller's basement was a prepper's dream. The old man had outfitted the space with a pantry loaded with canned goods, a chest freezer full of food, and a storehouse of potential weapons gleaned from the garden shed and the kitchen. Knives. A saw. Hammers. It was a bunker of sorts. The techs had processed the scene, and the body had been removed. With just Esther and Jake left, the space seemed to echo.

Clean and spartan.

"What was he doing?" Jake asked, picking through the strange assemblage of weapons. "The End Times or something?"

Esther wasn't sure. "Maybe something else."

They made their way through the main living space. The couch had obviously been used as the doctor's bed. A pillow was placed squarely on one end, a crisply folded Pendleton blanket on the other. Shoes sat polished and waiting for his feet to slip inside. Everything was in order— except for a large bloody smear that indicated where he'd fallen and cracked his skull on the polished concrete floor.

"Never regained consciousness," Jake noted.

"Paramedics said he murmured something before flatlining en route to the hospital," Esther said. "Not sure what it was. They think it might have been something about Diamond Lake."

A startled look flashed on the young man's face. "That's where his kid drowned."

Esther nodded.

"You think this has something to do with that?"

Esther looked over the garden tools and the assortment of medical scalpels and kitchen knives. "Probably not. Don't want to overthink motive anyway. Let the evidence guide us."

"So we might never know."

"That's the way it goes sometimes."

"Not very satisfying."

A quiet laugh escaped her. "Satisfaction's a lot to ask for."

"Yeah, but not knowing why Dr. Miller would pluck a neighbor kid from his yard and hold him captive . . . I don't know, that's a lot to never know."

"Yeah, it is."

They entered the room where Charlie had been kept. Like the rest of the basement, it was tidy. The bed was made up with vintage *Star Wars* sheets and an old blue chenille bedspread. Mount Bachelor skiing posters were positioned on a honey-pine-paneled wall behind the bed. A gooseneck lamp illuminated the far corner of the space. It was a replica of a child's bedroom from two decades before.

"He was in the army," Esther said, indicating the hospital corners on the linens and a trio of towels on a nightstand. "That or prison time ensures a man knows how to make a bed properly."

Jake was glad his bed was sloppily made, when he bothered to make it at all.

Across from the bed was a stainless steel table arranged with an array of surgical tools and medical supplies.

"Jesus, Esther, do you think he was going to do something to that kid?"

Esther didn't think so. "He must have injured Charlie when he took him. I think he was doing his best to fix what he'd done."

They stood there silently for a second, taking it all in.

"I never would have thought things would turn out like this," Jake said. "I was sure that the kid was dead. I thought we might have messed up on Brad Collins and he was the real perp. Or Carole Franklin . . . the blood on her blouse. Her friend Liz maybe covering up something to help her. My mind even went there. Never would have thought the boy would be here all along, right under our noses."

Big understatement, she thought.

"No one could," she said finally.

Jake poked around the medical supplies while Esther dropped down to look under the bed. "What do you think Liz Jarrett wanted to tell us when she came to the office?"

"Maybe she had her suspicions about her neighbor," she said. "Maybe she felt guilty herself about something or other. Guess it doesn't matter now." With a gloved fingertip, she tugged at a paint-splattered tarp and slid it out from under the bed.

"What have we got here?" Jake asked.

"A tarp," she said, stating the obvious and in doing so making her young partner smile.

"Oh, that's what those things are," he said, playing along.

She made a face. "We'll need to have the techs at the lab look this over for trace evidence. I suspect it's what the doctor used to conceal the boy when he first had him. Sure doesn't fit in with the perfect order he's established here in the basement."

"No, it doesn't," he said.

Esther studied the tarp for a very long time. She looked up at Jake and then back down at the mottled fabric.

He leaned closer. "What is it?" he asked.

"This," she said, pointing to a splash of color.

It was a pink hue darker than carnation, brighter than peony. It was distinctive and memorable. It was the kind of paint color people used to let the

446

world know they were not cookie-cutter types but purveyors of their own style. She'd come across that hue somewhere before, and had just realized where she'd seen it.

"The front door of the Jarretts' house is this same color," she said, again pointing to the spot, the size of a dime. "I'm almost sure of it."

"I didn't notice," he said.

"That's okay," she said. "I could be wrong."

Inside, she knew she wasn't.

"What do you think it means?" Jake asked.

"I don't know," Esther said. "But it's odd, isn't it? Everything here is cleaner than clean . . . except *this*. This dirty old tarp. Why is it here?"

"I guess we're going to find out. Right, Esther?"

She smiled. "We're going to try."

CHAPTER SIXTY-ONE
MISSING: NO MORE

Della Cortez was holding down the last three hours of a twenty-four-hour shift when Charlie Franklin and his mother were brought in by ambulance. The whole hospital was talking about it and a score of staff members came to have a look. They'd all seen every kind of medical drama in their careers, and they were excited about this unexpected happy ending to the story everyone in Bend had been following.

Hospitals seldom are the site of good news.

The boy's vitals were all in good shape, but some faint bruising on the back of his head concerned the trauma doctor enough to order an MRI. Not surprisingly, Carole refused to leave Charlie's side even for a second. Given the circumstances of his disappearance and miracle recovery, the hospital staff allowed her to remain with her son.

"I wouldn't let go of my child, either," one nurse said to a colleague who insisted that the mother was in the way. "Look, you don't have kids, so you don't get a say."

A nurse inserted an IV with a sedative before the procedure.

Charlie didn't even wince.

"Where's Daddy?" he asked, his eyelids fluttering as the sedative kicked in.

"He'll be here soon," Carole said, although she wasn't sure if he'd even been notified. She hadn't tried to reach him. She didn't care if she never saw him again. In fact, she hoped she wouldn't.

"He'll be scared in there," Carole said quietly to the doctor, gripping her son's hand.

"No, he'll be fine," Dr. Cortez said. "He won't even know the MRI is being done."

Charlie's mother didn't let go until the very last moment as the radiologist wheeled him through the double doors to the exam.

"He'll be out in twenty minutes," Dr. Cortez said.

Carole wrapped her arms tightly around herself and stood there, facing the doctor, her mind playing back every beat of the ordeal that had started with the phone conversation with the insurance adjuster. Deep down she knew that all of what had happened had been her fault. No matter what anyone said. She had left him alone. She had turned her back long enough for someone to take him.

And it hadn't been a stranger at all.

It was the man across the river.

"Who takes someone's child?" she asked the trauma doctor, a sanitized version of her thoughts.

"I couldn't begin to tell you, Mrs. Franklin," she said. "But Charlie's safe now. He looks good. He's young. He's healthy. He's back where he belongs." The doctor motioned to a nearby chair. "Please sit," she said. "This will be all right."

Carole brushed her fingers to her lips. "No, I'll stand. I'll wait right here." She planted herself outside the double doors, her eyes trained on the empty hallway beyond the glass. The weeks of the ordeal had beaten her down, her skin, her hair. She no longer looked put together. Yet no one who observed her at that moment saw anything more than the happiest mother on the floor.

The results of Charlie Franklin's MRI came shortly before Esther and Jake arrived at the hospital in search of Della Cortez. They found her just outside the room where the little boy was resting, his mother by his side.

"Is he going to be all right?" Esther asked after peering in the open doorway.

"Outside of a head injury, he's fine," Dr. Cortez said. "Well nourished. Clean. Obviously not victimized, at least in any physical way."

"No signs of abuse?" Esther asked.

"None."

"So why did that freak take him?" Jake said.

The doctor looked at Jake. "That'll be your job to figure out."

"The MRI," Esther said. "What does it tell us?"

The doctor picked at the film. "He was hit. It's been a while, but there's definitely the shadow of some bruising on the front and back of his brain. All of our brains float. Kids, even more so. It's a coup-countrecoup injury."

"What did he say?" Esther asked. "How's his memory of what happened to him?"

"Gone for the time being," the doctor said. "Maybe forever. It's missing from the time he was hit and abducted to the time he came to, and about the same amount of time prior to his injury. Retrograde amnesia is hard to understand. We just don't know enough about it."

"You mean he won't be able to tell us what happened to him?" Jake asked.

Dr. Cortez shook her head. "Not impossible, but I doubt it. I've seen cases like this before. Car accidents, a few serious assault cases. People forget everything in a window that's defined by the length of time they were unconscious and backward for the same amount of time prior to the incident."

"So he won't be able to tell us anything," Esther reiterated.

"My guess—and, again, it's only a guess—is no. While healed for the most part, his concussion was a severe one. Closed-head injuries like his are hard to understand because you just can't see how bad they are. A lot goes on hidden in the skull."

Esther looked at the scan, her eyes traveling over the areas of gray and black, stopping where the doctor indicated trauma had been picked up on the film.

"Not knowing what happened can be a great gift for some people," Dr. Cortez said. "That way they don't have to relive it over and over. Charlie is going to be fine. His family's a shambles, but that's another story. The boy will survive this. Kids are resilient. Adults can be another matter."

Esther thought of Dan Miller. He hadn't suffered a brain injury at Diamond Lake. Yet from what Liz Jarrett had reported to the officers who arrived first on the scene after finding Charlie, he'd never been able to get over what happened the day he left Bend with his son and a couple of neighbor kids for a day on his boat. It had been an enduring hurt festering below the surface.

"He told me that the biggest mistake he ever made was saving me instead of Seth," Liz had said. "By taking Charlie, maybe he thought he had the chance to finally undo what happened."

Chapter Sixty-Two
MISSING: NO MORE

Liz sat on the edge of the bed. Her shoulder injury from the battle with Dr. Miller had required just five stitches. The scar would be a lifelong reminder of what had happened. As if she'd ever need one. Owen had picked her up at the hospital and brought her home to change. She'd said almost nothing on the way there.

He sat beside her. "You're in shock," he said, patting her knee. "We both are."

She didn't respond. She just sat there, replaying everything in her mind and still unable to make sense of any of it.

"Dr. Miller saw us," she said at last. "He saw what we did, Owen."

Owen slid next to Liz and put his arm around her. She could feel the weight and warmth of his body, but it transmitted nothing to her. No comfort, no assurance. Nothing at all.

"And he's dead, Liz."

"Charlie's alive."

Owen persisted. "And he's a very little boy. What does he know? Really, what *could* he know? He was out cold when we put him in the field."

Alive, she thought. *He was alive.*

"He doesn't remember anything," he said.

Liz studied her husband's eyes. *Who is this man?* "That's now," she finally said. "He might remember later."

"He's only three." He was in salesman mode. "He won't be able to make sense of any of it. He's been traumatized. He's too little to put it together . . . and even if he could, no one could make sense of it. We're free."

Liz lowered her eyes and gazed at her lap. She pressed her hand against her stomach. She felt sick inside.

"Dr. Miller is dead," she said.

Owen relaxed his arm. "And thank God he is," he said. "He was a whacked-out weirdo. He was the only one who could put the pieces together. I'm not sorry he's dead."

Her feeling of nausea passed. "He thought he was doing right, Owen. He thought that he could somehow fix the past by taking care of Charlie."

"You can't fix the past. You can only go forward. We're going to do that."

"David is going to prison. That's on us."

"No. No, it isn't. It was a choice he made."

Liz turned to face him. "Because you told him about Brad Collins. Don't lie to me. I know you were doing what you do best, Owen. A button pusher. That's you."

"You're not thinking clearly," he said.

There was truth to that. Her mind had been firing nonstop since the fight in the basement. She knew it was all real, but she didn't feel like herself at all.

"Maybe," she said. "But I know for certain that what I did ruined David and Carole's lives. It was me, Owen. I was the one who started all of this."

"Right. I'll give you that. You also ended it."

Salesman again.

"Did I?" she asked. "Because it doesn't feel like I ended anything. Not for anyone. I can still see Charlie wrapped in that tarp. How could we have done that when he was alive? How could we have done that *at all?*"

"You need to stop thinking about this," he said. "It's over."

Liz knew better. She knew that it would never really be over. It would be like Diamond Lake, haunting her for the rest of her life. The lie would grow into a disease. Cancer, probably. It would come for her when she least expected it.

Although she would always know it was on its way.

Owen undressed for the shower. "We'll need to go back to the hospital," he said. "Carole will expect us to be there. They are keeping Charlie overnight."

"I can't face her again," Liz said.

"You have to," he said. "You are the hero. The press will be there. So will the detectives. You'll have to pull yourself together, Liz. This is done. You've been handed a gift. We both have. This is a happy ending."

Owen stepped out of sight into the bathroom and turned on the water. The old pipes creaked, and he stepped inside the shower.

It didn't feel happy. Not at all.

Liz picked up Owen's expensive jeans, which he had left in a heap on the floor. They were his favorite, dark dyed and not too skinny. She removed the leather belt and coiled it to place it in the top drawer. She'd grown to hate him since the accident. Shifting the contents of the drawer, she noticed some paperwork underneath his growing collection of cashmere and cotton socks. Her husband was becoming a clotheshorse. He dressed better than she did. He told her that he had to look the part.

"Dress for what you want to be," he'd said.

She'd wanted to be a lawyer. She would never be that.

A quarter-folded sheet of light blue paper caught her eye. She recognized it immediately as the stationery that Owen had bought for her birthday the year before. "Almost a dollar a sheet," he had said, in that grandiose way he had about certain things. It was teasing but true at the same time. "Don't waste it on shopping lists."

What was it doing there?

She looked over her shoulder at the bathroom

door as the water in the shower poured over her husband.

It was a typewritten note.

I'm sorry for all the pain that I've caused. I am a failure as a wife and friend. I no longer want to be a burden to anyone.

Her signature concluded the short missive.

Liz heard Owen pull the curtain back and step out onto the mat. She could feel her heart race.

Although she had imagined killing herself and even planned to do so, she'd never actually written a suicide note. She'd never taken that concrete step toward truly attempting what she thought was her only way out.

To save Owen.

To ease Carole and David's enduring heartbreak.

To fade away.

She sat there until Owen emerged, a towel wrapped around his waist. She turned and faced him, the slip of paper now unfolded in her hand.

"What is this, Owen?"

"I don't know," he said, running his fingers through his damp hair.

"Don't lie to me, Owen. You wrote a suicide note. For me. Why would you do that? What were you going to do to me?"

"Liz," he said, "calm down. I wasn't going to do anything. I thought you were going to kill yourself. You talked about it. I was thinking that if you did, then you should say something. You know, I thought you would want it that way. And you know they always blame the husband. I had to protect myself in case you didn't leave a note."

There he was again, doing what he did best. Lying. Looking for a solution that would sound good to others and absolve Owen of any blame. Liz was sure everyone at Lumatyx hated him.

"You wanted me to die," she said. "You were probably hoping the whole time that I would end it all so you could play the victim card and move on with your life. All that money. A dead wife. That's what you wanted, Owen."

"I didn't want a dead wife. I didn't want to lose everything. You did all of this to us and— yes, all right, I really did think that if you killed yourself . . . well, that it would be all right."

"How would it be all right?"

"I thought you killed Charlie. I thought we'd never, ever be able to undo that. If you killed yourself, out of guilt for what you'd done, I'd be able to move past all of this. Don't blame me. None of this is my fault. All of this is on you."

Liz could feel the blood drain from her face. "Owen, why did I even fall in love with you? I don't know who you are. You can't have changed so much from that man I married."

"Honey," he said, reaching for her. "I am the

man you married. I didn't know what to do. I was just trying to survive. Is that so wrong?"

"You wanted me dead, didn't you?"

"I didn't," he said. "I can't lie. You know me."

"Lying is all that you do, Owen. You must have been very disappointed that I'm still alive."

"No," he said, trying to hold her. She stepped back and held her hand out to stop him. "This is our chance to start over."

"We had our chance," she said. "We're done. You're going to leave soon. Not right away. I don't want anyone to make a thing about our breakup."

"What breakup?" he asked. "I don't get you at all. We're home free."

She sucked in some oxygen. It was like she could breathe for the first time.

"I want to be free of you," she said. "I know that you wanted me dead. I know that this whole thing was about your job at Lumatyx. The money. Well, it's not going to happen."

"You're insane," he said. "You've gone off the rails. I'm not going to be pushed around by the likes of you."

Liz didn't say anything for a long time. She just looked at the man who had played upon her weaknesses for his own personal gain. They had no marriage. He had a career path. The path to the big house on the river. He wanted to be like the Franklins.

"You don't even like me, Owen," she said.

"That's not true," he said. "I love you."

"You love yourself. There isn't room for you and me in this marriage."

"Fine," he said, his anger controlled but rising a little. "You stupid bitch. The only thing going for you was your looks, and we know those are fading fast. Pill popper. Boozer. It shows on your face every time you look at me."

"I took those pills because you gave them to me."

"Blame me. Fine. That's how weak you are."

"I *was* weak. I'm not now. I'm drawing a line, and I'm not going to budge past it. You are going to leave Bend for good."

"That's crazy," he said. "My job's here."

"You'll quit your job."

"No, I won't. Not going to happen. I'm about to get a shitload of stock, and I'm not going to leave that on the table."

"You *will* leave it," she said. "Or you will go to prison."

"What the hell are you talking about?"

"That night when we left Charlie out in the middle of nowhere, my phone accidentally took a picture of you, Owen. Remember that flash? It shows you carrying Charlie, his arm dangling out of the tarp."

"You're lying."

"Why would I lie?"

"There is no photo. We got rid of those phones."

"And you're the high-tech expert. The cloud, Owen. The photo was stored on the cloud. I sent it to my law professor. He's agreed to represent me if I need help in the future."

"You wouldn't do that," he said.

"I would and I have done it."

"You're bluffing!" he said.

"Want to bet?" she asked, finding some long-missing strength in herself. "Want to bet your life? You're going to resign from Lumatyx and you're going to leave town, or you'll go to prison for kidnapping and attempted murder."

Owen tightened his jaw. "No one will ever believe that I had a thing to do with what happened to Charlie. Besides, you were the one who killed him."

"He isn't dead, remember?"

Owen started pacing. Liz could see that his mind was working on what to say. What to do.

Looking for something to hit me with? A belt to strangle me with? A razor to slit my throat with? All of those things would require him getting his hands dirty. *Owen doesn't like to do that.*

"I could kill you right now, Liz," he said. "You've failed at everything you've tried to do. No one would give a shit if I did."

His true colors were ugly, but he had a point. Owen was always expert at pointing out her faults, be it with her relationship with her

461

brother—tenuous at best—or the fact that she'd failed the bar.

Technically, twice.

"Least of all me, Owen," she finally said. "The truth is I'm not sure I'll be able to live with everything I've done. None of it will ever leave me. I expect it will catch up with me. You, you're different. It didn't take but a single criminology class for me to understand you, though it's taken me a long time to face it. Who wants to admit they married a sociopath? But that's just what I did. Everything that comes from your lips is a lie. You'll start over. You'll do fine. You'll get that money. But you're not going to get it here."

"I'll drag you down with me if you mess with me," he said.

Liz wanted to laugh, but she didn't. Nothing about what happened to Charlie, the Franklins, Dr. Miller, and Brad Collins had been funny. "Owen, you'll quit Lumatyx and you'll leave Bend. If you don't, you'll go to prison and, as pretty as you are, I'm sure you'll make plenty of new friends there."

Owen stormed out, slamming the door so hard that Liz's grandmother's china hutch shuddered and a Blue Willow teacup fell to the floor.

She went over to pick up the shattered pieces. One piece at a time. Her own guilt and fear had made her a prisoner. Had made her weak. But in that moment of confrontation, Liz Jarrett had used one of her husband's most cunning methods of control.

She'd lied.

She'd never contacted any professor. There was no photo on the cloud.

CHAPTER SIXTY-THREE
MISSING: NO MORE

Within a few hours of Charlie's discovery in a neighbor's basement, the story of "Bend's Miracle Boy" was all over the Internet. News media trucks from Portland and Seattle had already staked out prime real estate at the hospital and along the street in front of the Franklin house. To all of the reporters' disappointment, there wasn't anyone central to the case available for a live shot. David was back in the kitchen at Sweetwater. Liz and Carole were at the hospital with Charlie. The police weren't talking. Not even the hospital spokesperson would comment.

The only one available was Owen, who'd left work because Damon had said the media was a distraction.

"And, really, shouldn't you be with Liz?" he asked.

Damon was marginalizing him again.

"But we have a conference call."

"You're optional. Now, do the right thing. Go home. I have it covered here."

Damon is a prick.

Despite the elated mood among the reporters

464

and the people on the street, Owen's countenance was grim. Sweat collected at his temples. He'd rather be anywhere but there. He'd especially rather be on the conference call to make sure Damon West didn't throw him under the bus.

He was speaking to the press only to get everyone to go home.

"The family is grateful for the return of their son," Owen said, gazing over the reporters and onlookers to avoid really looking into anyone's eyes. "My wife is not a hero but a messenger of hope that good has triumphed over evil and a little boy has been returned to his parents. Please leave and respect the privacy of all involved."

That last part was really his true message. To Owen's way of thinking, everything had become far more complicated since Charlie's miracle return. Directing the narrative was a feeble attempt to right a sinking ship. Everything would have been better if Charlie had died.

The kid has more lives than a cat, he thought.

Carole's phone pinged with a text from David.

Please let me come.

She took a breath and tapped out two letters.

OK.

He wrote:

Thank you.

Carole looked at their son, now sleeping in the hospital bed. She could see a little of David in his eyes. He was his father. He always would be. She patted the boy's warm little hand and then turned back to her phone to type a message.

It doesn't change anything between us. He's your son. You'll need to act like a father from now on. Room 346.

Liz stayed out in the hallway, thinking of what she'd say when she went into Charlie's hospital room. A couple of reporters tried to get her attention from an area just past the nurses' station, a horseshoe-shaped configuration that effectively corralled the media away from its most sought-after interview subject. She nodded politely when she inadvertently made eye contact with a woman from the Bend *Bulletin*. She hoped to God that she wouldn't have to say anything to anyone.

A young nurse came out of Charlie's room. "Mrs. Franklin needs you to come in."

"She does?" Liz asked. "Now?"

"Yes. Go right in."

Liz's hands started to shake, and she put one in her pocket. *It's over,* she thought. *Charlie*

466

must have remembered something and told it to Carole. Slowly she entered the room.

"Liz," Carole said very calmly from her place on the bed next to her little boy. Charlie was awake but quiet. Someone had given him a stuffed dinosaur, and he clutched it in his little hands. "You did this."

Liz's heart nearly jumped from her chest. She was going to die. Right there in a hospital. Carole knew! *I deserve everything that happens to me now,* she thought.

"I'm sorry, Carole," Liz said. "I'm so, so sorry." Her knees were weak, and she could feel her bones crumbling in her legs. She nearly lost her balance.

"Come here," Carole said, getting up and extending her arms. "We're all going to be okay. You did this, Liz. You made all of this happen and I will never, ever forget it. If not for you, Charlie might be gone forever."

Liz felt herself melt into her friend's embrace.

"How is he?" she asked.

"Doctor says he's fine," Carole said. "Scared. Confused. But fine."

The boy looked up at Liz and smiled. She smiled back. Inside, she could feel the horror of what she'd done rise up. Charlie was alive. She'd ended a tragedy that she'd ignited that day she backed out of the driveway. She wondered why she couldn't feel any real joy.

Shouldn't she?

Chapter Sixty-Four
TEN DAYS AFTER BEING FOUND

More than a week after the Bend miracle filled pages of newspapers and the feeds of bloggers and news sites, Esther still couldn't shake the loose ends of a case that continued to trouble her. She reviewed the tape that canoeist Matt Henry had made on his GoPro. It suggested that Dan Miller had been on *his* side of the river when the boy was abducted. It was possible that he'd come across the bridge and scooped up Charlie, but surely someone would have seen him. Plus the man was in his seventies. Physically, was he able to do what needed to be done? To carry a boy? Quiet a boy? Make sure that he got him home unnoticed?

And in broad daylight, no less.

It seemed like all kinds of impossible. And yet, there could be no other explanation for what ultimately occurred among the neighbors on the river. It was a fact that Charlie had been rescued from Dr. Miller's house. It was true that the three-year-old had been held captive there. That was undeniable.

She flipped through the reports that littered the top of her desk. Dr. Miller was dead. Liz

Jarrett had killed him. She'd told Esther and the responding officers that she fought for her life. There was no arguing that she'd been injured. There was no way to deny that she'd saved Charlie and brought him home.

But how? How was it that Liz was over at the doctor's house?

"I was worried about him," she had said. "I thought something happened to him. He'd pretty much vanished."

Jake poked his head into Esther's office.

"You look deep in thought," he said. "How about shutting it down along with the rest of us and going out for a beer after work? Decompress a little?"

Esther smiled faintly. "I need to take care of some things."

The young man looked down at the papers in front of his mentor. Among the documents were the DA's statement that Liz Jarrett had acted in self-defense when she killed Dr. Miller. She would not be charged with anything.

"You're still on the case," Jake said.

Esther picked up Charlie's photo. "I guess. Can't help it. When I step back a little from it, I still see a spiderweb." She tapped on the boy's face with her fingertip. "Charlie's in the middle. Carole and Liz and Owen and David are all caught up in it. Off to the side, we have Brad Collins and Dan Miller. All spun up. All of them."

"How do you mean?"

"We know that Owen told David he'd seen an Ohio plate at the park."

"Yeah, right. So?"

"I don't know," she said, still trying to work it all out. "I mean, David told his lawyer that the tip about the park was what had convinced him to go after Collins. Yet Collins never said he'd been at Columbia Park. If he had, he would have told us. He isn't a liar. No, I'm thinking Owen Jarrett fired David up and sent him after Collins—with a lie. Why would he go to the trouble of doing that?"

Jake pressed the side of his head against the doorjamb. "Or maybe he just saw some other Ohio plate at the park."

"Maybe. Maybe." She sat still for a moment. "And then there's Dr. Miller . . ." She fumbled through the photos and picked up the autopsy report.

Jake really wanted that beer, but Esther was working things out and he knew he had a lot to learn from her. "What about him?" he asked.

Esther looked up. "It doesn't make sense, Jake. I don't know why that old man would snatch that boy. But then again, my spiderweb. As you know, Liz had a history with Dr. Miller."

She pointed to the news clipping about Seth Miller's death.

"Right," Jake said. "The drowning of his son."

"Not just that," Esther said. "I mean, that too. Also the tarp. The tarp we found underneath the bed at Miller's house. How did it get there?"

She got up to retrieve the tarp from a box behind her desk. With Dr. Miller dead, there had been no criminal case to pursue. No real chain of evidence to consider from the artifacts found in the Miller basement.

"I get that the paint color matched the Jarrett front door, but so what? They probably loaned him the tarp," Jake speculated.

She was obsessed with the tarp and its proximity to the boy. She pulled it from the box. "That's possible. But I don't think so. They never talked, remember? Dr. Miller despised everyone on the opposite side of the river. He hated the Franklins for their new house, and now we know he didn't like Liz and Owen because she reminded him of what had happened at Diamond Lake."

"Speaking of Owen Jarrett," Jake said, "I just heard he left town."

"Seriously?" She set down the tarp.

"Yeah, my sister's best friend works at Lumatyx in accounting," he said. "Says that he walked in and gave his resignation a few days after Charlie was found. She said you could have knocked everyone there over with a feather. Not that they weren't happy about it. No one liked the guy. Constantly bragging to everyone that he was going to be rich. Made all the so-called team members feel like they were not a part of the same team. Left a boatload of money on the table."

Esther reached for her purse and pushed past Jake. "I'll catch up with you later. I need to try again to find out from Liz what she wanted to tell us that day she came in. We should've doubled back on that. It might have something to do with her husband."

"You don't think she was covering up for him? I mean, Dr. Miller acted alone, right?"

"Right," she said. "Of course. Something's been bothering me. That's all. Loose ends."

"What?" he asked.

"Not sure," she said, touching that pendant of hers. She took her coat and a scarf her mother had given her. It had snowed earlier that day, dumping six inches over Bend and turning it into a winter wonderland. The snow had a way of making even the darkest things pretty. Esther always liked the snow.

Clean slate, she thought.

It was almost dusk when Liz opened the door to find Detective Nguyen there, holding the rolled-up tarp she used to cover Charlie the morning she'd hit him with the RAV4. Liz didn't allow her eyes to linger on it, but it was there. Coming at her. A burning spear in a 3-D movie.

472

She wore a loose sweater and jeans. Her hair was greasy and pulled back. She wore no makeup. She was a far cry from the pretty young woman whom Esther had seen the day Charlie went missing.

The distinct odor of alcohol was on her breath.

"Are you okay?" Esther asked. "Can I come in?"

Liz opened the door wider, and the detective went inside. The house was filled with boxes marked with Owen's name.

"I heard your husband left Bend," Esther said, surveying the living room. An almost empty wineglass sat atop one of the boxes.

"It was bound to happen," Liz said, barely looking at the detective. "We'd been growing apart for some time."

"But he left town. Left his job too."

"He has other priorities now."

"But the money," Esther said. "I understand he was due for a windfall."

Liz shrugged. "Money isn't everything."

Esther made her way past the organized chaos of the living room to the window overlooking the Deschutes. An enormous **FOR SALE** sign was posted on the once-again perfect lawn rolling from the Miller house to the shore. It faced where passersby floating on tubes and dreaming of living in Bend would surely see it.

"That was fast," the detective said, motioning to the sign.

Liz eyed her wineglass but didn't reach for it. "I heard it's already sold," she said. "Buyers from California. Going to tear it down."

"And put up another one of those?" Esther cocked her head at the Franklin house, once a monument to what newcomers brought to the area with their piles of money and big plans, now a reminder of a near tragedy and its cavalcade of repercussions.

"No doubt." Liz offered the detective some coffee or tea. Esther declined. They stood facing each other silently for a beat.

"Go ahead and finish your wine," the detective said.

Liz picked up the glass and took a swallow.

"How are Carole and Charlie?" Esther asked.

"Good," Liz said, her words suddenly tight in her throat. She took another sip. "I saw them a few hours ago. Carole's going to take Charlie to see her parents. I think that's good."

"I've been thinking about something," Esther said, moving to the dining room table. She unfurled the tarp and spread it over the tabletop. She stopped when the fabric revealed the largest pink splatter. Her eyes met Liz's. "This color of paint is the same color as your front door."

"I wouldn't know about that," Liz said, stepping back, drinking some more.

Esther let silence fill the space. "The lab can confirm it," she finally said.

Liz could feel her face grow warm. It wasn't the wine. It wasn't merely what the detective was saying. It was something deeper, coming from far away inside her.

"It does look close," she said. "My mom loved that color. Called it Elizabeth Arden pink. Same color as her lipstick."

Esther ran her fingers over the stiff, plastic-coated fabric. "The other paint spots match the wall color over there." She pointed to the dining room, a celadon hue.

Neither woman spoke.

"Linda Kaiser at the bar exam was right, wasn't she? Something was wrong that morning and you didn't stay for the test. You were upset about something, but you couldn't have heard about Charlie yet."

Again silence.

"Isn't that right, Liz? You didn't know what had happened to him before the test."

No answer.

"You came to see me, Liz," Esther said. "But you left before telling me why."

Tears puddled in Liz's eyes. "I was worried about Charlie."

"Everyone was. You didn't need to come to my office to tell me that."

"I wanted to help."

"Maybe you did. But you didn't help, Liz. You came and went. You left so suddenly that you left your purse. And then when we dropped it by, you didn't have much to say. Your husband kind of stonewalled us. What was it that you were going to tell me?"

Liz left the table and returned to the window overlooking the Deschutes. As always, the river snaked past the old house, darkening in the early evening sky. *More early snow, maybe?* She considered the Franklin house. The lights were on. Carole was probably giving Charlie a bath. It was a routine that had resumed in spite of everything.

Everything she'd done.

"Detective, you're right," Liz said.

The space between them grew tense. Liz was digging deep. Esther had no idea where it was going.

"About what?" she asked.

Her lips trembled, but Liz knew she could do this. She pushed her wineglass away.

"There is something I need to say," she began. Each word increased her resolve. "Before I do, we need to go next door. Carole needs to hear this too."

Acknowledgments

Sometimes I think I'm the luckiest person alive. So much of all the good that comes my way is from the amazing network of support that surrounds me as I type away at my stories. I'm so grateful for the contributions of so many who offer advice and support. I can't thank each of you enough. Here are a few that are on my mind today: My buddy Matt Glass, who knows how much I love to use index cards to plot out a book, and who was an invaluable sounding board in the early stages of this novel. Thanks to Rand and Becky Hardy for some insightful medical details. Good people. Good wine too. Gratitude goes to Thomas & Mercer and its team of dedicated people who are transforming the storytelling process for authors—one book at a time. Special shout-out to Liz Pearsons, a devoted and brilliant editor, who has more than one trick up her sleeve. Thanks to Brittany Dowdle, my copyeditor. She's so smart! Finally, I've dedicated this book to David Downing, my developmental editor. David is flat-out amazing. I can't think of any other words to describe my appreciation for what he does.

But I know he could.

About the Author

#1 *New York Times* bestselling author Gregg Olsen has written more than twenty books, including *The Boy She Left Behind* and *The Sound of Rain*. Known for his ability to create vivid and fascinating narratives, he's appeared on multiple television and radio shows and news networks, such as *Good Morning America*, *Dateline*, *Entertainment Tonight*, CNN, and MSNBC. In addition, Olsen has been featured in *Redbook*, *People*, and *Salon* magazines, as well as in the *Seattle Times*, *Los Angeles Times*, and *New York Post*.

Both his fiction and nonfiction works have received critical acclaim and numerous awards, including prominence on the *USA Today* and *Wall Street Journal* bestseller lists. Washington State officially selected his young adult novel *Envy* for the National Book Festival; and *The Deep Dark* was named Idaho Book of the Year.

A Seattle native who lives with his wife and twin daughters in rural Washington State, Olsen is already at work on his next thriller. Connect with him via Facebook and Twitter or through his website, www.greggolsen.com.

Books are produced in the United States using U.S.-based materials

Books are printed using a revolutionary new process called THINKtech™ that lowers energy usage by 70% and increases overall quality

Books are durable and flexible because of Smyth-sewing

Paper is sourced using environmentally responsible foresting methods and the paper is acid-free

Center Point Large Print
600 Brooks Road / PO Box 1
Thorndike, ME 04986-0001 USA

(207) 568-3717

US & Canada:
1 800 929-9108
www.centerpointlargeprint.com